Vikings and Christian Franks, by a master storyteller'

Saul David, author of *Zulu Hart*

'Well researched... *Berserker* a whit...

The Saxon Wolf

Angus Donald is the author of the bestselling Outlaw Chronicles, a series of ten novels set in the 12th/13th centuries and featuring a gangster-ish Robin Hood. Angus has also published the Holcroft Blood trilogy about a mildly autistic 17th-century English artillery officer, son of notorious Crown Jewels thief Colonel Thomas Blood. Before becoming an author, Angus worked as a fruit-picker in Greece, a waiter in New York City and as an anthropologist studying magic and witchcraft in Indonesia. For fifteen years he was a journalist working in Hong Kong, India, Afghanistan and London. He now writes full time from a medieval farmhouse in Kent.

www.angusdonaldbooks.com

Also by Angus Donald

Fire Born

The Last Berserker
The Saxon Wolf

THE SAXON WOLF

ANGUS DONALD

CANELO

First published in the United Kingdom in 2022 by

Canelo
Unit 9, 5th Floor
Cargo Works, 1-2 Hatfields
London, SE1 9PG
United Kingdom

A CIP catalogue record for this book is available from the British Library.

Print ISBN 978 1 80032 189 2
Ebook ISBN 978 1 80032 188 5

Look for more great books at www.canelo.co

Printed and bound in Great Britain by Clays Ltd, Elcograf S.p.A.

I

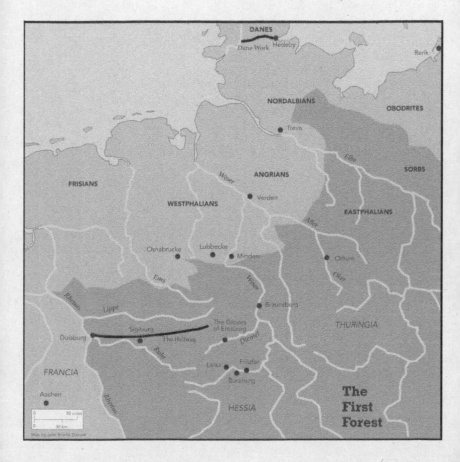

Part One

Spring 773

Prologue

Blackness rising

The shield-maiden stood perfectly still in the line of warriors, a warm trickle of shame running down the inside of her leg. This was not her first battle, by any means, nor was she the only fighter to have released her bladder in fear that day. But she was surprised at herself – revolted by her lack of control.

Around her stood several hundred of her comrades, folk of the North, all well-armed and armoured, and their commander, a Danish jarl, who stood to her left and a little behind the line of shields. The shield-maiden hoped no one in that press of humanity would recognise her abject terror. She had a reputation for fearlessness that she cherished – her features might be pretty, her body might be slender and short, her limbs wiry rather than powerful, but she could *fight*, and until this day she'd truly believed that she was dauntless.

Evidently not. The fear roiled in her guts like a poisonous eel, icy and ever moving. Her leather trews were soaked through now with her own sweat and wastes. And, were it not for the crush of warriors about her, she would have been tempted to run as fast as she could from this horror-filled gore-patch, to preserve her frail young life from certain destruction.

In the air directly above her, a lone red kite circled the battlefield, waiting for its reward, and away to her left, impatient crows hopped and squabbled among the fallen. The bully sun beat down, a great molten disc of metal in the perfect blue sky.

She stood in the second line, just below the crest of the small ridge. She and her comrades had not yet engaged in this life-and-death struggle. But it must be soon – the waves of battle must crash over her very soon. She could hear the sounds of slaughter: the rip and wrench of human flesh; the constant screaming; the shouts of rage and joy. The raw reek of shit and blood coated her tongue; the din of steel smashed against steel relentlessly, the rattle and slap, clash and clatter of blades pounding tattered mail and battered shields.

And nearby, a young man crying out softly for his mother.

Her body was shaking, despite the heat of the day. *Stop!* She ordered herself. *Stop this!* She bit a fold of her lower lip until the blood ran coppery-sweet. But her hands still trembled. She knew she would vomit again soon.

Abruptly the front rank of her comrades was swept away, the thin line of warriors hurled this way and that, shot down with evil, hissing arrows, or battered into bloody ruin by the whirling enemy blades. The battle noise, that awful din, was much louder now, and all around, suffocating, numbing – and suddenly there, revealed as if by a swiftly ripped-back curtain, stood a dread monster from a heathen nightmare, an enormous creature of black fur and fresh, dripping blood. Clad in gore-clotted mail and a vast, sodden bearskin cloak, and holding a bearded axe in one huge paw, the Rekkr threw back his great shaggy head, opened his maw and roared at the clear vault of the sky.

A bold champion stepped from their ranks to challenge this dread monster: a massive, shaven-headed fighter, a young, bare-chested warrior, strong as a full-grown ox, the trusted body-guard of her jarl. He bellowed his own challenge at the Rekkr and struck out hard at the creature. Behind him, the girl hefted her shield, snatched a quick instant to wipe the sweat from her brow, and when she looked again, the champion was down, the battle-mad *berserkr*'s axe buried haft-deep in the young man's bare chest.

Another warrior leapt on the monster's back, stabbing in hard, but the Rekkr plucked the attacker off like a cloak and, holding his head in one hand, he pulled out his seax, a long, brutal fighting knife, and jammed it into the squirming man's neck, before dropping him like a rag to the turf.

The monster's gaze now fell directly upon the terrified shield-maiden, his mouth grinning broadly. She could see bloody spittle and big square teeth in the blood-red hole. His eyes were black as jet, huge and mad. He took a step towards her, the bloody seax gripped in his right hand. He made a deep humming sound as he advanced inexorably on her small, trembling form.

She shouted: 'Bjarki! Stop it! You love me, as I love you. You know it, inside. Inside the real you. Stop! Come back to me. You cannot hurt *me*!'

The Rekkr did not seem to hear her.

Her comrades were fleeing, melting away before this appalling creature; she felt their absence, a space around her, and now stood alone on the grassy slope, face to face with this unholy being of such hideous power.

Her sword was forgotten in her hand. Her shield drooped.

She shouted a last time: 'No, no, please. Bjarki, it's *me*!'

'No *talking*!' the Rekkr bellowed. He slashed at her with his dripping seax. She stumbled backwards, tripped on her own feet, fell flat on her rump.

Bjarki leapt on top of her, landing like a cat on knees and elbows, straddling her winded body. She stared up into the twisted face, twitching, spattered with frothy blood; the face of the man she loved – the *monster* she loved – and felt his sharp steel pierce her belly and loins, again and again, a series of brutal punches.

She felt no pain, just his weight on her body, and a deep sadness. And an icy coldness, a void; blackness rising, rising till it filled her whole world.

Chapter One

A joyful reunion

When in doubt, go north. Bjarki Bloodhand lifted his heavy arms into the cold air and stretched out the knuckles of his aching spine. He pondered this maxim of his dead father – one of the few shreds of wisdom the battle-crazed old brute had passed on to his son during their short acquaintance.

When in doubt, go north. That was what the old man had said. So Bjarki duly stared out at the bruise-coloured, breeze-riffled surface of the harbour of Rerik, and beyond its wide bay to the Austmarr, the Eastern Lake. He watched the half-dozen fishing craft – tiny at this distance – as they scudded across the horizon. Out there somewhere, perhaps a hundred grey miles across the ocean, north and a little west, was his home – or rather the muddy flyspeck of an isle he had lived on for his first handful of years.

If Bjarki went north, as his father's ghost might have counselled, he'd be going towards Bago Island, and if not actually to his home, certainly into the Dane-Mark, the realm of King Siegfried. If he went back there, he would most likely be returning to the grinding tedium of life as a *bondi*, a free man but still a poor one, a drudge; and if not to the very same fish-stinking hamlet of his miserable upbringing, then somewhere similar. But worse than that, if Bjarki did go north, he would be admitting defeat; he would be conceding that his bright and shining dream was finally dead.

And Bjarki wasn't ready to do that. Not yet.

Rerik was a grubby, polyglot port on the north coast of one of the Wendish territories, east and north of the River Elbe, which was controlled by Prince Witzlaus, the lord of a local tribe known as the Obodrites. Ships from across the Austmarr – from as far east as the lands of the Estonians and Finns – stopped at Rerik to trade in thick furs, in sun-filled amber, bars of cold iron, hardy slaves and resin-scented pine trunks destined to become timbers for the dragon-ships that local wrights worked on along the shore.

The traders came, as well, to buy up the huge hempen sacks of precious salt produced here, and bundles of woollen cloth and barrels of herring and the several types of grain produced by Wendish husbandmen inland. The man Bjarki had laboured so long for on this chill day at the tail end of winter – a rotund fellow called Burik, a cousin of the local lord – had an enormous estate under the plough to the south of Rerik where hundreds of his poor thralls grew barley, rye and oats in vast quantities to feed the ships.

Bjarki bent down and hefted the last of the huge barley sacks; he jerked it up on to his shoulder with a soft grunt of pain, turned and began to plod under its immense weight into the gloom of the warehouse, a dozen yards from the slop of the harbour water. Each sack weighed as much as a small, limp man – a corpse, perhaps – and Bjarki had been doing this same lifting action, again and again, since before the first pinks of dawn. Now, as evening thickened the salty air, his gargantuan task was very nearly accomplished.

He entered the huge space of the warehouse and heard the familiar scurry and squeak of rats in the lurk of the shadows, an inescapable part of any place that stored grain. He staggered a little then, his knees buckling under the grind of this endless day, his breath coming in faster. Slowly, painfully, he began to climb the sagging steps made from piled sacks to the top of the barley mountain, where he dumped the last one in its place at the summit.

He rested for a moment, sitting on the bulging hemp, head swimming with the effort, his breath coming in soft pants. That was the last of them. The jetty was cleared. He was done for today. Tomorrow, the punishing labour would begin again: a merchant ship, of the type called a *knarr*, was expected from Gotland, his master had said, which must be unloaded of its cargo of oats. That was tomorrow. This day was over. Thank all the gods.

Drudgery. Hard labour. Dull, repetitive tasks. Day after day. He had been doing this work since the first frosts of autumn. All winter long, month after month, save for a few weeks just after Jul when the harbour had been locked by sea ice. Then all work had been suspended and he had taken shelter in the harbour ale-house owned by his master. He'd slept whole days at a time, wrapped in his fur cloak in a shed at the back of the establishment.

A brown scurrying form ran over his right shoe. He was too tired to kick it away. He stared unfocused into the deepening, dusty gloom of the warehouse, at the fine filaments of golden light that pierced the shingle roof and speared the huge hills of barley. These last gleams also painted a triangle on the threshold of the warehouse, a bold splash of reddish yellow. Perhaps he would just sleep here tonight. No need to go back to the fetid ale-house. He'd just lie here and close his eyes for a while. Just a little while.

His belly moaned. It was no use. That gnawing hollow urgently demanded his attention. He must eat something before he slept. He levered his body painfully to his feet and began slowly, carefully, more like an ancient cripple than a young man of only twenty-one summers, to descend the stair of sacks.

Whether he went north, to resume the life of a fisherman, or stayed on this unfeeling foreign shore, working like a mule day after day, it seemed he was doomed to drudgery. But there *was* an alternative, a voice whispered inside his head, a high, girlish, whining voice. There *was* one thing he could do that no other living man could. He was blessed with a talent that endowed him, on occasion, with extraordinary strength, stamina and animal savagery.

He quickly shut down the horribly familiar voice.

No. He was done with that. He had sworn it to himself: no more of the bloody madness. No more wading through other men's freshly spilled gore. He would stay here in Rerik. Remain in this dismal port, doing his daily mule's work. He'd earn his money with honest sweat, and save each penny. And when he had finally gathered enough coin, he would resume his search.

He would *not* give up his dream. He would find the long-haired man, the easy-talking easterner who called himself Goran; he would find the man somehow and do what was required to earn the prize he yearned for – the patch of free land Goran had offered him, the little house by the sea, the well-tilled barley fields and the fishing boat drawn up on the strand; the neat rows of leeks and cabbages planted; the contented pig tethered nearby. He wanted that with the whole of his heart. He would *never* give up his quest.

–

Bjarki sat at a small round table in the low, woodsmoke-filled ale-house, alone. On the wood in front of him was an earthenware jug of the local brew, a cup, some crumbs of rye and a bowl that had once held a thick fish and bean stew but was now scraped quite clean. There was also a pile of bright coins. A very small pile. The fruits of all his labours these past five months.

Burik, the Wendish landowner, a fat man of about sixty summers, had grudgingly paid him the usual paltry amount at the warehouse door and complained about the slowness of his work that day, and at the untidiness of the mountain of barley-filled sacks inside. He had seemed to be suggesting, ludicrously, that Bjarki should re-stack the entire shipload. Bjarki had said nothing at all to the old man's hints.

He understood a little of the Wendish tongue now, having been in these eastern parts for nearly half a year, but he had simply been too tired to argue. He had just stared at the grumbling Wend with his clear, honest, blue eyes, and held out his big hand for his hard-earned coins. He had not tried to use his unusual size or strength to be intimidating, nor had he bothered with curses or threats. Yet there was something about his huge, scarred form and impassive young face framed with longish, knife-cut dirty blond hair that had discomforted the Wend. Something lurking behind his eyes. Burik had eventually stopped huffing, his words petering out, and had meekly opened his purse and counted out the few coins he owed into Bjarki's hand.

Bjarki took another swig from his cup and stared at the sad little hill of ale-wet silver on the table. In his youth on Bago, he had rarely seen a coin of any kind, let alone silver ones like these Frankish *deniers*, pennies marked with a Christian cross on one side and a likeness of their king on the other; indeed, he'd been perpetually mud-poor and never owned any money at all.

Then he had travelled far south from his home in Bago and spent months training to be a warrior in the forests of Saxony; then was taken prisoner in battle and sent to the great city of Aachen, the capital of his enemies, the Christian Franks. There he had been befriended by their young king, Karolus – the very man depicted on these wet coins – and during *that* time he had seen treasure aplenty. Magnificent golden candlesticks, chased silver belt buckles, blue enamelled brooches, sword hilts studded with jewels – and coins, of course, rivers of shiny coins. When he had left the comforts of Frankish civilisation, heading east on a hero's quest to kill a monster, it had been with a purse packed tight with silver *deniers*. The monster was long gone, and so was his money. All the wealth he owned in the world was winking at him from the puddle of spilled ale on the table.

He knew he should get up and go out the back of the ale-house and wash his filthy body and curl up and sleep in his cot, but he was too tired to move. Instead, he refilled the ale cup and sank the contents in a single draught. As part of the arrangement with Burik, whose sister ran this tavern, Bjarki was given one plate of food in the morning and one at night, and allowed to bed down in one of the storerooms behind the smoke-filled common room.

He poured himself yet another cup and looked around the low, wood-walled room. It was a place of perpetual strangers, he thought; indeed, that was its function in this bustling seaport where every day a boatload of new men arrived seeking food and drink, sometimes women, too, and somewhere to lay their tired, ale-addled, salt-crusted heads.

It was a square building right on the waterfront, a dozen paces from the water, with a rectangular central hearth, a long common table and benches, two smaller tables, and a counter behind which lurked Manos, the unmarried sister of his master, a troll of a woman – balding, mean-spirited, flatulent – who peered out at her unsatisfactory world through shiny sunken eyes. She sat guard over her ale vat, a large cauldron in which she brewed her liquor once a week, and from which she doled it out grudgingly with an iron ladle.

There were only a handful of her clients in the common room that evening. A group of brash young Wendish warriors on the far side of the room, drinking and talking too loudly, either supremely confident or pretending to be so. They were clearly Witzlaus's hearth-men, soldiers from the forbidding fortress at the eastern end of the port. A swaggering gang of noisy youngsters with furs on their backs, colourfully embroidered thick felt tunics and heavy silver rings prominently displayed on their bare upper arms.

A Svear slave trader from Birka, a sly, untrustworthy-looking man who never held anyone's eye for very long, sat between Bjarki and the Wendish warriors, crouched over his cup. Even as Bjarki observed him, the fellow finished his ale, got up from his bench, pulled up his hood and hurried out of the door, a gust of icy sea wind swirling in as he exited, making the peat in the hearth fire flare. *I should go to bed*, Bjarki thought. *I must go to bed*. He scooped the coins into his purse, which he tucked under his belt, and just as he was commanding his legs to raise him, a leather-clad figure slipped on to the stool on the other side of his table.

It was a girl, perhaps nineteen years of age, red-headed and pretty as an elf, but marked with pale scars on her arms and face like a seasoned warrior. She slapped a soft, shapeless package on the table. It seeped a little blood on to the wood. The rank smell hit the back of Bjarki's throat like a slap.

'What is *that*?' asked Bjarki.

'Dead dog. Or part of one. Found it on the beach,' said the girl.

'Odin's hole! If you're that hungry, Tor, just ask Manos to give you something. Even her fish stew is better than rotting dog.'

'You are *so* funny! You know well enough who it's for.'

The girl seized the ale jug from the table and peered inside. She made a disappointed noise, a sucking of her small white teeth.

'I suppose you want a drink now,' said Bjarki.

'I walked all day,' Tor replied. 'I'm thirsty. Can you catch the old witch's eye?'

Bjarki waved an arm at the figure of Manos, perched in the darkness behind her wooden counter, far from the flickering light of the peat fire. The round dark shape neither acknowledged him nor stirred.

'I'll get another jug,' said Bjarki, but didn't rise from his stool.

'Any news, then?' he said.

'Nothing solid,' said Tor. She reached across the table, took Bjarki's ale cup, sniffed it, grimaced, then drained its contents.

'Well?' said Bjarki.

'No one in this salty little bunghole has ever heard of your man Goran, the long-haired servant of the Duke of Polans. No one has heard of his kind offer of free land for all who ask. No one believed me. Some just laughed.'

Bjarki frowned. 'I did not imagine it, Tor. Goran is real. He was there, last spring, in the main street of Brenna – you know it's true. He had his painted wooden board with the picture of the little cottage by the sea, and the forest and the fishing boat and the pig... I *spoke* with him.'

'I don't doubt your word, oaf. All I'm saying is that nobody in Rerik has heard of this fellow. I must have asked every man, woman and child.'

'You said nothing solid, which means you have *something*. That tavern keeper in Brenna – Valtyr's friend – he said in autumn he knew Goran and swore he'd be in Rerik at the winter herring fair.'

'Well, he wasn't, was he? The fair was a month past. And not a sniff of Goran. Could be dead. Maybe he went back to his duke.'

'Valtyr's friend said he'd be here.' Bjarki knew he was whining like a child, but he was frustrated; after many months, he was no nearer his dream.

'Maybe he lied. Maybe that old miser just wanted rid of us.'

Bjarki thought about this. It was possible. The man had feared him.

'Do you really think the fellow was lying?'

'I don't know,' said Tor. 'I do know this: I'm not going to languish in this fish-stinking midden for a moment longer than I have to.'

'But what choice do we have?'

'There is a jarl, I'm told, over in Hedeby, who seeks followers...'

'What are you saying, Tor?'

'I'm saying we should go to Hedeby, meet the jarl and...'

'No. If anything, I'll go south to Brenna. The spring market will be held in a week or two, and there is a chance Goran will be...'

'Hey, sweet buttocks,' said a voice in Wendish, 'why don't you come and take a cup of ale with us? Meet a few brave fighting men!'

Bjarki looked up and saw that one of the brash young soldiers from the fort was looming over them. He was swaying slightly, bright red in the face. His bicep sported three solid silver rings. A wealthy fellow, then.

'Fuck off! Leave us alone,' said Tor, barely looking at him.

'Sorry. We're in the middle of a chat,' said Bjarki in bad Wendish.

'Come on, lovely, join us. Have a little drink. Sit on my lap. I promise I won't bite,' leered the drunk. 'Unless you want me to!'

'No, thank you. We are both content to remain here,' said Bjarki.

'If you're looking for a whore who's not choosy about her customers,' said Tor, 'why don't you go round to your mother's house and join the end of what I'm sure is a very long queue?'

She said it in Norse, her native tongue. But it was obvious the swaying Wend understood the gist of the insult. He flushed purple.

Bjarki said: 'There's a chance that Goran will be in Brenna.'

'He could be anywhere,' Tor said. 'Could have been killed by bandits, or eaten by wolves... He could have fallen off a cliff.'

After a moment, Bjarki said: 'It is a possibility. He could well be dead. But I want to try for a little longer before I give up hope.'

The warrior was still hovering above them. It was obvious he wasn't used to being ignored. He scratched his beard, opened his mouth...

'Go away, you,' said Bjarki. He gave the words an edge of growl. He was feeling the first stirrings of anger. He was bone-tired. He was a little drunk too. He wanted to sleep for a long time – a month, at least. He didn't want to argue about the matter with Tor. Nor did he want her to leave him.

The Wend caught the menace in his words and meekly turned on his heel and tottered back to his friends.

'Bjarki, *please*, say you will sail east with me to Hedeby,' said Tor. 'Goran is as likely to be there as anywhere else in the Middle-Realm. If he *is* looking for landholders for the duke of the Polans people, why not seek him in Hedeby? There is to be a great gathering of warriors in a few days, and this jarl, well, he is a guest-friend of Siegfried. I know a shipmaster who'd take us both tomorrow for nothing. Two days' sail...'

'This jarl of yours would require me to fight for him, yes?'

'Is that such a bad thing?'

'Yes. You know I have turned my back on bloodshed. Ever since the battle at the Dane-Work... I've had enough of that madness. No more.'

'This duke, Goran's master, if you ever do find him, what do you think *he* will ask of you?'

Bjarki glared at her. 'That's different. I'd be fighting for my own interests, my own territory – new lands that this duke would grant me.'

'Is it? The Hedeby jarl would surely reward you, too. Come with me, Bjarki. Talk to him. Simply say no to his face if you don't like his offer.'

'Do as you like, Tor,' Bjarki said. 'I'm staying here in Rerik.'

She got up. She hefted the bloody cloth bundle.

'I'd better give him this,' she said. 'You promised me a drink. Can you at least do that for me?'

She walked towards the rear of the ale-house. One of the Wends, the fellow who had approached earlier, said something to her as she passed by him, and laughed. His friends all guffawed too. She stopped dead and turned and glared at him. The man got unsteadily to his feet. Almost immediately, he fell back on his bench, gasping. Tor had struck him once, a hard, stiff-fingered blow under his chin, which had knocked all the mirth out of him.

Then she turned and slowly stalked out of the back door.

Bjarki got up with the big ale jug and went over to the dark, round form of Manos. While the old woman ladled ale into his jug, muttering about lazy good-for-nothings who drank more than they should, Bjarki kept one eye on the five Wends, who were all clustered round the gasping man. He was still alive, Bjarki noted, but he wouldn't be speaking many drunken words of love any time soon. He turned to go back to his own table with his ale.

Out of the corner of his eye, he saw one of the warriors get up, a short, heavy man, and head towards the back door Tor had just passed through.

Bjarki immediately changed direction. He went towards them.

'You!' he said loudly in Wendish, addressing the short man at the rear of the ale-house who was just opening the back door.

'Take one step through that door and you'll regret it the rest of your life.'

He had meant it as a statement of fact. Tor could quite easily deal with this slab of pork. He meant it as simple truth. But it came out as a threat.

Suddenly violence was shimmering like gold dust in the air.

The five Wends – burly, drunk young men, bred for the slaughter – were on their feet, their breathless friend left still slumped on his bench.

They formed up in a loose, bristling semicircle around Bjarki, who stood perfectly still, feet apart, the full ale jug in his left hand, his right hanging casually next to the horn handle of the heavy fighting knife, the seax, he habitually wore slung across his loins.

'I don't want any trouble,' said Bjarki mildly. 'Why don't you take this jug and have a drink? No need for any unpleasantness.'

His words were soft. He smiled. He tried not to appear as any kind of threat; but inside his head a voice, a girlish, whining voice, began to chitter and squeak, like a caged rat overcome with rage and glee.

'We're going to fuck you up good, foreigner,' said one of the Wends, a scarred fellow with a lumpy shaven head.

'Then we're *all* going to fuck your scrawny slut.'

The little voice inside Bjarki's head was whispering urgently now: 'Kill them, kill them all – let's just open up *all* these lovely meat bags.'

'She's not a slut,' said Bjarki. 'She's my sister. And it makes me really upset when people call her that. And, trust me, *please* do trust me on this matter, you really do *not* want me to get upset with you.'

The shaven-headed Wend opened his mouth to retort and…

The rear door of the ale-house burst open and something huge, black and furry surged through into the middle of the loose semicircle of Wends.

It was a bear, already a sizeable beast although only half-grown. The animal let out a bellow, somewhere between a growl and a yelp, and bounded heedlessly through the five Wendish warriors, easily shouldering them aside, scattering them like skittles in an alley. Then it leapt up on to Bjarki, planting its paws on his chest, its weight tumbling him over.

From beyond the open back door came a woman's despairing cry: 'Garm, you naughty boy! Come back here now! Gaaaaaarm!'

The Wends were shouting in panic and scrambling for the ale-house's front door – even the would-be lover with the badly bruised throat. All six of them together bundled out of the door that led towards the harbour, each one blocking the other's passage, elbows flying, some yelling loudly, insanely about wild beasts, monsters and demons.

All the while, the bear was growling and snuffling at Bjarki's head, its pink tongue enthusiastically licking his big sweaty face, and Bjarki was laughing, gasping for breath, wrestling playfully with the powerful creature, trying to force its great shaggy bulk away from his prone and helpless body.

'Get off, Garm, your breath stinks of rotten dog. Bad bear, bad Garm!'

17

Chapter Two

A storm on the horizon

The freezing breeze that sliced across the Austmarr cut through Tor's thin cloak as if it were made of spiders' webs. But she did not mind the cold. She smiled, warmed by inner joy, the wind whipping her shoulder-length red hair, and she gripped the ship's mast a little tighter with her wiry left arm.

She was standing on a pile of thick tree trunks in the waist of the fat-bellied *knarr*, five dozen long pine boughs wrapped in waxed linen and bound for the wood-hungry markets of the Dane-Mark. Siegfried's maritime kingdom was always short of timber for shipbuilding, and this vessel's load reaped from the endless Svear forests would fetch a fine price in Hedeby.

Not that she cared about the shipowner's profits. The man, Lars, was a decent enough fellow, a Svear like her, although much older and more timid, and at that moment he was conferring worriedly with one of his six crew members at the prow of the *knarr*, pointing at a bank of dark grey cloud to the east that threatened a storm. She cared about rain even less than the cold. Her heart glowed because she was quitting that dreary Wendish port and going to the Dane-Mark, and had managed to persuade her oaf to come too.

She felt at last that her life was moving forward again – and Bjarki's life, too. He might claim that he had turned his back on bloodshed, but war was his *wyrd*, his destiny. Whatever the Fate Spinners had in store for Bjarki Bloodhand, it was not the life of a humble fisherman or dull, hard-working farmer. She knew it, even if he did not. He was a Rekkr, deep in his bones, one of the Fire Born – a warrior who could summon his *gandr*, his animal spirit, at need, which would grant him the ferocity of a wild bear in battle.

She had won her argument in Rerik and they were heading to Hedeby, to the great gathering of northern warriors. Once there, wise Odin, the Breaker of Spears, would set them on the right path, she was certain of that.

The All-Father had not yet smiled on her as he had on Bjarki. And although she had trained in the same spiritual school as her brother – the Fyr Skola – her *gandr* had never come to her. She was no Rekkr. Perhaps she never would be. Her role in this brief life, as she recognised it, was to follow her older brother and help guide him to his true path of glory.

If Odin smiled on Bjarki once more, he might find that elusive fellow Goran in Hedeby. Perhaps. Likely not. Tor's opinion was that searching for one long-haired fool who wandered the Middle-Realm selling his dream of happiness, and who might be anywhere in or out of this world, was madness.

But this was the argument that had swayed Bjarki the night before: that the dream-seller Goran might be in Hedeby for this gathering of warriors. That and the furious, spitting tirade from Manos about setting their pet Garm – a bear cub Tor had found in the forest last spring – loose in the common room and scaring off good, paying customers. Tor also knew that Bjarki, deep down, did not want to spend another instant hefting those barley sacks. He might dream of the simple, carefree farming life but the reality of it, the drudgery, the endless back-breaking work, day after day, was not for him.

And it never would be.

Tor turned her head and looked down the length of the *knarr*.

Bjarki was sitting hunched in the lee of the steer-board wall looking out over the furrowed grey sea flecked with row upon row of whitecaps. He was frowning, and seemed to be thinking hard. That usually meant he was going to be difficult about something. The young bear was in poor shape, too.

The animal was hunched in a pose of self-pity on the opposite side of the ship to Bjarki, a big black ball of furry misery. It had been excited to board the vessel earlier that morning, lumbering across the quay and leaping on to the cloth-wrapped logs and sucking down the familiar scent of pine. He had impertinently sniffed the crotch of Captain Lars, who had been somewhat taken aback to find that he was expected to set sail in an open craft with a dangerous wild creature. Even one that seemed well behaved.

But shortly after the fully laden *knarr* had slid out of Rerik harbour, under the big bellying red-and-white-striped sail, the bear had disgraced himself by shitting copiously in the bilges and scrabbling at the sides with his claws in an attempt to escape the wooden walls of his wave-rocked prison. It had taken Bjarki, a natural sailor who had grown up around fishing boats, the best part of an hour of stroking and soothing words to calm the beast and get it to accept the very moderate motion of the big trading vessel.

Yet the bear still seemed to be suffering terribly from his seasickness and was hunched down by the gunwale, cowering, mewling and shivering. At the prow, Lars was now coiling up a length of rope and speaking with two of his crew. By the hard glances they kept shooting down the length of the ship towards Garm, Tor surmised they were still complaining about carrying a ferocious animal on their precious ship. Frightened of her boy.

The bear looked anything but ferocious on this grey, windy day. It whined loudly in its discomfort, causing the helmsman, an elderly Finn who was sitting a yard or two behind the animal, to flinch nervously and allow the ship to give a little dance over the waves before he hastily corrected his course. Tor watched as Bjarki offered the animal some morsels of hard cheese, its favourite snack. But the bear daintily turned his snout away from the treat, like a high-born lord declining some awful peasant delicacy.

If Garm would not eat Bjarki's cheese, Tor realised, he really must be sick. They would have to do something about the poor cub. They could not travel far with it by ship. And on land, if they left it alone for too long, there was a danger it might hurt someone. The bear did not know its own strength, and disliked strangers. Maybe in Hedeby they could find him a good home.

Tor heard a shout then from the prow of the ship and looked forward to where Lars was pointing something out to his fellow mariner. She followed the line of his arm and saw, on the horizon, emerging from under the grey mass of cloud near the coast of the island of Lolland, a ship. It was a small, sleek vessel – obviously fast, and under the square black sail she could see the round painted shields of warriors hung over the sides.

She studied the ship for a few moments. She counted the shields: eight on this side and, presumably, eight on the other – sixteen warriors, at least. For a moment she toyed with the idea that the ship was harmless, that it was innocently making its way to Hedeby, as they all were, to join the gathering.

The strange ship was on the same tack as them, travelling in parallel, roughly north-east, on the same wind but moving a little faster than Lars's bigger, heavier vessel. Siegfried of the Dane-Mark had called for a muster of fighting men from across his wide, watery realm – perhaps this fine ship was just full of youngsters who were excitedly answering the Danish king's call.

Then the captain or helmsman of the other vessel caught sight of them. Tor saw men moving up and down its narrow length, their cloaks flapping in the breeze. The big black sail was swiftly pulled down and oars appeared, sprouting like weeds along its length, held vertically, then flashing down into the water in a smooth rippling movement.

They were a well-trained crew – even Tor, no sailor, could see that. The ship spun about and began to head directly for them. The wet oars sparkled as they rose and fell; its speed greatly increased.

There could be no doubt about its intentions now.

'Oaf,' called Tor, without turning her head.

'I see it,' said Bjarki.

Tor jumped down from her perch to the side of the ship and began rummaging in the hemp sack that contained her few belongings. She hauled out a byrnie, an ancient iron chain mail shirt that fell down to her thighs, and tugged it hurriedly over her head, feeling the comfortable weight settle on her shoulders. She pulled out a sword belt and buckled it on over the mail. Undid the ties on a bundle of javelins and picked out two of the straightest. She pulled out a heavy round wooden shield, which had been wedged against the side of the ship. Slapped on her plain steel cap.

Ahead of her at the prow Captain Lars was arguing with one of his shipmates. His hands were flapping. He shoved the man aside and came running down the length of pine trunks. His face was white, his eyes wild.

'We'll run. We must get the wind behind us!' he yelled as he passed.

The strange ship was a mere two hundred yards away now, and heading for them like a speeding arrow, their shining oars thrashing the sea white.

Bjarki came up to stand beside her in the waist of the ship.

Tor looked at him. He had no byrnie – he had sold his fine Frankish mail in Rerik, claiming he would no longer need it – but he had a round shield held in his left hand. In his right he grasped a bearded axe, a long-shafted weapon with a fearsome blade and a long lower part, shaped like a beard, that could hook an opponent's shield, pull it down and expose him.

His face was partially covered by a steel helmet with a nasal guard, and his grim blue eyes stared out over the glittering sea, watching the approaching enemy ship. A beautifully thick bearskin cloak, black as jet, soft as silk, clasped with a steel chain, fell from his shoulders to his ankles.

'Is your *gandr* close by?' she asked.

'I don't want her in me,' he said. 'I don't need her.'

Tor shrugged, causing her iron byrnie links to rattle.

'So we take the fight to them,' she said. 'They have the numbers on us, but if *we* board *them* their superior numbers are useless.'

The enemy was a bare hundred yards away now. Tor could see four men standing in the prow, brutal-looking, middle-aged men, bearded and grinning wickedly, with shields and armour, axes and swords. They were vikings, no mistaking them; lawless men who made their living by piracy in the Eastern Lake. Above their heads curved a beautiful wooden figurehead in the shape of a flame-spitting dragon. Behind them she could see the shapes of a dozen rowers' backs, all bent to the oar and straining on their sea chests.

Their own ship gave a wild, twisting lurch and swung round to the west, the freezing wind now coming from directly behind them. The *knarr*'s striped sail cracked once like an ox whip, but it didn't seem to Tor that much more speed was achieved from this change in the point of sailing.

Tor and Bjarki turned right to face the new direction of the enemy. Lars himself was at the helm now, hunched over the long tiller as if to drive the craft to greater speed with his own personal determination alone. The old Finnish helmsman was standing beside him, still keeping a wary distance from the seasick bear, and clutching a bow and arrow in trembling hands.

Garm appeared to be asleep, or in some kind of comatose state, wretched and unmoving, head tucked deep into its chest.

The enemy ship was gaining on them, now forty yards away and coming on fast. The four men in the prow were clashing their weapons rhythmically against their shields. Tor could see the black gaps in their mouths where they were missing teeth. They were *hoom*ing deep in their throats, or perhaps singing some battle song. Tor gave a little shiver – part cold, but also part fear, she admitted to herself. She took a firmer grip on her courage.

'Shouldn't you be humming too, oaf?' she said.

'I told you: never again,' said Bjarki, glaring at the oncoming foe as if he resented their obstruction to his vow to abstain from all violence.

'This could be our last battle,' Tor said. 'Only the Fate Spinners know. So let's make it a fine fight to secure us a place in the Hall of the Slain.'

The enemy was twenty yards away. In a dozen heartbeats, its sharp prow under the dragon-head would smash into their vessel about a third of the way up the steer-board side. Tor took two fast steps down the length of the ship, hefted one of her javelins and hurled it hard across the water.

The spear arced over the sea and plunged into the neck of the leading warrior, the blade stopped dead by the bones of his spine and the shaft waggling comically from under his huge black beard. Immediately blood gushed down the front of his leather breastplate. He sagged, coughing gore, and fell to his knees.

The old helmsman loosed an arrow, which struck fast into the lime-wood shield of the second warrior. The struck man roared with rage at this insult. Tor threw her second javelin in a fast, low trajectory, which missed the three enemies in the prow, slipping between them and vanishing into the ship.

The enemy vessel crunched jarringly into the side of their *knarr*. The impact made Tor stagger and almost fall. But Bjarki was ready for it, knees bent for balance, and his big hand steadied her too.

He gave a giant's roar, took one quick step down the length of the ship, then another shorter one, and leapt straight into the knot of armed men on the enemy prow, using his great bulk alone to tumble them all backward in a heap of snarling, cursing men, thrashing limbs and battering shields.

He was up in a flash, his big axe swinging, hewing at limbs, crashing his blade against steel helms. Tor, quickly recovered, was right behind him on his left, his shield side, leaping across and striking like a viper, her long sword flickering out and coming back red and glistening. Bjarki smashed his shield boss

24

into the face of one shouting man, and sank his axe into the ribs of another. He roared his fury. He pulled the axe free and split an oak shield.

The rowers with their backs to the action had now abandoned their oars, and these warriors too surged forward to join the fray in the prow.

All were fighting in the narrow front of the dragon-ship, a lethally cramped triangular space where no more than two warriors could stand abreast. Tor, in the shadow of Bjarki's shield, leapt forward to strike, time and again. She easily ducked a sword cut and lunged, skewering a red-bearded man through his unguarded thigh with her darting blade. The man fell sideways, spitting curses and, in falling, he blundered into Bjarki's left leg, catching him behind the knee and tumbling her brother into the bilges.

A spear reached out from the pack of jostling vikings to her front and screeched horribly over Tor's helmet, scoring the steel. She staggered back from the force of the blow, suddenly all alone. An axe looped out from the throng and crunched into her half-raised shield, kicking out a big splinter from the round edge. A second axe hacked into it, too, and the shield disintegrated into a bundle of boards. A sword clanged loudly against her helm again and she was knocked sideways, tripping over a dying man's legs.

The *knarr*'s Finnish helmsman, bow and nocked arrow in his hands, pressed forward bravely into her empty place. He drew and loosed. Sank his shaft deep into a charging rover's eyeball from only a bare yard away. Then a furiously hurled spear took the helmsman right through the left cheekbone, crunching into his skull, snapping his head back horribly.

Tor was still down and out, tangled with a coil of wet rope, a corpse and the remains of her broken shield. A big pirate, his bare chest thickly matted with hair, was standing right over her, a huge, double-handed sword raised high above his head, ready to strike...

Bjarki saw Tor take four hard blows in very quick succession. He saw her fall. He was on his back, too. He shouted: 'No, *no*!' and in a dreamlike state he saw a huge, hairy-chested warrior raise a massive sword above Tor's body, then the wetly glinting blade was slicing down and down, hacking towards her...

Bjarki suddenly felt very cold. He heard the familiar rushing sound like a huge tumbling waterfall in his ears and a sharp, high voice saying, 'Yes, yes! Let me in, man-child! Let me in now! You know you need me – now.'

He found he was humming, deep down in his throat, a dark, ancient, droning tune, a four-note melody. His vision became blurred, oddly tinged with streaks of red, then snapped into pin-sharp focus. He felt something huge and heavy swelling inside his chest; he could feel hot blood pounding in his veins. He felt suddenly light, buoyant, stronger than ever.

'Oh, yes!' said the little crowing inner voice, now deafen-ingly loud, crashing like gigantic waves inside his blood-red skull.

With a sliver of his still-human mind, Bjarki saw Tor snatch up an abandoned shield from the bilges beside her fallen body and hold it over her head. She somehow managed to block the first plunging blow from the massive sword. The blade screeched off the shield's boss and buried itself in the planks of the ship's hull beside Tor's head. But now Bjarki was consumed by his *gandr*. He was in his own world, scarcely aware of her or her plight.

And *his* world was moving very slowly. Time crawled. But Bjarki leapt lithely to his feet in one lightning-fast bound. He pulled the heavy seax from its sheath at his loins, and jammed the long blade into the belly of the bare-chested warrior still wrestling with the plank-stuck sword above Tor's body.

The seax slipped in easily, almost gently, slicing through the enemy's skin and muscle. Then Bjarki ripped the foot-long blade away, a hot gush of blood flooding over his hand. As the big warrior collapsed, Bjarki seized hold of his unwieldy double-handed sword and jerked the blade free of the timbers.

Then, whirling the long sword with one hand, bloody seax brandished in the other, he charged heedlessly into the dense ranks of his foes.

He bore down the very centre of the viking ship, stamping forward, hacking men apart with great wide sweeps of the sword and seax. He reaped like a scythe-man amid the barley; slashing, slaying and spraying blood in all directions. He was howling like a beast now, froth bubbling at his mouth. He was stabbing and killing, slaying and hewing. Moving forward; striking again. He killed them, he cut them, he struck them down in a welter of gore.

His long sword stuck once, briefly, in the ship's mast after an overly ambitious lateral stroke. So Bjarki simply stabbed the viking in front of him with his gory seax, plunging the knife lightning-quick into his throat, ripping away most of his neck in one sweep; then, with his right hand, he jerked the huge sword loose of the mast and cut down a cowering man with his next lethal swing.

No foe could hope to stand against him. None could face him and live. The Fire Born took blows here and there; now and then an opponent would catch him with a swift sword or cunning axe blow, but his bearskin, thick as double-wadded felt, springy as a willow basket, withstood the enemy insults.

They battered at him hopelessly, weakened by the certain knowledge of their doom; and, of the hurts he suffered, the Rekkr in his battle-joy was oblivious. He absorbed their feeble blows and replied to them with slaughter.

He hacked down all the men who stood in that narrow ship. Some men, recognising his true nature, jumped into the sea rather than face his wrath. They shed heavy shields, helms, mail and weapons and leapt into the grey waves, striking out for the distant mist-shrouded shores of islands, much preferring to risk almost certain drowning than be ripped apart by a Rekkr.

Yet the captain of these vikings, their chieftain, their lord, a man of deep pride, stood in the stern astride his tiller. He faced Bjarki with a savage snarl on his lips and a long axe in his gnarled and skilful hands.

The pirate waited for his moment and struck out at Bjarki with his blade. It was a fast, sweeping attack, a fine blow, which should have snatched his opponent's ribcage free of his spine. But Bjarki, nimble as a cat, swayed back out of the lethal path of the axe swing at the very last moment. Then, laughing like a donkey, between spitting insults at his foe, the *berserkr* stepped forward. The captain recovered his balance and slashed at Bjarki's leg, which the Rekkr lifted impatiently out of the path of the axe.

Then Bjarki struck, faster than a hunting weasel, a huge, diagonal cut with the double-handed sword, which started high and right and battered through his enemy's half-raised shield, driving down and down, continuing on into soft flesh, cutting into his body, almost dividing the chieftain in half.

They were all down by now, dead or bleeding, some flopping like fish, moaning, weeping, and still the Rekkr's rage was unsatisfied. Snuffling and growling, giggling and grunting, he prowled up and down the blood-slick planks, booting chests out of his path, stamping on broken limbs, crushing skulls, looking for any who might defy him and ripping their bodies asunder.

'Enough!' shouted Tor. 'Stop, Bjarki. Stop it, the battle's won!'

He recognised her slim form through the mad haze of his bloodlust, and saw that she was crouched over a smaller enemy: a little whey-coloured face, glimpsed beneath Tor's right arm, big blue eyes, a skinny body curled hard against the curve of the ship's side.

And this enemy was still alive.

'One last meat bag,' said his *gandr*. 'One more. Just for luck!'

Bjarki swiped at Tor with his forearm, the blow landing full against her cheek and knocking her out of his way, bowling her a good yard down the gore-washed vessel. He loomed over his last remaining foe – a child, he could now see, a terrified girl of eleven or so. The seax twitched in his fist.

'One more little one,' whispered the thin, cajoling voice.

The girl squirmed. Cowering, shielding her head with a slender arm.

Bjarki slashed down with the seax, the blade hissing through the air. And stopped, just inches from the little girl's soft white throat.

'I said, *enough!*' Tor's voice was now filled with a cold, bright anger. She was crouched down low beside the girl, and her two hands were clamped hard as a vice round Bjarki's brawny, swinging forearm, preventing him from completing his seax strike.

'You *will* let her live, brother,' she grated.

She put her shoulder under his meaty rump and, using all the strength in her legs, she surged upward and tumbled the utterly surprised Rekkr over the gunwale, out of the ship, into the freezing ocean.

Tor quickly checked that the girl was unharmed, and then looked over the side. And saw that her Bjarki, her brother, her oaf, was back. He was himself once more. Floundering in the sea, half tangled in his own heavy bear-cloak, gasping, coughing, swearing and spitting out salt water.

'Is she gone now? Your *gandr?*'

Bjarki nodded. So Tor extended a wiry arm towards him.

He looked up at his sister from the cold sea, at the big glowing red mark on her cheekbone. Then took her strong hand in his own massive paw.

A moment later, sitting in the blood-slick belly of the ship, now utterly deflated, he let the last dregs of his gigantic rage ooze from him.

Chapter Three

Land and glory

As she stirred the bubbling stewpot, Tor looked out of her good eye at the girl sitting on the sand, her arms wrapped around her knees, on the far side of the campfire. She was a pretty little thing, for sure: pale as milk, with fair hair framing an innocent face, and right on the cusp of womanhood – which was why she had immediately claimed the child as a thrall, the spoils of the battle. She had caught one of the crew members looking at the small, frail, quivering captive in a way that raised all the hairs on the back of her neck.

Other than that, Tor knew very little about the captive. She hailed from the limitless lands to the east, some kind of Slav; that was plain. She had spoken only one word since the battle, which was close enough to the Wendish word for water to be comprehensible, and thereafter she made not a peep on the short journey to the island of Lolland. Nor had she said anything when they had hauled the two ships up on the beach for the night and built tents from the sails, and she had carried the firewood without a single complaint.

She would not go near Bjarki, though. She was clearly terrified of the huge warrior who had so nearly ripped away her life, and when Garm had ambled over and given her a polite, enquiring sniff, she had actually loosed her bowels and messily soiled the raggedy shift, which was all she wore.

Tor had given her one of her own much-patched spare shirts to wear, and wondered what else she might do to reassure the child that she would not be harmed, so long as she behaved herself. But since the waif plainly did not understand the Norse tongue that Tor spoke – and Tor's Wendish was still very poor – she could not think of any suitable way to communicate.

She spooned a generous portion of the thick venison stew into a bowl and went around the fire to put it into the girl's icy hands.

As the girl began to scoop the hot meat and gravy into her mouth with her fingers, Tor put a hand on her own chest and said clearly: 'I am Torfinna Hildarsdottir – you call me Tor. Or mistress, if you prefer. That big man over there' – she waved a finger at Bjarki, who was lying on his belly on the sand, his head buried in his cupped hands – 'that is Bjarki Bloodhand. He's my brother. An oaf, yes, and fearsome in battle, but a good man. That is Garm.' She pointed at the cub, which was snuffling in a furrow of sand, digging with its outsized paws, happily investigating some exciting new scent.

'You belong to us now,' Tor said. She slapped her own chest again: 'Tor... Bjarki... Garm. So tell me now – what is *your* name?'

The little girl just stared at her with fearful incomprehension.

'I shall call you Inge,' said Tor. 'Inge – yes? Because you look a bit like a girl from my village who had that same name. Also because I like the name. You see those folk over there – those sailors – with Captain Lars?' She waved a hand over at a larger campfire around which several men were capering, clearly drunk. 'You stay away from those men. Stay close to me.'

The girl said nothing. Tor looked over at the figures dancing in the firelight to the beat of a simple kidskin drum, black shapes gyrating lewdly against the flickering light around their campfire. Captain Lars was a happy man that night. And he had broached a large keg of his strongest mead to prove it. Not only had Tor and Bjarki saved his ship and its valuable cargo of timber from the sea-rovers, but they had also provided him with another whole craft: the low, sleek, smaller but much faster

31

vessel, now emptied of the mangled corpses and body parts Bjarki had recklessly filled it with, and sluiced clean of bilge blood by many, many buckets of seawater.

Lars had made a heartfelt speech of thanks to Tor and Bjarki when they landed on the beach at twilight, praising their fighting prowess and courage. He had given himself up for dead,xhe confessed. He had believed his life thread had been cut by the Spinners. But now, not only was he alive and unhurt, he was also much richer into the bargain. He had only suffered the loss of one Finnish helmsman – who was easily replaceable, he said jovially.

'If there is ever anything I can do for you, lady,' he said, 'or for your mighty brother. If you ever need passage back to Rerik, to Uppsala, to the Little Kingdoms, anywhere in the Middle-Realm, I will gladly carry you!'

–

It was the black shame that was the worst, Bjarki thought. By far the worst of all he suffered. Much worse than the wounds taken – which were slight: a cut or two and some bruises – or the exhaustion that followed a possession.

The feeling of utter self-disgust that filled him when he recalled what he had done when the *gandr* had entered him, at the memory of all the lives he had joyfully ripped apart. It was a sick, oily, poisonous ache in his belly; a pounding in his head and heart, too. He could barely bring himself to look at Tor that evening. Her right eye was so badly bruised it was swollen almost shut. He had done that to his sister without the slightest hesitation. As for the little girl, he had been more than ready to rip out her throat in his *gandr*-driven rage. And the girl was no foe – she was just a frail life, a soft young creature that had had the misfortune to cross his *berserkr*-raging path.

One word kept popping into his mind – Galálar. It was a word that spread horror whenever it was whispered. It was the state when the madness that comes upon the Fire Born became permanent. A Rekkr who went Galálar had to be put down like a rabid dog. Without mercy. There was no other known cure.

Bjarki's father Hildar had been Galálar at the very end – he had gone completely insane after fighting in the Battle of Hellingar and had begun killing numbers of innocent men, women and children for the sheer pleasure of the act – and Bjarki had put him down, with his sister's help, about a year ago. But it was not that gods-cursed father-killing that made him feel so weak, so filled with self-loathing, on this bitter night, terrible as that crime was – it was the words his father had said to him beforehand that disturbed him the most. They had been angry, arguing, nose to nose, and Hildar had said to him: 'Do you know what you're looking at, boy?'

Bjarki, staring hard into his father's eyes, had not understood.

'You are looking at your fate, my son,' his father had said.

Those words had stayed with him. They still chilled his heart.

–

They came gliding into the inland lake in the last hour of the day, after a long haul south-west down the Schlei Inlet, with the marshy grasslands of the Danish mainland on either side of the *knarr*'s walls.

This long, shallow sea channel, which had in some places been only a few hundred paces wide, suddenly opened up into a wide expanse of calm blue water some five miles in length. It felt to Bjarki almost like discovering some hidden place, a new world that was meant to be kept a secret, and yet this place was the very opposite of secret – in the south-western corner of the lake, through a narrow bottleneck between two spits of land, sat the harbour of Hedeby, the second-largest town in the whole of the Dane-Mark.

There was nothing secretive at all about Hedeby, once you got within earshot of the score of bustling jetties and quays, which all pronged out like giant's fingers into the bay.

It was nearly full dusk when they arrived, but despite the gloom the quays were still thronged with thousands of people and hundreds of bawling animals, and piled with boxes and sacks of goods of all kinds. Along the harbour front the oil lamps were being lit. The dying sun did not mean the end of labour *here*. The winches and cranes shrieked, slave masters cursed, whips cracked, thralls sweated: this scene was repeated all along the shore.

There were hundreds of ships crammed into the harbour, tethered like fat ticks on a hound's belly to every available inch of landing space. The port was heaving. Thousands of folk had heeded Siegfried's call for warriors to gather in Hedeby; a multitude had assembled at his word.

Bjarki shaded his eyes from the red westering sun and studied the town from his position in the prow of the *knarr*, as Lars guided her efficiently into a space that had just miraculously opened up on the extreme northern edge of the harbour. A fishing smack pulled away, hauling up sails to catch the offshore breeze, at exactly the right time – clearly a blessing from Ran, the sea goddess. And a man in a jolly blue hood, who was coiling a rope in his own vessel, gave Bjarki a wave as his departing herring boat passed only a few feet from the *knarr*, gathering speed, heading off the way they had come.

'Welcome to the madness,' he shouted out in Norse.

For a few moments, Bjarki, still sunk deep in his after-battle swamp of misery, thought the fisherman was taunting him about his relationship with his *gandr*, and considered volleying back a vicious insult. Then he realised the fellow meant nothing more than a comment on the bustle of the harbour.

Bjarki had never viewed Hedeby from the sea before. He had glimpsed it inland, from the top of the Dane-Work fortification, at the time of the Battle of Hellingar – then seeing only a twinkle of silver sea and a scatter of distant ships – but this was his first time observing the port from the east.

The town was contained on the landward, western side within a high, semicircular earthen rampart and fence. It was cupped, you might say, as if in an enormous wine goblet, against the line of the sea.

The stem of the goblet was another higher rampart that ran directly west into the distance, with a fence and guard posts every few hundred yards along its length. This was the Dane-Work, a massive wall ten miles long built by King Siegfried and his predecessors to keep out their enemies to the south of the narrow Jutland Peninsula. Once these enemies had been the Saxon tribes, but now the mighty Dane-Mark was designed to protect against the Christian Franks and their many legions of red-cloaked troops.

The fortification stretched as far west as the River Treen, which ran out through impassable marshes into the open sea on the west of the peninsula.

In front of the Dane-Work, on the southern side, was an enormous ditch, a channel twenty-five paces wide and navigable to ships. This ditch – the Mark-Channel, as it was called – connected the two oceans, east to west. The fortification – the ditch and wall – was Siegfried's glory, as a friend of Bjarki's had once put it: the Dane-Mark's moat and ramparts all in one.

Inside the vast goblet, the town of Hedeby was set out in a grid of arrow-straight streets, paved with split timbers, running east to west, crossed at right angles with other avenues running north to south. Almost every space inside the grid was filled with long, low, straw-thatched halls, workshops and warehouses. There were taverns and ale-houses too, and shops selling everything from huge sacks of dusty charcoal or live chickens to fine-worked cloak-pins in silver and gold. There were many forges, as well, emitting smoke and the constant ringing of hammers. He could faintly hear singing, too, and the high tootling of flutes and the rumble of drums.

The town had greatly expanded, with buildings popping up like field mushrooms after rain, since Bjarki had last seen the place. Hedeby was a proper settlement now, as big and brash and loud as some of the towns he had seen on his travels in the Frankish lands. It was at least double the size of Rerik, and Bjarki guessed it must be home to five thousand folk, maybe six. And more folk were visiting it this month for the gathering of warriors.

–

They left Garm, still miserably seasick, tethered by his leather collar to a stout iron link chain, with a bowl of water close by, in a harbour warehouse owned by a friend of Lars. They left Inge behind too, with mimed orders to guard their belongings, a few spare clothes and weapons, and to keep an eye on Garm, but definitely not to go near him. Inge did not need to be told this: she was rigid with terror at even being in the same room as the young bear.

'If he gets hungry, give him some of this,' said Tor, handing Inge a bag filled with hard cheese. 'Just toss the pieces over to him.'

She had no idea if the girl understood, but she reckoned Inge was scared enough to keep her distance. Garm could be aggressive with strangers, and sometimes snapped his teeth at them. But they couldn't take her with them, not to the royal hall, where they had been told Tor's jarl would be that night.

Bjarki had a brief word with the owner of the warehouse before they bolted the big double door and departed for the town.

'It would be best if no man went inside this place while we are away,' he said solemnly to their host. 'The bear is not feeling well at present, and may grow fractious. The girl is my thrall and must not be molested. You understand?'

The Hedeby man, who had clearly heard a full account of the battle, was brimming with awe for Bjarki and anyone with him. He nodded eagerly.

'As you say, Rekkr,' he said. 'I shall guard the door myself.'

'No need for that. Just leave them in peace – maybe take the girl some food in a while. Soup or pottage, or whatever you have.'

Bjarki pressed a small silver coin into the man's hand.

'No, Rekkr,' said the man, handing back the coin as if it were red-hot. 'I could not accept your silver. It is an honour simply to have someone of your renown staying with us in Hedeby.'

Word of Bjarki's battle exploits seemed to have spread throughout the town, and as he and Tor strode out into the torchlit darkness among the throngs that filled the streets, they were aware of several sly glances, a host of furtive looks, and people making way for them as they passed by.

Sometimes they were greeted by folk they didn't know: 'Hail, Bjarki Bloodhand! Hail, the great Rekkr and his brave shield-maiden Torfinna.'

Bjarki found the looks unnerving after months of being treated like a dumb mule, then realised he was enjoying it. He was admired. People looked on him with *awe*. Tor hated it. She growled and glared at anyone who dared to look upon them as they walked through the muddy streets towards the centre of town, towards the King's Hall, which was the largest building in Hedeby.

One woman put out a hand to stroke the bearskin cloak that Bjarki wore over his tunic and trews, as if some glory would be transferred by the touch.

Tor knocked the matron's hand away, stepped in and snarled at her; and the woman, now terrified, staggered, tripped and sat down hard in the gutter.

By the time they reached the King's Hall, they had collected a score of followers: thanes, thralls and fishwives, townsmen and traders, even a pair of pretty maidens, who giggled and whispered to each other about Bjarki's impressive height and the breadth of his bearskin-covered shoulders.

They had no need to announce themselves. A fat little man, a merchant by his rich dress and the gold that adorned his neck and fingers, bustled forward importantly and informed the two guards who stood at the door to the huge hall. The two *hird*-men, gnarled old warriors in byrnies, leaning on spears, listened to the merchant, then looked long at Bjarki, measuring him. But even they had a gleam of respect in their hard eyes. The pair stepped aside smartly and held back the leather curtain that covered the door.

Bjarki gave each man a brisk nod and stepped into the King's Hall.

The sudden light and warmth was an assault on Bjarki's senses, particularly when combined with the scents of damp dog, sweat-drenched wool and woodsmoke – the homely smells of humanity. Someone was roasting pork, too, deliciously, somewhere in that space, but the hall was too crowded with men and women to see clearly more than a few feet in any direction. Tor seized two cups of foaming ale from a thrall who passed by with a loaded tray and handed one to Bjarki, who was wondering what he should do now.

He saw no one he knew well, although some of the faces in the throng seemed halfway familiar: they had perhaps, some of them, fought together with him at the Battle of Hellingar the year just past. Bjarki could not be sure – grief, horror and a fog of self-loathing still clouded his memories.

There were trestle tables laid out in the hall, and stout oak benches alongside them, but few folk were sitting. Most of the hundred or so people inside the loudly buzzing space – *hersirs*, thanes and freemen, a shield-maiden, here and there a few grizzled jarls, too, seasoned warriors all – were standing and talking in groups, drinking their ale, laughing, shouting at old friends and acquaintances across the smoky space.

Yet Bjarki and Tor's entrance had not gone unnoticed. No one approached them or offered any kind of greeting, friendly or otherwise; yet Bjarki sensed they knew who he was. He was aware of many swift sideways glances, and they were given plenty of room, far more than they needed, in which to stand and drink their ale.

At the far end of the hall, on a raised dais, there was a table with a dozen dignitaries, men and women, sitting facing the milling crowd, sipping from mead horns set in fine silver holders.

Here, at last, Bjarki recognised someone he knew. It was the king himself – Siegfried, Lord of the Dane-Mark – sitting at the centre of the long narrow table. He looked tired and perhaps a little bored. He wore a gold circlet around his creased brow which held back his long grey hair, and a twisted grimace beneath that, and he was conversing with a much younger man, a plainly dressed fellow with no jewellery, no arm rings, his very light brown hair arranged into two thin plaits that hung on either side of his blandly handsome, almost boyish face.

The king said something to the young man, who replied with a jest or pleasantry, and Siegfried smiled perfunctorily and put a hand on the youngster's arm in an almost paternal fashion. There was something about the man that struck a chord with Bjarki but he could not put a finger on it. He looked like any number of Danes or Saxons – regular features, blue eyes, pale complexion, fair hair – like a thousand men Bjarki had seen before.

The older man on the other side of the king was more striking. He had a lean, lined face and a black patch covering his right eye, which gave him a dashing air, an air of mystery, even of possessing some ancient wisdom. Bjarki knew him immediately. It was a friend: Valtyr Far-Traveller.

Bjarki's friend was speaking to an even stranger fellow: a small, ugly, misshapen man dressed in what looked like black rags, with a thin nose and animal bones and rings of iron knotted into his long grey-black beard. A line of some black paste was smeared under each shiny, birdlike eye. He looked like a sickly crow transformed into a human by some old magic, some *seithr*.

Bjarki grasped both his thumbs in the ancient sign to avert evil and looked away. His eye fell on a young woman, near the far left end of the table, who happened to be looking in his direction. Their eyes met and she seemed to incline her head slightly and smile at him, as if they were already friends. Her hair was the colour of the afternoon sun in winter, a dark shade of gold, touched with streaks of rose; it was thick, glossy and very long, partly held back by a band of gilt-embroidered cloth around her forehead, and it fell in a curtain about her finely cut features, framing them exquisitely.

Her neck was long and white as milk, her eyes were a dark blue, almost the purple of mountain heather, and intelligent. She held Bjarki's admiring gaze for a fraction too long, so it became a little uncomfortable for him. But he could not look away from her.

At that moment, Siegfried got to his feet. A bodyguard in mail, a royal *hird*-man, positioned behind his lord, stomped forward and hammered with his fist on the table, making the mead horns jump.

'Silence now, silence for the king,' the *hird*-man bellowed, and a hush expanded over the hall as every man and woman there turned to face the dais. The bodyguard stepped back and Siegfried lifted a hand high in the air.

'Greetings, my friends, subjects, allies and oath-men,' he began. 'Greetings to you all. You are welcome in my hall this cold night. I urge you to eat your fill, drink heartily and be easy in my company. And since our feast begins shortly, I thought I'd welcome our honoured Saxon guests, and name them, before the drinking begins. So you *remember* them!'

There were a few chuckles from around the hall at this jest.

'First, I extend a warm hand of welcome to my old friend Jarl Hessi of Eastphalia,' said Siegfried, 'who has made the arduous journey from his fine new hall in Orhum to join us this night.'

The king made a gesture to his right, further down the dais, towards a brutal-looking warrior of middle years with a badly scarred face and a tattoo of a red and blue dragon swirling around his corded neck.

Jarl Hessi nodded and then scowled round at the gathering as if he had somehow been mortally insulted by the king's words.

'I also greet my dear sister's husband, Jarl Ulf, lord of the mighty Nordalbian tribe,' said the king, the words aimed at a scrawny old fellow with a fat gold torc halfway down the other side of the table.

'The Angrians have sent us their Horse-Master Jarl Brun up from Verden – and it gives me great joy to see him here at my table.'

Siegfried nodded at a spear-slim, eagle-beaked warrior to his right, with the most impressively bushy eyebrows Bjarki had ever seen.

'Lastly, before we all fall to gorging, sluicing and general merriment, I present to you the husband of my lovely daughter Geva' – he wafted a hand at a plump, mouse-haired woman to his right – 'a man of honour, a warrior of high renown and noble blood, who now wishes to say a few words to you.'

He indicated with an open palm the pale-faced, plainly dressed youngster sitting immediately to his right. 'We all remember his heroic father, Duke Theodoric of Saxony, who was gathered by the Wingèd Ones from the bloody field last year and who now surely feasts in the Hall of the Slain by Odin's side. Friends, I present to you: Widukind of Westphalia!'

Siegfried said this with a flourish, as if expecting a storm of applause, then he abruptly sat down. But if the old king had been expecting a hearty welcome for the young warrior, who had risen to his feet by then, he was to be disappointed. There were faint cheers, and a lonely clap. But it seemed to Bjarki that few folk in the hall knew anything of this Widukind – and even fewer cared to hear him speak before they were served their pork.

Bjarki felt his own stomach growl like thunder. It had been a long time since their cold breakfast on Lolland. He hoped this mild-looking young warrior would not chatter away for too long.

'Thank you, O King,' said Widukind, 'for the great warmth of your welcome on this cold night. May Saxon and Dane ever be as true brothers and sisters in this hall – and in all others across the Middle-Realm.'

Bjarki's belly grumbled loudly once more. *Sit down now, boy*, he thought. *You've given your thanks to the king. Now sit and let the feast begin.*

'Many of you knew my poor dead father,' said Widukind, looking slowly around the hall, surveying the ale-flushed and bearded faces of the assembled warriors of the Dane-Mark. 'Some of you did not. Many of you loved him. Some of you did not.'

He had a very pleasant speaking voice, Bjarki admitted to himself, soft and sweet, like music – rhythmical and soothing. It reminded him of the humming that he'd learnt during his training to become a Rekkr. That was a strange connection. He recalled then that Duke Theodoric had been Fire Born and wondered if the son, too, was one of his ilk. This blessing – or curse – seemed to run in bloodlines. It didn't seem likely, judging by his manner. The bland youngster was still chattering away in his honey-sweet voice.

'...and on that day, on that bloody day, when my noble father fell, Saxon and Dane stood together in *unity*, all grievances forgotten, brothers in arms, standing shoulder to shoulder to face the common foe. And together we triumphed, *together* we faced the overwhelming might of the Christian hordes and sent the Frankish invader back home in bitter defeat and shame.'

Bjarki recalled those terrible days: the dreadful slaughter, the piles of warriors screaming in their throes. His own *gandr*-driven fury. In spite of himself, the man's words wrung from his heart an awful joy at the memory.

'Together,' said Widukind, his sweet voice growing stronger, 'all of us – all of us who fought on that bloody day – Saxon and

Dane – we plucked victory from the jaws of Death.' The young man raised a fist high in the air.

'My poor father perished on that day. But he died a good death, he died a warrior's death, with the bodies of his enemies piled before him, piled high like drifts of autumn leaves. He perished that bloody day so that we – Dane and Saxon, Jutlander and Westphalian – might all live on as free men, as true *brothers and sisters*, as members of one *family*, as members of one single *northern* nation, living under our own *northern* skies, under our own *northern* gods.'

Widukind unexpectedly smashed his fist down on to the table hard. And the clatter of the silver drinking horns echoed right round the hall.

'Theodoric *died*, so we might *live*. He died for our *freedom*.'

Bjarki felt a catch in his throat, the roil of emotion swelling in his heart. This fellow could speak like a skald – he had a powerful *seithr* in his words.

'I swear to you tonight,' Widukind boomed, his words winging across the whole hall. 'That my father's death shall *not* have been in vain.'

Bjarki looked discreetly around at the other men and women in the packed hall – every eye now on the passionate young man. All the various folk stood silent, rapt, eyes locked on the young warrior standing at the dais. Some were openly weeping. Up on the platform, Bjarki could see that Valtyr was mopping at his one remaining eye with a linen napkin. He turned to Tor to make a sly comment, and saw that she, too, was entranced by the fellow's words.

'We triumphed that terrible day of battle,' Widukind continued, 'and together we sent Karolus reeling back – but he was not killed. No! He was defeated by our combined northern strength, but he was not put into the cold earth where he belongs. He still rules in Francia, he still lives, and thrives, when so many of our own dear friends are dead. His people, his meek Christians, still infest our lands in the south, on the edge of the

First Forest, and in the west, too. Much of Westphalia, my own homeland, is now gone.'

Widukind paused for several painful moments. Then he said quietly, almost too soft to hear: 'I shall not allow that to stand.'

He lifted his chin: 'I mean to *fight*. I mean to fight with every beat of my heart, with every fibre of my being, to rid our lands of this foul Frankish curse, of this Christian intrusion. I mean to take back Saxony for the Saxons – for the Danes, too, and for all the good people of the North. I have nothing to offer you, my friends, but hurt and hardship. Blood, sweat and pain. And land – land for all who follow me!'

His voice was rising again, growing in strength and power: 'For those who do follow me into battle shall be richly rewarded if we triumph, *when* we triumph, with wide territories to rule over, when we have wrested them back from the beaten foe. I offer any man or woman who would join me *land*... and everlasting *glory*. Land and glory. I ask you here this night – I ask every man and woman of courage, every man and woman of true northern blood and bone in this hall to stand together with me: to fight, to struggle, to bleed – and ultimately to *triumph* against our oppressors.'

He paused again. Bjarki could hear a nearby warrior actually sobbing.

'So I ask you only this tonight: will you *fight*? Will you stand with me and fight, shoulder to shoulder, against our common foe? Will you fight, for your own *land* – and for your own *glory*?'

It seemed to Bjarki that every warrior in the hall that night – more than two hundred men and women – bellowed out their affirmation as if with a single voice.

'Land and glory! Land and glory! *Land... and... glory!*'

Chapter Four

Minds are made up

'No,' said Bjarki. 'I must refuse, my lord. I'm not interested. I wish you luck in recovering your territory from the Franks, but I cannot fight beside you.'

Her oaf was being particularly difficult this evening, Tor thought, as she sipped her ale and tried not to stare too hard at the handsome Saxon lord sitting across the table.

She would change Bjarki's mind. How he could ignore the appeal that this man – this extraordinary leader – had made was beyond her. In her heart, she had pledged herself to Widukind of Westphalia many times over. She would follow him even into Hel's freezing realm, if he only asked her.

The feast was in full swing; folk were gorging and drinking, shouting down the benches to their friends, and yet Widukind seemed to have forgone all food and drink. Before he had plonked down opposite Bjarki and Tor, he had been moving around the hall, greeting those folk he knew and receiving congratulations and offers of service from many he did not. His talk of land and glory seemed to have struck a chord with the warriors of the Dane-Mark. And it was, Tor considered, a most astute offer.

Siegfried's flat, marshy kingdom bred bold warriors: aggressive boys, and a few girls, brave as boars, savage as wolves, who sought glory and renown above all else – except for their own little piece of dry land to farm, or a small village to keep them in cabbage, ale and pork. The Dane-Mark had been sending adventurers off to war for generations, and there were always more bodies ready to fill the ranks of the shield wall. Land and glory, that's what they craved. And Widukind would provide it for them.

'You are an exceptional warrior, Bloodhand,' said Widukind, fixing Bjarki with his intense blue eyes. 'A Rekkr – the last of your kind. You already have renown and fame. Yet no lands to call your own. Why do you refuse me, when I have such need of you?'

'I'm finished with battle. I truly desire never to fight again.'

'But why? It is what you were born to do. You are Fire Born!'

'Look at her, lord,' said Bjarki, jerking a thumb at Tor's face, one eye purple and closed by the swelling. 'Look closely at my sister.'

For the first time since he had sat down, Widukind seemed uncertain. 'I heard tell of a sea battle – in which you vanquished a ship full of vikings. Your brave sister surely bears the honourable marks of that glorious encounter.'

'These are not the marks of battle, my lord. They're the marks of my fist. I did that to her. I struck her during the sea fight and might well have slain her, and a little child, as well, in my blind fury. This is why I must say no.'

Tor said: 'Bjarki – I forgive you. I've told you this a hundred times, it's just a stupid black eye. It will fade. In the heat of battle, you lashed out at me without thinking. It's nothing. I've had far worse hurts – as you know well.'

'You may forgive me, sister. I do not forgive myself. My *gandr* grows stronger with every fight, with every blow I strike while under her influence, with every man I kill. You *know*, Tor, what I fear to become, who I fear I *am* becoming. You cannot ask me to walk this path, knowing where it leads.'

Tor looked at Bjarki. He seemed to have tears glistening in his kind blue eyes. She knew what it was he feared. His fear had a face, his features familiar to both of them, and a name: Hildar Torfinnsson, their dead father.

46

She did not know what to say to persuade him he was wrong.

'You can't go through life afraid of what *might* happen,' she began. 'If we did that, we would never achieve anything of note, ever...'

Widukind put a hand on her forearm to silence her. 'Bjarki has no obligation to fight at my side, Torfinna. None whatsoever. And I would never force an unwilling man to follow me into all the pain and horror of battle. But I would ask one small boon of you, Bjarki, my friend...'

Bjarki looked at the Saxon lord. Tor could see the suspicion moving behind his honest eyes. 'What is it that you want from me?'

'I ask you only to take a morning ride with me. I ask only that you join me at dawn, at the West Gate of Hedeby, and that you accompany me for a brisk gallop, to take a little fresh air to blow away the ale fumes.'

Bjarki looked unsure, as if he foresaw some devious trap.

'I cannot ride with you, lord. I have no horse,' he said.

'I shall bring one for you. Dawn at the West Gate, yes?'

–

They sat at a long trestle table and ate and drank. Vast platters piled high with roast pork and crispy crackling were brought out by relays of thralls, and bread and stews and various pottages and mounds of vegetables in melted butter were borne forth too, and the sweet, nutty ale flowed like a river in spate. The warriors of the Dane-Mark ate and drank like heroes and bellowed their boasts to each other. Or raised their cups in friendship. Many of their words were in praise of Widukind – the Saxon Wolf, they called him – or were expressions of joy at his war against the Franks. But none of them approached the place at the middle of the table where Tor and Bjarki sat. There was a circle of emptiness around them.

'So that was your Hedeby jarl, then,' said Bjarki.

'That was him. And you said no to his face. Happy now?'

Bjarki said nothing. He speared a thick slice of fatty pork with his eating knife from the platter and took a large bite. He'd already eaten his fill, and more; his blond beard glistened with golden fat as he chewed.

Tor waited till he had finished his mouthful, then she said: 'I am going with him, Bjarki. I will fight for Widukind. I've found my captain, my jarl.'

'You want land and glory?' Bjarki said, wiping his mouth with the back of his big hand. 'Is that truly what you want, Tor?'

'I want something. I don't know what. I can't simply trot around after you for the rest of my life. Maybe I need a good cause. Maybe the cause of Widukind and the North will fulfil me. Maybe this is what I truly need.'

'Sounds like an excellent idea,' said a new voice, and a lean man with a black eyepatch sat down in the empty space that Widukind had recently vacated on the far side of the long table.

'Are you behind all this nonsense, Valtyr?' asked Bjarki. 'Are you encouraging Widukind to take on the Franks in battle? We've had peace now for a year since Hellingar. Are you trying to start it all up again?'

'How nice to see you again, Bjarki Bloodhand,' said Valtyr. 'I have missed you, too. Yes, I'm in good health, thank you for asking.'

Bjarki ignored the old man's lumbering wit. 'Widukind will never win. Karolus is far too strong. You know how many *scarae* he commands, how many regiments of Red Cloaks. If Karolus wants to possess Saxony, there's nothing Widukind, for all his fine, stirring words, can do about it.'

'The Saxon will do everything he can,' said Valtyr. 'He will fight.'

'Widukind cannot win a war against the king of the Franks. You are sending him and all these drunken fools here to their deaths.'

'So?' said Tor. 'It is a fine cause, oaf. You want to live for ever?'

'We did manage to beat the Franks last time, I seem to recall,' said Valtyr, selecting a bronze curl of pork rind and crunching on it.

'We can't expect the Franks to oblige once again by attacking the Dane-Work, our strongest fortification. And, in truth, we didn't beat Karolus himself. We beat Gerold of Swabia, a proud young fool who underestimated our strength. And we only *just* won that battle. This is quite different.'

'You have some idea how vast Karolus's territories are, Bjarki,' said the old man. 'But you don't know the whole of it. A small slice of Saxony is nothing to the king of the Franks. Not a thing. Right now he is eight hundred miles away from us – *eight hundred miles*, a good forty- or even fifty-day march – in north Italy, slaughtering Lombards, claiming their lands, fighting in a distant war, in a distant land. If he were to lose a patch of Saxony while he is away, it would mean little to that overmighty monarch.

'Yet it would mean *everything* to Widukind to regain his ancestral lands. Men will fight hard for this Saxon Wolf. Fight to the death. And the folk to whom he gives the recaptured lands – they will strive even harder to keep them. We do not seek to defeat the whole of the Frankish kingdom, Bjarki, we only seek to deprive Karolus of a tiny corner of it. I say we can win against the Franks, Bjarki. We shall win. You could be part of it.'

Bjarki helped himself to more pork, and a spoonful of buttery turnips.

'It's not my fight,' he mumbled. 'Besides, I've made up my mind. And you couldn't possibly understand my true reasons anyway, old man.'

'I might understand them better than you think, Rekkr.'

But Bjarki had turned back to the platter of pork and would say no more.

–

While Bjarki set his mind to eating, Tor and Valtyr exchanged news. The one-eyed old man had wintered on Gotland, an island east of Svealand, at the hall of their king, Floki the Lame. A drunken fight ending in a killing had enlivened one of the Jul-tide feasts.

'Can you guess who the killer was?' said Valtyr.

'I know nobody on Gotland,' replied Tor, with a puzzled frown.

'It was the traitor, Snorri Hare-Lip,' said Valtyr.

Tor pictured the man: a fat, spittle-spraying braggart, a turncoat who had secretly become a Christian and tried to open the gates of Hellingar Fortress, the key to all the Danish defences, to the Frankish legions in the great battle the year before.

'Odd he should have ended up in distant Gotland,' she said.

'Siegfried put a bounty on his life – a big one. Bring the king his severed hare-lipped head and you will receive the weight of that head in silver. He was going about calling himself Olaf the Bold, and I believe he thought no one would recognise him out there on an island in the middle of the Austmarr.'

'Who did he kill?'

'One of Floki's men who discovered who he was. He accused Snorri in the great hall in front of everybody, and was immediately gutted like a trout for his pains. And that black-hearted traitor is on the run once more.'

'You were hunting him? You alone? Were you planning to lop off his head and claim all that silver from King Siegfried?'

'I heard some rumours and thought I might check if they were true.'

Bjarki let out a thunderous belch, then took a deep swallow of his ale. Tor ignored her boorish brother and looked narrow-eyed at Valtyr. She'd always thought of him as a mild man, wise and well travelled, but not one to boldly hunt down malefactors single-handed and bring them to justice.

'Are you still looking for Snorri Hare-Lip?' she said.

'If I saw him, I would happily hack off his head and claim the reward. Who wouldn't? But I have much more pressing concerns at present.'

'Widukind's war against the Franks?'

'Among other things. The Franks are sending an embassy to Hedeby.'

'A what?'

'An embassy. They are sending some of their great lords here to parley with Siegfried under a flag of truce. It's all arranged. Hostages have already been exchanged – Siegfried sent his younger brother to the Frankish capital at Aachen, and a couple of Karolus's cousins are being held up in Viby. But the embassy is coming to Hedeby. I thought I should be here for that. To make sure that our king is given the proper advice concerning the Franks.'

'You seek to manipulate the talks between Siegfried and the foe?'

'I simply want what is best for our northern peoples.'

Tor made a scoffing noise. 'Will this affect Widukind's plans?'

'I don't think anything could stop Widukind doing whatever he wants – you mean to go south with him, Tor, and his war band, yes?'

'Yes, I'll go,' said Tor. They both glanced over at Bjarki, who was still sitting there staring miserably at the empty, grease-slick pork platter.

'I'm heading back to the warehouse,' he muttered. 'I need to sleep.'

–

Tor and Bjarki walked back to the harbour together in horrible silence. They had been in each other's company almost every day for nearly two years now, and both of them – although neither would admit it – agonised over the thought of the parting they knew was imminent. Life without the other sibling would be strange for both of them. Yet neither would beg the other to change their plans. Their minds were made up. Tor would be heading south with Widukind in a few days. While Bjarki was going back to Rerik by sea, then down to Brenna on foot to continue his search for the elusive Goran.

It was almost pitch-black that night except for a few torches outside the ale-houses and larger halls, yellow-glowing islands in the darkness where snatches of drunken singing could faintly be heard. The elm boards of the paved walkways squelched under the heavy tread of their feet. Occasionally they stepped over a man or woman who had taken too much drink and slept in the muddy street, or was huddled up in a cloak against the walls of a hall.

Bjarki tried to break the tension between them. 'I do hope poor Garm hasn't caused any trouble,' he said, giving a wholly false chuckle.

'The bear is chained up,' Tor said tightly. She was coldly furious with Bjarki. 'And Inge won't go anywhere near him. She's far too frightened.'

As they came out of the narrow street and on to the empty wooden deck in front of the big warehouse they had borrowed from Captain Lars's friend, they heard a weird eldritch keening noise.

Bjarki looked at Tor, frowning. She shrugged.

'It sounds,' he said in a puzzled tone, 'a bit like someone singing.'

'I do believe that's a lullaby,' said Tor. 'An old Slavic lullaby.'

Chapter Five

A trot down memory lane

The horse between his thighs was large, strong and clearly loved to run. Bjarki gripped the animal tightly with his thighs, and focused on not being hurled from the saddle-blanket on this joyfully galloping creature's broad back.

Ahead of him he could see two riders, fifty yards distant, knee to knee, and clearly relishing the speed of their superior mounts. He saw the young warrior – Widukind of Westphalia – lean over and shout something to the young woman. The exquisite long-necked golden girl who had taken his eye at the King's Hall feast: Edith.

She was no longer dressed like a noblewoman; her long legs under a man's thigh-length tunic were wrapped in cross-gartered trews, just like her brother Widukind's, and as he watched she laughed at whatever quip he had made and drummed her heels into her horse's flanks and easily pulled ahead of the grinning Saxon prince. It was obvious she was the better rider.

He had been rather surprised to see her there when he had turned up with matted hair, sleep-creased and short-tempered, at dawn, at the West Gate of Hedeby. Indeed, when he saw Widukind and the lady waiting by the open gate, already mounted, he wondered if the Saxon had forgotten his invitation and was riding out with a lover, or perhaps even with his Danish wife.

But this was Edith, younger sister of the Saxon Wolf, and possibly the most entrancing individual Bjarki had encountered in an age.

Bjarki's mare splashed through a stream, her churning hooves spraying rainbows, then she lurched up the far bank, nearly dislodging him from the padded saddle-blanket as she hauled herself and her rider on to higher, firmer ground. He cursed under his breath that he had ever agreed to this morning torment. He hated riding at the best of times. He had a poor seat, and his dislike of this form of travel meant he avoided it whenever possible. He had not imagined this wild cross-country scramble. He had thought he would have to endure a short gallop with Widukind, listen to a repetition of his heartfelt call to arms, politely refuse the young lord, then go back to his nest of warm blankets in the warehouse for a few more blissful hours.

He wondered if Tor was still asleep. The sun was only now peeping above the horizon, and when he had left their lodgings in the predawn grey she had been snoring next to Garm and Inge, girl and bear cuddled together.

That had been quite a surprise. When they had entered the warehouse a little after midnight, they had found Inge sitting hard against the back wall with the bear's black head resting on her lap. She had been stroking his soft fur and singing a tune to him. It was a sweet, unfamiliar melody, something from her homeland – a lullaby, just as Tor had recognised. Garm seemed to be enjoying the girl's odd, high-pitched singing and the gentle stroking of his fur, and gave them only a small sleepy yowl in welcome. As far as Bjarki could determine, the two young creatures appeared to have formed a sort of bond, a kind of friendship even, while he and Tor had been at the feast.

The two riders ahead had reined in and Widukind was gulping from a flask when Bjarki rode up to them. He was grateful that they had stopped, and for the first time – now that he was in less danger of being unceremoniously tossed from the saddle and made to look like a fool – he began to look about him. The landscape they were in was very familiar. They had set out from the West Gate heading roughly north-west on muddy tracks and narrow pathways, following the thick reed-banks on the coast of the Schlei Inlet, and had gradually come around in a wide semicircle until they struck a proper highway – the Ox Road, as he knew it was called.

It was a broad, dry thoroughfare. Used by herders since the time of heroes, hence its name, and slightly raised above the flat, surrounding farmlands.

It led due south towards the Dane-Work.

Widukind tossed him the flask and Bjarki drank – a pleasant belly-filling concoction of ale boiled with oats and a little honey – and allowed his big mare to crop the lush grass at the roadside.

'How did you like Skinfaxi?' said Widukind, smiling at him. 'She has a bold, fiery spirit, does she not? I thought she might suit you – Fire Born.'

Bjarki took a few moments to realise that the Saxon was speaking about the horse he had provided for him that morning.

He passed back the flask and said: 'She seems a fine animal.'

'If you like her, she's yours,' said Widukind. 'A gift to you.'

Bjarki said nothing. He knew it would be rude to refuse such a gift and, despite his determination to resist his blandishments, he liked the Saxon and did not wish to offend him.

'He doesn't want a mare,' said Edith. 'He clearly doesn't like horses and he has no use for one, do you, Bjarki? He's going on a trading ship back to Wendland in a few days. What is he supposed to do with a feisty mare on a cramped *knarr*? If you offer him Skinfaxi, he either has to refuse you, which would be boorish, or sell the horse before he leaves, which might be seen as an insult. You have put him in an impossible position.'

'I beg your pardon, Bjarki,' said Widukind. 'That was foolish of me.'

'Yet I honour you for the kind gesture,' said Bjarki. Then he smiled at the woman, who warmed his heart by returning his grin.

'You fought here yourself last year,' said Edith. 'At the big battle. You did great deeds here, Bjarki Bloodhand. Am I not correct?'

'Not exactly… here,' said Bjarki, gesturing at the high road.

'Let's go up on the ramparts,' said Widukind. 'Return to the place where we both bravely faced the foe in the Battle of Hellingar!'

They were off again, this time at a more leisurely trot down the arrow-straight Ox Road towards the Dane-Work, which seemed to rise up before their eyes as they approached. It took the form of two great black bars across the horizon, each stretching away into the distance, and between their two dark, sloping shoulders lay a fortress of timber and thatch: Hellingar.

This was the place where a few thousand Saxons and Danes, and their Norse allies, had faced the overwhelming might of the Franks under their commander Gerold of Swabia, the brother-in-law of Karolus himself. Now that he was confronted with the reality of the Dane-Work, Bjarki's memories came tumbling back – this Widukind, this young prince of Saxony, had indeed stood beside him in their defences on the Western Rampart, and he had charged with him, too, in a desperate attempt to avert catastrophe when the traitor Snorri Hare-Lip had opened the gates of Hellingar to the enemy.

As he approached the fortress, Bjarki saw a lone sentry on the gatehouse above the northern gate. Widukind, up ahead, was already speaking to him, identifying himself and smoothing their path. A man-sized door opened in the double gate and a second soldier came out, bowed respectfully and took Widukind's white stallion and Edith's gelding, and when Bjarki trotted up a moment later, took the reins of Skinfaxi, too.

–

Bjarki stood on the summit of the Western Rampart and gazed down the grassy slope on the other side of the wooden fence. Below him, the Mark-Channel, a ditch that spanned most of the Danish peninsula, east to west, was green with algae and weed-choked. He wondered if it was still a viable way for ships to travel between the Western Sea and the Eastern Lake.

Probably it was, he thought; King Siegfried was a prudent ruler who had spent a fortune on the Dane-Work, and since it had saved his land from the Franks only the year before, he was unlikely to have abandoned it so soon.

He turned east and squinted down the line of the Dane-Mark. He could glimpse the sea two miles in that direction and the brown smear of smoke over Hedeby. The sun was now a hand's breadth above the glittering water. The wind was fresher up here on the rampart. He could smell baking bread.

Much nearer, only a stone's throw away, was the circular shape of the great fortress. Somewhere down there a baker was at work, making the garrison's staple for the day. Bjarki saw only a few warriors walking about casually on the timber-paved streets of the interior, and a handful of sentries up on the circular walls – it was clear that the fortress was now only lightly defended. He remembered it as teeming with warriors, hundreds of them crammed in, and he himself suddenly placed in command of them all. Then the red-cloaked legions of the Franks had swarmed up against the walls...

'I do relish the view from up here,' said Widukind, shocking him from his reverie. 'I feel I'm standing on the lip of Saxony – my own beloved homeland – and looking godlike over the whole of it. As far as I can see was once my father's domain. Well, this part here was – and is – Jarl Ulf's territory of Nordalbia, but he swore an oath to Theodoric, as did Jarl Hessi of Eastphalia and Jarl Brun, Horse-Master of the Angrians. They were all independent rulers, but my father was their overlord. A king in all but name.'

Widukind paused then, and shot Bjarki a sly glance.

'It is a great shame, I think,' he continued, 'that not one of those brave and noble jarls has renewed that oath to his only son.'

Bjarki said nothing. *Here it comes*, he thought. Here come the stirring words, the heart-squeezing appeal to join the young Saxon's growing war band. He set his jaw. Clenched his teeth to keep the angry words inside.

'I had thought that at least one of those powerful lords of Saxony, who were once such great warriors, such champions of their people, I thought that at least one would prove steadfast to my father's memory. Alas...'

Bjarki turned on the young man. 'Save your breath to cool your broth, Saxon,' he said. 'I have already given you my answer.' He found that he was now struggling to hold on to his temper. 'I shall not make an oath to serve you. I shall not unleash my *gandr* in your cause. I shall not choose the path of the Fire Born, a doomed path, to save your notion of family honour.'

'I know that,' said Widukind. 'I heard your answer last night. I did.'

Bjarki was taken aback; he had expected more resistance from this young warrior. 'Then I do not see what we have to speak about,' he said.

He saw that Edith was fifty paces away, out of earshot, gazing at the landscape. She had evidently decided to give them some privacy.

'You do not know what an honour it is just to be in your company, my friend. You're Bjarki Bloodhand, the last Rekkr of the Middle-Realm.'

Bjarki stared hard at Widukind. 'You seek to flatter me now.'

'I do not. I speak the truth. Will you allow me to tell it to you?'

Bjarki shrugged.

'It is true that I was planning to remind you that we fought here together, shoulder to shoulder, on this very spot. I was, in fact, going to remind you it was I who persuaded my father that you be given command of Hellingar Fortress. But I chose not to.'

'Yet you have just done so.'

'True. It is also true that I do seek your help in my struggle against the Franks. But I beg you to allow me to tell you *why*. Will you let me make this one last appeal for your services?'

Bjarki waved a hand vaguely in the air. It might have meant 'go ahead' or 'I can't prevent you'. Either way, Widukind forged onwards: 'Thank you. But first let me tell you what it is that I can offer *you*.'

'Land and glory – right? I wasn't asleep in the hall last night.'

'Land, yes. I believe you may have already had your fill of glory. So what I offer you is a position of great authority, of complete command over the whole of the south of Saxony. I want you to be my jarl from the River Rhenus as far eastward as the River Weser – all of Saxony south of the River Lippe will be yours to rule. You can call yourself the Jarl of the Three Rivers, or the Warden of the First Forest or... I don't care what you take as your title. You would have sole authority, under me, of course, over that huge swathe of territory. All the villages, all the farms, all the *hersirs*, would pay their taxes every quarter to you, personally, the money yours to spend as you choose. And you report only to me – to me alone.'

Bjarki was suddenly frozen; the word 'jarl' was spinning around in his head. He'd never imagined such a high honour, in even his wildest dreams.

'I know what you would say,' said Widukind. 'That this land is now mostly under the control of the Franks – indeed, you may already know that they are building a great fortress at Sigiburg, a bastion to guard their road, the Hellweg, the artery along which their legions march when they seek to despoil Saxony. These lands are not mine to give, that's what you may say.'

Bjarki was, in fact, pondering his new title – Bjarki Blood-hand, Warden of the First Forest, or Jarl Bjarki of the Three Rivers. But he had the wit to keep his mouth shut and just listen to the Saxon's speech.

'You would be right to make this valid objection,' said Widukind. 'But I'll give you six hundred people – good warriors all, a mix of Saxons and Danes, and a few others, to take Sigiburg Fortress from the enemy and to garrison it with our own people. I shall be engaged in the west, in the Stolen Lands, but I will give you this small army to cut their highway, the Hellweg, in south Saxony and keep the Franks out of our lands, *your* lands.'

'My answer stands,' said Bjarki, summoning all his reserves of will.

'You're not yet persuaded, I can see that,' Widukind continued. 'You fear you will become Galálar – I believe that is the correct word – like your father Hildar, whom you had to kill. I know the story, you see. Valtyr told me. But let me tell you this. You knew *my* father. You knew he was a Rekkr, of the Boar Lodge. So answer me this: what age was my father when he died?'

Bjarki pictured Theodoric in his mind: a hefty, red-faced, oldish fellow.

'Sixty years?' he said.

'He had seen sixty-four summers when he died on that very spot right there,' said Widukind, pointing over the rampart at a patch of grass near the edge of the Mark-Channel, a mere hundred paces away.

'He died an old man. That's my point. Yet he was a Rekkr. If he chose, he could have died in his own bed. He did *not* wish to do that.'

'I don't follow,' said Bjarki. 'What has this to do with me?'

'It's simple,' said Widukind. 'I *do not* want you to fight. I *do not* want you to kill – or risk death – for me. I want you to lead others, as my father did. No one questions your valour. No one doubts your battle skill or your courage. All men respect you – they fear you, too, which is no bad thing…

'I am saying you could lead six hundred bold warriors into battle in south Saxony and never once unsheathe your sword. I saw you here, this time last year, when Snorri Hare-Lip opened the gates and revealed himself a traitor. You did not hesitate. You charged down the slope and thwarted the Frankish attack. The other folk up here came with you. I was among them. That's why I recommended you to my father, that's why I persuaded him that you should be the Master of Hellingar. You are a born leader of warriors. You have that rarest of all qualities.'

Widukind put a hand on Bjarki's shoulder and squeezed.

'I do not require you to personally slaughter legions of Franks for me in some terrible Galálar blood-frenzy. I want you to live till you are as old as my beloved father. I want you to *lead* six hundred of my people in this coming war. And I want you to lead all those warriors to victory.'

—

Bjarki did not remember agreeing to Widukind's offer. But he must have done so because his will to resist the Saxon had completely evaporated, and both men knew it. Perhaps it was the promise of great wealth and power that turned his head, or the knowledge that he would not be obliged to summon his *gandr* and join in the slaughter – unless he wished to. Or perhaps it was because he did not wish to abandon Tor, his only kin, and he with no other plan except to go back to Brenna and hope to simply run into Goran by chance – something even Bjarki knew deep down was most unlikely. Whatever reason, he was committed to the cause now. He was Widukind's man – his jarl. He silently rehearsed his new appellation in his head: Bjarki Bloodhand, Jarl of the Three Rivers *and* Warden of the First Forest.

On the ride back to Hedeby, the three of them all abreast, they spoke amicably about the huge area of land in the south he was to rule as Widukind's new jarl.

'Karolus will come at the Groves of Eresburg again,' Widukind said. 'And a large part of your task must be the protection of the Fyr Skola and its folk. It is a powerful symbol for all of us in the North – and their king surely understands this very well. He tried to destroy the Groves once before, but he failed to fortify it or leave a garrison up there. I am told they now have about thirty people on the Eresburg, some Barda, one or two *gothi*, even a couple of Rekkr candidates. I want you to strengthen the Groves when you have taken Sigiburg and cut the Hellweg. We can't afford to lose it. The Groves of Eresburg are the heart of Saxony, Bjarki. While they stand, we fight on.'

Bjarki nodded. This talk of the Fyr Skola had roused his deep emotions: the Groves of Eresburg was the place in which he had first felt a sense of self-worth. The Fyr Skola had laid the foundations of the man he was today: Bjarki Bloodhand, Jarl of the Three Rivers and Warden of the First Forest.

'I will defend it, my lord,' he said. 'I think I understand the mistakes that were made last time the Franks came at us there. But you are wrong to think that a mere *place* – one single location – is the heart of the North.'

'What do you mean?' asked Widukind, frowning.

Bjarki said nothing for a while. Then he said: 'If we lose the Groves of Eresburg, will you stop fighting? Will you surrender?'

'No. Never. Not while I have breath in my body.'

'And others will also continue to fight alongside you?'

'Yes. Oh, I see what you mean,' said Widukind.

'As long as one stout-hearted warrior of the North stands with his feet planted on his own lands,' said Bjarki, 'ready to defend them against all, ready to die for them, then we are not defeated. We will *never* be defeated.'

'Beautiful! You're as poetic as a skald, Bjarki Bloodhand,' said Edith.

Chapter Six

Old friends, old enemies

The Frankish embassy arrived in Hedeby the next day. From the high walls beside the West Gate, Tor watched the procession wind up the road to the banging of drums, the squawk of trumpets and even the clash of cymbals.

The Franks approached from the south-west on an offshoot of the Ox Road, which split from the main road about a mile south of Hellingar.

There were about sixty of them, Tor reckoned, mostly warriors but with half a dozen priests or monks around their leader, a tall, handsome fellow mounted on a fine black horse and wearing a high starched linen hat marked with a black cross, and gorgeous flowing robes of gold and scarlet and blue.

'Do you recognise that fellow?' said Valtyr, who was standing beside Tor, leaning on the wooden parapet and eating an apple.

'How could I not?' said Tor. 'It's the same superior, smirking bastard who captured Bjarki and me, who humiliated us. It's Karolus's priest...'

'Bishop Livinus,' said Valtyr. 'Now Francia's most senior prelate, and personal chaplain and chancellor to the king of the Franks. We are honoured by a visit from such a great and powerful fellow, it would seem.'

They watched the procession in silence for some moments. Apart from Livinus in his bright, ostentatious robes and high bishop's mitre, most of the rest of his followers were in plain, even drab robes. The priests wore white or black, and were bareheaded, displaying the Christian tonsure – a patch shaven on their skulls to give even the youngest the semblance of old men.

Their troops, a full company – or *cunei* – of *Scholares*, the king's elite guards, wore sombre black cloaks over their thigh-length scale mail, and each man marched with two swords at his waist, one long, one short. Tor knew these soldiers well. The *Scholares*, or the Black Cloaks as they were often called, were the finest troops in Francia, hand-picked to serve Karolus.

The bishop and one or two mounted monks formed the centre of the long column, with squads of *Scholares* on foot before and behind them. But there were also four very different warriors in a square formation around the central core of religious envoys. And they looked magnificent. Their helmets were polished to a dazzling shine, with snow-white wings or polished bull's horns attached to the sides. Their iron cuirasses shone like lady's mirrors from recent polishing; their sword handles were fashioned from gold and silver and adorned with jewels, ivory and enamel, so magnificent that even the dust of a day's march could not seem to besmirch them.

Tor knew these troops too, although she had no regard for them as fighters.

'Odin's hairy arsehole,' she breathed. 'It's only the Auxilla!'

She watched the obedient *hird*-men of King Siegfried swing open the West Gate and allow the sixty-strong embassy to march through the doors, noting the huge white flag that fluttered above the procession, along with the standard of Livinus, a red, blue and gold banner emblazoned with a cross.

'Why have they come?' she asked Valtyr. 'What can they possibly hope to agree with Siegfried? The last time they met was at the Dane-Work and they threatened to invade his lands, depose him and take possession of his throne. Now they think he is willing to parley with these same Franks?'

'Parleying is always good,' said Valtyr. 'We may yet uncover what is in the enemy's mind. We may divine his secret intentions. But I'd better go now, to Siegfried's side. He will need

64

my wise counsel in the coming rounds of talks. When do you set off with Widukind?'

'The day after tomorrow. We all muster at Verden on the River Aller, I'm told, as a guest in the halls of the Angrian Horse-Master Jarl Brun.

'Widukind thinks there will be a good turnout there after his speech the other night. Jarl Brun is with him now – he has been persuaded to make his loyal oath and call him overlord, and more than forty *hersirs*, thanes and freemen of the Dane-Mark, mostly landless second sons, have also pledged to his cause in Hedeby. And if they are joined by friends and relatives...'

'Widukind will have a good-sized force to begin his war.'

'You will join us too, Valtyr?'

'Yes, when I'm done here. But make sure Widukind knows he cannot attack the Franks while this embassy is taking place – nor while they journey home. The day after they leave Hedeby, I will come south to join you at Verden. Tell Widukind. It is important, Tor. We must not break this truce.'

She shrugged. 'I'll tell him, but he has a rare fire in his belly...'

'Then I'll speak with him myself. I'll come and see him tonight.'

When Valtyr had gone, Tor amused herself by observing the reception of the Frankish embassy, which was standing in rigid formation in a space behind the West Gate. An aged jarl, one of Siegfried's uncles, was giving the visitors a long, slow and nearly inaudible speech of welcome, droning on about the time-honoured traditions of guest-friendship, honour between even the bitterest foes and the rules of a truce blessed by the gods...

Tor looked down at the four members of the Auxilla, standing quite still in their square formation around Bishop Livinus and two of his senior priests. Their shields, which were usually painted in bright, bold colours and depicting fierce beasts or martial symbols, had been painted pure white to signify they came in peace. She thought she recognised one of the Auxilla warriors – a dark fellow called Brandt, whom Bjarki and she had known in the barracks they had shared in Aachen, when they had been part of this unit.

She remembered him as one of the more competent members of their ramshackle company. A north Jutlander, she recalled, one who had run from his home after a killing and who had ended up in Karolus's service as a kind of ceremonial guard. All the members of the Auxilla were non-Franks, most of them northerners. It was a small regiment, or *scara* as the Franks called it, their poorly trained ranks filled with all sorts of men and women who came from outside the wide Frankish territories: refugees and runaways, mostly.

It made sense to include Brandt in this embassy to the Dane-Mark, Tor thought. He would have insights to offer Livinus about local customs, and he could help if any translation was required – although the Frankish tongue was close enough to the Saxon to be comprehensible to all folk in the talks.

She thought she recognised another of her Auxilla comrades: a young Hibernian girl called Yoni, a pretty, giddy little blonde who could not fight her way out of a pile of wet hay. But Tor could not be sure. The shield-maiden she was looking at had a full-face helm with nasal guard that obscured her features and a mirror-bright cuirass, both items chased with silver and gold and inlaid with images of wild boars and wolves. It was certainly a beautiful panoply, and Tor sighed, looking down at her own badly scratched and scuffed leather armour. If wars were always won by those fighting in the shiniest outfits, she reckoned, then the Auxilla would be invincible.

–

Bjarki faced the bear across the empty space of the warehouse. He scowled, growled and waggled his head comically. The animal growled back at him.

Garm was on all fours, his black furry back arched, the hairs slightly raised. The young bear had a length of rope between its teeth, a chewed, drool-slathered foot of thick hemp that Bjarki had cut from a coil they found among some old ship's stores. The bear shook his head, the length of rope lashing back and forth as if he meant to taunt the man.

Bjarki responded to the implied taunt – he struck.

He leapt forward and rolled on his shoulder, coming up lithely just in front of the bear's long snout. He feinted with his left hand, waving the fingers beside the animal's head, and snatched the length of rope with his right, wrenching it from the bear's mouth, before leaping away.

Garm barked with displeasure, and bounded after the man, catching him effortlessly and bowling Bjarki over with a knock from his powerful shoulder. The bear bent over the now-gasping man lying on his back, and ripped the soggy length of rope from his unresisting fingers, then shuffled back to his corner, yowling softly to celebrate his victory.

Inge, who was sitting cross-legged on a big wooden box, safely out of the path of the two battling creatures, shouted: 'Bear! Bear!' as if awarding points to one of the contestants. She had picked up some odd words of Norse in the few days she had been with Bjarki and Tor. And her strange friendship with Garm seemed to have given her a whole new charge of self-confidence.

'I'll grant you this round, Garm,' said Bjarki, slowly and painfully getting to his feet. He had stripped to the waist for the bout, and scars and bruises and a few freshly sewn and bandaged wounds covered his fish-white skin like a patchwork. He hobbled over to the bear and hugged the animal round its neck and, while the trusting cub accepted his embrace, Bjarki's thieving hand crept up to his muzzle and seized the slobbery knotted end of the rope. He snatched, jumped away, rolled once again and bobbed up in his own corner of the dim warehouse, laughing.

'But *this* round, I believe, must go to me!' said Bjarki.

He shook the thick, sodden rope in the air in his triumph.

'Bad man! No good!' shouted Inge. 'Steal! No good.'

The bear seemed to agree with his new little friend. He stood up on his hind feet, his paws with their long black claws clearly displayed, and roared. It was a full-blast meaty trumpet of sound. He peeled back his black lips to reveal his long white teeth in blood-red gums – and Bjarki, for the first time ever while playing with the creature, something he had done most days of their acquaintance, felt a real frisson of fear scurry down his back.

The animal's eyes, normally a friendly light brown, almost a yellowish colour, now seemed to glow with furious fire. The young bear lumbered forward; he snarled, teeth fully exposed. And Bjarki glanced nervously over at his weapons, his axe, sword and seax, which were piled on his mound of bed-blankets three yards away. Too far away.

'Bad man. Give bear!' shouted a still-outraged Inge. 'Give!'

The bear was a yard from Bjarki now, still growling most horribly. The voice-tone was different: deeper, menacing. For an instant, Bjarki thought the animal might actually come for him, attack him in earnest.

So the mighty Rekkr meekly held out the damp length of ship's rope at arm's length in front of him.

'All right, boy, you win,' he muttered. 'Here's your prize.'

Garm ducked his head forward and delicately took the knotted hemp in his long teeth, and flicked it out of the big man's grasp. Then the bear turned and shambled across the warehouse, now mewling with obvious pleasure.

Bjarki looked up at the girl on the box. 'Hey, little one, whose side are you on, anyway?' he asked. 'Who rescued you from those nasty pirates?'

The girl lifted her tiny nose in the air and turned her blonde head away from him. 'You steal!' she said. 'Bad Bjarki! Good Garm!'

Bjarki was very deeply asleep when the knocking roused him from his blankets. He had been totally exhausted after his rough rope game with the bear, and much of his body still throbbed from hurts taken in the sea battle.

But he was at peace in his own mind for the first time in some weeks. He would remain with his sister, and now he had a real purpose in life. The prospect of fighting the Franks – so long as he did not have to summon up his *gandr* and risk going Galálar – was not entirely unappealing. He had an old score to settle with Karolus and his legions. Yet most satisfying of all, to his mind, was that he was now Bjarki Bloodhand, Jarl of the Three Rivers and Warden of the First Forest. He was a man of consequence. He was somebody – no longer the poor fisher boy from Bago; nor the wandering vagabond forced to work like a mule for pennies. He was a jarl of Saxony. A great man. And he was grateful to Widukind for making him feel this fine about himself. And, perhaps as a result of all this, his sleep was dreamless.

The knocking at the door was Valtyr, in unusually high spirits.

'How go the talks with the Frankish embassy?' said Bjarki, yawning, scratching his balls and ushering his beaming visitor inside the warehouse.

The bear lifted his black furry head and opened one eye. He briefly examined Valtyr, snorted once loudly and went back to sleep. Inge, who was curled up beside Garm, enjoying his body warmth, did not stir at all.

Bjarki wondered where Tor was.

'Lots of fine words, little substance. The usual stuff. And it will go on for some time, I believe. A few weeks, anyway. I think Livinus – did you know it was Bishop Livinus in charge of their embassy? – I think Livinus is eventually going to make some sort of offer to King Siegfried before the start of the fighting season, something to keep him out of the war in Saxony. A big pile of gold, probably. Or a massive chest of silver coins. Some kind of grubby bribe. I don't know what. But I do know Siegfried will refuse it, whatever the bribe is. He's far too proud, our beloved king. Anyway, it is too late now to stop a war.' Valtyr was grinning at Bjarki like a drunken pirate. 'Widukind has recruited more than enough warriors and is on his way.'

'Wait! Widukind has already left Hedeby?'

'No, but he'll be off soon. He took Jarl Brun's oath of fealty, did you know? And more than a hundred of Siegfried's folk have agreed to follow him.'

'That's good.'

'I heard he offered you six hundred warriors and the title of jarl. And you accepted. Is that right?'

For an instant, Bjarki felt a shaft of doubt. He wondered if he had just accepted 'some kind of grubby bribe'. He pushed that ugly thought aside.

'Are you sure Siegfried will say no?'

'Certain. I think even Bishop Livinus would be astonished if our king accepted. This is about feeling the enemy out, trying to get a look inside his private mind. Livinus will have his spies with him, sneaking around, asking our people cunning questions. The Christians will be taking the measure of the Dane-Mark over the next few weeks, testing its will to support the Saxons. That's all this is about. It's a scouting mission, dressed up in fancy clothes.'

It seemed a lot of time and effort, to Bjarki, to discover the mood of the Dane-Mark. Anyone who had heard Widukind's speech in the King's Hall could give Livinus his answer.

'You want ale?' he said. 'I have a little stew left if you're hungry.'

'No. I'm for bed. But I'd be grateful if you, Jarl Bjarki, would do something for me. For Widukind, if you prefer. A service for our noble cause.'

Bjarki wondered if Valtyr was mocking him.

'I'd already taken to *my* bed. I need to rest before we march south.'

'No lamb for the lazy wolf,' said Valtyr with a smug little smile. 'Now, listen to me closely: the Frankish delegation have been given use of the old hall near the street of the silversmiths for the duration – it's just a bowshot from here. Why don't you go up there and see some old friends of yours, and welcome them to the Dane-Mark? Bishop Livinus brought some of the Auxilla with him as an honour guard, did you know? Go and pay your respects. Ask how things are in Aachen. See if you can pick up gossip. See if you can learn anything useful to us about the comings and goings of the Frankish court.'

'You want me to spy on them?' said Bjarki, a little shocked.

'No, no, nothing like that. Well, in fact, yes. But think of it as a chance to see some old friends. I brought you something to take along as a gift.'

–

Bjarki wondered if other jarls were pushed around in this abrupt fashion – who was Valtyr, anyway? A simple trader, a travelling man who dabbled in portable trinkets? He was not even a *hersir* in rank. He had no position at all in Widukind's circle, so far as Bjarki knew, nor a post in Siegfried's court.

Valtyr had once told Bjarki that he was something called a Guardian of the North, a member of a fellowship that protected the people. Did that give the old man the right to order a jarl around as if he were some ignorant thrall with straw in his hair?

Yet Bjarki was an obliging fellow at heart, and Valtyr was a friend, so he left Inge and Garm snoring peacefully in the warehouse and, grabbing a cloak and tucking the small wooden cask of mead – Valtyr's handsome gift – under his arm, he stepped out willingly into the dark streets of Hedeby.

–

Any disgruntlement that Bjarki might have felt towards his old friend was soon washed away on a tide of laughter, friendship and mead. Bjarki, sitting at a rough-hewn pine table in a cramped hall in the northern quarter of Hedeby that had been set aside for the use of the four members of the Auxilla, soon realised he was enjoying himself enormously.

At the table with him sat Brandt, a grim-looking warrior who was in truth a fellow of good spirits, and even humour, once he had taken a drink or two; a man named Ringast a serious older warrior from Scania, the most easterly part of the Dane-Mark, who claimed that he had joined the Auxilla because he wished to see more of the world; and Yoni, a very pretty girl he had known in Aachen – a person for whom he had, at times, harboured desires.

It was evident that his three hosts – the fourth member of the Auxilla honour guard, a fellow named Nils, was fast asleep at the end of the hall – were more than pleased to have his company, and to be able to partake of his mead, which turned out to be the finest quality, sweet and strong and clear.

'The last time I set eyes on you, Bjarki,' Yoni said, fixing him now with those same eyes, very large, luminous bright blue ones, that had been delicately underlined with black kohl, 'you were heading off with your grumpy girl to fight a dread monster. What happened next? Captain Otto never returned to the Auxilla, and *your* name was never spoken again in the barracks. Did you kill the monster? Tell us all about it.'

She had a most charming Hibernian lilt to her voice, Bjarki thought.

'Tor was never my *girl*,' said Bjarki. 'Not in that way. Which is just as well. We did not know it at the time, but it turns out she's my own half-sister. We would have been like Freyr and Freyja. We had the same father, you know. In fact, Tor is in Hedeby right now. I'm sure she could be persuaded to come round and see you here, to catch up with old friends, if you should like that...'

No one said anything in reply to that for just a little too long.

'You must tell us all about the dread monster,' said Yoni.

'You went to a place called Egg Town, wasn't that it?' said Brandt.

So Bjarki told a half-true version of the story. He talked about the great wounded she-bear they had met and battled and slain. How the creature had tragically killed Captain Otto, at that time the leader or *hersir* of the Auxilla. However, he did *not* mention that he had discovered his *gandr* inside the huge she-bear, Garm's mother, and personally slaughtered two dozen pursuing Black Cloaks, as well as eviscerating the commander of Karolus's personal guard, the King's Shield, a fearsome Wendish ogre called Lord Grimoald.

He made it sound a bit like a fairy tale, an adventure in the deep, snowy woods of Thuringia. In fact, he made it sound altogether a little too fanciful.

'So why did you not return home to us?' asked Brandt.

Bjarki covered his confusion by taking a slurp of mead, then refilling his cup and everyone else's. After killing Lord Grimoald, the King's Shield, there was no way they could return to Aachen even if they'd wanted to.

'I felt I could not return to Aachen because there was so much more of the world to see. Like you, Ringast, I wanted to travel...'

It was not a satisfactory answer. His three hosts frowned and scratched their heads. 'But you did *not* travel, you went back to the Dane-Mark,' pointed out Yoni. 'I heard that you even fought against the king in the great battle at Hellingar. Several Red Cloak officers recognised you there.'

'It's the religion, isn't it?' said Brandt. 'The worship of the Christ god they insist on. That's why you left us, Bjarki, am I right?'

In a flood of relief, Bjarki assured them this was perfectly true.

'I am Odin's man,' he said. 'I remain true to the old ways.'

And thankfully the talk then moved on to other matters.

'So who replaced Otto as *hersir* of the Auxilla?' Bjarki asked.

'We had a *nithing* called Svein the Red, who died of fever this last Jul-tide,' said Brandt. 'But now we have a new captain. A bold, swaggering fellow – a jarl, no less. He claims he has grand plans for the Auxilla. He wants to turn us into a fighting unit. He brought a dozen warriors with him when he joined, and he has been recruiting more folk ever since. It was he who persuaded Bishop Livinus that we should be a part of this embassy.'

'It's very different now, Bjarki,' said Yoni. 'The *hersir* has us training hard every day, morning to night. We have to keep all our kit spotless, not just the expensive ceremonial gear. You wouldn't recognise us.'

'He sounds like a fine, efficient captain,' said Bjarki. 'And what is the name of this paragon of military virtue, if I may ask?'

'He's called Snorri,' said Yoni. 'But he's not all that fine to look at – he is rather too fat in the belly, to be honest, and his upper lip is split in two like a hare's – but it's true that he *has* completely transformed the Auxilla.'

'Jarl Snorri Hare-Lip? *He's* your new captain?'

'That's our man – why, do you know him?'

–

Bjarki left in the dawn with a leathery mouth and an aching head. But also suffused with the marvellous glow of pleasure received and given. He left Yoni sleeping in her blankets, her mouth wide open and a thread of drool running down her cheek. He kissed her lightly on the forehead before he left, and wondered if he'd ever see her again. It seemed unlikely. They had both readily acknowledged the fleeting nature of their union the night before.

Yet it had been a very satisfying bout. Bjarki had not enjoyed a woman's body for some months, and he felt both exhausted and filled with a warm, slow energy by the encounter. He could feel the itch of the scratches she made on his back – and that made him smile like a simpleton.

'Had a good night?' said Tor, when she flung open the warehouse door. She sniffed the air around him. 'Yeuch! You get *any* sleep at all?'

Bjarki beamed at her.

'Well, good for you, oaf. But you'd better wash your balls and pack your gear. We are leaving at noon. All of Widukind's people.'

'I thought we had a day or two,' said Bjarki.

'Change of plan. He wants us on the road today.'

Chapter Seven

The building of an army

The day was magnificent – a bursting, full-blossoming, muscular spring morning. The hawthorn was in flower with dark, gnarled branches covered in clusters of tiny white petals like half-thawed snowdrifts. There were vivid blue crocuses thrusting out beneath the shady roots of oak trees, and creamy narcissi, with glowing yellow hearts, nodded like royal syco-phants on the lush verges of the wide road along which they marched. They were now a force more than two hundred warriors strong, Tor reckoned, a proper army of young Danes and Saxons all heading south through the flat lands of the Nordalbian tribe, the most northerly territory of all Saxony.

It was a good haul for a few days of passionate talking in the halls of Hedeby. And there would be many more men and women following them in the next few days and weeks. That was clearly Widukind's greatest gift, she realised. He could talk as skilfully as Loki. Like the trickster god, the Saxon prince seemed to be able to persuade anyone of absolutely anything.

And she had fallen in love with his moving words the moment she first heard him open his mouth: his shining vision of a united North – Saxon and Dane together – triumphing over the perfidious Christians. His message spoke to her heart. But she had been astonished when she discovered her oaf had also agreed to join his band, and delighted. Although, of course, she could not tell Bjarki how happy she was that they would not now be parting.

He knew it, anyway. She was sure he did.

She was less than delighted by the company Widukind was keeping that golden spring day. The female bulk who was riding next to his white stallion on a solid grey pony, her wide body jiggling like calf's foot jelly on a platter. Geva was the milch cow's name, and Tor loathed the sight of her.

She was, however, Widukind's lawful wife, and the daughter of King Siegfried, to boot, the embodiment of the alliance between Saxon and Dane. For this reason only Tor had decided she would not slit the fat sow's throat.

Tor knew that Widukind could not truly love her – she was simply too flabby, too graceless, too relentlessly jolly for any real man to find at all interesting. She saw that he had sacrificed his own happiness for the sake of the North; he only lay in her doughy arms at night so that Saxon and Dane might march arm in arm against the Christian foe. Tor knew she ought to revere this royal wife of her lord. But she hated everything about her, from her great wobbling bosoms to her blocky calf muscles, which were visible under the silver-stitched hem of the unsuitable purple gown she wore on the march.

Beside Tor that day rode Bjarki, his face sagging like butter in the sun.

He was still smiling, though, albeit faintly. Whichever Hedeby hussy he had been rutting with the night before seemed to have transformed his mood, and she was glad of that. She herself had experienced lovemaking only once. In Rerik, when she was bored and lonely during the long winter nights, she had bedded the son of a grain merchant from Scania but had found the experience briefly painful, mildly embarrassing and horribly unsatisfying.

After that one grisly encounter she had decided she would not bother with all that nonsense again. For some reason, most of the men she liked, the right kind of men, seemed to find her unapproachable. Some even admitted they were frightened of her – and that immediately turned them into the wrong kind of men. The obviously wrong kind of men always fell for her hard and made idiots of themselves, which meant she could not respect them. So that was that. Then there were the unabashed pigs – and she tended to knock them flat on their arses immediately so there could be no misunderstanding.

'Do you know why we left in such a hurry?' said Bjarki.

'There's an important ceremony being held in Verden in a couple of weeks, or so Widukind says. He needs to prepare for that. He also said something about wanting to blood his new troops as soon as possible.'

'So you *don't* know.'

'You're the big man in our war band, the jarl, the Warden of the Three Forests or whatever your stupid new title is – why don't *you* go and ask him?'

'He said something about the Frisians. How important they were to our cause. But my head was still humming from all the mead I drank last night, and I didn't pay full attention. I heard him say Verden, that's all.'

'So you don't know either.'

'No doubt he'll make a stirring speech about it tonight at camp.'

'No doubt he will,' said Tor.

She turned her horse and headed down the line to check on Garm and Inge, who were trudging along at the very rear.

–

Widukind did not make any kind of speech that night. They bivouacked in a sheep pasture near a copse of elm and a babbling stream. Widukind and Geva slept in a makeshift tent made from a few riding cloaks, and everyone else slept on the turf around several bonfires. The next morning they were off again, without a word from their charismatic young leader.

The bear seemed to enjoy the journey, and even allowed Inge to ride on his back for a part of the way, like a horse, the girl clinging on to his leather collar, before shaking her off after a mile or two with an impatient growl.

It felt good, though, to be on the march again, Tor thought. Bjarki had fully recovered from his debauch, and had a new lightness or buoyancy to him that lifted the hearts of all who spoke with him. There were many, she saw, who wanted to befriend the famous Rekkr, the new jarl, now that they saw he would not rebuff them. Bjarki also spent time riding with the other leaders of the war band – Abbio, the strange crow-like man, all dressed in black rags, who was Widukind's closest adviser, and the haughty Jarl Brun, lord of the Angrians, whose fine hall they were heading to at Verden.

'I think he practises *seithr*,' whispered Bjarki the next night, as they lay side by side in their blankets in a stand of ash on the marshy south bank of the Elbe, which had taken all afternoon for the Saxon army to get across.

'Who – Jarl Brun?' Tor found it difficult to imagine the aristocratic horseman indulging in the dark arts. He looked as if he would find all that messing around with the cauls of newborns and toads' skins and packets of dried virgins' monthly blood far beneath his immense and chilly dignity.

'No – not him. Abbio. Widukind's friend.'

On the other hand, Tor could easily imagine *him* as a practitioner of any amount of dark sorcery. The man muttered to himself like a grandfather. And smelt appalling – even compared to the rest of them after two sweaty days on the road.

'What gave him away?' said Tor. 'Was it the magical iron staff he always carries? Or the spooky dried bird bones in his beard?'

'Don't joke about it. That sort of thing makes me uneasy.'

'Bjarki, half the folk here genuinely believe that you turn into a wild bear every time you lose your temper.'

'What is your point?'

'No point. Just stay away from Abbio, if you don't like him.'

'I would. But he seems to be hanging around Edith a lot. I worry that he is putting some kind of a bewitching spell on her. A glamour, perhaps.'

Edith – Tor had often seen her older brother mooning around Edith. Grinning foolishly, laughing, making bad jokes just to amuse her. He had even picked some spring flowers for her, which she wore in her hair until they fell out.

A thought struck her – surely Widukind's sister could not be the energetic hussy Bjarki had been ploughing the night before they left? No.

'I don't think Edith is in any danger,' she said. 'Abbio, even if he does dabble in the dark arts, would not dare to harm the sister of his friend. No one in their right mind would risk Widukind's wrath by even touching her.'

She gave Bjarki a significant stare. Her brother was oblivious.

'I just don't trust that man,' he muttered. 'He's... simply *wrong.*'

–

They arrived at Verden on the evening of the fourth day. In the dying light of the sun, the smooth, limewashed walls of Jarl Brun's hall seemed to shine like sheets of beaten gold.

The hall stood at the centre of a large complex of lesser halls and houses, storerooms, granaries, kitchens, brewhouses, forges and stables – many, many stables, both large and small.

The whole sprawling settlement, built beside an ancient fording place on the north bank of the slow River Aller, was surrounded by a circular rampart and stockade with four wide gates – one facing in each direction.

They had ridden all that day through the famous horse pastures of Angria. Wide fields of short-cropped grass populated by huge herds of equines, hundreds in each herd, guarded only by small near-naked boys and girls who rode bareback as if they were a part of the dashing creatures between their thighs. Tor was entranced by the spectacle of the children, yipping and hallooing and rounding up the galloping masses, turning them this way and that, guiding the herd into large paddocks nearer the town, where smiths with portable forges were busy, separating individual steeds and roping and swiftly shoeing them. The warm spring air was filled with the din of hammer on anvil and the sizzle of red-hot iron on hoof.

Tor had never seen so many horses together in one place – hundreds, perhaps thousands of them. This was the true wealth of Angria.

Bjarki, who could not wait to get down from his own mount after four days of riding – he had reluctantly accepted Skinfaxi as a gift – was less impressed with this seething ocean of horseflesh.

'A warrior should fight on his own two feet,' he pronounced, when Tor expressed joy at the sight of all these cavalry mounts. 'It's more natural.'

'Just because you're a high-and-mighty jarl now, oaf, doesn't mean you need to talk like a pompous old grandpa,' she said.

–

They found out the reason for the mass round-up of horses later that night, when Widukind summoned his captains for a council after supper.

'Beginning thirty miles west of here, beyond the Hunte River but east of Ems River, is a wide tranche of good pasture we call the Stolen Lands.'

Widukind stood at the centre of a long table with a dozen men and a couple of women gathered around him. He drew two lines in the spilled ale on the wood, to indicate the rivers that bounded the territory he had named.

'This was the Westphalian heartland until two years ago. Now the local people have either fled east into Angria or been enslaved by the Franks and set to work in their fields. And our enemy has built three fortified churches there, the kinds of settlements that are called *castra*. One is situated here,' he indicated a spot on the wood with his wet finger. 'Another one is here,' another ale dot. 'And the largest one in the south – about here – is the strongest manned and fortified and oldest

Christian settlement. There is now a good-sized market there, too, in the place which is called Osnabrucke.'

The warriors round the table leaned in and peered at the wet lines and dots on the worn wood. Widukind let them absorb the map for a moment, then he said: 'To the north of the Stolen Lands is Frisia, which is now firmly under the thumb of Karolus. But Frisian folk are like our own people – people of the North – they worship the same gods we do, those who have not been corrupted by the poison of the Christ god. When they look southwards, they see the rich lands of the Saxons now overrun by the Franks. They see the Stolen Lands occupied by our Christian enemies, and their hearts fail inside their chests. They think: if the mighty Saxons can be so easily defeated, how can little Frisia hope to stand against the Frankish legions?

'Our first task this year is to give our Frisian brothers and sisters new hope. Ultimately, we must unite with Frisia to drive back the Franks once and for all. But this fighting season, I mean to take back the Stolen Lands. And, to do that, I must take these three Frankish settlements, here, here and here.'

He put his finger once more on the ale-wet dots on the table. 'I mean to destroy them all – all three of these *castra* – in a single lightning campaign.'

There were many gasps, and some murmurs of approval too.

'The key to the victory will be speed. The key to speed, my friends, is horses. Many horses. The swift, bold steeds of Angria.'

As Widukind outlined his ambitious plan, which involved three large mounted forces, attacking the three enemy *castra* one after the other in very quick succession, Bjarki began to feel uneasy. He hoped that he would not be expected to lead a cavalry attack on a fortified town. He had attacked a *castrum* once before on foot, and it had led to the massacre of a Saxon war band and the death of many friends. But he felt he could make no objection. He was fully committed to Widukind's cause now – for good or ill.

Widukind continued, speaking about the size of the forces necessary for this western campaign, and how they hoped to move very quickly on horseback, after taking the first *castrum*, to attack the second, and on to the third, with luck *before* the news of the Frankish defeats had reached the other targets.

Widukind named the captains, three seasoned warriors, two Saxons and a Dane, none of whom Bjarki knew well, who would lead the three contingents – and the Saxon Wolf promised them that after the triple victory they should have possession of these recaptured western territories as his local thanes.

There was a brief discussion of the numbers of warriors and remounts required, talk of what would constitute adequate fodder and food and ale to provision them, the possibility of living off the land and how to divide all the booty they captured. Widukind went through detailed instructions of each of the routes of march, so all three forces would converge on Osnabrucke for the final assault, and then the council came to an end, with Widukind telling his captains to pick their lieutenants and be ready to ride in about a week's time.

'We shall depart the moment we hear word that the Frankish embassy has left Hedeby,' the Saxon Wolf said. 'We cannot leave before or we risk breaching the terms of the truce.' All around the long table grizzled heads nodded in solemn agreement.

Bjarki frowned as he saw that the gathering was breaking up. He realised he had not been mentioned once in the discussions, and he was overcome with a feeling of dizzy disorientation, as if this gathering of warriors inside Jarl Brun's hall was just a dream.

What was his part in this campaign? Did he even have a role? As soon as the council meeting broke up, he approached Widukind.

'You're not a horseman, Bjarki,' said the Saxon. 'I mean no offence by this. But you're not the man to lead any part of *this* campaign in the Stolen Lands.'

'What am I to do then?' Bjarki asked.

'There will be much work for you soon in the south,' said Widukind. 'Beyond the River Lippe. That is where you will win your own glory. I said I'd give you six hundred recruits. And I will. I want you to build me an army out of them.'

The next day, Bjarki set to work.

—

There were fresh volunteers coming into Verden every day, small groups of three or four men trickling in, sometimes lone warriors, sometimes whole bands of armed folk, and Bjarki greeted each of them personally, with Tor glowering at them from his side. Many were from the Dane-Mark, poor, landless folk, or just young men and women in search of adventure. They had heard of Widukind's promise of land and glory and it had lit a fire in their hearts. A larger proportion of the incomers came from all four corners of Saxony – refugees from Westphalia, who had been dispossessed by the invading Franks over the past few years, but also Nordalbians and Angrians from villages within a few days' walk of Verden, and who had heard the rumours – or been sent to war by their ambitious fathers. There were even some fighters from the wild borderlands of distant Eastphalia.

Bjarki made them all run – even the horsemen. Following the rigorous training regime he had undergone in the Groves of Eresburg, he made every recruit join in the exercises. Any who refused were turned away.

They ran in the dawn for seven miles around the low hills of Verden, rain or shine, with Bjarki leading the pack and Tor at the rear, verbally nipping at the slow ones' heels like a terrier. Then they trained all morning, lifting heavy boulders and manhandling logs to build up their strength, and solving problems in groups to create a sense of comradeship: building log walls then dismantling them, vying with each other to be the fastest to complete a task. Constructing bridges to allow them to cross small rivers dry-shod. They all ate at noon and rested till evening, when Bjarki and Tor gave them instruction in the use of weapons.

It quickly became apparent that many of the recruits, although eager to fight and win land and glory, had next to no training with weapons. There were a few sons of *hersirs* or of thanes among them who had been well schooled in sword and shield from a young age – and provided Bjarki found them congenial, he made them group leaders – but most were clumsy peasants who had wielded nothing more deadly than a scythe in their lives.

'They know less about swords than I did when I came to the Groves,' said Bjarki to Tor, one evening over ale and grilled river trout in the small longhouse they shared with Inge and Garm, inside the Verden compound but a little bit away from the great hall.

'Oh, they're not *that* bad, oaf,' said Tor, through a mouthful of hot buttered fish. 'At least they have a notion which is the sharp end.'

'Was I truly as bad as that?'

'I wouldn't say you were utterly gormless...' said Tor.

'Thank you!'

'But you weren't exactly stacked to the rafters with gorm.'

The next day, Bjarki gathered his recruits – more than four hundred of them – in a horse pasture just outside Verden. He addressed them from the broad back of Skinfaxi.

'Have any of you ever hunted game?' he asked. More than half of the recruits lifted hands. 'What implements do you use?'

It turned out almost half had used bows and arrows to bring down marsh fowl, hare or deer – a weapon of war that Bjarki had not considered. And a number of the others had hunted with light javelins or spears.

He divided his force into three unequal parts: a regiment of bowmen, one of spearmen and, finally, those who were reasonably competent with sword, axe and shield – the elite, to his mind – he formed into a *hird*, a personal guard of about fifty warriors. An older man, an experienced warrior from Eastphalia called Eckhart he made the captain of the bowmen – the Yew Regiment, it was named, after the powerful five-foot yew-wood bows its members carried. A steady fellow called Kveldulf was made captain of the Ash Regiment – the spearmen. Bjarki was puzzled by his name, which meant Night Wolf, a shape-shifter, one who turned into a wolf after dark.

'You're not Fire Born?' he asked Kveldulf over the noon pottage, after congratulating him for beating the Yews in a foot race.

'No, lord,' said the young man, grinning shyly. 'But I was named after my grandfather and he was a famous Rekkr – a member of the Wolf Lodge in the Fyr Skola. He died before I was born but my father wanted to honour his memory.'

'A fine name,' said Bjarki. 'I'm sure you'll bring great honour to it.'

Tor was placed in charge of Bjarki's *hird*, and she brought all her natural ferocity into turning this group of men – and two sturdy women – into as skilled a company as she knew how. She treated them with scorn and offered insults and a measure of rough affection. They, in turn, adored her.

Bjarki's army was taking shape.

More recruits still came in almost daily and Bjarki, after a brief meeting with them, disposed of them either to the Yew or Ash Regiments or, more rarely, to join his *hird*. Yet despite this promising beginning, all was not well in Bjarki's world. He came home to his hall with Tor after a long, hard day to find Inge sitting in the branches of a tree in the yard, weeping as if her heart would break – and Garm munching noisily on a bloody object at its roots.

Chapter Eight

The old sacrifice of the young

'I deeply regret, Jarl Brun, that I must report a tragic accident to you.'

Bjarki was standing in the hall of the lord of Verden, facing the great man himself, who was sitting bolt upright in a carved chair. Jarl Brun was looking magnificent that evening, in a fine sea-green tunic and a scarlet mantle lined with marten fur, clasped with a gold brooch. His hair and beard were freshly barbered, his moustaches were plaited into neat ropes either side of the line of his mouth, but his wild eyebrows were as untamed as a storm at sea.

'An accident, you say?' the elderly jarl seemed to be looking down his long nose at Bjarki. 'Tell me what has occurred, then.'

Bjarki was suddenly aware that he had come straight from the training ground, where he had been demonstrating some basic wrestling techniques to members of his *hird*, without changing his filthy clothes.

Behind the imposing form of Jarl Brun, his two wives, one roughly the jarl's age and another much younger and prettier, were chatting together amicably with Geva, Widukind's ever-cheerful wife.

'My pet bear, Garm,' Bjarki began, 'it seems, that he... uh.'

'Spit it out,' said Brun, frowning. 'What did your animal do?'

'It seems Garm – who is only a young cub, really, and still wilful. He has, ah, he has killed and eaten – I'm sure he did not mean to. An accident, as I say. But he gets hungry, and out of sorts...'

'Come on, man, I haven't got all night.'

'It seems that Garm has killed and eaten one of your thralls, my lord. A boy. I am sorry, and I will pay you recompense for your loss.'

'Your bear *ate* one of my house slaves?'

'Yes, lord.'

'Don't you feed the creature? By the way, since you are a jarl, you don't need to call me lord. We are equal in rank, you know.'

'Yes, lo… I mean, yes. We do indeed feed the bear, and very well, but he grows fast and…'

'Hmm,' said Jarl Brun. 'You'd better tell me what happened.'

So Bjarki related the story he had pieced together from Inge's incoherent, snot-filled account, and his own and Tor's knowledge. The unfortunate thrall, he said, was a lad of nine or ten summers called Mirko, a Sorb captured some years back in a raid conducted by an Eastphalian war band and subsequently sold on to labour as a groom to Jarl Brun.

Mirko, who worked in the nearby stables, became fascinated by the young bear, who spent most days chained up outside Bjarki's hall.

He had watched from the stables each night as either Tor or Bjarki unbuckled the bear's collar, fed him his ration of fresh meat and playfully wrestled, or played the rope game with him, until Garm was tired.

That afternoon, when he had finished his duties in the stables, and Tor and Bjarki had been busy several miles away training their recruits in the Angrian pastures, trying to get them to form tight shield walls at a word of command, Mirko had decided to play with the bear cub all on his own. He had been warned not to approach the animal by Tor, who had seen him hanging about watching them as they fed and cared for Garm. But Mirko had ignored the warning and had loosed the bear from its chain, found the gnawed piece of ship's rope and, according to Inge, had begun taunting the bear with its toy.

Boys will be boys, you might say.

Bears will be bears, too.

The hungry animal had made short work of the boy. By the time Bjarki and Tor had returned to their hall in Verden, there was very little left of young Mirko, just a limb or two and some bones and bloody rags.

'Well, it can't be helped,' said Jarl Brun, when Bjarki had told his tale. 'What's done is done. And it was only a thrall. And not a very clever one, by the sounds of it. But I really cannot have a hungry bear roaming loose around Verden. I could lend you a team of carpenters and have them build a wooden cage for your beast to live in, I suppose. How does that sound?'

It sounded terrible to Bjarki. He had once been caged himself.

'I thank you for your offer, lo… Brun. May I think on it?'

'Think away. But keep that bear safely chained up while you do. I don't want any more of my servants eaten alive. Do you hear me?'

Bjarki nodded.

Then Jarl Brun did something rather odd. He turned in his chair and beckoned his younger, prettier wife and said something quietly to her, and she nodded and slipped away in a delightful rustle of silks.

He said: 'Jarl Bjarki, I have been remiss. You have been my guest here for several weeks and I have not treated you with the level of respect you deserve. I have some fine wine in today, a rich brew from southern Francia, and I ask you to share a measure with me, and perhaps we might get to know each other a little better.'

A while later Bjarki found himself clutching a delicate green glass cone in his paw, filled with a sweet dark liquid, a nectar that he'd not tasted since he was a privileged prisoner of Karolus in Aachen more than a year ago.

'Did you know,' said Brun, 'that some *gothi* claim that Odin at his ease in his Hall of the Slain, surrounded by the heroes, only drinks wine? He doesn't need to eat at all. He gets all his nourishment from wine.'

At that moment, Bjarki's empty belly gave a loud gurgle.

'However,' said Brun, smiling at his young guest, 'since neither of us is, quite yet, feasting in Asgard, let us have some food brought in!'

–

'He gave me a comb,' Bjarki said later that night to Tor. They were sitting together by the hearth fire in their own longhouse and Bjarki passed her the object. It was a beautiful piece, a carved square of brown and white mottled ox horn with the top, where the user would grip it, cut into the shape of two elegant horses' heads.

Tor examined it closely by the light of the hearth fire, turning it over in her hands, and made a tooth-sucking noise of approval.

'Is it significant?' Bjarki asked. 'I am not accustomed to gift-giving. Does it mean something?'

'I should have thought it obvious. Look at the state of you!'

Bjarki looked down at his clothes; his tunic was badly torn under one armpit where a novice wrestler had grabbed him that afternoon when he was teaching him unarmed combat. He sniffed himself gingerly, and recoiled.

'You know you have dried mud in your hair?' she said.

'It is bath day tomorrow – I'll get clean then.'

'I do hope so,' said Tor, sniffing loudly too. 'And next time you dine with a fellow jarl, at least change your linen and comb your hair.'

To change the subject, Bjarki told her the information he had gleaned during his meal with Jarl Brun.

'He said Widukind should be back by the full moon from his Stolen Lands campaign with about half of his horsemen. That's in five days. They captured two of the three *castra* easily but met stiff resistance at Osnabrucke. They're besieging the town now.

Widukind was obliged to come back here – apparently there's to be an important ceremony, which we must all attend. Valtyr will be there.'

There had been excited reports coming in over the past three weeks of Widukind's actions in the field. Several wagons of booty – sacks of grain, great slabs of salted pork, big smoked cheeses, barrels of wine and sacks of dried fish, as well as hacksilver and real silver coins – had arrived in Verden, spoils from the two successful battles, accompanied by strings of dejected slaves, Christian settlers captured by the victorious Saxon horsemen. This influx of loot had been fortuitous, since the swollen population in and around Verden had been eating through Jarl Brun's stores of grain like a plague of mice.

Bjarki had set both his Yew and Ash Regiments to hunting game on the fringes of the First Forest, forty miles away – partly as a training exercise, partly as a foraging expedition – and they returned from time to time with hare and deer meat, and once a massive young wild aurochs. But even so, the stews and pottages served out to the regiments at noon each day were beginning to become thinner and ever more watery.

'I'll be glad when Widukind is safe back here with us,' said Tor.

Bjarki gave her a knowing glance.

'What sort of ceremony?' she went on, ignoring his sly look.

'Widukind is being initiated into the Guardians of the North – the mystical fellowship that Valtyr belongs to. Sounds like a lot of nonsense to me.'

Tor said nothing at all to that. She yawned and stretched.

'We need to talk about *him*,' said Bjarki, jerking his chin at the humped form of Garm, who was asleep, and chained to one of the central posts of the hall. 'Brun was very decent about his thrall, but he wants me to build a cage for our hungry boy to live in.'

'No,' said Tor. 'Out of the question. No cage.'

'I feel the same. But what do we do?'

Two days later, Bjarki, Tor, Inge and Garm stood in a sheep pasture and gazed at the forbidding green wall of the First Forest a hundred yards to the south of them. This was the primal woodland of Saxony, older than Man, according to the legends, and it stretched almost unbroken from the marshes of Frisia in the west in a wide sweep for hundreds of miles all the way to the Slavic lands east of the wild Frankish province of Thuringia – and beyond.

Bjarki did not know if it even had an end.

Somewhere to the south and west of them, about ten days' travel through the dark and tangled forest, was the Diemel Valley and the Groves of Eresburg, home of the Irminsul, the One Tree, and the Fyr Skola. Candidates for the honour of becoming Fire Born had for centuries had to prove themselves by surviving in the First Forest, naked and alone, with only an animal pelt and a knife.

Many did not survive.

Bjarki always had a feeling that the forest itself was watching him. Perhaps, even now, there was a half-starved young man or woman, clad only in a tattered fur, looking out hungrily at them. He saw that the local peasants maintained the practice of nailing the carcasses of animals to the trees, a *blot*, or sacrifice, to keep the spirits of the First Forest inside its borders.

'Come on,' said Tor. 'If we're doing this, we'd better do it.'

Inge, who was sitting astride the bear's neck, drummed her heels into his shoulders, urging him to lollop forward. Tor took a hold of his leather collar and tugged hard. But it seemed the bear did not want to move. Bjarki shoved at his hindquarters. It took the combined force of all three humans to get Garm to stumble down the slope of the pasture towards the wall of trees.

'You'll have a good life in here,' said Bjarki, stroking the cub's round furry ear. 'Not so many stable boys to eat, but there are deer and rabbits, and maybe even a fox or two. There is wild honey to be found in here. You *love* honey, Garm. All you have to do is sniff it out and ignore the bees' stings. You'll make friends, too – there'll be other bears...'

They walked the cub deep into the gloomy interior of the forest and found a small clearing, and there they said their goodbyes.

Inge, whose command of Saxon was growing every day, said: 'You are a good bear, Garm, a brave bear,' before breaking down and sobbing her heart out. Bjarki hugged the animal tightly and gave him his mangled bit of rope. Garm looked into his face with his big yellow eyes and whined.

Bjarki could feel the animal silently accusing him of betrayal. He looked away. But Tor, who was made of stronger stuff, dumped a haunch of venison on the turf, then cuffed the bear's cheek, really quite hard.

'You can't stay with us, boy. They'd lock you in a cage your whole life. You'd die of misery. I'd die too. You belong here in the forest.'

She slipped a rope under Garm's leather collar and, walking a few paces away, she tied it to the bole of a small tree.

The bear was too busy investigating the venison to notice.

'Are you sure he will be able to get loose?' said Bjarki.

'He can chew through that rope easily enough. Farewell now, Garm!' Tor's eyes were stinging as she grasped the young bear's head, pulled it up from the raw meat and kissed him on his wet black nose.

Garm made a little mewing noise.

'We must go, right now, before I change my mind,' she said.

And the three humans turned and quickly walked away, back out of the gloom of the trees and into the cold, sunlit world of men.

–

The path that led out of the Verden compound north towards the sacred grove by the lake was lit every ten paces with burning pine torches. They were largely unnecessary as a light source since a huge silver disc of moon shone above the route. The path wended through the horse paddocks and sheep fields to the sacred little wood, where for centuries the lords of Verden had held their holiest rites.

Bjarki felt a little uncomfortable striding along in his fine new clothes – lavish gifts from the freshly returned Widukind, flushed with his successes in battle. Bjarki had bathed long and washed thoroughly, combed his hair and beard and Tor had trimmed them both with a pair of shears and he had donned his fine attire. He wore his long, thick bearskin cloak, a scarlet tunic with silver buttons at the neck, dun-coloured trews cross-gartered neatly below the knee, and a magnificent silver necklace of bear's teeth.

Tor walked beside him, almost as primped and primed as he. Her fiery hair was freshly washed and she wore a yellow gown that fell to her ankles, a heavy blue woollen mantle over the top, pinned with a pair of silver brooches connected by a silver chain over her breasts. She looked like a traditional Saxon woman – some warrior's dutiful wife, even – and only the heavy boots on her feet, and the seax that hung at her side, said otherwise.

However, her green eyes, lined with kohl, were veined with red from the bouts of savage weeping she had indulged in since the abandonment of Garm. Bjarki, although he sorely missed the bear, had been dry-eyed and gruff for the past few days. Indeed, neither of them felt very good about their decision to free their beloved pet.

The gathering for the initiation ceremony was larger than they had imagined it would be. Bjarki estimated that there must be at least fifty adults – no children allowed – mingling in the moon-dappled clearing. He stood to one side with Tor, unsure what to do, eyeing the chattering throng uneasily when a dark, slender form glided up beside him.

'Greetings to you, Bjarki Bloodhand, Jarl of the Three Rivers and Warden of the First Forest. I trust you are in the most excellent fettle?'

'Oh, it's you, Valtyr. How long have you been in Verden?'

'Some days. I've been readying the grove,' said the old man.

'So what can we expect tonight?' said Bjarki.

'Majesty, mystery, magic. Tonight the gods join us in—'

'I meant will there be any food. It's been a very long, hard day.'

'I don't know why I waste my breath on you, Bjarki. You look pretty tonight, Tor. Still managing to keep this chunk of mutton out of trouble?'

'Barely. What news from Hedeby?'

'Oh, nothing much to report,' said Valtyr breezily.

'How did the talks with the Frankish embassy go?' asked Bjarki. 'Did they offer Siegfried a big fat bribe, as you predicted?'

'They offered to give him Nordalbia, the impudent bastards. Bishop Livinus said he could draw the new border of the Dane-Mark at the River Elbe and everything north of that would be King Siegfried's domain, as far west as the Wendish lands of the Obodrite tribe, almost all the way to Rerik. But everything south of the Elbe would be Karolus's business. They offered the king of the Danes a quarter of Saxony not to back Widukind.'

'He said no, didn't he?' Tor spat out the words.

'He did. The Dane-Work will mark the border, as always.'

'That's a relief,' said Bjarki.

'Not really. Siegfried is nobody's fool. He would never trust Livinus – nor would he betray Widukind. We did learn, too, that the Franks know all about our Saxon Wolf's ambitions to take back his father's lands. Their spies were busy – just as ours were. I also learnt that Karolus is still in Italy and is set to remain there for many months, perhaps even until next year.

'This is the time to strike,' Valtyr went on. 'Their king is elsewhere and the court at Aachen is bitterly divided. Karolus's wife Hildegard – you met her once, Bjarki, did you not? – and our saintly Bishop Livinus are locked in a struggle for power, with Gerold of Swabia, Hildegard's brother, standing ready to pounce on either one from the edge of the battlefield. He's recovered from his chest wound, apparently, but is still rather sickly. These three are all vying with each other to rule Francia while Karolus is in Lombardy. Now's the time to hit back at the Christians, my friends, while their leaders are at odds with each other. Now's the time!'

Bjarki's mind was cast back to the Frankish capital at Aachen, and to the pampered queen, Hildegard, reluctantly entertaining him in her chamber. She was imperious, high-handed and a little stupid, he thought. But did she want to rule? Yes, he would imagine that she did. So, she and Livinus and Gerold were jostling with each other for power…

'Tell us about tonight's ceremony, Valtyr,' said Tor, breaking his chain of thought. 'Is Widukind truly ready to join your little gaggle of mystical heroes?'

For an instant it looked as if Valtyr might take real offence at Tor's teasing words. But instead, after a beat, he merely shrugged.

'Widukind of Westphalia will be initiated into the ranks of the Guardians of the North this very night. He will undergo the ancient rite and make his vows, then be welcomed into our fellowship. You two will not be required to do anything but bear witness – although you may never speak of this ceremony to anyone afterwards. And there will be food aplenty, Bjarki – more than enough – when the ceremony's done.'

The full moon was still rising in the east, and topping the highest branches of the trees, it filled the clearing with a silvery light. Bjarki was able to see quite clearly the other people gathered in this place around the edges of the clearing. Most of them were warriors of the better sort – thanes and *hersirs*, although he did recognise his captain of spearmen from the Ash Regiment – Kveldulf. And Jarl Brun, in all his refined glory, braided, combed and dressed in purple majesty, was there, speaking to Widukind, who in contrast was wearing merely a simple white linen shift and looked rather cold.

Edith was beside him, head held high, in a shimmering green cloak and golden coronet. She looked every inch the princess. And at her side was the hunched form of Abbio the Crow, as Bjarki privately thought of him, in his filthy black rags, bones in his beard, rings of kohl around his beady bird's eyes. He noticed Bjarki looking at him and stared back, hard-faced, unsmiling. Bjarki shivered; ice melt seemed to run down his spine.

There were a dozen other *gothi* in the gathering, too, some in robes adorned with weird sigils and symbols, some carrying staffs with intricate ironwork heads, others with wax-stiffened hair, their faces painted in odd whorls and stripes of white and black. There was a pen, half hidden by the trees in the direction of the lake, and Bjarki could make out the constant movement and gentle snorting of several large animals – horses, he thought – inside a square timber corral.

Somewhere a bell was struck three times, soft at first, then three more, louder, then three more again, very loud – clanging even. Nine rings of the iron bell, the sacred number, the clamour summoning the spirits of the wood to this ceremony, the hidden folk, the sprites and *gandir*, alerting all the gods, too, the Aesir and Vanir, inviting them to witness the solemn rites of mortal men.

Abbio stepped forward alone into the centre of the clearing.

In a loud, clear voice he said: 'Hear us, Odin, Wise Wanderer, hear us Thor, Giant Slayer, hear us this night mighty Tiw, who shatters the shields of his foes. Honour us with your presence, grant us your favour this hour.'

The bell rang out again, three times.

Widukind, now completely naked, stepped out. Abbio the Crow seized the Saxon Wolf's right hand and lifted it high in the air as if he were a champion of the hazel square who had just killed his opponent.

'Behold this man, O Aesir, who now stands before you sky-clad as he was at his birth. Behold this warrior, O Vanir, who humbly begs your protection in battle. See this man, Theodoric of Westphalia, son of Theodoric, grandson of Theodoric, who is called Widukind, the Wolf of the Woods. See him, you gods. See him, you spirits of the wild. See him, you folk now gathered here.'

The bell tolled three more times.

'Theodoric of Westphalia, who is called Widukind, speak now, and speak true. Do you freely choose to join this hallowed fellowship of warriors who call themselves the Guardians of the North? Do you pledge your life to our people? Do you swear that you will not stint your blood till all our foes be vanquished?'

'I do choose and so swear,' said Widukind in a calm, clear voice.

Tor found she was gazing at the contours of his well-muscled body in the moonlight, at his smooth white flesh with an intriguing nestle of shadow at the groin. She found she was breathing hard.

Two elderly *gothi* appeared from the edges of the clearing, their faces madly painted, hair spiked up in clumps. One had something small, dark and moving tucked under one arm; it seemed to be softly clucking.

Abbio took the dark object – a cockerel, Tor could now see – and handed it to Widukind. Another *gothi* handed him a small knife. Abbio stood by with a bowl as Widukind slashed through the cockerel's throat. The blood spurted blackly and Abbio gathered the running gore in the copper vessel.

Tor realised that many of the scores of shadowy people now gathered around the clearing in the moonlight were singing. It was an odd feeling because she could not remember them beginning the song. Stranger still, she found that she too was singing the familiar words. It was 'Weyland's Blade', a song about the hero Sigurd, who used a magical sword made by a legendary smith to slay a fire-breathing dragon that threatened his hall, his land and his people.

Abbio dipped a sprig of mistletoe in the copper bowl of hot blood and spattered Widukind's white body with a few drops.

He moved sunwise around the circle of watchers, scattering droplets over the congregation.

The crowd sang on. The bell rang out again.

Next a yearling pig was brought out on the end of a rope, grunting softly, and a sword was pushed into Widukind's hand.

He knelt briefly beside the pig, muttered a prayer and sliced upward and opened its throat like a trained slaughterman. Abbio was again beside him immediately, catching the gushing blood in his big copper bowl. This time the delicate spray of bloody droplets, scattered by the *gothi* and his mistletoe, hit Tor squarely in the face and she felt a shock of revulsion at the hot, thick liquid that was now dribbling down her cheeks; *then* she felt an enveloping sense of warmth and well-being, from her toes to her scalp.

This was the blood sacrifice to the undying gods themselves; they were here in this clearing. She was a mortal participant in their sanguinary feast.

A horse came next – a magnificent white stallion from the pastures around Verden – and a long, bearded axe for Widukind to use to dispatch the creature. He split the steed's skull with one fine blow – and as ever Abbio was there to catch the sheeting blood, splash a little over Widukind's gore-slick body and sprinkle the other participants liberally in this communion.

The bell rang out – three times three, this time; nine strikes.

The horse's big corpse was dragged away with ropes, as the two other sacrificial beasts had been, towards the lake. Through the trees Tor could see the glow of several fire trenches. Was it her imagination, or could she already smell meat cooking and hear the delicious sizzle? Her sacrilegious belly grumbled in anticipation.

Then the prisoners came out, escorted by two warriors each. Nine men.

Their arms were lashed to six-foot-long poles that rested across their shoulders. Their faces were white and terrified. One of them began to cry weakly. The singing had reached its peak, 'Weyland's Blade' was coming to its stirring conclusion, when the hero leaps fearlessly into the mouth of the dragon and plunges his magical sword deep into its red-hot, fiery throat...

The nine men were all Franks, Tor assumed, prisoners of war captured in the Stolen Lands and brought back here by Widukind or his soldiers. One of them, an older man, was a priest or a monk, or so she guessed by the way his sparse grey hair was shaved in the Christian tonsure.

The nine were all hauled up into the trees by the long poles that their arms were lashed to. There were plenty of willing hands to pull the ropes and raise the victims. They looked as if they had been crucified, like images of the Christ god that she and Bjarki had pretended to worship in Aachen.

'No!' said Bjarki. 'This isn't right. No, not like this!'

She turned to look at him in amazement. She had, in truth, been utterly lost in the drama of the scene before her. Bjarki's face was speckled with black spots of blood. He looked furious; he looked indeed as he did in battle, on the cusp of madness, before his *gandr* came to him.

His mouth was a grim, determined line.

'Not like this,' he said again. 'These are men, not dumb beasts.'

He bunched his right fist, and for a moment Tor thought he would fly at the gang of a dozen people who were hauling the nine prisoners, one by one, up into the trees. She grasped his forearm with both hands to restrain him. On the other side, she heard Valtyr speaking into his ear: 'These are our foes, Bjarki, these are the people who stole our lands. They deserve death.'

Now Widukind, naked, blood-spattered, was standing in front of the nine men, all up on their individual trees. He had a long spear in his hands. He approached the first one, a young, handsome fellow of not much more than sixteen summers, barely able to shave. The Saxon Wolf lunged up very fast. The spear tip sliced into the victim's belly, surging on upward through skin and muscle and under his ribs and deep into his lungs.

The young man gave a great scream, only partially drowned out by the loud singing. The other eight victims were also now shrieking and bellowing in their fear. All except the older priest, Tor noticed, who had his eyes tight shut and was mumbling something to himself. Widukind took one stumbling step sideways; he struck again, piercing the second man with the spear.

Valtyr was still speaking urgently into her brother's ear: 'The gods can see this, Bjarki, they're here this night. If they did not approve, would they not send a sign? Odin requires this sacrifice, this *blot*, he demands it. He will grant us a great victory in exchange for the blood we shed here.'

Widukind stabbed up again, skewering the belly of a third victim. The prisoners' wailing had grown in volume. The singing had reached its final verse – the screams somehow adding to the impact of the slow, heroic beat of the ancient song. The Saxon Wolf was increasing the speed of his work, perhaps recognising the hymn was nearly done. He stabbed up again, again.

Valtyr was still whispering: 'You are destruction made flesh, Bjarki. You are Death incarnate. But Odin himself granted that power. You're beloved of the All-Father and he bids us to honour him. Do not shame us this holy night.'

The air in the clearing was filled with the metallic stench of blood and emptied bowels. The sixth, seventh and eighth man were quickly dispatched; now only the priest remained alive. Abbio was circulating with his bloody bowl and his mistletoe – he splashed Bjarki and Tor, and Tor heard her brother give a strangled moan as the hot blood spattered across his face.

He reached up his left hand to wipe the gore away, and in so doing effortlessly hoisted up Tor, who was still clinging on to his arm, with the easy movement. He seemed not to notice her dangling weight at all.

Widukind sliced his glistening red spear blade into the belly of the final victim, the old Christian priest hanging in the branches of the oak tree, and Tor heard the man shout out a few last words in clear Frankish: 'Into thy hands, O Lord, I commit my spirit.'

Then the fellow went limp.

Chapter Nine

Jarl of the Three Rivers

Bjarki stumbled away from the clearing and into the darkness. His face felt as if it were on fire, as if the blood that had spattered him were some poison that was burrowing into his skin. He felt sick and ashamed, almost as if his *gandr* had come into him and he had destroyed every living thing in that foul clearing. Would that have been better? To have let loose his killing rage?

No, that would have been the end of everything.

But his rage was still right there, simmering just beneath his skin. The expressions of fear on the faces of the young men as they awaited their fate were etched into his mind. And why did they have to die? So that the Aesir gods, the *gandr* and woodland spirits might be briefly amused by their gory endings?

Bjarki was not a deep thinker – no one ever had accused him of that – but he did know that the nine murders he had witnessed were an abomination.

It was one thing to face an enemy in battle, and to use all your strength to slay or to subdue him. It was another to accept that warrior's surrender, then drag him hundreds of miles from home and hang him on a tree like a Jul-tide hog and disembowel him for the entertainment of a mystical society and a few woodland spirits. It was wrong. Worse, it was dishonourable.

As he walked the dark path back to Verden alone, and made his way to his longhouse, he wondered if he had been mistaken in joining Widukind's army and accepting his grand titles and honours. Perhaps, he thought, he should climb on to Skinfaxi's broad back and ride away, never to return.

'Let him go, Tor,' said Valtyr. 'Just leave Bjarki be for a little while and he will eventually find his own path to peace with this.'

As she watched her older brother stump off furiously into the darkness, away from the sacrificial circle, Tor felt a mix of relief and sadness. Relief that he had not allowed his *gandr* to come into his heart – that would have been a catastrophe – and sadness because she realised that something new had come between her and her brother, her only living kin, something dark and powerful that could not be dissolved by sweet words or sleep or time.

The moonlit clearing was emptying now, with Abbio leading all the people out towards the glitter of the lake and the glow of the cooking fires. She glanced up briefly at the nine pale bodies hanging limply in the trees, and saw that at least one of them was still alive, kicking feebly and quietly moaning. She hesitated, wondering if she ought to end their suffering.

Valtyr was by her side. 'Leave them be, their pain is a part of the sacrifice,' he said. So she shrugged and followed after the rest of them.

They all trooped down to the lake and Widukind walked straight into the black water until it was up to his waist. Tor could now definitely smell the cooking meat from the three trench fires to her left, tended by thralls. For an instant she wondered what they thought about the fate of their nine fellow slaves this bloody night. Did they fear a similar painful and public ending? Probably. A terrible image of Garm leapt into her mind then, and his ghastly meal beneath the tree outside their hall. Then she forced herself to dismiss these unpleasant thoughts: the lives of a few thralls were quite unimportant.

Three of the *gothi* and Abbio followed the Saxon Wolf into the water, and after chanting the names of several major gods and some that Tor was unfamiliar with – presumably the names of the individual spirits of this lake – they handed Widukind the bloody knife he had used to kill the rooster. He hurled it far away into the pale grey of the night. It barely made a splash. The gory sword and the bearded axe followed a similar trajectory. Last of all, Widukind shouted: 'Odin, All-Father, Spear-shaker, Lord of the Undead, accept these nine lives as our humble sacrifice to your everlasting honour!'

And the Saxon cast the spear far out into the glitter of moonlit water.

The *gothi* seized Widukind then and plunged him under the surface. They held him there. The moments inched past. Abbio was chanting a prayer to Tiw, the God of War – it was a long prayer, and just as Tor began to be concerned that they were drowning her lord, Abbio gave a great shout and pulled Widukind up, spluttering and coughing, from the black, icy depths.

And it was done.

Widukind was dried and dressed in a rich black gown trimmed with marten fur, and presented with a fine enamelled sword belt, which he strapped over the robe. Every member of the Guardians of the North took turns to embrace him and kiss him on both cheeks. Tor counted eight of them – nine now Widukind was among their number. And the feast began.

Tor found she was ravenously hungry and she ate and drank as if she was already in Valhalla, feasting with the heroes of old and the eternal gods themselves. There was mead and ale, and even wine, too, and the roast flesh of the horse and the pig – she never got a taste of that lone cockerel – along with pottages and fruit and bread and cheese. The fifty or so celebrants sat at the long tables set out on the shore of the lake, lit by pine-resin torches and the cooking fires, with a thousand stars glittering above like a blanket strewn with tiny jewels and the big moon beaming down upon them all in approval.

Soon the drink began to have an effect and her world began to blur and slip. She discarded her mantle and loosed the belt around the yellow dress. Some men and women were slipping away into the darkness of the sacred grove, on urgent business of their own. Other folk, who had drunk their fill, snored on the sand with their mouths wide open. And just as she was contemplating rising to her unsteady feet and negotiating the path back to her longhouse in Verden, she found that Widukind was standing before her, and smiling.

He reached out a hand and took hers. It was warm and soft but strong. Without saying a word, he led her away from the vast human roar and the dancing firelight, and drew her deep into the cool, dark woods.

—

Inge woke him with a light hand on his neck, and Bjarki opened his crusted eyes and wondered where in the Middle-Realm he was.

He was in his longhouse, in his bed, fully dressed in last night's finery and with an aching head and a mouth like an old purse. He remembered then that he had begun to drink deeply the night before, trying to wash away the shame of the ceremony, and once he started, by downing a gallon jug from the ale barrel, he found he could not stop. He drank until he knew no more.

Inge, in her rough Saxon, said: 'Woman. There is a woman.'

Bjarki groaned and rolled out of the rope-strung cot and got to his still-booted feet. A shaft of white lightning shot through his temples, and he nearly collapsed back into the bed, felled by the pain. He steeled himself.

'Water,' he said, squinting at Inge. 'Bring me water.'

The woman was Edith, and she gazed about the small, fusty-smelling longhouse while Bjarki made himself more presentable, splashing water on his face and drinking several large cups, too, in an attempt to wash the ale-sickness out of his body.

'I had imagined it to be much more squalid,' said Edith. 'I thought it might resemble a wild bear's den, to tell you the truth. But this house is nice. It would even be charming, if you threw open the shutters and let the air in.'

'That would be Inge's work – the thrall. She keeps the place neat.'

'I congratulate her. And you for employing her in this fashion.'

'Do you want food? Or ale?' said Bjarki. He liked this woman; indeed, he found her extremely attractive. But the morning-after feeling was making him gruff.

'Is there any ale *left*?' said Edith with a wicked little smile.

Bjarki shrugged. He waited for his visitor to get to her point.

'I saw you leave the *blot* last night,' she said. 'You looked… uh… not entirely pleased with the ancient rituals of the Guardians of the North.'

'I was disgusted, if you want the truth. I was sickened by it all. I *still* feel dirty. I feel shamed by the murder of those nine prisoners.'

'I see. Well, thank you for telling me the truth, Bjarki. Sorrow eats the heart if you cannot tell someone close your whole mind.'

'Are you going to inform me that Odin requires this filthy bloodbath?'

'I don't know what Odin requires – and anyone who tells you different is a liar. But I do know that those deaths served a purpose.'

'What purpose?'

'Their deaths brought Widukind into the Guardians. They have made him stronger, part of a blood-sanctified fellowship. Those deaths have also united powerful factions of our people, united them in a single purpose – to defeat the Christian Franks. Did you see the man with the white hair and red cloak?'

Bjarki shrugged again. He remembered seeing an old man like that on the far side of the clearing before the bloodletting began.

'That venerable fellow is called Raedbad. He is the grandson of the last king of the Frisians. His folk were forced to accept

Christianity many years ago – at the point of a Frankish sword. Widukind has shown Raedbad, at least, that we Saxons still adhere to the old ways. That many good and powerful men still worship Odin in the traditional way and will fight – and kill, even sacrifice men – to uphold the beliefs of our grandfathers.

'Now Raedbad will go back to his lands – back to his poor, oppressed Frisian people – with a new fire of hope in his saggy belly. Perhaps when we call on him and his folk to fight, they will join us. Perhaps the deaths of those nine have brought our victory over the Franks that little bit closer.'

Bjarki said nothing. He could remember the old man's hungry, almost lustful look – the excitement in his eyes. A new fire in his loins, perhaps.

'But even if Raedbad proves deaf to our call, the bonds between all the men there, all the Guardians of the North, were greatly strengthened. There were men from all across Saxony united by that bloodbath – that quite *disgusting* bloodbath. Yes, I found my own stomach was sickened by it too!'

'How could you allow it? How could you not do your part to persuade your brother to forgo the evils of that night?'

'I suffered the spectacle for our cause. For the North. Those Franks were dead men already. They should have been dispatched on the battlefield – but they were spared. They were spared for that night, for that sacrifice. *That* was their fate. That was what the Spinners had in store for them.'

Bjarki said nothing; he could feel his certainty ebbing away.

'You have killed men in battle, Bjarki,' said Edith. 'I have not. Yet I would do so, if I were called upon. Let me ask you this before I go. Were all the men you killed deserving of their deaths? Sometimes I think it is just blind chance – or, if you like, the will of the gods – that one man lives and another dies. I do not pretend to know the will of Odin – but I *do* know that if he chose, he could have saved them. He did not do so. And so they died.'

Bjarki looked at his boots.

'I will go now and leave you to your hangover, but hear me when I say this, Bjarki Bloodhand, Jarl of the Three Rivers and Warden of the First Forest: we need you. The North needs you. Perhaps the gods need you, too.'

—

A full month had passed since the bloody ceremony of the Guardians, and still Bjarki had not quit Verden. He had, indeed, come to a reluctant acceptance of the barbarities of that night. To take it out of his mind, he had thrown himself anew into the task of training his Regiments to the highest level and preparing them all to face the horrors of battle.

He had them running and lifting weights from dawn till dusk. He had them forming shield walls, at a single word of command, then breaking formation suddenly and charging their imaginary foes in a tight mass, all shouting their furious battle cries. He gave lessons in sword craft, basic moves and then more advanced techniques; he taught them simple battle tactics, how to read a battlefield and some tricks of unarmed combat. And every day Tor was by his side, exhorting them all to be faster, stronger, better.

But since that blood-drenched night, his relationship with Tor had changed subtly. They were more reticent around each other – more guarded. His relations with Widukind had altered, too. Bjarki now avoided his company, and the Saxon seemed to recognise this and accept it, never unnecessarily forcing his presence on the ill-tempered Rekkr.

Yet Tor and Widukind were both now standing beside him on the *thing*-mound, a low, wide dome of earth in a horse pasture just to the south of Verden, which was the place where traditionally the tribal leaders and the mighty horse-lords of Angria held their assemblies, enacted their laws and discussed matters of the greatest import.

A little way down the slope of the dome, astride a huge warhorse, sat Jarl Brun, in his full battle finery, mail and greaves, spear and shield, his face hidden under a splendidly engraved helmet crowned with the likeness of a savage boar. It was in his honour that they were gathered there that day.

He had come to review Bjarki's troops, his newly made Saxon army – the six hundred and sixty-three warriors who were now paraded in neat lines on the worn pasture in front of him – before their imminent departure.

On the left stood the Yew Regiment, two hundred and sixty-five bowmen and women, all armed and trained alike, with lethal five-foot-long yew-wood bows, a leather quiver filled with twenty-four arrows and a short sword, hunting knife or hand axe tucked into their belts. These were Bjarki's light troops, which he meant to use for scouting, skirmishing and ambushes.

On the right stood the Ash Regiment – three hundred and thirty-three folk armed with seven-foot ash-shafted steel-tipped spears and round lime-wood shields, and an assortment of side arms ranging from swords to axes to the brutal, single-bladed fighting knife, the traditional Saxon seax.

Behind Bjarki, on the reverse slope of the *thing*-mound, stood the sixty-two members of his personal *hird*, the most skilled of his warriors, the more experienced men and women who acted as his bodyguard and shock troops. They were all under Tor's command.

Widukind stepped forward, raised a hand and filled his lungs and smiled. As the Saxon Wolf began his inevitable speech, Bjarki looked over at his sister, watching her closely as she gazed adoringly at their lord.

She had a look of absolute devotion in her eyes, Bjarki realised. There was no doubt about it. His sister was deeply in love with Widukind. He wondered if the Saxon was aware of and even reciprocated her affections.

The young lord was speaking of land and glory again – and a united North – and his heroic father, and Bjarki stopped listening. He had heard it all before, many times, the same phrases trotted out whenever Widukind sought to inspire a gathering of followers.

He was not sure how he felt about the man. He no longer wanted to ride away from Verden and never come back. But his respect for Widukind had been shaken by the cruelties of the *blot*, and while he had been moved in the past by the fellow's powerful words, he knew that it was just a learnt skill, a kind of trickery, a way to persuade simple folk to fight and die for him.

Yet he had to admit that he also felt admiration for this energetic fellow, who was filled with such confidence, possessed of such a sure vision of how the Middle-Realm should be ordered. He knew Widukind would do anything, sacrifice anyone, to fulfil his dream of a united North. There was something terrifying about this, but also comforting.

Widukind was talking about the war again – about how these brave and honest northern men and women gathered before him now would shortly be heading south in a new campaign to wrest the great fortress of Sigiburg from Frankish hands and to reclaim all the lost Saxon territory south of the River Lippe. It seemed the Saxon Wolf was trying to put a little heart into Bjarki's still-raw troops:

'Some of you will surely die,' he boomed.

Bjarki frowned – it seemed an odd thing to emphasise to folk about to face all the pains and perils of battle.

'Some of you may be horribly wounded,' Widukind went on.

Bjarki opened his mouth to interrupt his lord.

'But only a *coward* believes he'll live for ever,' the Saxon Wolf bellowed. 'The coward is wrong, of course: old age won't grant him a truce even if the enemy spears do spare him in battle. Cattle die, pigs die, sheep die, kinsmen die. All of you, my friends, will die – *one day*. But he who wins word-fame in battle will surely live for ever!'

Widukind's words were met with a cheer from more than six hundred throats. *He* does *know what he's doing*, Bjarki thought.

There was a stir behind him, shouts of alarm. Bjarki whirled. The men of his *hird* were shouting and pointing southward.

At first Bjarki could not see what all the fuss was about. Then he saw it: a dark object in the distance was coming towards the open pasture. At first he thought it was a horse, because of the speed of its approach, but as it drew closer, he recognised it.

'Garm!' shouted Tor. 'My beautiful boy. Come to me!'

The bear was bounding along, mouth open, long red tongue lolling with every stride. The ranks of the *hird* split before it, parting like a hall's shutters thrown open at dawn, and Garm charged straight up the small hill.

For the first time, Bjarki saw that Widukind, the silver-tongued Saxon, the wizard of word-play, the skald of West-phalia, was at a loss for something to say. His exhortations died away. Garm bounced up to Bjarki and threw himself on to his chest.

—

'It has to be the wooden cage,' said Bjarki. 'Has to be. There's no choice.'

He and Tor were alone in their longhouse some hours later – Inge and the excited young bear playing happily outside in the courtyard.

'We can't take him into battle with us,' said Tor. 'But I have a better idea. Not a cage, as such, but an enclosure. We ask Jarl Brun to lend us his carpenters and we convert that big paddock behind the hall into a roofed enclosure and build Garm a hut at the back of it. Inge can stay here and make sure he is well fed. And I have the perfect steward to look after them both.'

The man Tor picked for the task was one of the older warriors from Bjarki's Yew Regiment, a grandfather of sixty summers called Ulli. He was a fine bowman, a marksman, and Tor explained to him that, as part of his duties, he would be required to hunt regularly so that Garm would never lack meat.

'You are to take care of the girl, Inge, too,' said Tor. 'I know she is just a thrall but I will allow no man to take advantage of her.'

Tor brandished a finger. 'Hear me: if any harm does come to her, I'll cut your pizzle off. Your balls, too. Don't think I won't.'

'I'll watch over her, mistress,' said Ulli.

'And don't you get any ideas about creeping into her bed on a cold winter's night, either, or I *will* cut your manhood off when I get back.'

'No, mistress.'

'And make sure the bear cub, if he is ever taken out of his nice new enclosure, doesn't eat any more of Jarl Brun's servants, or...'

'You'll cut my private parts off. I understand. But do not fear, mistress, all will be well. I will guard them both with my very life.'

'Well, then,' said Tor. She looked over at a frowning Bjarki. 'What now?'

Tor smiled at him. 'Let's go to war, brother.'

Chapter Ten

A cold wash of darkness

Bjarki had forgotten just how much work was required to travel on foot through the First Forest. The last time he had attempted it, it had been just him, Tor and Valtyr, threading their way through the close-grown trees and underbrush, occasionally cutting a low-hanging frond or obstructing branch, but treating the ancient woodland with exaggerated, almost reverential care.

As with last time, he had Valtyr as his guide, but this day in his train were more than six hundred troops blundering along behind him, creating a swathe of destruction, the column stretching out over a half-mile of territory along with the hundred or so packhorses and mules that carried all their food, spare kit and weapons. It was a completely different kind of journey.

They had crossed the Aller at the ford at Verden, and heading due west crossed the River Weser a couple of hours later, and then they swung around southward following the line of the river, where the marshes permitted it.

This area between the Weser and the Hunte was the ancient heartland of Westphalia, but a day's march to the west were the Stolen Lands, now at least partially recovered by Widukind. And the farmlands they passed through on this left bank of the Hunte had a raggedy, war-torn look, and the folk were suspicious of foreigners, particularly of a horde of mostly young men on the march. Somewhere to the south-west, perhaps two or three days' travel, was Osnabrucke, which was still besieged by the Angrian horsemen.

Bjarki kept his men heading roughly south for two hard-slog days and then stopped at a low-lying, boggy and ill-kempt hamlet called Lubbecke at the foot of a steep forested ridge. At the approach of the Saxon army the people who lived in that muddy fish hole of a settlement ran away.

They had camped that night on a small ridge a few miles west of the village, a vantage point overlooking most of the local area, and Bjarki ate his supper looking south at the dense wall of woodland that rose up before his eyes. It was the beginning – the northern border, in fact – of the First Forest.

They rested for a day on the ridge at Lubbecke, Bjarki ensuring that every company of thirty to fifty warriors, a unit called a *lith*, was prepared for the rigours of a forest march. Then, the next day, they plunged into the thick trees at a little after dawn and began, very laboriously, to ascend the first ridge.

Within an hour or two, Bjarki was exhausted, sweaty, irritable and scratched by branches and brambles, and his people were straggling out in several long lines behind him down the slope. He called a halt in the late afternoon, and climbed a tall tree and looked back down the slope they had conquered. He saw with a sinking heart that his force had only travelled about six or seven miles as the eagle flies that day. And his troops were already worn out and could go no further. Despite Valtyr's protests, Bjarki allowed them to cut wood from the forest and cook their meals over fires.

'Do you even *have* a plan?' asked Tor, spooning out a bowl of beef and mushroom stew from the small cauldron over their campfire.

'A plan? Oh, do you think I need a *plan*?' said Bjarki, wide-eyed.

'Odin's arse, you stupid...'

'I have a fucking *plan*, Tor. Indeed, I have more than one.'

Relations between brother and sister had often been strained since the night of the *blot*, and had not improved much over the three hard days of the southward march. Bjarki had been feeling a little unsure of himself – he was not comfortable with this role as the commander of so many near strangers, and he disliked the creeping realisation that their lives were solely in his hands. He fretted every hour that he was making errors. Tor had been mostly silent as they travelled south, and less than helpful – lost in her dreams of Widukind, Bjarki silently assumed. They'd barely spoken except to bicker.

'Like to tell me, then, what your brilliant plan is?' said Tor.

'No, thank you,' said Bjarki. 'You'll only piss all over it.'

'Come on, oaf, I should know what's in your mind, in case...'

Bjarki swallowed a mouthful of hot stew. He knew he was behaving badly but he did not seem able to stop himself.

'I'll tell you the plan when I inform all the other captains,' he said.

'Do you still intend to dodge the actual fighting?' she said.

'I'm not dodging anything,' he replied hotly. 'I plan to *lead* the troops under my command to victory. Widukind said that I wouldn't even need to draw my sword, that I was a natural *leader*...'

'They've found a body,' said Valtyr, plumping down beside Bjarki and hungrily sniffing at his bowl of beef and mushrooms.

'What do you mean, a body?' said Tor.

'A dead human being. A man – a boy, in truth,' said Valtyr. 'Naked. Few shreds of animal skin and a rusty knife.' He helped himself to the stew. 'The remains have been eaten by something large – a bear, most likely.'

'Someone out Voyaging!' said Bjarki. 'The poor fellow.'

'How far is it to the Groves?' asked Tor. She remembered her own miserable, frightening time alone and naked in this forest, when she'd been trying to summon her own *gandr*. She had failed.

'Three days' march, due south,' said Valtyr. 'The boy didn't get far.'

'We must bury him,' said Bjarki.

'No need,' said Valtyr. 'Hungry foxes or the wolves will dispose of him in due course. Or possibly rats.'

Bjarki was suddenly furious with Valtyr. 'I'm going to see the poor lad buried anyway!' He rose and stomped off into the trees.

'Hey, rats need to eat, too!' said Valtyr, to his departing back.

–

Tor had to wait a full day until the next camp to hear Bjarki's plans for this southern campaign. It had been another long, hard, frustrating day struggling up and down the covered slopes of the mountainside through thick, dragging foliage that often felt like virgin forest. In the slanting light of late afternoon, Bjarki summoned Tor, Captain Eckhart of the Yew, Captain Kveldulf of the Ash and Valtyr Far-Traveller to his side while he outlined his strategy.

'We are going to capture the fortress of Sigiburg,' he began. 'Which is roughly *here*, overlooking the River Ruhr. *Here.*'

He pulled out his seax and drew a crude map in the earth at his feet.

'I believe we should be able to take the fortress without too much difficulty with a straightforward assault over the walls. They have about a hundred troops in there, or so Abbio's spies have informed me, so we easily outnumber them. The problem, I think, will be holding on to the fortress afterwards. The Franks have been active along the River Rhenus recently, moving troops in response to Widukind's fight in the Stolen Lands, *here…*

'They have also been using a fine, straight, well-made road – called the Hellweg – which runs below the Lippe about *here* – to transport their troops very swiftly into the heart of Saxony.'

The men and Tor craned to look at his scratchings in the dirt.

'As you can see, the Hellweg runs east to west along a ridge above the Valley of the Lippe and passes a mile or two north of Sigiburg. *Here*. They use their road to resupply the fortress. The very moment they hear that Sigiburg is under attack, they will dispatch troops along the Hellweg to come to the aid of the defenders. Or if they're too late, to retake the *castrum*. So this is where we lay our trap. Right on the Hellweg itself, about *here*.'

There were some murmurs of approval at this.

'I want Captain Eckhart to take a strong force – most of his Yew bowmen, two hundred of them, say, and a hundred Ash spearmen, too, and lay an ambush at a point that he chooses along the Hellweg. Anywhere between *here* and *here*. I want you to stay out of sight, Eckhart, until you see a substantial force of Red Cloaks; nothing less than a hundred men. Then you must attack and destroy them, if you can. You think you can do that?'

'I was born to kill Franks,' said the captain, with a cruel smile.

'Good. After you have successfully sprung the ambush, send word to me at Sigiburg, and prepare to hold the Hellweg and deny it to the enemy. Keep moving up and down the line of the road and attack any Franks you see. If they come in numbers, then you just harry them, nip at their heels, butcher the stragglers, shoot a man or two down and retreat into the forest before they catch you. And keep me informed. That is crucial. If a sizeable Frankish force does get past you, I need to know very quickly. You know how to wage this kind of hit-and-run war, I think, Captain Eckhart?'

'I've fought like this for much of my life,' said the grizzled Eastphalian. 'Strike and run away. Swoop and escape, having reaped lives and looted the baggage. I know exactly how to do this, jarl.'

'I believe you. And I'm giving you almost half my troops. Try to preserve their lives. We're going to need them in the months ahead. The rest of us are going to capture Sigiburg. Now, does anyone have any questions?'

'The months ahead?' said Tor. 'What happens after Sigiburg?'

'When we have taken the fortress, we will command the Hellweg. Our task is to deny both to the Franks,' said Bjarki. 'Once they're secure, we go to the Groves of Eresburg and strengthen them with the troops we have.

'Those are the three pillars of our position in south Saxony – Sigiburg, Hellweg and the Eresburg. We hold those three and drive all new Frankish settlers out of the region. All the territory between the Rhenus, the Lippe and the Weser, which was once Saxon land, shall be Saxon land once more. Our task – my task – is to hold that swathe of territory in the name of Widukind.'

Tor said: 'Well, that's ambitious, oaf. No half measures, eh?'

'I am the Jarl of the Three Rivers and Warden of the First Forest. I intend that to mean something. I *shall* rule my lands. Any more questions?'

No one said anything.

'Good,' said Bjarki. 'Tonight, Captain Eckhart, you may choose your warriors for the Hellweg ambush and make ready. Tomorrow you split from the column and go east. Good hunting, my friend. May the Bear guard you!'

–

Widukind was on her mind that morning, three days later, as Tor looked up at the palisaded fortress – the *castrum* – on the oval hill to the south.

He was on her mind most days, in truth. The one night they had spent together was burnt eternally into her heart, branded into her spirit.

She cherished the memory of the rough scratch of his beard against her cheek, his hot, urgent breath on her neck, the solid weight on top of her and the all-filling hardness of him inside her; the grinding, the wild bucking, the breathless, building rhythm of their movements, growing, growing, and the glorious, liquid madness of release in the final moments of their coupling.

She forced herself with a vast effort of will to concentrate on the task at hand. Widukind was in the Stolen Lands, at Osnabrucke, vanquishing his foes. He might even be dead – no, that was a thought she could not face.

Concentrate. There was a major battle unfolding before her eyes.

Tor looked up the steep slope of the small hill at the long, wooden barrier of the Sigiburg fortifications and the rows of helmeted heads that looked back down at her and her comrades gathered in the valley below. Bjarki was standing a little to her right on a hillock, a bald knoll, and was also staring up at the fortress on the summit, five hundred paces above them.

His Saxon troops were moving forward now, in full view of the enemy, the two hundred or so spearmen of the Ash Regiment, commanded by Captain Kveldulf, supported by a score of Yew archers. There was no element of surprise this day – and none had even been attempted.

She wondered if Bjarki had considered a night attack or some sort of ruse or subterfuge, rather than this basic frontal attack, and then chided herself for second-guessing her brother. He needed her support at this time, not her criticism. She had been a bad sister of late. She would hold her tongue, fight hard for him, and help him achieve a notable victory this day.

The twenty Saxon archers were in range now, and showering the top of the palisade with their slim shafts. The enemy heads were ducking back, the Red Cloaks taking cover behind the breast-high wall, crouched on the walkway behind, she assumed. They were right to do so; the arrows rattled like thrown twigs against the face of the wooden walls or flew, presumably harmlessly, over the top of the battlements, falling into the interior of the fortress. A few of the bowmen were shooting their arrows almost vertically in the air, aiming to drop their points on the sheltering Franks, but too few hit the target to make much of a difference. And for most of the archers the angle was quite wrong. Tor opened her mouth to speak – and closed it.

She looked over at Bjarki and saw that he was chewing on his right fist in his anguish, the bleeding knuckles shoved hard in his mouth.

She heard the rattle of drums and the bellow of the wolf-horns – the big, curved instruments that some of the *lith* commanders carried to relay orders to their warriors. The large mouth of the bronze horn was shaped like the jaws of a wolf and, to her ear, the sound was indeed just like a wild lupine howl.

The ladder men now began their run – a hard journey indeed. The slopes of the hill on which Sigiburg was situated were steep and bare, cleared of trees and undergrowth so that the defenders could see the enemy approach. The shiny helmets were back on the line of the walls, scores of them, with glimpses of red attire beneath, too, and Saxon arrows were answered in kind from the ramparts, accompanied by showers of spears.

The ladder men were trying to run up an almost vertical slope carrying the heavy wooden frames they had constructed the night before. It was ten warriors to each ladder, all of them now puffing and panting as they laboured up the steep hill, struggling under the weight of the ladder as well as the encumbrance of shields on their backs and weapons in their belts.

The first of Bjarki's men were now in range of the defenders' missiles – and Tor saw a young man shot right through the neck with a black shaft, release his hold on the ladder and fall to the ground stone dead. A second man carrying the same piece of equipment a yard behind him was struck in the shoulder by a hurled javelin, and as he fell back screaming, the ladder was dropped and the rest of the men had to stop their charge, pick the heavy equipment up again and, under the shouts of their leader, carry on up the hill.

The enemy missiles were showering down now, a storm of death, a blizzard of arrows and spears. The Red Cloaks were even leaning out over the wall to hurl their javelins down with greater force, like Thor's mighty thunderbolts. Ladder men were dropping down bloody, here and there; there were bodies of wounded and dead already strewn all over the hillside. The screams of pain were clearly audible from the knoll. But now the nearest ladder was finally at the foot of the wall, and the Saxons were hoisting it up, up, up, leaning it precariously against the rough pine logs of the wall, and they were climbing as fast as they could, scrambling up the wooden rungs, desperate to get to the top and escape from the barrage.

A boulder – a jagged lump the size of a pig – now plunged down from the wall above and smashed into the leading climber, catching the Saxon full in the chest. He was swept down, tumbling into the fellow behind him, and the one below that, stripping the ladder clear of men in a single heartbeat.

A rain of other missiles followed the boulder, spears skewering men already broken by the crunching fall of the rock. A second ladder went up, further along the wall, and a second bold squad began to climb – which was devastated by a fresh volley from the side, a dozen arrows that hissed into the line of climbing men, sweeping them away, hurling them off the rungs.

The Saxon bowmen below were still loosing, plucking shafts from their arrow bags, nocking and releasing, aiming high and dropping their shafts almost vertically on the walls, and one or two had even found their mark in Frankish bodies. Tor watched as a Red Cloak tumbled down the palisade and smashed on to the bare earth below. The Saxons cheered. But if the Yew archers' aim was to keep the Franks cowering behind their wall, they failed.

Kveldulf was standing alone, twenty paces from the base of the walls, beckoning his men to hurry forward, to get their ladders up and begin the hellish climb. His shield was on his back and facing the enemy. An arrow struck the lime-wood boards and remained there, quivering. Some of the Saxons were answering Kveldulf's call; brave northern warriors were still coming forward carrying their ladders, ready to risk their lives once more.

But many were not.

Knots of Saxons were hanging back, hovering foolishly around their dropped ladders, dithering. One man was pretending to tie and retie the leather straps of his shoe. Others were slowly edging backward, down the slope. The row of heads on the walls above them seemed to thicken; the curtain of missiles continued to fall like a grotesque waterfall of death.

A swift-hurled javelin struck Kveldulf on his iron helmet and knocked him to the ground. Tor saw one man throw away his shield and simply run back down the hillside. Other men were doing the same; the best of them stood fast, but the attack was clearly stalled. None were moving forward. The dead and wounded lay in scores on the bloody grass before the walls. Some moving feebly. The merciless arrows and spears continued to fall on them.

Tor looked over at Bjarki. His whole body was shaking. His face was red and glistening with sweat. His right fist, now streaming with blood and spit from where he had savaged it with his own teeth, was still stuffed hard in his mouth. His eyes were wide as platters.

She stalked over to him; put a hand on his shoulder.

'You don't want to let *her* in?' she said.

He stared at his sister blankly, as if he'd never laid eyes on her before. Then he removed his red-wet fist from his mouth and blurted: 'No, but she is screaming at me. Yelling. She's banging on the door to my heart, so close now, so very close. And she wants me to do these terrible...'

'Be calm, oaf,' said Tor. 'You are stronger than your *gandr.*'

She took a deep breath. 'Give me the *hird*. And I'll do it for you.'

Bjarki goggled at her. He seemed to be about to refuse.

'You want this *castrum*? Give me the *hird* – now, brother.'

Bjarki stared at her a little longer, then he shook his head wildly. 'No!' he said. 'No, this is my task. They are all dying up there – and for *me*.'

He drew his sword from its sheath with his bloody fist and raised the blade high in the air. 'The *hird* will advance,' he yelled. 'Ad-vance!'

Tor was already shouting follow-up orders to the waiting warriors behind who made up Bjarki's bodyguard, waving them all forward.

Out in front strode Bjarki; he walked, he simply walked up the slope as if he were out for a morning stroll. He had his sword pointed in the air, as if indicating the general direction of travel. And the sixty men and women of the *hird* were hard on his heels, flowing forward behind their jarl into battle and streaming up the slope towards the great fortress of Sigiburg above.

They met stragglers from the first wave coming back down, spearmen, bowmen, some wounded, more trembling and unsure. Many terrified.

'Come on, you cowards,' Tor bellowed at them as they passed. 'Come with us, you *nithings*. Do you want to live for ever – is that it? Attack!'

She hauled out her own sword, brandished it high. 'For the North. For Widukind. For Jarl Bjarki. All together now. Charge!'

She pelted up the slope behind her brother and the swarming *hird*.

A wolf-horn bellowed, then another joined the wild chorus.

And, astonishingly, it worked. The retreating warriors stopped moving backward. They saw the ranks of the *hird*, the best of them, the elite unit, streaming up dauntlessly towards the walls of Sigiburg – and followed. They stopped to pick up their abandoned ladders and surged against the walls of the fortress. Tor saw that Bjarki now had a ladder propped against the base of the high wall, and his booted foot was planted on the first rung.

He held his big round shield over his head for cover and the painted leather-faced surface was already thick with enemy shafts.

The arrows, spears and javelins flew – dense as a murmuration of starlings.

Tor ran forward as Bjarki was about to begin his climb. She seized his shoulder, pulled him back and went past him, yelling, 'I claim the honour!'

As she ran up the rungs, barely touching them with her hands, she did not think for an instant of the horror that awaited her at the top. She held the image of Bjarki's face in her mind. His mouth grim. His blue eyes glittering – but not with the usual madness. There was no sign, she thought, of frenzy.

He is stronger than her, she thought. *He is the master of his* gandr.

Around her the other ladders were swinging up, and the Saxons were climbing, surging up their rungs on either side of her. But she was the first. She burst through a cloud of Frankish missiles, batting a spear away with her shield, and exploded over the wall. She vaulted the sharpened wooden points and crashed into a terrified Red Cloak. She fell to her knees on the walkway. He staggered back, drawing back his spear to skewer her as she crouched. She came up fast, driving with her sword, plunging the point into his belly.

He screamed, and fell. She stood upright, alone, on the enemy wall.

But not for long.

A dozen men of the *hird* were also on the wall now, bringing their hard-practised skills to bear on the enemy. And the spearmen of the Ash Regiment were now joining them, pouring over the battlements by the dozen, by the score, half a hundred now, shoving defenders back, slicing, cutting, killing.

Bjarki was just ten yards away. He was hacking at a big Red Cloak officer, a fine red plume nodding on his shiny helmet. His sword-work was good, she noted, precise, skilled. He blocked a blow, slipped his long blade past the officer's guard and sliced it up the inside of his upper arm. The man howled in pain and Bjarki ended his suffering with a fast, lateral slice across the throat. As his dying opponent sagged, Bjarki booted him off the parapet.

Their eyes met. Bjarki flashed her a tiny smile before turning to bellow at his people, ordering them onward, urging them on to sweep the last remaining Franks from the walls. *He is stronger*, she thought. *He really is.*

Something black flickered in front of her eyes. She felt a blow like a kick from a horse in her leather-armoured chest and she was hurled back against the inside of the palisade. She looked down in wild surprise and saw a slim, almost insignificant shaft protruding from her armour, high and to the side, blood welling around it. She stared at the Frankish arrow, stunned, bemused, and slowly, slowly her sight began to dim, darkening, narrowing, becoming focused only on her chest and the blood – no pain; just a numbness.

Her left leg, too, she saw, looking down, was sheeted in wet blood from some wound that she had not even noticed, taken while climbing the ladder. Now, a freezing blackness was rising around her, filling the soft edges of her vision. She gasped out: 'Odin, heed me – heed my deeds this day of battle!'

She sagged, quite suddenly; only her left arm hooked over the stakes of the barricade kept her body upright, her right hand still slackly gripping her bloody sword. She must not let go of that. Even in death, she would hold it.

She looked along the wall to see her brother. To say goodbye. And saw him already looking at her. His mouth black and wide in shock. His face was somehow changing: swelling, becoming far larger, filling with blood and rage and hatred. She heard him release a she-bear's roar, the howling of a battle-maddened beast, and thought she could feel the walkway shuddering beneath her feet as he thundered towards her. His body seemed even bigger than usual, a dark shape approaching, a terrifying monster of fur and steel, sword in one paw, seax in the other.

No, she thought, *I was wrong.* She *is stronger than him.*

Then all the darkness in the world crashed down upon her.

—

Now the Rekkr was loosed inside the fortress of Sigiburg and, such was his fury, even his own folk kept their distance. He savaged and slew; he howled and hewed; he sliced and slashed at the foe, opening them all up one by one.

He hurled himself at knots of Red Cloaks in the court-yard, blades whirling, bloody spittle flying, carving them into butcher's joints. He burst through armoured men hastily formed into shield walls, sweeping them all before him, then turning to kill and kill again, as he leapt from man to man.

His sword and seax were soon sheeted in gore. His arms were dripping red to the elbow, his huge body slathered, and still his lust was not sated.

When he'd cleared the courtyard of the last of them – some Franks were wise enough to surrender to members of the *hird* and were shown the now-open fortress gates and told to run for their lives – the *berserkr* roamed the halls and storerooms seeking those who attempted to hide from his fury.

He found a Frankish servant cowering in one grain stor-eroom, hiding under a pile of old sacks; a terrified older man, too old for battle, in all truth. This doddering fellow, revealed when the oat sacks were torn away, and faced with a gore-splashed giant, frothing at the mouth, wielding two red, glistening blades, had had some kind of seizure. He clutched his chest in agony, called out weakly to his Christ god and collapsed to his knees before Bjarki had so much as breathed on him. The Rekkr cut his head from his skinny torso anyway. He left the spattered storeroom and roamed the open courtyard, howling and spitting curses, grunting, snuffling, hunting. Till, at last, the Rekkr sank exhausted to his haunches and let out one final terrible war cry. A simple name ripped from his swollen, broken, once-human heart.

'Tor!'

Part Two

Summer 773

Chapter Eleven

Return to the Groves of Eresburg

Bjarki sat on a stool beside the cot in the Frankish church with his head in his hands. The morning sun streamed through the window high on the eastern end of the building, which stood at the centre of the courtyard of the fortress of Sigiburg, and formed a golden pool on the floor of the large, mostly empty space.

Through his fingers he could see the utterly still form of his sister, lying before him on the cot, her face as pale as snow, her eyes peacefully closed. The blankets were pulled up to cover her breasts, but he could glimpse the layers of bandages beneath that swathed her pathetically thin upper body.

Valtyr Far-Traveller was fussing with a rag and a bowl of water, dabbing Tor's temples with the liquid and muttering under his breath. Bjarki wondered if he was intoning a magical healing spell, but realised that it was more likely to be a complaint about the unsatisfactory state of the world.

He knew Valtyr wanted to leave Sigiburg and return to the Groves of Eresburg, three days' march to the east, but he had forbidden the old man to depart – and now that he truly was Jarl of the Three Rivers, in command of Sigiburg and most of south Saxony, Valtyr was obliged to do as he was told.

Perhaps, Bjarki thought, he was misjudging the one-eyed old man. Valtyr loved Tor as much as he did, and Bjarki had kept him here because he had relied heavily on his skill as a healer, which was considerable, in the perilous days and nights after Tor had been struck down. It had been two weeks since the battle – and Bjarki's usual feelings of all-engulfing shame and sickness after this latest bout had subsided eventually and left him only with a sense of helpless sadness, a melancholia, centred around the near-mortal wound Tor had taken, but also spiked with shaky memories of his actions when his *gandr* had taken full control of his body and he had come roaring and slaughtering throughout the Frankish fortress.

Mercifully, much of what he had done in his frenzied state was erased from his mind. But the fragments that did remain were horrible enough: the bloodbath of enemies, the stink of shit and piss, the screams that echoed long after all the victims were dead, the sound of flesh tearing... The folk of the Ash and the Yew had watched aghast as Bjarki had howled and hewn, sliced and slain; now they looked on him with mingled fear – and respect.

Tor opened her eyes. She tried to rise but Valtyr was there to gently hold down her shoulders.

'Don't move, child,' he said. 'You will rip out the stitches.' Tor turned her russet head and looked over at Bjarki, who was now for some reason weeping silently but copiously, his big mouth hanging open like a simpleton.

'How long have I been...' she whispered.

'Not long,' Bjarki sniffed loudly, trying to master himself.

'Did we take the *castrum*?'

Bjarki nodded. 'We did. You're in it now. But you must rest.'

Tor closed her eyes. Valtyr held a bowl to her lips and made her drink.

'I thought I was truly dead,' murmured Tor. 'I saw the All-Father himself, surrounded by a bright shining light. He smiled at me...'

'Don't try to talk now,' said Valtyr.

'He looked like you, old man,' she said and sank into a deep sleep.

The arrow wound she had taken was high in the chest on the left side, just below the joint of the shoulder. The shaft had sunk deep into her flesh and severed a major artery, which had led to swift and dangerous blood loss. But perhaps Odin had been guarding her because the point did not puncture her lung, which would most likely have been fatal. She also had a nasty, deep gash in her thigh, from a hurled javelin, probably taken while she was climbing the ladder, which had also considerably weakened her.

Valtyr had spent many hours tending to her, cleaning and stitching her wounds, bandaging them and making sure that she drank down little sips of warmed ale and honey at regular intervals. Now, it seemed, his patience and diligence had been rewarded.

'She will live, Bjarki,' said the old man, getting up from Tor's bedside with a soft grunt. 'With the All-Father's help, she will recover.'

'I am grateful, Valtyr,' said Bjarki.

The old man nodded and patted his shoulder.

Bjarki got up and went to a bench at the side of the building and returned with a large bundle. It was his bearskin cloak. He spread the fur over Tor's sleeping body and said: 'May the Bear guard you, my sister!'

'But what about you, Fire Born?' said Valtyr, peering into his face. 'Does the Bear guard *you*? I can tell something is not altogether right with you. What is roiling around inside *your* bony thought-cage these days?'

He gently tapped Bjarki's forehead with one finger.

The younger man said nothing. Then: 'I am lost, Valtyr. I am truly lost. I don't know who I am any more. When the *gandr* takes me... when she gets into me, all of *me* is pushed out. I'm just her toy. The *me* ceases to exist. I'm just this big bag of meat and bones for her to play with.'

'You have won a notable victory: you have taken the enemy fortress of Sigiburg. You are a man of great power now – that's who *you* are.'

'You're right, old friend, I have no good reason to complain. Tor will live. I took Sigiburg, as I intended to. It's just that...'

'What?' said Valtyr.

Bjarki looked around the big, almost empty church; there were a few folk gathered at the far end but no one close enough to hear his words.

He spoke softly anyway. 'It's just that *she* is so much stronger than me. I know it. My *gandr* took me over completely in the fight, just slipped into my heart, and I had no choice about it at all. I thought *I* could master *her*. I thought I could keep her out, and be a warrior, a leader, even a hero, and... not a blade wielded by *her*, a blood-crazed maniac, a mad butcher...'

Valtyr looked at him sympathetically. 'I know what troubles you, son,' he said. 'All Rekkar dislike the loss of control when their *gandir*...'

'It is not just that – although that is utterly terrifying. It is as if I'm no longer myself. I'm no longer Bjarki. I'm some other horrible thing.'

'I understand your suffering. I really do.'

'You *cannot* understand,' said Bjarki. He suddenly looked as if he were about to weep again. 'No one can fully grasp my pain, unless—'

'I understand your pain better than any other living man. But hear me now: I also know of a way by which you *can* master your *gandr*. Trust me. If you choose. It is possible. There is a dangerous method, an obscure ritual, by which a Rekkr might expel for ever, or even kill his *gandr*...'

'Tell me,' said Bjarki.

'It is perilous. You must offer up your life to Queen Hel...'

'Tell me!' Bjarki seized Valtyr by the collar of his robe.

'I must go to the Groves of Eresburg. Soon. I've neglected my sacred duties for far too long. I swear I will tell you *everything* at the Fyr Skola.'

Bjarki released Valtyr. 'Yes, you *will* tell me,' he grated. 'And you shall go to the Groves – but I will go with you. Once we are there you will tell me all you know, and we will face this desperate peril together and kill my *gandr*. Agreed? The women of the *hird* will watch over Tor here and, when she is stronger, I will send her back to Verden to recover fully from her wounds. We ride out before dawn tomorrow, old man. Be ready.'

–

They rode north-east at first light, following the north bank of the wide Ruhr, with the dark, living mass of the First Forest on their left, to the north. Across the river was the rich land called Hessia, Valtyr informed Bjarki, in one of their few conversations. A place of cosy farmlands and fortified villages and thickly forested hills, it was a fertile land that had been settled and controlled by the Franks for some generations and which the Saxon tribes to the north – Westphalians and Angrians mainly – had customarily raided as a way of blooding their young men and acquiring rich booty.

They were passing along the traditional border between pagan Saxony and the Christian lands, Valtyr told him, as they walked their horses along the bank at an ambling pace with which even Bjarki, on Skinfaxi's back, was happy. And he *was* feeling happier that day. He had a sense that he was patrolling the limits of his new fiefdom like some predator marking his territory, which delivered a pleasant jolt to his pride. And Valtyr's words by Tor's sickbed had offered hope, a soothing balm to his anguished mind.

They were not travelling alone. Two hundred Saxon warriors marched with them, mostly spearmen from the Ash Regiment, and a few companies of Yew archers, too, and about a quarter of his original *hird* – the company that had endured the worst casualties in the storming of Sigiburg. Bjarki had left a strong garrison at the fortress, some two hundred shields, and all his sick and wounded, under the command of Captain Kveldulf – the young warrior had been knocked unconscious during the battle but now claimed he was entirely recovered – and the Sigiburg garrison stood ready to defend the *castrum* should the enemy attempt to wrest it back from them.

Word had reached Frankish territory within days of the loss of Sigiburg. As Bjarki had rightly predicted, the Franks responded swiftly, sending a full *scara* of Red Cloaks – about three hundred troops – across the River Rhenus and speeding along the Hellweg.

And, on that road, Captain Eckhart had done his jarl proud.

Five days after they had captured Sigiburg, they received word that Eckhart had ambushed and massacred the entire Red Cloak *scara* sent out against them. The archers had hidden in companies in the thick trees of the First Forest and had decimated the *cunei* as they hurried along the Hellweg. Eckhart had spread his men along the route over nearly a quarter of a mile, so the whole column could be attacked simultaneously by his archers.

The Christians had perished in their scores, ripped apart by the arrow storm that lashed out from deep cover. Then a devastating charge by Eckhart's massed spearmen had shattered their hasty formations. The Frankish survivors had either fled into the forest – to an uncertain fate – or been cut down on the road by Eckhart's victorious and blood-maddened men. It seemed unlikely they would attempt another incursion by this route.

To cap it all, a joyful rider had come in from Widukind's besieging force at Osnabrucke two days ago to say that the town's stubborn defences had finally fallen to the Saxon Wolf. The smell of victory was on the wind.

It occurred to Bjarki, as he rode by the placid River Ruhr in the golden sunshine of that late-summer day, that Widukind had reclaimed almost all his patrimony in the space of a few short months. Bjarki's earlier pessimism had been swept away – he could barely remember why he had believed the Saxon Wolf must be doomed to fail. They were triumphant on all fronts. Odin smiled on them. This he found to be a particularly pleasing thought.

They left the banks of the Ruhr in the afternoon of the second day and headed due east, following a smaller tributary, and camped that evening, tired but filled with a sense of accomplishment, beside a large lake, which Bjarki learnt from a spearman who knew these parts was known as the Möhnesee.

It was a place of such beauty and tranquillity that Bjarki felt strangely calmed, and his mind began to wander strange pathways. The shame and sickness that always attended him after a bout with his *gandr* had receded; indeed, it was almost completely gone. As he washed the crusted sweat and dirt from his body in the cold, clear lake waters, he wondered if Tor was awake yet, and whether she was feeling any stronger now.

He splashed the icy water all over his naked body and looked down idly at the patchwork of yellowing bruises, scrapes, cuts and angry, recently stitched wounds that covered almost all his skin. He remembered how, when he had arrived at the Groves, he had been intimidated by the Rekkar he met, and how he had marvelled at their collections of scars and burns, bumps and divots. He realised he must present a similarly battered landscape of flesh.

He wondered, then, if the Groves Rekkar had faced a similar struggle for control over their own *gandir*. But of course they had. They must have done. Had any managed to master their Beast? He would never know. They were dead now, all killed in battle. He was the last. The last of the Fire Born.

Later that night, lounging by the fire, unusually relaxed, after one of the *hird*-men had brought him a horn of ale and a bowl of stew, he began to think seriously about his own future for the first time in months.

He did not fear death – truly he did not – but neither did he seek it. He knew that talk of word-fame immortality was a lie. Who now remembered Angantyr, the once-mighty Father of the Bear Lodge, a ferocious, dauntless Rekkr? Only a handful of folk recalled him, and he was in the ground not much more than a year. One day, they who did remember him would be dead, too, and no one would then know of the man who had been so vital, so terrible in the flesh; a man who had so impressed Bjarki with his strength.

He did not fear death – he was fairly certain the warlike deeds he had already done would grant him a seat in the Hall of the Slain – but he wanted to live his life for a season or two before he was done. And perhaps even die at sixty-something years like Theodoric, Widukind's heroic Rekkr father.

He had abandoned the impossible dream of finding Goran, and gaining the idyllic farmstead in the east, to follow Widukind. And he did not regret it. He liked his grand new titles and his responsibilities and, in truth, his new-found power, too. So might it not be possible to create a longish life here in south Saxony as Jarl of the Three Rivers and Warden of the First Forest?

Against all his expectations, Widukind seemed to be winning this war. His enemies were divided; bickering among themselves while Karolus was in Italy. In both the west and the south of their territories the Saxons had been victorious. Widukind had quickly taken back the Stolen Lands west of Verden and east of the River Ems. And since the victory at Sigiburg, Bjarki controlled almost all of lower Saxony. If they stood fast, held their ground, and their nerve... If they faced down the inevitable counter-attacks from the Franks... If they could weather the storms of battle that must come, and defended their lands with determination... might there be a chance that Bjarki, like Theodoric, could live a long and happy life? There just might, he reckoned. But it could not happen while war raged with the Franks. First it would be necessary to arrange a peace: a fair, lasting peace with their enemies.

–

They travelled slowly up the Diemel Valley, entering from the south-west the next evening. And when Bjarki saw the Eresburg mountain rising out of the distance like a vast whale breaching the surface of the sea, he felt a pang of longing for his old life in the Fyr Skola. The sun set as red as blood over his left shoulder, washing the whole valley in its gory hue, like an omen. But

Bjarki ignored it, entranced by the sight of the extraordinary plateau on which the Groves stood. It was a very curious geological structure, an oval flat-topped mountain thrusting out of the valley floor, with almost sheer sides. There were buildings up there on the flat top, halls with thatched roofs, that Bjarki could just make out. He could also see, in the centre of the plateau, the stark outline of one enormous tree, towering over everything – the Irminsul – the One Tree – the Mother of Trees – the axle of the world.

This huge living thing was the focus of the Groves. It was here, as a nervous candidate for enrolment in the Fyr Skola, that Bjarki had begun to truly understand his own strengths and his weakness. It was here that he had been set on the very hard and painful path to becoming Fire Born.

He was pleased to notice, when he was within a mile of the Groves, that there was a group of spearmen in dark green cloaks, off to his right, who were watching the advance of his column from the edge of the First Forest.

And, when he waved an arm in a friendly greeting, one young spearman came running down the slight slope towards them, and jogged swiftly across the valley floor to investigate them more closely.

These green-cloaked watchers were Barda, Bjarki knew, the Fyr Skola troops tasked with defending the Groves, and standing with the Fire Born heroes when they went off to war. The other Barda quickly disappeared, presumably to report their coming. So the Groves of Eresburg were alerted, Bjarki noted with approval, to the presence of a potentially dangerous force.

'Welcome home, Bjarki Bloodhand,' said the green-cloaked young man. And Bjarki saw with a surge of pure joy that it was his closest friend from the Fyr Skola days – Gunnar – once his mop-headed clown and confidant, now a much more sober and soldierly figure.

'Well met, Older Brother,' said Bjarki, using the old title of his one-time mentor, as he reached down from the saddle to clasp hands.

'I hear I'm supposed to call you jarl, these days,' said Gunnar.

'I hear you're now the captain of the Barda,' replied Bjarki, 'lord and high commander of all the mighty warriors of the Groves.'

'All sixteen of them – yes,' said Gunnar with a familiar grin.

'So you've recruited more since I left?' said Valtyr.

'Two recruits came in from Westphalia two months ago, Mikelgothi,' said Gunnar, bowing low to the old man. 'But we still have not a single Rekkr in our halls. Not one Fire Born now in the Fyr Skola – unless, Bjarki, you've come to honour our little community...'

'Oh, he's far above that sort of thing now,' said Valtyr, grinning at the young man. 'He's ruler of all southern Saxony. Far too grand.'

'I *shall* be staying at the Groves for a while, Gunnar,' said Bjarki. 'If you'll have me. And, of course, I shall be glad to help out in any way I can. I'm here to see to the strengthening of your defences. But I think I can spare a few warriors to swell the ranks of the Barda. If that would be acceptable.'

'Acceptable? By Thor's great hairy cock – that will be more than acceptable. Bjarki, old friend, you can stay with us as long as you please!'

–

The ancient Groves of Eresburg were in many ways pleasingly the same – and yet in many others uncomfortably different. When Bjarki and his two hundred men had toiled up the dusty slope to the main gates at the summit of the plateau, they were greeted by the whole Groves community with a song of welcome, a stirring dirge in a forgotten tongue which Bjarki remembered well, and which set all the hairs on his body immediately standing upright.

They were conducted by the captain of the Barda and the three Groves *gothi* – none of whom Bjarki knew – to the Irminsul, the One Tree, the axle legends claimed connected the Nine Worlds of the universe from the eagle-inhabited heavens to the freezing depths of the realm of the goddess Hel.

The last time Bjarki had seen the One Tree it had been a sad, blackened skeleton, a statement of the agony of the whole Saxon people. But after the Franks had overrun the Groves the spring before last, and slaughtered its inhabitants, the foe had then departed and the Irminsul had revived itself.

The huge oak tree was now covered with green leaves once more and, although the trunk was visibly charred, it was obviously far from dead. The community of the Groves and the Fyr Skola was another matter entirely.

Once the plateau had been covered with lines of trees, trimmed into intricate patterns, which marked out the various zones of the Fyr Skola.

Novices had spent hours of every day tending the lush, elaborate topiary of the Groves with much incantation, animal sacrifice and prayer. All that was gone – all that remained were a few scrubby, sad-looking shrubs and dusty uncared-for bushes.

Once there had been three imposing Lodge Houses for the three different types of Fire Born – the Bears, Wolves and Boars – and a Thing House for all their meetings, and a venerable shrine, which marked the spot where Odin himself had rested after his ordeal hanging on the One Tree, and which was stuffed with silver and gold trinkets – the wealth of the Groves.

All that had been swept away by the Franks.

The summit of the plateau was ringed with a sagging wooden fence of pine stakes, and there was a rickety watchtower beside the entrance gate that, admittedly, gave a magnificent view over the whole Diemel Valley.

There were two large, solidly built longhouses with thatched roofs, and a few huts, and kitchens, bakeries and storehouses. A rutted and churned-up exercise ground had been marked out with small whitewashed river stones. The only structure to have survived the Frankish onslaught was the Fyr Pit, a large rectangular basin lined with stone slabs and filled with grey sandy ash, where some of the bloodier rituals of the Fyr Skola had been enacted.

After the hymn of welcome and some long prayers in the shade of the Irminsul led by Valtyr – who despite his peregrinations was the Mikelgothi, or high priest, of the Groves of Eresburg – Gunnar showed Bjarki around.

'We've only managed to construct two Lodge Houses so far,' Gunnar said. 'One for the Bears, one for Wolves. You'll be put in Bear Lodge, obviously. But there were no members of the Boar Lodge left alive after the... anyway, and we have so few people here now that it has taken us all this time just to do what we have done.'

'How many people *do* you have now?' Bjarki asked.

'Twenty-eight, counting Valtyr, but he's so often absent.'

'No Rekkr at all? Have you any candidates for that honour?'

'We sent out three boys Voyaging over a month ago. All of them Wolf Lodge. They seemed ready. But none has yet returned.'

'I'm sorry to tell you, Gunnar, but we found one of them dead in the forest, three days' march north. Blond boy. Very young. I buried him with his wolf fur and sent up the proper prayer to Odin from his grave.'

'That would be Frederic. I'm sad to hear that. He was so keen.'

'And what was your plan if the Franks did ever attack you?'

'We hoped to spot them early, run into the First Forest and hide.'

'There'll be no more running and hiding,' said Bjarki grimly.

He grasped Gunnar's shoulder, squeezing it hard: 'I promise you, old friend, that together we are going to restore the Fyr Skola to something resembling its former pomp and glory. That is what I'm here for, mainly. I have enough good, willing folk to achieve this, but we have a great deal of work to do. Are you with me, Older Brother?'

'Till the end, old friend!' replied Gunnar.

Chapter Twelve

The unexpected travels of an apostle

Tor's shoulder was paining her badly, but she was determined not to show her agony to Gerta, the sullen, middle-aged *hird*-woman who had been given the task of escorting the wounded shield-maiden safely back to Verden.

They had travelled slowly on horseback and had taken two weeks over a journey that should have taken only five or six days, and despite their absurdly snail-like progress, Tor found herself exhausted at the end of each day's ride, often falling asleep while Gerta was making the nightly pottage.

It was a month since the storming of Sigiburg and, while Tor knew she was very fortunate to be alive, she found herself increasingly frustrated by her own weakness and the difficulty she still had in doing the most ordinary of things. Even the morning emptying of her bladder and bowels was an undignified and painful chore, involving gripping a convenient low-hanging tree branch to avoid having to squat on her sore, wounded thigh for too long.

However, her heart quickened as they splashed across the ford on the Aller late one afternoon and she glimpsed the grey palisade of Verden through a copse of ash on the far side of the river, and a flash of golden sun reflected from the high, limewashed walls of the house of the Horse-Master.

Widukind would be here.

They went straight to the small longhouse on the edge of the town that Jarl Brun had given for their use and, as Tor dismounted, she was greeted by Inge, who came pelting out of the main door shrieking with childish glee at her unexpected return.

That put Tor in a better mood. And her reunion with Garm in his large new enclosure was equally touching – the bear seemed to sense that she was not at full strength, and after sniffing her all over he began to gently lick her face and neck, as a mother might wash its cub.

However, Tor's good humour was plunged into the mire again later that night when the elderly steward Ulli told her over supper that Widukind was away on the north coast, paying a visit to Raedbad, venerable lord of Frisia.

'What is he doing up there?' she said, perhaps a little angrily. 'While we fight in the south, he's taken time away from his duties to visit the sea?'

'Don't know, mistress,' Ulli said. 'I don't have much to do with the fine folk of the hall. Jarl Brun is here, though, should you need anything.'

It was good to be home, though, and after they had eaten a pair of plump mallards Ulli had bagged in the Aller marshes, Inge sang songs from her land while Garm and Tor drowsed contentedly by the hearth.

Inge woke her in the late morning with a mug of ale and a piece of buttered bread and honey, and Tor luxuriated in her blankets, enjoying the thought that she had nothing to do that day, or the next, or the one after that, but rest and recover from her wounds and the rigours of the hard journey.

–

Princess Geva entered the longhouse at noon like a force of nature; she came in with a gust of wind and a tumbling gale of kind words.

'Phew! What a fug! Smells like a garrison whorehouse the day after a victory. We must get those shutters open immediately. Never mind, never mind, a little stink never hurt anyone.

You there, girl, get that hearth fire stirred up and set some water on to boil. I shall need hot water, plenty of it. I've never seen the like: you Norse folk live like pigs... Oh, is that a *bear*?'

Tor was on her feet – perhaps not as nimbly as she once might.

'What in the name of Odin's sweaty arse-crack do you mean by bursting in here, woman, and ordering all my good people about...'

'Don't give me any of your smutty backchat, my girl. Jarl Brun has ordered me to nurse you back to health, and nurse you I shall. My own dear Widukind also told me before he left to make sure you lacked for nothing. Huh! Ordering people about? Ordering! I haven't begun yet. First things first: get those nasty, smelly man-clothes off and you into a hot tub. Where is that hot water? You there, old man – build up that fire good and hot. Don't dilly-dally, come on, come on, come on... Must I do everything myself?'

Inge was already scurrying to obey her commands. Old Ulli was now outside fetching firewood. And Gerta was hauling out a huge round wooden half-barrel bathtub from one of the recesses at the back of the hall. Even Garm seemed bemused by this whirlwind-like arrival. He let out a small barking cough. And Tor opened her mouth to give this bustling invader a piece of her mind and... instead, she just meekly surrendered to her.

Tor's mother had died young and the shield-maiden's half-forgotten memories of her were for ever tarnished by the brutal beatings the poor woman had taken at the hands of her father Hildar, a Rekkr, who was even then halfway to being Galálar.

Tor had had few older female friends over her years of growing, and not one of them was even vaguely maternal towards her, unless you counted Valtyr, and Tor did not. So now she found herself oddly comforted by the energetic presence of Geva, bossing her servants, arranging hot baths and healthy food, making her go to bed early and changing her dressings with a brisk tenderness. She found she enjoyed the feeling of being mothered.

One thing she did not like was that poor, sweet Garm was banished back to his cage-like paddock enclosure, and she had to hobble across the large courtyard every morning after breakfast just to see him.

The other fly in her ointment was, of course, Widukind.

She recognised that she was in love with Widukind. She spent large portions of each day thinking about him and recalling their one frenzied night together. More than anything she longed to have him with her again. Yet Tor could not see Geva as a genuine rival for Widukind's affections. The princess was the opposite of Tor in almost every way: she was loud and large, rich and jolly; she was soft and feminine, bosomy, and always smelt of lavender. But while Tor had not yet seen this, one quality they did both share was a cold, steely ruthlessness, a driving desire to get their own way.

Most of the time Tor accepted Geva's kindnesses, allowing her to order her life in Verden without complaint. Widukind, she believed, could not truly love this ever-bustling woman. Whatever they shared, it was not love, not passion, not a true meeting of mind and body, of the kind she and the Saxon had achieved in the sacred grove that magical, blood-soaked night.

It simply could not be true. In some remote part of her mind she knew that they must have lain together in the marriage bed at least once. But it could not be a true union – it was impossible – Widukind was a part of *her*.

Sometimes, when she lay in bed watching Geva busy herself around the longhouse, or when the older woman was spinning raw wool into yarn by the hearth, and mainly when her wounds were paining her, Tor thought about telling Geva what had happened between her and Widukind on the night of the *blot* – just to see what reaction it might produce. But every time she contemplated it, she shied away from voicing the hurtful words.

Her love for Widukind, she decided, was her secret. Not to be shared with anyone, least of all this flabby, interfering, too-cheerful milch cow.

Two months after Tor's return to Verden, with the wet, musty smells of late autumn in the air, when she was able to be out and about on her feet most of the day, and was beginning to train her body for combat once more in the yard each chilly dawn with Ulli, word came that Widukind was back at last.

Geva gave Tor one last vast, smothering hug and a kiss and she was gone: back to Jarl Brun's hall to welcome her returning husband home.

Tor waited in her little house for the call from the Saxon Wolf. She expected, at least, that she would be asked to report on Bjarki's situation in south Saxony, or to describe the taking of the fortress of Sigiburg. She imagined, perhaps, that she might receive a reward, a gift from Widukind for her role in the battle. There was also a large part of her that longed for a midnight meeting, alone, just the two of them in his private quarters, when the rest of the hall was fast asleep. So Tor waited; she waited patiently.

Then she waited some more.

A week passed, and then another, and the bone-like trees emerged from under their cloak of dead leaves to announce that winter was finally at hand. And still Widukind had not summoned her to his side. Inge reported in her ever-more confident version of Saxon that there was a feast being prepared in the great hall for full moon. Tor waited for her invitation. It did not come.

Ulli told her that the horse troops of Jarl Brun's *hird* had been ordered out to hunt, to fill the jarl's larders with fresh meat. Still no invitation came.

On the night of the full moon, Tor's long patience turned to rage.

She dressed herself carefully. She washed and braided up her fiery red hair and donned her old leather trews and tunic, and a green cloak over that, pinned with a silver brooch shaped like a pair of deer, the only jewellery she possessed. She slung her seax across her waist and hung a sword at her side to remind her lord that she was a renowned warrior, and not some kitchen trull to be bedded after a drunken feast then dismissed in dawn's cold light.

She walked to the great hall and demanded entrance from the *hird*-men at the door. With Gerta at her side, she stalked inside.

The hall was packed, with folk seated at the long benches, hundreds of them, and standing around the walls – most unusually they all seemed to be sober. She looked to the end of the hall, at the dais and table where the jarl and his family sat, and there she saw a solemn scene being enacted.

A lone harpist plucked his instrument softy, and she saw Widukind seated in a huge chair, a throne, with Geva standing by his side, her plump hand possessively on his shoulder. A grim-looking warrior, scarred and shaven-headed, was kneeling before him, offering his sword, a magnificent naked blade with a silver pommel, hilt first. Tor recognised the warrior from his battered face and bold dragon neck tattoo as Jarl Hessi of Eastphalia.

Widukind accepted the beautiful sword and admired it for a moment or two. Then he got to his feet and, lifting the kneeling jarl upright, he solemnly presented the sword back to its owner. He raised the older man's hand in the air and with his other hand he beckoned another fellow from the wings, a thin, sickly-looking man with a fat golden torc around his neck. Tor knew him from King Siegfried's feast in Hedeby as Jarl Ulf of Nordalbia.

When Ulf was next to him Widukind lifted both men's hands in the air.

Tor suddenly understood the full significance of this night's great feast before Widukind even opened his mouth to speak.

'Friends are good on the day of battle,' the Saxon Wolf began. 'And I have few better friends than these two brave warriors here with me today: I accept the oath of my cousins Jarl Ulf and Jarl Hessi, and swear that I will be a generous lord to them all my days, and will spend the last drop of my blood to lead them, and their valiant men, to victory over our Frankish enemies.'

Then Jarl Brun stepped forward dramatically from the black shadows behind Widukind's chair. The timing was so perfect that Tor wondered if they had practised this part of the traditional oath ceremony beforehand.

The Horse-Master of Angria said: 'Theodoric, only son of Theodoric, known to all as Widukind, has now received the solemn oaths of the jarls of Eastphalia and Nordalbia this night. He already has *my* sacred oath. We have seen him triumph in the west – he has recovered the Stolen Lands, as he swore to do. We've seen him triumph in the south: his Warden of the First Forest, the mighty Bjarki Bloodhand, has taken the Frankish fortress of Sigiburg and is holding the Hessian march for us. So therefore I hereby proclaim that Widukind is the overlord of all Saxony, not merely by his name and lineage, nor by his territorial claims, but in cold, hard, undeniable truth. I say it is time for him to take on the mantle of his father. What say you, good people of Saxony, what say you, folk of Westphalia, bold warriors of Eastphalia, Angria and Nordalbia – do we now acclaim him as our duke?'

The roar of approval that echoed around the hall struck Tor like a blow. Her anger was forgotten and she was gripped by wild excitement. She found that she, like hundreds of others, was yelling: 'Wi-du-kind… Wi-du-kind!'

For all Saxony was now united behind this magnificent man – her man!

—

Tor had no idea how she managed to keep her countenance for the remainder of the feast. She ate and drank in a dream, and made small talk with Gerta and the folk sat around her. Inside, she was raging with a fire for her lord.

The Saxon warriors gorged and drank in the usual manner and, after an age, they began to wander away to sleep, or find bedfellows. Gerta burped a gust of ale and said she was going back to the longhouse. Tor dismissed her and remained at her bench, waiting, waiting for the word from her man.

She had no doubt at all that it would come, in due course.

She knew that Widukind must have seen her in the hall. Perhaps when Geva had retired for the night, he would summon her... So she sat and sipped her ale, making it last, on and on into the night. The hall was nearly empty, and the walls redounded with the sounds of snoring. The hearth fire had burnt low. Abbio was standing in front of her like a small shaggy bird.

'He wantsss to sssee you,' said the strange little man. His voice sounded as if he was hissing rather than speaking. She saw that he had lost two of his teeth in the centre, and the others had all been filed in grooves, from some sort of magical ritual, she assumed, which gave his voice that weird sibilance. She realised she'd never heard him utter a word and had always assumed his voice would match his look and he'd croak like a raven.

She got up without a word and followed the shabby fellow, threading through the benches, past all the warriors stretched out on the wooden slabs.

Abbio led her to the back of the hall, and through a leather curtain to a small chamber. She was not surprised to see Widukind in there, but she was astonished that he was not alone. Four men sitting there on stools around a glowing brazier, drinking mead from silver-chased horns: jarls Brun, Hessi and Ulf – and their leader, the newly acclaimed Duke of Saxony.

'I think you all know Tor Hildarsdottir,' said Widukind, beckoning to a hovering servant to bring a stool and a drinking horn. Tor sat down; another thrall came and filled the elaborate vessel in her hand from a jug. She sipped the drink – a very strong honey brew.

'She was first over the wall at Sigiburg,' Widukind went on, 'and is recovering here from the grave wounds she took in that battle.'

The three other men nodded at her politely. Jarl Brun offered her a grim smile. Out of the corner of her eye she saw Abbio the Crow whispering with a man in the garb of an Angrian rider at the far side of the room. Tor, as was her habit when she did not know what to say or do, glared fiercely at all four seated men in turn, holding their eyes with hers, but saying not a word.

There was an awkward pause, then Widukind said: 'You are perhaps wondering why I asked to see you – so late, and in private.'

Tor frowned at him, and shrugged as if she cared not. But she held her tongue lest it betray her. If he wanted to pretend there was nothing between them, no bond, she would not make a fool of herself by saying otherwise.

She took a sip of her mead.

'I think Abbio can explain best what we hope to learn from you this night,' Widukind said. 'But first, I must ask this: am I right in thinking that you and Bjarki spent last winter in Rerik?'

Tor nodded. Inside, she was astonished. This was the last thing she had expected to be asked. She kept her face expressionless and seemed to have lost the capacity for speech. Her silence compelled words from Widukind.

'As you may know, Abbio serves me in a variety of helpful ways,' he said, almost babbling, 'but one of his most important duties is the gathering of information. He has cultivated a host of informants in halls across Saxony and beyond… He collects bits of gossip and snippets of news, and, uh, he tracks the movements of various folk, friends and enemies, that we may one day have an interest in. He also, I think he will not mind me saying, uses the power of divination to reveal the truth of things far away. So, anyway, he has heard something strange, and we wondered if you or perhaps Jarl Bjarki might be able to shed light… and since the Bloodhand is not with us…'

Abbio was back. He had acquired a long horn of mead but no stool. He paced up and down behind Widukind, back and forth, like poor Garm when he was restlessly patrolling the bars of his enclosure.

'You were in Rerik for sssome monthsss, yess?' said Abbio. 'All lassst winter long?'

Tor nodded again.

'Did you have any dealings with Prinss Witzlausss of the Obodrites?'

Tor found her voice: 'No. We were too unimportant to mix with such a man. He was a prince. We were beneath his notice.'

Jarl Hessi of Eastphalia growled: 'You didn't miss anything, shield-maiden. He is a snake – a dirty cattle-thief. His young warriors have raided my lands for years. He steals away with my good beasts and runs...'

'Yes, well, the girl says she doesn't know this Witzlaus fellow,' said Jarl Ulf. 'There seems little point...'

'I should add that Bjarki served the prince's cousin, Burik, a grain merchant, for some weeks at the end of our stay there,' said Tor. 'He is a greedy fool. Untrustworthy. But neither of us met the Obodrites' prince.'

'Iss that ssso?' said Abbio. 'You are ssssure it was Burik?'

'Bjarki said it was him.' Tor shrugged. 'He would not lie.'

'What did the Rekkr do for Burik, the richessst man in Rerik? He was his personal bodyguard? His asssassin? Did he train his warriorsss?'

'He shifted his grain sacks,' said Tor. 'He unloaded all his trading ships and stored the big sacks of grain in a huge water-front warehouse.'

To Tor's surprise, all the men began to laugh. And then laugh some more. Jarl Brun had tears in his eyes and slapped his thigh. 'Ha-ha! A Rekkr... working... ha-ha-ha... working like an ox.'

Tor suddenly felt tired. She had been hoping for a night with Widukind. She did not enjoy her brother being the butt of a stupid joke.

'Is this why I was summoned?' she snapped. 'To tell you amusing stories about how Bjarki and I struggled to put bread in our mouths when we were starving? If this is all you require from me...'

'Peace, Tor, peace! Our apologies,' said Widukind. 'We hold your brother in such esteem that, well, it *is* amusing to think of him labouring...'

Tor pushed back her stool. Her expression hard as stone.

'Wait, woman,' said Abbio. 'Tell me, what did Burik do with all the grain that your brother shifted ssso *heroically* for him?'

'He kept much of it in a great warehouse – as big as this hall. And some of it was taken to another vast depot on the edge of Rerik.'

'That issss a great deal of grain. He filled a warehouse as big as this hall with grain, you sssay?'

'Yes, easily as big as this place. Filled to the rafters. And there was another outside the town, too. Perhaps several more places besides.'

'That is enough grain to feed an army,' said Widukind.

The air in the chamber had suddenly grown rather chill. Brun leaned forward and poked the brazier with a poker, stirring up the red coals.

'What does this mean?' said Tor. She looked in turn at all the faces there. All the good humour was now gone.

Widukind said: 'When in Rerik, did you ever see or hear of any wandering Christians? Any missionaries? What are they called: apostles?'

'No one like that. Their gods are like ours – a little different, odd names for Thor and Odin, but still very far from Christ worship.'

'You know Bishop Livinus, Tor, from your time as a prisoner, and perhaps also from Hedeby?' said Widukind. He now sounded rather sad.

'I know him. A leader of the Franks. A fanatical Christian. He's a cold-hearted and cruel bastard, too. Dangerous, I would say.'

'I would say so, too,' said Widukind. 'It seems that after the Frankish embassy to Hedeby – which was merely a sham, by the way...'

'They offered Siegfried Nordalbia, my lands,' said Jarl Ulf, clearly offended, 'but my cousin told 'em to stuff it up their—'

'...*after* the embassy was over,' Widukind's words rolled right over Ulf's high whining, 'the Frankish contingent did *not* go south and west, back to Aachen, as we had expected them to do. They went *east*. I was occupied with the campaign in the Stolen Lands at that time, and did not order them watched. An error. And it seems the embassy travelled east into Wendland, into the territory of the Obodrites. I'm informed that they spent a month with Prince Witzlaus at his powerful fortress in the port of Rerik.'

Nobody responded to that. Then Jarl Hessi said: 'I still have friends across the Elbe – I will send to them there to see what we can learn. But this information is not good, my duke. Not good at all.'

'I have sssome people too in Wendland, my lord,' said Abbio. 'I will set them to discovering what took place between Livinusss and Witzlaus. Do not fear, my lord, we shall dissscover their planss.'

The men drained their mead horns and handed them back to the thralls. One by one, they got up and bowed before making their way out of the new duke's chamber. Finally, only Tor and Widukind were left in the dark room, both staring blindly into the dying brazier, deep in their own thoughts.

'Do you need anything, Tor?' said Widukind, finally getting to his feet.

'Why did you not call for me sooner?' she said.

'I meant more food or a healing salve, or bandages or something. You still look pale. But Geva said you were on the mend. She was impressed.'

'I thought you might call for me, uh, for a report on Sigiburg.'

'I've already had a dozen reports on the battle. It was well done, that action. Very well done. But you are correct that I have been remiss...'

'Yes, lord,' said Tor, a little too eagerly.

'I have not thanked you for the heroic part you played in that fight. First over the wall – that is quite a feat, with all the brave warriors gathered there on that bloody day. I salute you, Tor!'

'You salute me?'

'Yes, I do, and I have this for you. A fine gift!' Widukind fumbled in the leather pouch at his waist. He pulled out a shining silver arm ring, the metal cleverly segmented, intricately worked, and the two big end-pieces beautifully shaped into fierce dragons' heads.

'A mark of my great esteem for you, Tor Hildarsdottir...'

'Widukind,' said a new voice, and Tor looked beyond her lord to see a figure at the rear of the chamber.

It was Geva. Her hair was loose and formed a glossy chestnut cloud around her face. She was wearing nothing but a light linen sleeping-shift that clung to her ample shape. And for the first time ever Tor realised that she was indeed attractive, even beautiful.

'My dear,' said Geva softly, 'will you be much longer at this?'

'I'm coming to bed now, my love,' said Widukind, smiling lovingly at his wife, and he turned back and tossed the arm ring over to Tor.

'You are the bravest of my warriors, Tor Hildarsdottir, and I am most fortunate to command your service. I thank you.'

His words were earnest but he could not look her directly in the eye. 'If you do require anything at all,' he continued, 'do not hesitate to ask... ask one of my personal attendants or my thralls. Or my dear wife. I'm sure she can provide anything you need to, uh, speed the healing of your wounds.'

'Oh yes, indeed,' said Geva. 'But I will bid you good night now, dear, sweet Tor. Sleep, rest – you'll be back to your old self very soon, I'm sure.'

The honeyed words spoken by the big Danish woman might have been kindly meant – but Tor knew the sound of gloating when she heard it.

Chapter Thirteen

The return of the twins

Bjarki's arrival at the Groves in the late summer with two hundred warriors infused the place with a bolt of energy. He immediately set his people to work, first building barracks on the plateau for them to take shelter in. Grey autumn was approaching, with winter breathing icily on the back of its neck.

Once the first rudimentary halls were raised, mere flimsy waterproof sheds, in truth, which took a matter of a week or two to erect, he set one full-strength company, or *lith*, of fifty fighters to strengthening the defences all the way around the perimeter of the Groves.

Their task was to make the flimsy fence much higher and more formidable, with a walkway inside that ran a full mile around the whole circumference. Yet more folk were put to digging a wide ditch across the earthen ramp that was the final part of the road up to the main gate.

Bjarki planned to replace the solid dirt road with a wooden bridge, at least one cart-width wide, which could be removed by a system of ropes if they were attacked, like a drawbridge. This would leave the Groves with sheer sides all the way round, and a palisade that could be easily defended.

Defending such a long perimeter required warriors – a lot of them. If they only had one shield every one or two paces, Bjarki calculated, they would still need a thousand folk to complete the full circuit. And there was no way that Bjarki could ever find a thousand spears to permanently guard the Groves. Even if he could, how would they be fed? He decided to follow part of the cautious strategy devised by his friend Gunnar. He built three more watchtowers, three times the height of a man, equally spaced around the perimeter, and manned them day and night. From the top of a watchtower a sentry could see six or seven miles easily, and give ample warning of an enemy army's approach from any direction, except through the thickets of the First Forest to the north. But even the efficient Franks would not be able to bring their men through the wilderness in any numbers.

He decided that rather than trying to guard every inch of the perimeter, there would be a permanent garrison of a hundred and fifty, in three *lith*, who would take turns to man all the watchtowers, all the time. If, indeed when – Bjarki was under no fond illusions – the vengeful enemy came in sight, the Groves commander, warned by the watchtowers, would mass his troops to repel them at whichever point they tried to scale the sheer cliffs.

Let them come now, Bjarki thought, *and we will show them*. He would not make the same mistake his predecessors had and come down from the Groves to give battle in the valley. *Let the Franks attempt our walls now, if they dare, and we will dispatch them all to their burning Christian hell.*

His two hundred hard-working Ash and Yew warriors were already eating through the stores they had brought with them at a terrific rate. And so, when much of the initial building work was completed, Bjarki sent out *lith* to forage in the surrounding lands. They were ordered to stay out of the forest, and to attack only lands newly settled by Franks – not their own folk. In this manner, Bjarki hoped to drive away the incomers and feed his own men, *and* accumulate stores to feed everyone in winter or in case of a siege.

Amid all this bustle, Bjarki had not forgotten his conversation with Valtyr at Tor's bedside in Sigiburg. One evening, shortly after their arrival, he interrogated Valtyr about the method he had mentioned for killing *gandir*.

'You once asked me who I was, Bjarki,' said the old man, 'and I gave you an answer. I told you I was a trader, a gatherer of information, and a Guardian of the North – all this is true – but I did not tell you everything. I never told you, for example, how I came to be connected with the Groves of Eresburg and the Fyr Skola, did I? And you never once thought to ask me.'

Bjarki scratched his beard. They were sitting in one of the newly built barracks, sharing a jug of ale after a hard day. 'So tell me, then!' he said.

'You know I fought as a young spearman in the battle in the mountains, at Blundfjell, with your father, when he smashed the shield wall of Anders Black-Tooth single-handed?'

Bjarki nodded – he knew the story. It was one of the only tales about his Rekkr father Hildar that showed him in a heroic light.

'I was impressed by Hildar, by his strength, his ferocity and courage. He was the first Fire Born that I ever met. I was a stripling then and wished to be a great warrior. So I asked permission of my king, Harald Fox-Beard, to journey south to the Eresburg and enrol as a novice in the Fyr Skola.'

Bjarki found it hard to imagine Valtyr as an impressionable youth, eager to become a Rekkr, but he nodded his agreement anyway.

'I came to this place and made my oath in the shade of the Irminsul and was accepted by the Mikelgothi. But I was not a good candidate. I learnt the humming and fought another boy in the Fyr Pit. I did the exercises diligently – well, you know, Bjarki, what it is like when you come here and dream of becoming Fire Born. I was so eager.'

'You became a Rekkr?' said Bjarki. 'I did not know *that*!'

'No, Bjarki, I never became a Rekkr – I wasn't even allowed to join the Barda. I was destined, it seemed, to become a servant in Wolf Lodge. And when I came to this realisation, I was crushed. I wept, I raved, I even cursed the gods. Then *she* came to me.'

'Your *gandr*?' Bjarki frowned at the old man.

'Not a *gandr* – a girl. A real, flesh-and-blood girl, who was a novice in Boar Lodge. Her name was Skymir. She was tall, slender and very beautiful, with long, shining hair the colour of bronze.'

'Not the same Skymir who was the Mikelgothi when…'

'The same. She came to the Fyr Skola a few weeks after me. For some reason, after a little while she chose me as her lover. And we spent every day together. We were inseparable. It was perfect love – for both of us equally.'

Bjarki tried to picture Valtyr as a handsome swain in love with a pretty girl for the first time. Obviously, Valtyr had been young once, but… no, it was beyond him. To Bjarki, he'd always be this annoying, skinny old man.

'She was a better Fyr Skola candidate them me – by far. She soon mastered the humming. She learnt the First Forest myths and all the old *berserkr* lore, and trained in healing, too, under the *gothi*. They said she learnt *seithr*, as well, the dark arts. Then one night her *gandr* came to her while she slept – she said she was a great white sow with skin pale as snow.'

Valtyr paused and took a sip of his ale; he wiped his mouth.

'Go on,' said Bjarki, 'you can't stop there!'

'The one thing to know, to understand Skymir,' said Valtyr, 'was that she was a deeply gentle person. A loving woman. She understood the necessity of war and violence, and she was a fine fighter in the Fyr Pit, and in training, but she took no pleasure in the spilling of blood. She did her Voyaging in three quick days and the White Sow came to her in the forest – and the Boar Lodge Mother declared her to be a true Rekkr – but she did not relish it. She fought only once as a Fire Born, a skirmish against the Franks in Hessia, I think – I forget the details. When she returned, she told me, weeping in my arms, how she felt shamed by the things she had done. Sickened.'

Bjarki was tipped forward on his stool, his eyes burning bright. 'So she rid herself of her *gandr*? She did that? She banished the White Sow?'

'She did.'

'How?'

'She killed herself.'

Bjarki's mouth fell open. 'What? No! I knew her. She was alive and well when Tor and I came to the Fyr Skola. What do you mean?'

'I am very tired, Bjarki, and an old man must have his rest. I will tell you the remainder of this tale on another occasion.'

'Oh no, you don't. You will tell it me now, old man.'

'She was the only woman I ever truly loved and it burns my heart to remember her. Her once-sweet memory brings only pain to me now.'

'Valtyr, I'll bring you a great deal *more* pain if you don't...'

The old man smiled slyly at him. 'Very well, Bjarki, if you insist, I shall tell you just a little more tonight. It was like this...'

–

One day at the end of autumn, when Bjarki was discussing the placement of signal fires along the valley with Eric, one of the few surviving Barda of the original Groves, he became aware of a commotion from the centre of the plateau, shouts of alarm, and then, oddly, snatches of some strange singing.

He hurried over to the shade of the great Irminsul and saw a crowd of folk gathered admiringly around two extraordinary figures. They were two young men, both as thin as skeletons, with their skin bruised, torn and scratched almost everywhere. All they wore were a few tatters of grey fur around their loins. They both bore the same look of grim triumph on their gaunt, filthy faces – faces that were unnervingly alike, indeed, identical under the same thatch of grey-shot black hair. They both possessed extraordinary eyes that were the pale, washed-out colour of summer clouds.

Gunnar said: 'Bjarki – this is Fidor and Fodor, two novices of the Groves that were sent out Voyaging. They are returned safe to us. The Wolf has spoken to them both, they say. They will become our first new Rekkr.'

'Not so fast,' said Valtyr Far-Traveller. 'I must examine them first personally, as the Mikelgothi of these sacred Groves, to see if they have truly met the Wolf and summoned their *gandir*.'

One of the twins turned his head slowly towards Valtyr – and growled. It was a horrible sound. Even Bjarki felt an icy shiver down his spine.

–

They met in the Wolf Lodge, all the more senior members of the Groves of Eresburg. Bjarki was struck once more by how few of them he truly knew. There was Gunnar and Valtyr, of course, who were old friends, and Eldar, a healer of considerable skill; Erik, a powerful but slow-witted Barda, who was the only surviving member of the now-defunct Boar Lodge, and who had been made an honorary Wolf, and a raven-haired young woman called Katla, a strange, tight-lipped *gothi*, coldly beautiful, who stood in for Valtyr as the spiritual leader of the Groves when the trader was on his travels. The other half-dozen faces of the Wolf Lodge were all almost strangers to him.

Valtyr opened the proceedings: 'Describe for us if you will what occurred after you left the Groves of Eresburg in the summer. The more detail you can give the better – the more likely that you will be believed.'

The twins, sitting side by side, on a bench at the side of the Lodge, stared at Valtyr. The silence stretched out uncomfortably. Bjarki saw that one of them, Fidor, he thought, had a tiny brown mark, a mole, on the right side of his face. It was as far as he could see the only way to tell them apart.

Fodor – the one without the mole – said: 'It is no matter if you believe us or not. The Wolf came. He spoke to us. We *know* this.'

Valtyr began angrily: 'Tell us of your experience, or you—'

Bjarki interrupted him. 'Before you came to the Groves, Fodor, when I was a novice here, there was one called Ivar Knuttson of Boar Lodge.'

The twins fixed Bjarki with their pale eyes. Fidor nodded. 'We have heard of him. He was a Rekkr, Father of the Boar Lodge.'

'He was no Rekkr – he was, in fact, a coward, a false *nithing*.'

The twins looked shocked. 'How could this be?' asked Fodor.

'He lied,' said Bjarki. 'They questioned him in the Boar Lodge and he invented a story about his Voyaging. He claimed the Boar came. It did not.'

'Do you say we too are liars – like this... *nithing*?'

'No,' said Bjarki. 'I do not. But we *must* ask questions, hear your tale. Do you see why you must tell us of your Voyaging?'

The two men looked at each other for several moments, eerily engaged in a silent conversation. Then they turned back to Bjarki.

'You are a true Rekkr – we *know* this – we can see the Bear in your eyes. We believe you will see the Wolf in us. We will speak.'

–

'It was high summer when we left these Groves of Eresburg, with another fellow, a frightened little boy called Frederic,' said Fidor.

'My brother and I had both dreamed of the Wolf three nights in a row. He howled in our heads all night, each of the three nights, calling us to him and inviting us to join his spirit pack.'

'The little boy went away into the forest on his own – he was seeking his Bear *gandr*, he said. He too said he had seen it in his dreams, and in his nightmares. We saw that he was weak, fearful, too, but we thought the Bear might give him strength. We never saw him after that first day of leaving.'

Fodor took over the tale. 'It was strange. Once we were in the First Forest, and all alone, the dreams just stopped. The Wolf had called us but when we left the Fyr Skola, for some reason, all our visions, the howling, the calling of us to join his pack, they all went away. We felt we were...'

'...unworthy of the Wolf,' Fidor said. 'That *he* wanted to test us.'

They both fell silent for a while, staring at the floor of the Lodge. Just as Bjarki was about to invite them to continue, Fidor said: 'It was hard. The hardest thing we've done. The hunger, the cold, every day growing worse.'

Bjarki tried to picture them, two boys alone in the First Forest with no food or clothes. Nothing but a wolf pelt and a knife apiece.

'We began to hunt – deer, sometimes, we made our knives into spears. A boar piglet we tried to catch, but its mother was close and it was too dangerous. But we ate anything we could catch or find. Worms, fungus, acorns – a dead fox once. We scared a bear off its kill, an elk, by making fire and screaming till he left. It had mostly finished anyway, and the meat was near putrid.

'We became sick, for many days we were too sick to move. I thought my brother would die. But he did not. And worst of all, we never even saw a wolf – not once. You walk for a week in the woods and you hear one calling almost every night – and maybe see one or two, even a hunting pack. We saw none. Heard none. It was as if all the wolves were avoiding us, shunning us. It made us afraid. Perhaps the Wolf *gandr* would never come to us. We talked about going home, back to the Groves, in our shame. But we held on. We always thought, one more day, one more day...' Fidor stopped.

'How long did you Voyage for?' asked Bjarki.

'There is no time in the First Forest,' said Fodor. 'We were in there till we came out. I don't know. One moon, or two, perhaps?'

'They were gone for more than three months,' said Valtyr.

'So then... three months.'

'But the Wolf came to you in the end?' said Bjarki.

'He did,' said Fidor. 'It was cold and we had not eaten for days and we made a fire to get warm and... the pack came to us.'

'We heard them calling to the moon, not very far away,' said Fodor. 'Then they stopped and, in a little while, we saw their eyes, out in the darkness, all around. Yellow eyes between the trees.

'There were eight of them and the pack leader – the *gandr* – a huge white and grey beast twice as large as the rest of them. Nine of them, in all. And the *gandr* spoke to us silently inside our heads: he asked us why we had come to his lands, and why we children of men came to disturb his people at their hunting. We told him that we sought to join his pack – and the Wolf growled and said we were weak. He said we were not worthy of that honour.'

'What did he sound like?' asked Bjarki, who was utterly entranced.

'He spoke inside our heads,' said Fidor, 'but he sounded...'

'He sounded like a blade scraping against stone,' said Fodor.

'Yes, like that, cold and cruel. Is that what your *gandr* is like, Rekkr?'

'No,' said Bjarki. 'Nothing like that. But, please, do go on...'

'They began to circle us,' said Fidor, 'slinking in and out of the shadows and firelight. And we stood back to back, with our knives out, and we began to hum, just as we had been taught to do in the Fyr Skola...'

'They came closer and closer – not the pack leader, he stayed away, watching us. They came in ones and twos, darting in, snapping at our legs.'

'That was when it happened,' said Fodor. 'We hummed and the *gandr* of the Wolf came into us. One *gandr* came into both our bodies at the same time. I cannot say how. He left the pack leader and came into us. And we were filled with his strength and ferocity. I cannot describe it – our blood became fire, our breath cool as meltwater, our bones turned to iron. The wolves sped at us, all at the same time, snapping and biting, and they seemed slow to us, slow as honey in winter, and we killed them, we cut them and slashed them open. We opened up their bellies and severed their throats.

'Even the pack leader, now weaker because the *gandr* was gone from him, came at us and he died in a few moments. They all died, all the wolves, except for two who ran whining into the darkness. When it was done the *gandr* told us to cut into the chest of the leader and rip out his heart...' Fodor paused.

'And we ate its dripping meat while it was still warm,' said his brother.

—

They built the facsimile of the dragon-ship in the Fyr Pit, complete with a carved wooden prow in the shape of a scaly snake-mouth and protruding tongue, and they filled the vessel with cut logs, pots of rendered pork fat, straw and kindling. And three days after hearing the tale of the twins in the Wolf Lodge, Valtyr assembled all the Groves to witness the fire-ordeal.

The Bear Lodge stood on the right side of the square, stone-lined pit; the Wolf Lodge stood on the left, and at the head of the Fyr Pit stood Valtyr and Katla and the rest of the *gothi*, some of them manning huge wooden barrels filled with river water ready to be freely poured over scorched flesh.

Further back and all around the pit stood all the warriors of the Yew and Ash Regiments in the Groves save those two score men who had drawn the short straws and been given sentry duties on the perimeter walls and in the four high watchtowers. Yet even they were constantly turning their heads to look into the centre of the plateau to catch a glimpse the Fyr Ceremony.

Bjarki stood at the rear of the square pit between the two Wolf Lodge candidates, both of whom were naked. Bjarki could clearly see the marks of half-healed wolf bites on their pale, emaciated legs. This was the final test, and if they managed to pass through the burning ship and live, they would be welcomed into the community as Fire Born – as fully fledged Rekkr.

There had been no dissenting voices at all in the Wolf Lodge after hearing the story of their harsh Voyaging – not a person there had any doubts that they had indeed met their Wolf *gandr* in the First Forest and been jointly inhabited by that great spirit.

The twins were both shivering now in their nakedness – it was freezing cold, a grey snow cloud lowered above the plateau, making the Groves feel enveloped, enclosed and private, and Bjarki felt a pang of sympathy for the boys. He himself was dressed in his full *berserkr* glory, in his long, heavy bear pelt – which had been fetched specially from Sigiburg by a rider for the occasion – and he wore a helmet fashioned by Eric the Barda of a huge bleached bear's skull and jawbone, and his torso and thighs were covered by shining scale mail that had once belonged to a fallen defender of the Frankish fortress. Around his waist hung a scabbard containing a yard-long Frankish pattern-welded sword, sharp, strong and flexible – another trophy of battle garnered from the dead at Sigiburg.

Lodge servants were now lighting the straw and kindling with torches. Bjarki put a hand on a shoulder of each of the twins, partly to restrain them from going into the ship too soon, before it was properly alight, and partly to reassure them, should they be fearful.

'You do not have to do this!' he said quietly, and not for the first time. 'There is no shame in refusing to undertake the ordeal.'

Fidor turned his head and looked up at him, an expression of scorn in his pale eyes. But he said nothing. Bjarki saw that fat snowflakes were now gently falling on them all. They hissed in the flames crackling aboard the dragon-ship. The twins' teeth, he saw, were now chattering uncontrollably.

At the far end of the Fyr Pit, Valtyr, who had been mumbling a long prayer that Bjarki had not been able to hear, straightened his spine and spoke out loudly: 'Let both candidates now prepare their bodies for the ordeal of Fyr. On my command, both Fidor Ulfricksson and Fodor Ulfricksson will enter the flames together and willingly offer their lives to the Wolf spirit. If they are worthy, the *gandr* will protect their frail flesh from the pain and hurt of the fire. If not, they will die a hero's death. Are you ready?'

The twins each gave a jerky little nod. Bjarki lifted his big hands from their shoulders.

'Go when you will – and may the Wolf guard you,' he said.

The twins shared one quick, silent glance with each other, and both plunged into the inferno of the pit at exactly the same time.

Bjarki watched as the two boys charged into the orange wall of fire, the flames licking up against their white bodies, the black smoke roiling away above them into the close, grey dome of the sky. He well remembered his own encounter with these very flames, and winced, his flesh recoiling at the memory of the awful pain.

The twins reached the halfway point of the ship in a matter of moments, the hair on their heads burning like two torches, and then something very strange seemed to happen. They suddenly fell on to their hands and knees and, before Bjarki's eyes, the two young men seemed to be utterly transformed. Their white bodies became covered with a thick grey coating, almost like the thick pelt of a wolf, and they bounded forward from plank to plank, dodging the most fiercely burning patches, leaping through the blazing ship with a wholly animal grace and speed. The transformation – if it had indeed happened at all – lasted only for a moment, one or two heartbeats at most, and they were leaping out of the other side of the ship, hurling themselves from the flames to land on the soft turf at the feet of Valtyr Far-Traveller, while the men at the water barrels on either side hurled bucket after bucket of freezing water over their smouldering carcasses.

The grey fur was immediately washed away by the torrents of water and their white and red scorched bodies were revealed underneath. Bjarki rubbed his eyes. Whatever had taken place in the flames – whether these two strange young men had indeed transformed into wolves – one thing was in no doubt at all. They were Rekkr. These two odd young men were *ulfhethnar*.

Chapter Fourteen

'We come not in conquest but to collect our due'

Tor had never felt so cold. Even in the deep winters of her childhood in northern Svealand she had never felt this level of numbing icy misery. Wrapped in a heavy woollen cloak and a blanket over the top of that, she still felt the fingers of cruel winter creep all over her blue and white mottled body. The flanks of her horse were crusted with snow as well as frozen sweat from a hard gallop, and feathery flakes still fell from the leaden skies.

I should have stayed in Sigiburg, thought Tor for the twentieth time, as she kicked the horse's ribs to get him to increase his pace. Two hours more and they would be at the Groves, where hot food and shelter surely awaited her.

She had left Verden as soon as she was strong enough to ride; perhaps a week after her midnight discussion with the Saxon jarls and Widukind. She had not slunk away like some dirty thief, but boldly informed the duke at his court that she would be returning to her brother's side in the Hessian March, and asking if he had any messages, news or orders that she might deliver personally to the Jarl of the Three Rivers and Warden of the First Forest.

Widukind had accepted her unexpected departure with a bland smile, and Geva even had the gall to come round to her longhouse with a woollen shawl she had knitted and a basket of food to sustain her on the journey.

Tor only just managed to stop herself punching the bitch's teeth into the back of her ever-grinning mouth. One thing was crystal clear to her: Geva knew about her night with Widukind. The duke must have confessed to his wife and begged her forgiveness, and they had then closed ranks against Tor.

She knew that some men had more than one wife – Jarl Brun had two, for example, who lived in peaceful amity, and some warriors had concubines, too, alongside the mothers of their children – but Tor was not the sort of woman who could ever share a lover with another.

Widukind had obviously made his choice – the bastard.

So she left Verden before she did something that she would regret, leaving Inge and Garm under the care of Ulli and the *hird*-woman Gerta.

The snow had started to fall when they were just leaving the fortress of Sigiburg the day before, and a more sensible rider would have turned back and spent a few days snug and warm in the erstwhile Frankish fortress. But Tor had a powerful urge to see her brother – something to do with being wounded deeply by love, and seeking out a kindly face, a friend, a man she could completely trust. So she pushed on through the worsening weather.

She had had one bad night beside the frozen Ruhr, when she was forced to bury herself, shivering, in a snowdrift, covered in all her blankets and clothes. But now she was nearly at the foot of the Eresburg and more than ready for a roaring fire, some hot food and hearty companionship.

–

Tor was deeply impressed with what her brother had achieved over the past three months. When she had last seen the Groves, it had been a site of dismal devastation, overshadowed by the blackened living skeleton of the Irminsul. Now the place was a bustling military camp, with a formidable perimeter wall, a dozen new buildings and hundreds of people crammed into the new barracks. It had taken her a while to locate Bjarki – who had been teaching a class in grappling techniques to a group of Ash spearmen inside one of them.

Tor sidled in and stood at the back, watching silently as her brother demonstrated – rather well, she thought – a simple across-the-hip wrestling throw that she remembered teaching him herself.

'You may find yourselves disarmed in battle,' said Bjarki, a few moments later, addressing a dozen sweaty, red-faced young men who were all stripped to the waist. 'Pray to Odin that it should not happen to you – but it does *not* necessarily mean the end of your effectiveness as a warrior.'

Tor saw the young men were hanging on his words. The way they looked at him went beyond respectful. It bordered on hero-worship.

'If you find yourself without a sword, spear or seax,' Bjarki said, 'and facing a foe with a shield, you might like to try this. Come up here, Red Karl, face me and hold up your shield like this, as if two opposing *skjaldborgir* had just clashed together on the battlefield. No, hold it a little higher. There.'

Then Bjarki seized the shield rim with both hands and twisted it like a wheel. Red Karl let out a yell of pain. Bjarki immediately released him. 'You can break a man's arm with this move,' he said. 'So have a care when you practise. And once his arm is broken you can even use the foe's own shield as a weapon against him. Karl, get back up here again – come on!'

Bjarki seized the nervous young man's shield with both his big hands again and jabbed the upper side of the protector at his 'enemy's' face. The surrounding metal rim stopped a whisker from Karl's nose. 'Now he has a broken arm *and* a broken nose,' said Bjarki, 'and if you want to take his sword from him – or his life – he'll most likely be unable to prevent you.'

A while later, not long after sundown, Tor and Bjarki sat by the wonderfully crackling hearth in Bear Lodge, sipping bowls of hot leek soup.

'It's not as pretty as the old place,' said Tor, looking at the unadorned walls. 'You need a few pictures of bears or a nice carving or two. Or maybe some antique weapons hung up on the wall. It looks... well, a bit drab.'

'We'll get round to it,' muttered Bjarki. He was very fond of his sister, but he sometimes wondered if she had *ever* paid him a compliment. He had worked almost without ceasing, day and night, to get the Groves into a state of war-readiness, and she seemed to have barely noticed. He refilled her mug of ale and put down his empty soup bowl. 'What news from Verden?'

'Not much to report. Widukind is busy as a honeybee consolidating in the Stolen Lands – I suppose we shouldn't call them that any more, now we have them back again. The Recovered Lands. No, that doesn't sound right. Lands between the Hunte and the Ems... anyway, you know where I mean. He's planning a new campaign for next spring. Or perhaps in the summer.'

Bjarki looked hard at his sister. There was something different about her. She seemed somehow softer, a lot less focused, almost indifferent to the progress of the war she had been so ardent about only a few months ago.

'Are you all right?' he asked.

'I'm fine,' she said.

'You haven't fallen out with Widukind, have you?'

'No,' snapped Tor. 'Why would you think that?'

'Are your wounds healing – they're not paining you too much?'

'I. Am. *Fine!*'

'All right – I believe you. Tell me all about Widukind's campaign in the spring. Or perhaps in the summer.'

'He says he will join you in a month or two, and together you two will attack the Franks over the border in Hessia. He says you are to get ready, get your men ready to march next year. He'll tell you more when he gets here.'

'In a month or two – is that what he said?'

'Something like that. I think that's what he said.'

Bjarki looked at her again.

'You must be tired,' he said. 'I've had them prepare a bed in the back of the Lodge. If you need to sleep, don't mind me.'

Tor ignored his words. 'Do you ever think about Hildar?'

'Sometimes – I think about what he did when he didn't know what to do,' said Bjarki. 'He used to go north, to the Sami, to my mother's people. He went north to the soothing ice and snows, as he called them. I sometimes try to find some wisdom in his words. But I'm not sure there is any.'

'I think about what he did to my mother, the beatings, all the fear and tears. I can *never* forgive him for that.'

'He is dead now – and we took revenge for your mother,' said Bjarki.

'It doesn't help. But just as you fear you'll become like *him*, I fear I'll become like *her*. Weak, fearful. In thrall to some bad man.'

Bjarki turned on her very fast. 'Did someone hurt you?'

Tor shook her head. She bit her lip hard. There was something in Bjarki's face now that was terrifying – she knew he was only a hair away from a cataclysmic rage.

'*Tell* me. Did Widukind hurt you? Or another man?'

'No, not like that. No one has laid a hand on me.'

Bjarki subsided. 'If someone *were* to harm you, you tell me and…'

'I can look after myself, oaf,' Tor said. 'You know that. But thank you…' Then she reached over and pulled his big head down towards hers.

She kissed him very lightly on his bearded cheek.

–

They celebrated the winter solstice and festival of Jul by hauling two huge trimmed tree trunks up from the First Forest and setting one in the central hearth of the Bear Lodge and the other in the Wolf Lodge. The logs were blessed by both Valtyr and Katla, who sprinkled them with the blood of two cockerels, and then set them alight to burn for the twelve days of celebration.

There were feasts and songs and poetry competitions, and nights of ribald drinking and telling riddles, and indoor wrestling matches, on which wagers were placed, the winners praised and the losers jeered. Bjarki held himself aloof from those contests and nobody urged him to compete, wisely.

One small fellow, a Wolf Lodge Barda, who was humiliated in a poorly matched wrestling event, lost his temper and seized a knife and killed his ox of an opponent. The friends of the murdered man fell on the furious little wrestler and slew him with their bare hands – and after that, Bjarki called a halt to any more wrestling bouts. They ran foot races in the snow, instead, and threw javelins at targets, and played traditional word-games in the hall.

On the sixth day of the celebrations, they enacted the age-old Jul ceremony in the Bear Lodge, with all the senior men and women invited. The guests of honour were Eckhart, captain of the Yews, who travelled in from Sigiburg with Kveldulf, who was now the commander of that fortress.

A dozen members of the Yew Regiment made themselves outlandish animal masks to disguise their faces and long capes of twigs and leaves, and capered in front of the guests, beating shields with wooden staffs and chanting 'Jul, Jul, Jul,' as their war cry, as they mimicked a great spiritual battle between various kinds of *gandir*.

It was a good time – a happy time. No work was done and Tor relished being in such a gathering, and in Bjarki's company.

She found it fascinating to observe the twins, Fidor and Fodor, newly acclaimed as Wolf Lodge Rekkar, and who were made a great fuss of by all during this period of jollity. She felt a little jealous, if she was quite honest with herself, for she had once hoped desperately to become a Wolf Rekkr like them. But she felt something else beside that envy when she watched them; another emotion less easy to identify. They made her deeply uneasy.

The way they acted in front of their Wolf Lodge comrades, and held themselves aloof from the rest of the warriors, was somehow jarring – they strutted and preened before their friends as if they were already heroes, already the victors of a dozen battles. Perhaps it was jealousy, she mused. The Fire Born had always been accorded high status here – the creation of Rekkr was the purpose of the Fyr Skola – yet these two seemed too arrogant.

A week after the Jul celebrations, when the pale sun had come out in a chilly but perfectly empty blue sky, Bjarki gathered his captains for a council of war in one of the bigger barracks, a last gathering before the captains Kveldulf and Eckhart departed to Sigiburg Fortress to return to their duties there. About thirty men and women were gathered, including Tor, several other members of Bjarki's *hird*, Valtyr and Katla, Gunnar and the twins Fidor and Fodor, and half a dozen of their Wolf Lodge followers. The leaders of the various Ash and Yew *lith* were also present.

Bjarki, standing on a stool, addressed them all.

'Winter has now turned the corner,' he said. 'The days are growing longer. It is time to prepare for the coming of spring and make ready for the beginning of a new campaigning season.'

He has grown into a true leader in the past few months, Tor thought. The Bjarki she had first met almost three years ago would never have had the easy confidence of this man in scale mail and bearskin, commanding the attention of thirty oak-hard seasoned warriors.

'Widukind has sent word that he and his men will be here within two months. And he commands that we be ready to march by then, if not before. So our watchwords during these next few weeks must be training, training and yet more training.'

There was a murmur of approval.

'I should like each captain to devise a particular routine for his people – a training schedule to be adhered to every day...'

'Can we go into the First Forest?' asked one captain of a *lith* of Yews. 'I should like to practise stealthy movement in woods.'

'Yes,' said Bjarki. 'But only in daylight – I don't want anyone getting lost, or going off Voyaging by mistake...'

There was general laughter.

'Can we raid a little in the south, over the border into Hessia?' said another captain. 'My warriors are eager to wet their blades.'

'No, I do not want to forewarn our enemies of the campaign. Nor risk any unnecessary losses before Widukind arrives here.'

The captain looked crestfallen but slowly nodded agreement.

'I propose that we maintain our current dispositions on the Hessian March until Widukind arrives,' said Bjarki, 'and then, when we know what is in his mind for this season, we can respond accordingly. So... Kveldulf will continue to hold Sigiburg with his two hundred men, Eckhart will continue to patrol the Hellweg with his Yew companies, and will both deny the road to the enemy and give us warning of any Frankish movements – but Captain Eckhart, you are to rotate your men regularly, with frequent rest periods in Sigiburg. I don't want to lose even a single warrior to frostbite, hunger or fatigue. Captain Kveldulf, are you well provisioned at Sigiburg, enough for your folk and Eckhart's?'

'My storerooms are all filled to bursting, Jarl Bjarki,' said the young commander, grinning. 'We stripped the Ruhr Valley clean as a bone before the first snows. There are no Frankish settlers within thirty miles of my folk. They all went south into Hessia – or back across the Rhenus into Francia. And left us all the richer in grain.'

'Excellent,' said Bjarki. 'And the Hellweg – I take it there has been no fresh troop movement. Is that correct, Captain Eckhart?'

'Quiet as a forgotten grave,' said the Eastphalian. 'It's snow-blocked along much of its length. No traffic for weeks – not even all the usual local traders, pedlars, cattle drovers and the like.'

'Good, well, if there is nothing more, I suggest you—'

Fidor put up his hand, and Bjarki stopped mid-sentence.

The twins were looking particularly fine this day, Tor noticed, in new wolfskin cloaks, with warm hoods made of the heads of the animals, oiled leather chest plates, leather vambraces and greaves. Both had new tattoos, long wolf-face-shaped triangles inked between their black brows, and expensive swords at their sides.

'Yes, Fidor? What do you wish to say?' said Bjarki.

Tor saw Fidor swallow, as if summoning up difficult words.

'We're in the Groves of Eresburg,' he began, speaking a little too loud for the gathering. 'Standing in the shade of the Irminsul. We are, in fact, at the centre of the Fyr Skola. The spiritual home of the North.'

'I am not unaware of that,' said Bjarki, to a ripple of laughter.

Fidor flushed.

'You're a Rekkr, Bjarki Bloodhand. Fire Born, beloved of the Bear. I would never deny your right to speak or to lead in battle.'

'Thank you,' said Bjarki. 'That all you wished to say, Fidor?'

'But my brother and I are also Fire Born – we too are Rekkar, you have acknowledged us yourself. Yet we have not been asked to speak. We have been ignored, while lesser men dribble out their thoughts like weak piss. So we now ask – we demand – the right to speak in the Fyr Skola and the Groves, in the same way that you do.'

There was grumbling. Someone said: 'Who you calling lesser men?' Someone else said: 'Our words are piss now?'

Bjarki looked at Fidor, long and hard. Tor could see him thinking.

'I am the Jarl of the Three Rivers and the Warden of the First Forest. I have been placed in command of all the southern Saxon forces by Widukind. I do not believe that you have been given any command by any lord at all.'

'In the Fyr Skola, we are no lesser men than you, Rekkr,' said Fodor, 'and far greater than most others.'

Tor could see Bjarki struggling with his thoughts once more.

'You're right,' her brother said at last. 'I've been discourteous. Speak your minds to the council, I beg you. Your status as Fire Born requires it.'

Bjarki waited, standing still on his stool, towering over everyone. Fidor swallowed again. He looked over at his brother.

'All I will say, at this time, is that my brother and I fully agree with all Jarl Bjarki's wise suggestions. We should maintain our dispositions as they are until Widukind arrives. Then we shall see what our lord has in his mind.'

'Well, that *is* a relief,' said one sarcastic voice in the crush of warriors. 'The wolf pup gives us his permission to carry on as before.'

Fodor whirled round: 'Who said that? Who dares insult us?'

No one owned up. The silence stretched into awkwardness.

'I will say one more thing,' said Fidor. 'My brother and I will be recruiting a special *lith* of wolf warriors, not only our Wolf Lodge Barda, but any other brave fighters who choose to join us will be most welcome. When we go to war in the spring, our wolf *lith* will win the greatest honour of all!'

–

The only light in the freezing cavern came from a single beeswax candle. By its flickering flame, Bjarki examined his surroundings. Before him was a roughly circular pool, a dozen yards wide, the surface covered with a sheet of thin grey ice which reflected the candle's light. On the far side of the pool, sitting cross-legged on the stony ground and wrapped in a voluminous sheepskin robe was Valtyr Far-Traveller, his breath streaming from his mouth like dragon-smoke. He held an iron staff in both his hands, a yard-long piece with an intricate head of spiralling metal strands forming an egg-shaped cage below an iron knob. The Mikelgothi's staff of office.

Beyond the sphere of candlelight, all was darkness except for a dim half-disc off to the right that indicated the entrance of this cavity in the side of the huge Eresburg rock formation, a hole in the holy mountain, and a glimpse of the grey winter afternoon outside.

However, the candle's flame did clearly illuminate the ceiling of the cave, two yards above Bjarki's head, a thick spider's web of sinuous black roots that twisted throughout the soft, yellowish rock of the ancient cave and covered the domed roof, as if caging it in its woody embrace.

'Those roots up there,' said Bjarki, 'are they the roots of...'

'The Irminsul,' finished Valtyr. 'Yes, son, those are the roots of the One Tree above our heads, protecting us – and this sacred cave, the old legends say, is one of the many entrances to the realm of Queen Hel.'

Bjarki shivered. Not just from the cold. He was naked, his scarred and battered skin grey-white and pimpled like a plucked goose. Hel, the daughter of the trickster god Loki, presided over a freezing afterworld at the base of the One Tree, or so he had been told, where she was served by the spirits of the dead, those unfortunates who were not admitted to the Hall of the Slain.

He clutched the long handle of the bearded axe in his right hand more tightly. It was certainly chill and eldritch enough in this space to be the actual entrance to Hel's realm, he thought. But he wasn't dead. Not yet.

'This is where you came with Skymir all those years ago?'

'This is where she expelled her *gandr*, the White Sow.'

Bjarki recalled the night, two months ago, when Valtyr had told him the extraordinary story of Skymir and how she had divined the techniques for controlling her *gandr*, by meditating on the lore and practice of the Groves and consulting the wisest and most learned of the *gothi*. It was all bound up with the eternal duality of the world, Valtyr had said. Opposites, pairs of opposites. 'Yet I cannot claim to fully understand it, even now,' he had said.

'The masters of the Spirit World are the Sami,' Valtyr had continued, 'and Skymir journeyed to the north to consult them about her *gandr*. She refused to tell me what wisdom they imparted, but I did witness her struggle on this very spot, here in Hel's cave, below the Groves of Eresburg.'

It had taken a great deal of persuasion to get Valtyr to attempt this ritual – he had asked Bjarki again and again if he truly wanted to give up his *gandr*, and all the power the Bear conferred on him. Ultimately, Bjarki had convinced the old man he was committed to this path, and so here they were, Bjarki and Valtyr, in a freezing hole at the roots of the Irminsul, while all the Groves folk snoozed by their hearths a hundred feet above their heads.

'So what do I do?' said Bjarki. 'And may we make it quick – I am turning into a lump of solid ice.'

'From what Skymir *did* say to me, I learnt this: *gandir* are repelled by their opposites. Rekkar are born in the fire, as we both know, and the opposite of fire is water, just as the opposite of heat is ice. Fire and Ice, there are the two opposing elements.'

'Fire and Ice – yes, I understand, so what do I do?'

'Have patience: the second pair of opposites is Hate and Love. You must hold in your mind, while you do the ritual, an image of the person you love most in the world. Your lover, perhaps. Hold fast to her in your head. Skymir admitted she thought of me when she underwent this same ordeal.' Valtyr smirked a little at the memory.

'Love and Hate – got it. What next?'

'First smash the ice in the pond. Keep your loved one in the centre of your mind at all times. Next, you summon your *gandr*. When the Beast is inside you, you jump in the water. This external coldness, combined with the warm love inside your heart, will force the *gandr* from you – and it may perhaps even kill her. You may, like Skymir, never hear from her again. For the very last time of asking, are you sure you wish to go through with this?'

'Yes, I'm sure, Valtyr.'

'Skymir killed the White Sow in this cave and renounced her Fire Born status. Soon afterwards she became a *gothi* – as I did – and, eventually, she became the Mikelgothi. Is this the path you now choose? Be certain.'

'I don't want to be a *gothi*. But if I don't kill my *gandr*, my *gandr* will one day kill me. I want an ordinary life. I want to *live* before I die.'

'So be it. Smash the ice. Summon the Bear.'

Bjarki swung the axe, again and again, the blade cracking against the solid surface of the pool. A few moments later, he sat down cross-legged on the cold rock once more, looking at the pale shards floating in the rippling black water. He began to hum. A four-note tune, ancient, familiar...

At the same time he tried to think of someone he truly loved, a lover, Valtyr had said – and the last person he had made love with was Yoni. But that had been a casual affair, a one-night encounter. Or had it? Did he love her, deep down inside? He thought of her sometimes, when he felt lonely. She was pretty; no, she was beautiful, kind and loving. He held her in the centre of his mind as he hummed. On and on. The ancient summoning tune. He tried to focus on Yoni and hum at the same time, droning deep in his throat. It was not easy. But he was also very aware of Valtyr praying loudly: 'Hear me, O beings of the Spirit World,' he said. 'Hear me, O *gandr*!'

He increased the volume of his humming, thinking of Yoni, reaching his senses out blindly into the void, stretching out invisibly to grasp at...

'Free this brave man, this fine warrior, from your invisible grip,' intoned Valtyr. 'Great Bear Spirit, O Mother Bear, you know Bjarki Bloodhand well, you have visited him often. Now it is time to loose him from your power. I command it. I, Valtyr Far-Traveller, Mikelgothi of the Groves of Eresburg, command it in this sacred place. The goddess Hel, whose holy shrine this is, she also commands it. The All-Father, Odin himself, commands it – loose your jealous grip now on this mortal man. Allow him to go free!'

Bjarki opened his eyes. He could see Valtyr on the other side of the pool, standing like a hero, the sheepskin cloak hanging loose around his widespread skinny legs, the magical iron staff brandished high in the air.

The candle flame flickered, although there was no breeze at all.

'Quick!' the old man said, 'Into the pool! Into the cold now!'

Bjarki lurched to his feet, took two steps forward and jumped.

The shock of the icy water was like a thunderclap to his whole body. He felt his heart squeezed in a giant's fist; he felt his vision shrink black, then return in full, glorious, exploding colours. He came to the surface and gasped out a desperate breath. He began to splash and struggle, skill forgotten, towards the edge of the black pool where Valtyr stood, still lofting the old iron staff.

'Stay in,' the old man said, pointing the Mikelgothi staff at Bjarki's bedraggled blond head. 'You must stay in the water till the Beast is gone.'

Bjarki goggled at him. His breath was coming in hard pants; his brain was too frozen with shock to form any words with his open mouth.

He kicked his legs in the water. Already he could not feel his toes.

'How...' he managed to stammer, 'how... long?'

'I recall that Skymir remained in this pool for about the time it might take to milk three morning cows.'

'No...' gasped Bjarki. 'I... can't. It's not poss—'

'Do you want the *gandr* gone or not?' There was an edge of cruelty to Valtyr's stern words. 'If not, please come out, Bjarki, don't waste my time. Come out, I'll wrap you in my cosy sheepskin. Think how snug you'll be!'

Bjarki made a noise, somewhere between a snarl and a moan. He gritted his teeth, set his jaw and remained in the icy pool, kicking with his legs, sweeping his spread hands to keep his head above the surface.

The moments passed, very slowly, marked only by Bjarki's loud, laboured breathing. He could feel nothing now below the waist. His chest felt tight, squeezed. *How long had he been in this pool?* In his long agony, he was aware that Valtyr was praying again: 'Hear me, O Spirits of the Void, hear me, O *gandr…*'

He found he was sinking; his whole body felt encased in solid iron. He kicked up to the surface again. Took in a great cold blast of air. But he could feel the darkness encroaching, growing with every heave of his breath. He summoned his strength. He dug deep to find a grim resolve inside. He breathed deeply, and then deeper still. Ice nails were driving into his spine. He could feel the strength flowing from him, like ale from a burst barrel.

'Hear me, O Queen of Death,' Valtyr was saying. 'Hear me, Hel Lokisdottir – accept this *blot* sacrifice to your eternal glory. Take the spirit of this brave man Bjarki down into your eternal icy embrace…'

Bjarki fought the cold, and the exhaustion, of course he did; he fought them with everything he had, but gradually he could feel the strokes of his leaden arms begin to slow. The water felt like thick syrup. His churning feet now felt they were moving through a sack of fleeces, tripping, tangled; the kicks slowed, slowed again, then stopped.

Somehow the water now seemed to be growing a little warmer.

He looked up at Valtyr, and could only see him through a small tunnel of white light, as if he were looking up at the old man through a tube of leather. That was funny. So very funny. He giggled. He sighed. The water was truly warm now, as if he were submerged in a hot bathtub on washing day. It was actually quite pleasant – or was it? Now it was maybe even a little too hot. He was about to make a jest to Valtyr about this discovery, some funny words, the old fellow had always liked a joke, but irritatingly his head was too heavy and it seemed to have slipped below the surface. He was falling, down and down, the lovely warm bath growing grey, then black as pitch.

Down he went. He could hear a voice calling his name. *Bjarki, Bjarki.* Was that Queen Hel herself, welcoming him to her Realm of the Dead?

'Bjarki, Bjarki – come back. Bjarki – will you wake up now?'

The young warrior realised someone was slapping his face. Hard. He opened his eyes. Raising his wet head slightly he saw he was covered with Valtyr's sheepskin cloak and his own bearskin was flung on top of that. Parts of his body felt as if they were burning. Flames on his fingers and toes.

'Did you feel her leave?' said Valtyr, peering deeply into his eyes.

Bjarki just groaned, and tried to sit up. He wiped his face with a corner of the bearskin. He felt dizzy, exhausted – and suddenly nauseated.

He leaned to one side and vomited a thick yellow stream.

'Do you think we did it?' said Valtyr. 'Bjarki, did we get her out?'

'I don't know,' he mumbled. 'Maybe.'

'But can you feel your *gandr*'s presence in you now?'

'No. I can't feel her.'

'That's good. I think we did it. I think *you* did it, Bjarki!'

On a pale blue day, six weeks later, Widukind of Westphalia, Duke of Saxony, arrived at the Groves of Eresburg. He did not come alone. Four hundred seasoned Westphalian and Angrian warriors, all fully armed and well provisioned, marched there with him.

Valtyr arranged a ceremony of welcome under the branches of the Irminsul. The ancient hymn was sung by all gathered there – many hundreds of folk. He and Katla intoned prayers to Odin, to Tiw and Thor and to the Irminsul, the Mother of Trees. And Abbio, who had arrived with his master looking even more dark, raggedy and eldritch than ever, sacrificed a pair of newborn lambs and sprinkled their blood over the roots of the One Tree.

Then they feasted in the open air – scores of men and women, captains and above only – and gorged on a whole roasted ox, and hare pies, mutton stew and cheese and ale and mead and fresh bread. In the centre of the table, under a waxed linen canopy in case of spring rain, Bjarki sat in the place next to Widukind, and they offered each other the choicest cuts of the meat and clashed their drinking horns together in many toasts to good fellowship.

Tor, who had found a humbler place further down the table, watched them. Widukind, the bastard, was looking rested, well fed – as handsome as ever – plainly married life with Geva the milch cow suited him.

When most of the eating and drinking was done, Widukind rose to his feet and lifted his mead horn to the entire table.

'My friends,' he said, 'you must eat and drink your fill this day, for I come to you girt for red war, with my sword at my side and vengeance in my heart. I come to take you into battle, to take the fight to the halls of our foe.'

He paused for a moment, then said: 'The day after tomorrow the Saxon army will drive south into Hessia, deep into the lands of our enemies. Their territory is rich – in crops and animals, in fruit and corn. Their churches are filled to bursting with gold and silver, and we shall capture many thralls, too, to work your lands. We shall take all we desire and bear it home to Saxony.'

The table erupted in cheers, but Tor saw Bjarki was frowning again.

'It has been many a long year since Hessia felt the righteous wrath of our people, but that season is upon us – as our vengeance is upon them. For years the Franks have raided our lands and settled them with their folk, built their churches and enslaved our folk. Now the tables are turned. We ride into Hessia to take back what is rightfully ours. And in the autumn, when the fighting is done and winds turn cold, we'll ride back into Saxony, to full larders and happy halls. We will come back to our own lands with tales to tell and glory to spare. But remember this: I seek not to steal the Frankish lands for myself – only to teach them to fear us, and grow rich in slaves and booty. We come not in conquest but to collect what is due for years of hurt.'

He hoisted his horn into the air. 'I give you a final toast this happy day, my friends. Let us drink to... other men's *lands* and...'

Before Widukind could finish, someone shouted, 'And *glory*!'

And every warrior at that table rose up roaring to their feet.

Chapter Fifteen

The reluctant Rekkr

'I can't explain, Tor, but this feels like foolishness,' said Bjarki. 'It doesn't seem planned or organised. Not like a proper war, or a serious campaign. It's just one long drunken raid to seize thralls and silver.'

'The other captains seem quite happy about it,' said his sister.

'Of course they're *happy*. They get to plunder undefended farmsteads, to sack villages, to burn peasant homes to their hearts' content and fill their wagons with booty. Of course they're *pleased*. What warrior wouldn't be?'

'You're a warrior – at least, you used to be.'

Bjarki gave her a sour look.

'I keep asking myself, what's the point of all this destruction?' he said, and waved a hand at a Frankish hall, with an adjacent barn and stables, all of which were crackling merrily, with smoke pouring out of the shutters. He pointed at the dozen wolf pack warriors, men who followed Fidor and Fodor, reeling about outside having discovered a wine store. There were bodies, some distressingly tiny, scattered around the blood-spattered yard.

'That *is* the point,' said Tor. 'To make Widukind's folk happy. To make them rich. And the richer he makes them, the happier he makes them – and the more they will all love him.'

'Is that what he's trying to achieve – to be loved by all?'

The instant he said it, Bjarki knew he was treading on very dangerous ground and so, when Tor did not respond, he let it drop with some relief.

They were sitting alone together on a small wooded knoll above the burning farmstead, sharing a skin of ale and some cheese. The stench of smoke was strong in their nostrils, and a taint of fresh blood and dung, too.

For the past month, Widukind's forces had ravaged Hessia, driving south-west down the Diemel Valley then due south into the Frankish lands beyond the Ruhr. They had overwhelmed dozens of farms and a handful of villages with their sheer numbers, burning and slaying as they pushed on southward. Widukind's four-hundred-strong army making the vanguard and main column of the attack, and Bjarki's force – about half that number after strong garrisons had been left both at Sigiburg and the Groves – coming in behind and sweeping up any resistance. They encountered many folk who had run from the marauders initially and hidden in the thick Hessian woods, but Bjarki also spent much time dealing with the long, lumbering trains of wagons piled high with loot, and the miserable columns of men, women and children who were yoked together and bound for the markets in the north.

'The other thing I don't understand,' said Bjarki, 'is why the Franks have not responded *at all* to our incursion. We are killing their people, hundreds of peaceful, prosperous folk, and Widukind insists on burning every church he can find, any building with a cross on it, in truth. It is a bold provocation – surely they cannot allow it to go unpunished. But we have seen almost nothing of them these past weeks. I've barely seen a dozen Red Cloaks. While I did see two Black Cloak *cabellarii* last week, they were fleeing as fast as their horses could carry them. Why aren't they retaliating?'

'I wouldn't complain, if I were you,' said Tor. 'Maybe they're scared. Or don't have enough troops to face us in battle. Could be many reasons.'

'We both know – as does Widukind – how powerful Francia is. What did they send against us at the Dane-Work, two dozen *scarae*? Three dozen? Something like eight thousand fighting men, if I rightly recall.'

'And we sent them packing with half that number.'

'Yet here we are, rampaging happily over a plum Frankish territory with barely five hundred warriors. Something's just not right, Tor.'

'When did you become such an old woman?' said Tor. 'I feel I hardly know you. We're winning the war, aren't we? We're ravaging their lands, freely, and they dare do nothing. It smells very much like victory to me.'

Bjarki kept silent. He wondered whether his sister was right. Had he truly cast out his *gandr* in Hel's freezing pool and become a weak and whining old woman? Was he just being nervous and worrying over nothing? No. He was sure. The lack of response from the Franks did not make sense.

He was summoned by the Saxon Wolf two days later, invited to join his lord in an as-yet-unburnt hall in a village called Leisa.

The duke was eating mutton stew at a long trestle table when Bjarki arrived. Widukind waved at the bench with his mouth full; he shoved the ale jug towards Bjarki and mumbled something through his food. He poured himself a cup and sipped, waiting for his lord to swallow his mouthful.

'You don't look happy, Bjarki. Why's that?' said Widukind.

Bjarki thought for a moment. 'It's all been too easy, lord,' he said after another pause. 'We've met almost no resistance from the Franks.'

Widukind nodded. 'There is good reason for that. But if you don't mind, my friend Abbio here will explain it to you. I want to eat my dinner.'

The weird crow-like man came shuffling out of the gloom at the far end of the long hall. He stared at Bjarki with evident distaste, sat down on the bench opposite and helped himself to ale.

'Jarl Bjarki says it has been too easy – tell him why, Abbio,' said Widukind, and then he applied himself to his steaming bowl again.

'Consssentraysshion,' said Abbio.

'What?' said Bjarki.

'He means they have gathered all their troops in one place,' said Widukind. 'There is a fortress five miles down the road, south-east of here, a strong one. Buraburg. On a hilltop. Tough place to get into. Called Buraburg – did I already say that?'

Bjarki saw then that Widukind was very tired; and possibly drunk, too.

'I've heard of the place,' said Bjarki.

'They have been concentrating there for several weeks. One sniff of a hairy Saxon arse and the Franks all run for cover in cosy Buraburg.'

'Can't say I blame them,' said Bjarki.

'It's full of loot, you know. Packed with it. All the good, portable stuff – gold, jewels, every single *denier* a hard-working Frankish husbandman can scrape up, he has carried down to Buraburg. It's all there behind those walls.'

Bjarki shrugged. 'We've taken plenty of booty – more than enough, I'd say.'

'I'll tell you when we've taken enough,' snarled Widukind, suddenly furious. 'We've taken enough when we possess every silver penny in Hessia.'

Bjarki said nothing.

Widukind spooned another mouthful of stew into his face.

'I'm going to take Buraburg,' he said, spitting out a few droplets of gravy. 'I'm going to tear down the walls and slaughter every man, woman and child inside. No quarter.'

'I must advise against it,' said Bjarki. 'We're not equipped for a siege – and we don't have enough folk to storm a powerful fortress.'

'You don't undersssstand,' said Abbio. 'Bishop Livinus hass named it his official *sseat*. His Episcopal sseat for the whole region. A few days ago, he proclaimed himself Archbissshop of all Sssaxony.'

'Bishop Livinus is in there?'

'Buraburg is his base,' said Widukind, pushing his bowl away. 'He claims jurisdiction over all Saxony from there. That's why I *must* take it.'

Bjarki nodded. He understood. It was a grave insult and therefore must be answered. 'How many troops does Livinus have in Buraburg?'

'At least three *scarae*, a thousand Red Cloaks, plus whatever refugees have managed to get in there to safety over the past month. Say another five hundred, farmers not fighters, but still. Men of their hands. Not weaklings.'

Bjarki stared into his ale. 'It cannot be taken, lord,' he said.

'It can,' said Widukind. 'And I will do it. With or without you.'

—

Later Bjarki and Tor attended a formal council of war in the same hall in Leisa. A dozen captains attended, some dirty, many tired and some burdened with minor wounds. Ale was served in abundance but no food.

'I must tell you again, my lord, I am against this attack,' said Bjarki. 'We can ride away from Buraburg. Livinus hopes we will attack him in this strong, ready-prepared position. It is quite obviously no more than a trap.'

There was a curious silence after Bjarki's words.

One of Widukind's Westphalian captains, a fellow called Bildur, spoke up: 'By claiming his foul Church has spiritual power over all Saxony, this Christ-worshipper has insulted our duke. That insult must be expunged with blood. I say we storm the fortress and hang the bishop from his own walls.'

'It's only an insult if we choose to take it as one,' said Bjarki. 'It's a stupid claim – Saxony is not a Christian land, and it never will be – this absurd proclamation by Livinus should be treated with derision.'

'It must be answered by the slaughter of all Christians inside!' said Bildur. There were a few half-hearted cheers around the table.

'I'm told there's a great deal of Frankish coin inside Buraburg,' said another captain, an older one, whose name Bjarki didn't know. 'A very large quantity of silver *deniers* – is this true?'

'I do not believe we *can* capture Buraburg,' Bjarki said. 'We would destroy ourselves against its walls. We don't have the strength. We have only four hundred fit and able warriors. I say we take our wagons of booty – each of you has already done very well from this campaign – and go home.'

'There are three or four hundred fighters lying idle in Sigiburg and the Groves,' said Widukind, looking at Bjarki. 'If, as you say, we need more troops to storm this Christian fortress, we know exactly where to find them.'

'We cannot strip Sigiburg and the Groves of their garrisons,' Bjarki said. 'What if Karolus should send his Red Cloaks down the Hellweg. Our whole strategy is based on...'

'Karoluss iss ssstill in Italy,' said Abbio. 'Hisss wife ruless Francia – if you can call what she doesss ruling. Duke Gerold of Swabia iss sssick in his southern mountain realm. Bissshop Livinusss is before us *now* – he iss our most dangerous foe... I ssay we wipe him off the tafl board. Now.'

Suddenly many voices were all speaking at once.

'My boys can take it. There isn't a rampart they cannot scale...'

'Could you please confirm, duke, that there are indeed substantial quantities of silver coin inside Buraburg itself...'

Bjarki felt a small hand on his elbow. 'Listen to them all. You've lost *this* battle, oaf,' said his sister. 'He's decided to attack. Best just let it go.'

He heard someone mutter: 'For a famous Rekkr, our new jarl seems somewhat reluctant to fight!' But he couldn't tell who had spoken.

Bjarki made one last attempt to change Widukind's mind. He lingered till all the captains had gone and approached. He bowed very low.

'My lord, may I make a proposal before the matter is decided.'

'The matter *is* decided, Jarl Bjarki,' said Widukind crossly. 'You heard them all – we *shall* take Buraburg, once we have fetched more troops from Sigiburg and the Groves. I don't have the patience for any more quibbling.'

'My proposal is this, my lord. That I take a small embassy to Aachen, just myself and Tor, travelling fast and light, and we offer a peace treaty, a fair and honest one, to the lady Hildegard, to agree in her husband the king's absence. I know her. It makes the most sense – you know it does, lord. At this moment, we hold all of northern Hessia, all except Buraburg, and we are now a powerful threat inside their territory. But if we offer to return Hessia to the queen and withdraw our forces north of the Ruhr, everything would go back to the way it was before this campaign except that we retain the booty and the spoils. Everyone wins, we hold on to south Saxony...'

'You don't understand, Bjarki. Livinus is there, in Buraburg, with an army on my doorstep, thumbing his nose at me, insulting all of us. You think he will leave us in peace, *just because that silly Swabian slut in Aachen tells him to*? Are you mad? I've a chance to destroy my worst enemy – the jarl of all the Christian Franks – a man who *dares* to call himself Archbishop of my Saxony. I have him in my palm – and you would advise me to let him go?'

Bjarki dropped his eyes. 'I am thinking only, my lord, of the future of our people,' he said. 'I'm thinking of a Saxony not racked by war with these same Christians. This is the only way I can foresee a victory – of any kind. We cannot defeat the might of the Frankish legions, even if we beat them in battle after battle. The only way for us to live together is by making peace. And *now* we have the advantage, *now* we can negotiate from strength...'

'I expected a lot more from you, Bjarki,' said Widukind wearily. 'I really did. I did not expect all this sheepish bleating from a man like *you*!'

The Saxon duke took a deep breath.

'I shall not expect you to fight at Buraburg, Jarl Bjarki Blood-hand – but neither shall you share in the glory when we have crushed the Franks and Bishop Livinus is a corpse dangling from his fortress's walls. That is all I can take from you for tonight. I'm tired. Now go, remove yourself from my sight.'

—

Bjarki went to collect the troops needed from Sigiburg and the Groves himself. He knew he was doing it partly to get away from Widukind, and partly to appease him. But he took his own time about the errand, spending two weeks selecting and gathering the warriors and leading them south into Saxony, hoping that something would change during the time he was away.

As he led a column of three hundred warriors of the Ash and the Yew Regiments south, he could not shake the feeling that he was leading these people, who trusted and relied on him, to certain death. Yet he also had a suspicion that Widukind thought he was a coward – which was intolerable.

He shared his fears with Gunnar, who was commanding the hundred-strong Fyr Skola contingent, and who rode his chestnut mare beside him.

'If he thinks you're a coward, then *he* is a fool,' said Gunnar stoutly. 'And you do not *know* that Widukind will fail to capture Buraburg. He might win. He might take the place. He is a wily campaigner, or so those who have fought with him before have told me. He will surely not just throw away the lives of his own people for no good reason.'

Yet when he arrived with his reinforcements at the sprawling Saxon camp that lay before Buraburg, all his worst anxieties came tumbling back.

On the morning of the attack, he and Tor and the sixty or so members of his *hird* took their positions in the treeline a few hundred paces north of the River Eder. In front of them ran a short grassy slope, which went down to the brown river and up the other side to a small hill that was crowned by the fortress of Buraburg. There was a stone bridge across the Eder, wide enough for four men to cross abreast, which the enemy had abandoned to the Saxons. It seemed they put all their trust in the strong walls of Buraburg.

Bjarki had been brusquely ordered by Widukind to form a battle reserve, which could be called upon at need. The twins Fidor and Fodor and their wolf pack of thirty warriors – all Groves of Eresburg men who had made an oath to serve the two Rekkar – stood a dozen paces to the left of Bjarki and Tor and the *hird*. All the ninety-odd folk of the reserve watched the Saxons down in the valley below them as they prepared for the attack.

Widukind was on his beautiful snow-white stallion on the north bank of the Eder, with the narrow river between them and Buraburg. He was addressing his folk, who were gathered in a loose group around him. There seemed to be fewer Saxons there than Bjarki had imagined, only some four or five hundred warriors.

'Where are the rest of them?' he asked Tor.

'I don't know – ravaging the countryside, I should imagine.'

It was too far to hear what Widukind was saying to his troops, although Bjarki could imagine the words of glory, of striking a blow for freedom, and all the usual fare. Widukind was dressed magnificently this day in a long coat of scale mail that had been polished till it shone like a rippling mirror.

He wore an ankle-length cloak the colour of blood and had a fine sword at his side, the hilt gleaming with gold and silverwork and displaying a large square red jewel at the pommel. He had a round wooden shield painted black, white and red with a design of a wolf staring out from the centre.

'Look at his helmet,' said Tor. 'He can't seriously be going into battle in that ridiculous thing. It would catch on every blade swung at it!'

Widukind's helmet was a most extraordinary confection of polished brass, which shone like gold, with a brass eagle's head rising from the centre and two real golden eagle's wings attached on each side and sticking out a foot from the dome. Bjarki found it very hard to tear his eyes away from it.

Now Widukind had drawn his magnificent sword and was gesticulating with the shining blade, as he made his white stallion rear up and prance on its back legs. Bjarki looked beyond the river and up the slope a few hundred yards to the walls of the fortress. They were thick with Frankish heads, some helmeted in steel, some bare, some covered in caps or hoods.

It seemed that every Christian in Buraburg had lined up on the walls this morning to catch a glimpse of the godless foe that menaced them. Then Bjarki, in a rare flash of insight, realised what Widukind was hoping to achieve.

It was a distraction. It was all a ruse.

Whatever speech Widukind had been making it was over and, with a wild flourish of his flashy sword, the Saxon Wolf was clearly ordering his troops across the narrow river. Scores of troops were piling on to the bridge and surging across to the other side. Some jostling Saxons seemed *so* eager for battle they knocked each other over the edge of the bridge wall and splashed into the brown water, and had to be rescued before they drowned. The attack was noisy, undignified, chaotic – a marvellous spectacle to behold.

About half of the troops were now on the southern bank, forming up into their *lith*, thirty or forty men in a gaggle, trying to regain some sort of order after the undisciplined swarming across the bridge. Here was Widukind, still in his winged helmet, making his horse caracole again, the well-trained creature seeming to actually dance on its hind legs.

The Saxon Wolf was exhorting his people to climb the grassy slope, to charge and attack the tightly closed gates of Buraburg – and some of the *lith* were now indeed beginning to drift up the slope. Bjarki lifted his eyes and saw, with amazement, that those closed gates of Buraburg were creaking open. He was astonished. This was not at all what he had expected. When the gates were flung wide, out of their black maw poured a stream of Frankish horsemen.

They were big, armoured men on huge mounts – the elite troops known as *Scholares* – heavy horsemen who formed Karolus's personal bodyguard.

A hundred riders spewed out of the gates in a thundering column. They carried two swords, Bjarki knew, a long blade and a short, and wielded nine-foot, needle-tipped lances from behind spiked shields with terrible efficiency.

They cascaded down the slope, black cloaks flying out behind them, speeding towards the half-assembled, still-chaotic Saxons on the south bank. Some of Widukind's troops were about halfway up the slope; but most were only half formed. And a good two hundred folk were milling around on the *north* bank of the Eder – on the *other* side of the river.

Bjarki shoved his right fist hard in his mouth and began to chew. This was about to be a bloody catastrophe. The *cabellarii*, as these elite heavy horsemen were sometimes termed, crashed into the loose Saxons massed on the slopes, slicing through them like a swung axe through a mouldy turnip. Warriors were hurled here and there, many skewered right through by the long lances, even pinned to the green turf. Others were just ridden down.

The horsemen shattered the Saxon *lith*, slashing left and right with their blades as they passed among them, flaying the flesh from Saxon faces, cracking bones, shattering shields, driving warriors before them like sheep.

There were already a dozen Saxons lying still on the slope, the blood puddling around them. Others were running for the river and jumping in.

The remaining north bank Saxons were hurrying across the bridge to join in the fight, but their timing was disastrous. Widukind's force was divided – half on one side of the river, half on the other. They'd been caught in the middle of a manoeuvre by a wily enemy who'd done the unexpected.

The *cabellarii* were relentlessly cutting down the few hundred disorganised Saxons on the south bank. The carnage was appalling to watch.

Yet it was not all one way. Widukind had gathered a dozen thanes around him now in a defensive circle, spears out, and they were doing great destruction to any horseman who came near, slicing with their leaf-shaped blades. Widukind, up on his fine white horse, a rallying point visible to all, was bellowing for men to form up in their companies, form up now. Archers were picking off Black Cloaks, one by one; others were scurrying into the safety of the hastily formed rings of spears and continuing to loose shafts.

Bjarki saw an individual Frankish horseman try to force his terrified mount into Widukind's spear circle, his sword hacking down at the footmen, but the animal baulked, a spear penetrated its underbelly and the *cabellarius* himself was seized by a dozen Saxon hands and ripped from the saddle.

He was bloody meat in a matter of moments.

'Should we not go across and help them?' Tor asked.

Bjarki did not reply for a moment. 'We wait,' he grated. 'We wait till we are called. Look, up there on the right, by the trees.'

Inexplicably, there were now Saxons pouring from a patch of woodland near the summit of the hill, only a few hundred yards to the left of the black bulk of the fortress. Bjarki thought he recognised young Captain Kveldulf in the lead, and many spearmen of his own Ash Regiment following swiftly behind him. The Saxons on the hill were racing for the still-open gates of Buraburg.

This was Widukind's ruse. While the Saxon leader made a conspicuous demonstration in front of the fortress, a small band of his folk – who must have been spirited across the river during the night – would attack the town from the side, or the rear. With luck, they might have got over the walls with little resistance and been able to open the gate, to allow Widukind's force in.

It was a sound plan, Bjarki acknowledged with half his mind, but the enemy's surprising move in opening the gates to allow the massed *cabellarii* to charge down the grassy slope had utterly spoiled the Saxon Wolf's game. Even so, Captain Kveldulf and his Ash folk were now only a few yards from the open gates.

On the south bank, the Saxons had now mostly recovered from the initial shock of the cavalry assault, and some discipline had asserted itself. The Saxons were grouped into three rough circles now, shields up, spears out in a kind of hedgehog formation. Widukind was at the centre of the largest ring, still mounted, with two of his *hersirs* at the heart of each of the others. The *cabellarii* roamed about the field like wolves, hunting anyone not inside a steel-tipped hedgehog and slaughtering them without mercy.

'Bjarki, we *must* go to their aid,' said Tor.

'He ordered us to wait here,' said her brother. 'He said he would summon us over the river with a trumpet call, if it proved necessary. He was insistent. He repeated himself twice.'

'We going to fight or not?' Fidor called from Bjarki's left.

'Wait, wolf-boy!'

Kveldulf and his men had now reached the open gates. But they were met, and stopped there, by a solid wall of Frankish shields. Bjarki could even glimpse the individual red cloaks of the troopers in the bristling double line. Kveldulf screamed a wild challenge and threw himself bodily at the centre of the shield wall, his long sword slicing down at a red-plumed head, his solid young body crashing against the bulwark, buckling it inward a little.

An instant later his people were all around him, slicing wickedly at the foe, boiling right up against the enemy line.

From high above, on the walls, spears and arrows rained down like a waterfall, dropping on the scrum of Saxons at the gates, plunging deep into leather-clad shoulders and backs, scraping sparks off iron helmets. Saxons were falling here and there now, tumbling down, kneeling, bloody, maimed – and the Frankish wall held firm.

Kveldulf was fighting like a maniac, crunching his sword again and again against the implacable line of Red Cloaks, their shields still locked tight – then a sword jabbed out from the wall, a low blow, and he was down.

At the bottom of the slope, Bjarki saw that the *cabellarii* had broken one of the smaller hedgehogs, and their big horses were trampling over the ruin of two dozen brave Saxons. The two larger circles held firm, drawing themselves in tighter. Archers from across the Eder, Yew Regiment folk, Bjarki saw, were now dropping their killing shafts on horsemen's heads.

A wolf-horn trumpet echoed out over the battlefield, a bold but oddly anguished note, like a lonely howl from the wild animal itself.

'That's it,' said Tor. 'That's the call from Widukind.'

'I'm not deaf,' said Bjarki. He looked then inside his heart – half expecting to feel a familiar, hot, heavy pressure, a chittering voice, a dark, malevolent presence. Nothing. Nothing at all. So *she* was truly gone, then.

'The *hird* will advance on my order,' he yelled. 'Ad-vance!'

They began to pelt down towards the river. To his left, Bjarki was dimly aware of the twins Fidor and Fodor, who were already howling like wolves, strangely in tune with the urgent trumpet calls. And the other members of their wolf *lith* threw back their chins to follow their example.

The twins had found their *gandr*. He, it seemed, had banished his.

Chapter Sixteen

The long road to a lasting peace

Tor watched Bjarki out of the corner of her eye to see if the Bear spirit would force its way into her brother's heart. But Bjarki seemed oddly normal, given the circumstances. His mouth was a grim line, jaw tight with determination. But there were none of the mad, bulging features and protruding eyes of *gandr* possession. He seemed strangely calm.

As she jogged down the slope, she looked across the narrow river at the scores of broken bodies littering the torn and bloody grass. At the two Saxon spear circles still intact, at the *cabellarii* orbiting them – pointlessly. Occasionally a horseman would ride in, smash at the bristling hedgehog, swiping at shields and helmeted heads with his sword, then ride clear of the jabbing spears – shouting insults, urging the foe to come out and fight him.

The *hird* swept across the stone bridge in a tight pack, Fidor and Fodor in the vanguard, howling and snarling, with Bjarki just a pace behind them. She felt the familiar rush of battle excitement, the exhilaration, the belly-fear and raw anger mingled in her hot, pumping blood.

'For Saxony,' yelled Bjarki beside her. And she echoed his war cry.

They erupted on to the south bank of the River Eder – nearly a hundred running warriors led by a pair of snarling, frothing Wolf Rekkar – and hurled themselves en masse at individual scattered horsemen, each of whom seemed somehow to be taken completely by surprise by this infantry assault.

They swarmed over the first Black Cloak rider in a wave of fury and flashing steel. The unfortunate Frank was engulfed, ripped apart by stabbing blades in an instant; his horse too was hacked apart. All that was left a moment later was a mound of black cloth and blood on the ripped green turf.

The *hird* split into several groups then, rushing individual horsemen, swamping them – a dozen warriors to each *cabellarius*. Tor spotted a likely fellow, ran towards him and rammed her spear hard into his scale-armoured back, just as three or four other Saxons moved in on him too. He was dragged from the saddle in moments by a sea of Saxon hands. But her spear blade was wedged in the man's spine, and the long shaft was ripped from her grip as he fell. She looked around. Bjarki was in the thick of it, she saw, swinging his bearded axe with a merciless precision, striking at horse and rider alike, blade sinking into flesh, battering down his foes one after the other. He ducked under a swung sword and hacked his axe into the passing *cabellarius*'s lower back by way of reply. The man yelled out, arching in agony, while the horse carried him thudding away. Bjarki was now looking out for his next opponent, scanning the battlefield left and right. He seemed to Tor to be almost entirely without emotion. Chillingly calm. As if he were performing some routine, even boring everyday task.

She too was forced to quickly dodge under a blow as a Black Cloak slashed at her head with his long sword; she whipped out her seax, lunged at the man and plunged the blade into his left calf. His scream was drowned by the blast of Frankish trumpets. She ripped her knife free and stepped back.

The *cabellarii* were pulling away now, called by the trumpets, the horsemen coalescing into one tight black group about halfway up the slope.

They were retreating. Not *retreating* – they were turning their mounts, forming a neat line and *charging* back up the slope! Back up towards the fortress of Buraburg. They appeared to be attacking the gates of the fortress, making straight for the mass of Saxons still surging round the shield wall of Red Cloaks who denied the heroes entry. Tor stood panting, dripping seax in her fist, and watched in amazement. Their control was extraordinary.

The living *cabellarii* had all quit the field at the foot of the slope. And, a moment later, the neat black wedge of galloping horsemen reached the summit and the gates of the fortress and crashed full pelt into the backs of the battling Saxons fully engaged at the Red Cloak shield wall. The cavalry tore into them, hacking down at blond heads with their swords, slicing through their unguarded backs. Kveldulf's folk were thrown this way and that. Then the Frankish defence line suddenly collapsed, apparently sucked backward into the fortress by some invisible force, just as the rampaging *Scholares* cavalry punched straight through the middle of the melee, destroying it entirely.

There were dead and dying men now scattered in a half-circle all round the gates of Buraburg – but not one warrior standing in the entrance – there were pools of gleaming blood, heaps of abandoned weapons, kit and shields. A few shocked Saxon survivors were staggering down the hill towards the river.

The big double gates of Buraburg were swinging shut. They snagged on a couple of corpses, and four Red Cloaks immediately ran out and began dragging the limp bodies away, making the path clear for the closing doors. Then they too disappeared inside and both double gates banged shut.

Tor looked around for Bjarki and saw him leaning on his bloody axe, breathing heavily, not far from the old bridge. She looked up the slope beyond him: the gates of Buraburg were shut once again, the rows of black Frankish heads once more lined up along the battlements, and, except for the bodies scattered across the ripped-up slope, the puddles of gore and the moaning of the wounded, there might have been no battle at all.

'Fall back, fall back!' Widukind had broken up his spear hedgehog and was hobbling back down the slope towards the bridge, leading his beautiful white horse behind him by the reins. The animal had a deep cut, a sword wound perhaps, in its right haunch, which was dribbling gore. Tor saw that one of the eagle wings on Widukind's ridiculous helmet had been broken, snapped, and now flopped down by his cheek like a puppy's ear.

'Back, everyone!' shouted Widukind. 'Back safe across the river!'

Tor saw Widukind walk right up to Bjarki and put a big hand on his mailed shoulder. Her brother seemed dazed, almost confused by his touch.

'You might as well say it,' Tor heard Widukind say loudly to him.

Bjarki turned then and looked directly at his Saxon lord. Tor could see her brother's face clearly. He looked miserable, somehow bereft of all joy.

'Just say it – I will not hold it against you, Jarl Bjarki.'

'I do not understand you, my lord. Say what?'

'Say I told you so,' said Widukind.

He clapped Bjarki on the shoulder and strode past him, leading his poor wounded horse clattering on to the old stone bridge.

–

They recovered their wounded that afternoon under a flag of truce – and there were a great many of them, far more than the dead, who still numbered four score and three, a terrible toll. Then they all retreated across the river and pulled back up the slope to the original Saxon campsite in the woods.

It was a demoralised council that met by candlelight in Widukind's big campaign tent to assess the day's losses. The Saxon army had taken a serious mauling but it was not entirely decimated.

'We go at them again – first light tomorrow,' said old Bildur, an ox-brained near idiot, if not actually insane, in Tor's considered judgment.

'We swarm the walls with all our remaining strength in the morning. Ladders. Ropes. Grappling hooks. Up and at 'em!'

Widukind stared at Bildur, but he said nothing for an uncomfortably long time.

'Does anyone else have anything to offer?' he said eventually.

There was complete silence.

'We mussst retreat back to Sssaxony,' said Abbio.

There were murmurs of agreement around the table.

'Bjarki – you were vocal at our last meeting. What say you?'

'If you ask us to attack Buraburg again tomorrow, we'll do our duty.'

'I would expect no less of you, jarl. What is your counsel?'

'You've already heard it. I've not changed *my* mind this day.'

Widukind made a wincing face.

'Yes, I deserved that,' he said. 'There are many good folk who have fallen today because of my rashness, and more who'll not live to see dawn.'

The general gloom seemed to chill the air inside the big tent.

'So, this is what we will do,' said Widukind, his tone brisk. 'We will begin withdrawing back into Saxony, but it will not be a swift retreat: we will raid and forage and strip every town and village bare in all northern Hessia – all the ones we missed on the way down. We will take every single item of value that we can lay our hands on. And if the coward Livinus dares to come out of his rat hole and fight us, we will oblige him. Otherwise we will go home richer and perhaps wiser. Our first target is Fritzlar Abbey, two miles east of here. Bildur, I want your men to lead the attack, and you may take half the spoils.'

The assembled captains murmured their assent. Bjarki just nodded.

'Good, then: dismissed. Jarl Bjarki, would you remain a while, I want to talk to you privately about a certain young lady.'

'Have you ever noticed,' said Bjarki, 'how a day can change everything?' He looked across at Tor, who was walking her horse in Skinfaxi's shadow.

'What I mean is that, at sunrise on that black day outside Buraburg, exactly one month ago now, we had a victorious army that was penning in the Franks, intimidating them. We were the masters of all northern Hessia, and Bishop Livinus was up there in his fortress trembling before our might, and hiding like a *nithing* behind his walls, unwilling to face us in battle...'

Tor snorted in amusement.

'Yet the next sunrise,' she said, 'we were a beaten rabble, with a third of our people dead or wounded, shamefully retreating north, burning and looting everything in our path. Yes, I do understand you, oaf. But, mark me well, it wasn't a *day* that made a difference – it was a single *decision*.'

They were riding along the western end of the Hellweg in the last days of summer, on a sunny, sluggish afternoon. On either side of them the First Forest presented a thick, high wall of dense foliage, which made it feel at times as if they were travelling inside some kind of channel. Behind them on the highway marched a Saxon *lith*, thirty warriors, members of Eckhart's depleted Yew Regiment, who had accompanied them from Sigiburg and who had orders to see them to the banks of the River Rhenus and no further.

'Widukind made a bad decision at Buraburg,' said Tor. 'He should have listened to you. Is that what you're saying?'

'No. We all make mistakes,' said Bjarki. 'Even great men such as your friend Widukind. It just shows he's human. And, to be fair to him, this is the first serious mistake he has made since he took up his dead father's mantle.'

Tor said nothing.

'And he did listen to me on *this* matter,' Bjarki went on. 'On the far more important matter of this peace mission to Queen Hildegard.'

'If he *had* listened to you, oaf, and not spent his strength in that ill-advised fight, we'd be in a better position. As it is, we're the ones penned up in our own territory and cowering in fear of Livinus's roving *cabellarii*.'

–

The retreat from Buraburg had started well enough. Bildur's men had ransacked Fritzlar Abbey of its gold and silver, burnt the church and slaughtered the few remaining monks. But, as the rest of Widukind's army began moving away north – splitting up into small bands to forage efficiently and wring the last drops of loot from a ravaged countryside – Bishop Livinus had indeed come out of his rat hole, or at least his ferocious heavy cavalry had emerged, and the scattered Saxon forces had begun to die.

Widukind had few horsemen in his column and, time and again, his foot soldiers had been surprised in their drunken looting by *cabellarii* – and the Frankish light horsemen too – who swooped down on them, slaughtered a dozen Saxon warriors and rode off before they even knew they were in a fight.

One day, two weeks after Buraburg, after a morning in which another score of his scavenging men had died for no good reason, Widukind had called all his surviving folk together and formed a huge shield wall on the south bank of the Ruhr. They had formed up in the face of the enemy cavalry, waiting for them to attack the *skjaldborg* – inviting them to do so.

They had declined the invitation. Widukind, after waiting all day and night, finally ordered his army to break up the massive wall, turn about and march the five miles across the river back to the safety of the Groves.

A week ago, when Bjarki and Tor had set out on their diplomatic mission, with orders to present a tempting offer of peace to Queen Hildegard in Aachen, Widukind's army was only half the size of the force he had set out with so optimistically in the spring. And now it was indeed cooped up in the fortresses of Eresburg and Sigiburg, while the Frankish cavalry roamed and roared over the Diemel Valley and north of the Ruhr.

'Since we are talking about the battle at Buraburg,' said Tor, 'what was it like to fight the Franks without your *gandr*? Did you miss her?'

'No.'

'You looked very detached. I've never seen you like that in battle.'

'It was... extremely odd.'

'Do you think she is gone for good?'

'I don't know.'

'But you did the ritual with Valtyr in Hel's cave. You nearly drowned yourself in that icy pool – like an idiot. She's gone. It must have worked.'

'The truth is, I'm not sure that my *gandr* was even there that day. I did the humming but I did not feel her presence, and when Valtyr said, "Jump in the pool", I did so. Do you remember Brokk, the mad old Rekkr from the Fyr Skola? He said something to me once. He said: a *gandr* is not like a dog, you can't whistle and it comes. It's better to say that you are your *gandr*'s dog. Sometimes it doesn't want to come into you, so it won't. Sometimes a *gandr* likes to play little games with you. For fun. And I sometimes wonder, if you want to know the truth, if my *gandr* is just playing with me. Hiding from me, you know, to amuse herself.'

'Nonsense – you're thinking too much about this. You are now free of her. But maybe you do miss your *gandr*, now it's gone.'

'That's not it,' said Bjarki. And they fell into silence.

They rode along for a quarter of a mile without speaking.

'Tell me, Tor,' said Bjarki, eventually, 'after all I have told you about it, do you still wish your Wolf *gandr* had come to you when you were out Voyaging,' he waved a hand at the green wall, 'in there alone in the forest?'

Tor did not answer.

–

Two days later they had almost reached the end of the Hellweg. The dense woodlands had petered out and, on either side, now there were golden fields of stubble, basking in the late-summer heat, recently shorn of crops. There were villages here too, but the houses were of brick, with red-tiled roofs, not timber and thatch.

There were Frankish villas, as well, every dozen miles or so, great sprawling mansions of marble and stone with rows of columns in the front and gangs of miserable slaves bent and sweating out in the fields. Both Tor and Bjarki had travelled part of this route years before, as captives of Bishop Livinus, transported in a rolling wooden cage – not a very pleasant memory.

When they caught the first glimpse of the River Rhenus, a shining patch of water in the distance, the *lith* commander, a tubby little fellow named Olav, sheepishly told Tor that he must take his thirty back into Saxony – on Widukind's orders – for they were now deep in the realm of the enemy, and any encounter might end in loss of life. They bade Olav farewell and watched as he and his warriors marched away in a drifting cloud of dust.

'Well, oaf,' said Tor, 'I think we had better hoist up the flag.'

From their packhorse she rooted out a flagpole and banner, a sheet of pure white linen with a pennant on top depicting a grey wolf, to signify they were Widukind's representatives. Then they climbed back on their saddle-blankets and began to canter at a gentle pace on a smaller road that led off the highway, slanting down gradually towards the great wide river.

The road took them almost due south along the banks of the Rhenus. There was no doubt they were in Francia – the language of the few people they met on the road was still comprehensible but more flowery and soft, even refined somehow, like the landscape through which they were passing.

Next day they were stopped by a suspicious *cunei* of fifty Red Cloaks, a road patrol and the first body of troops they had seen on this journey.

The red-plumed officer eyed their weapons and dress, looked up at the white flag Tor was holding, noted the white-painted shields, too, that indicated peaceful intentions, and curtly asked them to state their business.

Bjarki showed him a letter, written in Latin on fine vellum, penned by Widukind – with only a little help from Valtyr – to which a heavy black wax seal depicting the crude mask of a wolf had been clumsily attached.

'An embassy?' said the young Red Cloak officer incredulously. 'From the barbarian warlord of Saxony? The Ravager of Hessia?'

He stared at the half-unrolled calfskin in his hands, evidently unable to read the words. But the heavy seal gave the message gravitas.

'We have been sent as personal envoys of Widukind, Duke of Saxony,' said Bjarki, 'with rare and precious gifts for Hildegard, Queen of Francia, and an offer of a fair and honourable peace between our great peoples.'

'Have you now?' said the Red Cloak. He frowned at Bjarki, head on one side. Staring into his big, sunburnt, bearded face for the longest time.

'I know you, soldier, don't I? I know you from somewhere. Wait, wait, don't tell me...'

'I am Bjarki, known as Bloodhand, Jarl of the Three Rivers and Warden of the First Forest, and I am the personal representative of...'

'Beast-man,' shouted the Red Cloak officer happily. 'You're the beast-man who slew all those Avars in the amphitheatre. By Christ, I remember *you*. I was on duty on the main gate. I've never seen anything like it in my life. Beast-man, here, what an honour!'

He seized Bjarki's hand and began pumping it vigorously.

'Hey, lads,' he shouted over his shoulder at the file of gaping Red Cloaks, 'you'll never guess who *this* is...'

–

The Red Cloaks escorted them along the riverside road all day to the bridge at Cologne, a massive wooden structure more than four hundred yards long that spanned the mighty Rhenus. Tor was feeling short-tempered by the time they had all crossed the long bridge and presented themselves at the wooden tower that guarded the entrance to the sprawling town on the western bank.

All day the Red Cloak captain had been loosing a barrage of admiring questions at Bjarki – about his prowess, and about the process of becoming a Rekkr – questions which Bjarki dodged or gave only half-true answers to, again and again. But the dim-witted Frank wouldn't let it go, and insisted on reminiscing endlessly about the fight in the amphitheatre against the Avars.

Not once had he noticed that Tor was the other person who had fought beside Bjarki in the amphitheatre – and that she was the one who had done most of the killing of those unfortunate tribesmen from the Pannonian Plain.

Tor told herself not to be petty. She ought not to care what this soldier-boy thought of her. If he seemed to hero-worship Bjarki, what was that to her? But it would have been nice if the idiot, who seemed to remember every cut and blow, every feint and strike, had acknowledged her participation.

They were handed over to a scowling squad of Black Cloaks – a *scara* of *Scholares* cavalry – at Cologne, and were given food and accommodation.

The Black Cloak captain told them that a galloper would be sent off to Aachen for further orders, and glared at them like an ogre with a toothache as he bid them good night and locked the door of their room, as if to suggest that their lives hung in the balance, which Tor supposed they did.

Yet she was unconcerned as she rolled herself into her blankets. From what little she knew of Queen Hildegard – Bjarki had met her, she had not – she was unlikely to order their deaths; at least, not until they had delivered her gifts. It would also be an unthinkable breach of her personal honour, not to mention the ancient laws of hospitality, to harm them. Franks and Saxons had observed the law of the white shield – of safe parley between foes – for centuries. They were fairly safe, Tor thought, as she fell fast asleep.

Two days later, surrounded by a score of dust-covered Black Cloak cavalry, they arrived at the huge gate in the high walls of the city of Aachen.

Chapter Seventeen

'I could never love a murderer'

They were assigned a small hall in the compound of the Auxilla, right next to the new church. Bjarki was astounded by the way the place had changed over the past three years, since they had first set eyes on this unusual Frankish unit. This *scara*, known by all as the Auxilla, was one of a dozen units in Karolus's standing army permanently based in Aachen. It had been a much-neglected outfit when they'd reluctantly joined its ranks, commanded by a tiny, incompetent buffoon, with only about thirty fighters in total.

These thirty members of the Auxilla had been a random gathering of flotsam from all over the North, murderers on the run from local feuds, vagabonds, adventurers, oath-breakers, charlatans and sell-swords…

It had since grown into a very different beast: bigger, for a start, but also a real fighting force, a unit of professionals – and Bjarki was impressed.

The first indication of the Auxilla's new status could be seen on the parade ground at the centre of their compound. This square of baked earth was where Tor and Bjarki had once tried to instil the rudiments of combat into the maladroit members of the old Auxilla, quite unsuccessfully.

On this day it seemed a full pitched battle was in progress.

More than a hundred warriors were engaged in a melee, smashing swords against shields, lunging at each other with spears. The clash of steel and the clatter of blade on wood was almost deafening, as were the war cries of the combatants. So enthusiastically did they battle with each other that it took Bjarki a few moments to realise they were not in earnest.

He saw that some had strips of white cloth bound round their upper arms, and others had strips of red cloth, and moving between them all, inviolate, were half a dozen men in blue cloaks, carrying wooden batons.

Fight marshals, Bjarki presumed. Law-givers of this odd game of war. Occasionally, after several blows had been exchanged, one of the marshals would tap a combatant on the shoulder with the baton and the recipient of the tap would immediately slink off the parade ground. Some of the warriors did actually fall, some bled real blood – then the marshals would intervene in the duel, stop it, and either carry or help the wounded one out of the square.

Bjarki was entranced. He had never seen a full-on mock battle before. And these fighters were *good*; some were indeed exceptionally skilled.

'They've come along a fair bit since our day,' said Tor.

Bjarki nodded, rapt. He watched as a tall, dark-haired warrior, a fellow wielding two swords, one short, one long, in either hand, but with no shield or armour, fought two duels simultaneously with two opponents, a man and a woman. He fended both of them off easily in several dizzying exchanges.

Then he went over to the attack. First he blocked a sword swipe, came inside the fellow's guard and dealt him a crunching blow with the flat of his steel blade to the man's ribs, which had the nearest marshal hurrying over. Then the dark warrior feinted, stepped right, left, and tripped the woman opponent with his left foot and stood over her body with his sword point an inch from her panting throat.

Bjarki found himself applauding. The warrior glanced over at him swiftly – and smiled. Bjarki recognised him. It was Brandt, a fellow Dane, a man he had last seen in Hedeby during the Frankish embassy's visit. He lifted a hand in greeting and

Brandt flicked one sword tip up in response, then the warrior was back in the thick of the whirling melee.

Bjarki looked around and saw that he and Tor were not the only observers of this contest. Apart from those fighters who had been adjudged 'dead' by the marshals, and who now stood on the far side of the square watching their 'surviving' comrades battle it out, there was an odd pair standing twenty paces away as enthralled by the bite and clash of the fight as Bjarki and Tor.

They were a strikingly mismatched pair, Bjarki thought. One was weed-thin, dressed all in sombre black robes and wearing the tonsure of a priest. The other was jowly as a pig, round as a ball of wool, and wore a brilliant yellow tunic and red-and-white-striped trousers, all topped with a sky-blue cloak, like the marshals' attire. This fellow's top lip was split into two parts like a hare's and was partially covered by a long ginger moustache. His balding, ginger-fringed head was crowned by a thick gold circlet worn around his forehead. A sword hung from his belt, the hilt crusted with gemstones.

Bjarki knew him, too. It was the traitor, Snorri Hare-Lip.

He nudged Tor with his elbow and indicated the new *hersir* or captain of the Auxilla with a sideways jerk of his head.

'Remember what we discussed on the road?' he said quietly. 'All that stuff I said about courtesy and decorum. And the role of an envoy in parley?'

'Do you think I'm going to walk over and insult him?'

'No. I'm sure you will behave yourself well, Tor. But remember...'

'I'm not a child, oaf. You don't have to tell me to behave.'

Bjarki wisely kept his mouth shut.

Tor said: 'But if this embassy doesn't work out, I might slip into his hall, hack off his fat head and take it back to Siegfried. Think of all that silver!'

'Tor, please...'

'Joking, oaf, just having a little fun. Let's go and greet him!'

As they walked towards Snorri Hare-Lip, a trumpet blew somewhere off to their left and immediately every warrior on the parade ground stopped fighting. They helped the fallen to their feet and separated into two loose groups, the white armbands in one gathering and the red in the other. One of the marshals made a count of the 'survivors' and hurried over to Snorri.

'My lord count,' said the marshal, bowing low before Snorri. 'It would seem the Whites have the day. Shall I award the honour?'

'Very well, Griffo, you may award it to the Whites,' said Snorri, spraying a fine mist of spittle as he spoke. He did not bother to look directly at the marshal as he did so. His eyes were fixed on Bjarki as the young warrior strolled over to him, smiling genially, his right hand holding out his vellum scroll of credentials.

'Jarl Snorri, I bring you the greetings of my master, Widukind of Westphalia, Duke of Saxony, under a flag of truce. I am Jarl Bjarki Blood—'

'I know who you are,' interrupted Snorri, ignoring the offered scroll. 'Your pretty little friend, too. But you do not seem to know *my* correct name and title. I am no longer a pagan jarl. My true title, graciously bestowed on me by King Karolus himself, is *Comes*. I am Count Simon of Herstal. The regional count – or *comes* – of the lands around Herstal. I have renounced my heathen names. You may address me as my lord count.'

'As you wish, my lord count,' said Bjarki, bowing low. Tor favoured Jarl Snorri with a tight little sneer, which, viewed in a kindly light, might just have been mistaken as a polite smile of greeting.

'I'm told that you barbarians have been foisted on me by the palace,' said Count Simon, 'and that I am to feed and house you at my own expense until Queen Hildegard condescends to grant you a personal audience.'

'We have been granted that honour,' said Bjarki. 'I hope that we shall have the pleasure of renewing our acquaintance with you in the coming days.'

Tor made a scoffing noise in the back of her throat.

'You've become quite the smarmy little arse-licker since I last saw you, Bjarki Bloodhand,' said Snorri. 'When that pretty Saxon bum-boy made you his jarl, did he show you how to get your tongue all nice and shitty, too?'

Bjarki stared at the Count of Herstal in astonishment. Then the full disgusting meaning of his words registered properly in his brain. For the briefest moment, he considered drawing his sword and avenging the insult, there and then. Chopping the fat bastard down. He put a hand on his hilt...

'Courtesy and decorum, oaf,' whispered Tor, trying not to laugh.

The slender priest glided forward. 'My lord count is, of course, pleased to jest with you, Jarl Bjarki. That is all his remarks meant. The count is well known in all of Francia as the possessor of a marvellous, a unique sense of humour. Allow me to introduce myself to you: I am Father Alwin. I'm entrusted with tending to the spiritual needs of the members of the Auxilla.'

'If you think I'm joking, barbarian, you are even stupider than you look,' said Snorri. 'I know why you're *really* here! You *and* the little bitch.'

'You are beginning to make me angry, my lord count,' said Bjarki. 'I'm sure you would not like it if I became even more upset with you.'

'You think I'm frightened of you, Rekkr? I have a hundred warriors at my beck and call.' He indicated the folk gathered on the parade square.

Bjarki's hands were now clenched into tight fists. Father Alwin stepped between the count and the furious, pale-faced ambassador.

'Perhaps you will permit me to give you a brief tour of the Auxilla compound, since you shall be our guests for some days,' the priest said. 'Let us take our leave of the good count. He is so busy today with the training, so many urgent duties on his mind...'

Bjarki and Snorri exchanged poisonous looks, then Bjarki inclined his head slightly and walked away with the priest. Tor gave the count a scathing glance from calf to crown, turned her back on him and strode after her brother.

'I hope you will forgive the, ah, *brusqueness* of the count,' said Father Alwin. 'He has many concerns at the moment. If I may be candid, he believes his enemies in the North have put a large price on his head. He even suspects, erroneously I'm sure, that you've been sent to assassinate him. That would be unfortunate – the count is a favourite of the king, who would take it as a gross betrayal of trust if anyone should attempt to harm him under a flag of truce. The response would be rapid and, I fear, um, quite disproportionate.'

'We're not here to murder that fat sack of pig shit,' said Tor.

'You have my word of honour that we came with no intention of harming him,' said Bjarki, just about holding on to his temper. 'We wish to discuss an honourable peace with the queen, that's all. We have precious gifts for her. Do you know when we might be granted a hearing? The sooner we meet Queen Hildegard, the sooner we'll be gone from here.'

'I will inform the palace that you are eager for an audience.'

Father Alwin's accent was odd, though his words were comprehensible: 'You are an Anglecynn, Father?' said Bjarki, after a while. 'Like Bishop Livinus? From the Angle and Saxon kingdoms across the West Sea?'

'For my sins,' said Alwin, with a modest smile, 'but I'm not filled with quite so much zeal for battle as our good Bishop Livinus. I, too, favour making an honourable peace with our Saxon brethren. A heathen converted to the worship of Our Saviour at the point of a sword, in my view, makes a poor Christian. One that is likely to slide back into the old ways. However, like our bishop, I was called by God to minister to the heathen, so here I am.

'Please, make yourselves at home in the Auxilla compound,' Father Alwin continued, 'and if I can be of any service to you during your stay, please do not hesitate to call on me. I can most often be found at that church yonder, and I would be happy to oblige you in any way I can. Now, allow me to show you the stables, where your horses are being cared for, and later we will visit the brew yard, where we might enjoy a cup of fresh ale and a bite of bread...'

It took Bjarki the rest of the day pacing up and down inside the small hall they had been allocated to rid himself of his fury at the insults he'd had to swallow. Having lectured Tor on the journey about preserving decorum and courtesy in all their dealings with the Franks, he was now filled with a strong desire to pay a short and bloody visit to Snorri Hare-Lip – or Simon, or the Count of Herstal, or whatever it was the pot-bellied bastard called himself now.

'Did you think it would be easy?' asked Tor. 'A few weeks ago we were burning farms in Hessia, taking their women as thralls. It would be odd if there were no animosity. We're lucky the Red Cloaks didn't butcher us.'

'The tradition of white-shield parley is absolutely sacred,' said Bjarki. 'You know this as well as I do. They can't touch us while we are here and, sadly, we cannot chop the fat head off that traitorous ginger pig's bladder.'

'You still think making peace is worth all the humiliation?'

Bjarki breathed out, long and slow.

'Yes, I do,' he said. 'It has to be. I still believe the same as I did in Hedeby. Despite our victories, we cannot ultimately win a long war against the Franks. They are simply too powerful. All we can hope to do is make a good peace that allows us to prosper, tend our fields and raise our children.'

'You want children now, is that it?'

'You know what I mean.'

'The home-loving Rekkr!' scoffed Tor. 'Dandling a tribe of snotty little babies on his battle-scarred knee. I can see why your *gandr* left you!'

Tor's jokes were not helping his temper.

'What else is there? Would you rather fight and struggle and slaughter the whole world – until you too eventually fall?'

'I want a good life,' said Tor, 'a free life, in which I'm no man's thrall. And I'm prepared to fight for that. At the end of that good life, I want a good death. And a seat in the Hall of the Slain. You used to want that too, oaf.'

'Did I? I don't know what I wanted. I wanted to be special, I think, to be admired by all. That's truly why I wanted to become Fire Born. I wanted to be respected. And now, now that my *gandr* has gone, I feel... I feel that I never really understood what life was all about. It's so brief, so fleeting. I liked the fame, all the respect. I *hated* the slaughter. I hated being the *plaything* of a being so much more powerful than me. You said I missed having a *gandr*. I don't. Truly. I'm glad she is gone. But I don't know what to replace her with. Perhaps a woman to love, and babies – why not?'

Tor was quiet for a while.

'You asked me on the Hellweg, brother, if I still wished that a *gandr* had come to me when I was out Voyaging. And I did not answer.'

Bjarki looked attentively at her.

'The answer is yes. For all the terrible things that *gandr* possession entails, all the horrors you've described, I'd rather be a short-lived Rekkr, even a spirit's plaything, but a warrior of great renown, than a nobody whose long, dull life is unremarked upon and very soon forgotten.'

'Well, you can have mine,' said Bjarki, 'if you can find her.'

Their laughter was interrupted by a loud knocking on the hall door. When Bjarki opened it, he saw Yoni standing there, with flowers in her hair.

'Thought you might like to visit a wine shop in town,' said Yoni, after they had hugged, and hugged again, and enquired after each other's health.

As Bjarki pulled on a travelling cloak, and shoved his seax into his belt, he caught Tor's knowing eye. She was grinning at him and making a rocking motion with her linked arms, to indicate she was cradling an invisible baby.

—

The wine was sweet and strong, and the wine shop, a stone's throw from the half-finished palace of the king, was packed with drunken customers. It was a dark, barrel-filled cave of a house squashed between two residential 'islands', the curious towers several storeys high which housed a dozen families, one living above the other. There were several other members of the Auxilla in the wine shop that night – it was clearly a favoured venue – including Brandt, the dark swordsman Bjarki had watched fight with two blades.

He came over to greet them in a most friendly manner, but sensing some silent message from Yoni, declined Bjarki's invitation to join them at their table.

'I saw you swapping angry words with our count,' he said, grinning.

'He thinks I'm only here to murder him in his bed,' said Bjarki.

'Are you? I'm not sure anyone would mind – no one in the Auxilla, anyway. Can't stand the man myself. We call him Simon the Snake. That fat, oily turd would stab you in the back as soon as look at you.'

'Truly?'

Brandt put his head on one side.

'It's true I don't like him – and few of the others do either. But if you were really trying to kill him, I suppose we would have to stop you. He made us all swear a personal oath to him to protect him with our lives in battle, and so on. To him, personally, not to the king, not to the realm of Francia, but to the great Count Simon of Herstal.'

'I can't imagine Captain Otto asking that of the old Auxilla.'

'He'd never have dared. None of us would have made the oath anyway. But things have changed since then. Up at dawn every day for a run, training with weapons, Whites against Reds. Like proper soldiers.'

'I saw,' said Bjarki. 'Very impressive, Brandt – two against one!'

The man blushed. 'That was nothing. Just a pretend battle.'

He turned and made to move away, then he turned back: 'I know you are here with an embassy and all, but, if you were to – um, accidentally – murder Simon in his bed, you could take over his position. I'm sure all the Auxilla would follow you. Karolus would pay you well. I think all the boys and girls would swear an oath to *you*, if you asked them. Just a thought.'

When Brandt had gone, Bjarki said: 'What an odd thing to say.'

'You are something of a legend here,' said Yoni. 'Those of us who remember the old Auxilla have been talking about you, quite a lot. Sure you wouldn't like to rejoin? Brandt was only half joking.'

'I'm here for peace talks with the queen,' said Bjarki. 'And wine.'

They drank and talked long into the night, and Bjarki found he was able to be at ease with Yoni in a way that he could not with any other person, even Tor. She seemed interested in his life, in what he thought about the world, and the prospects of a peace between the Franks and the Saxons. He was careful to be very discreet, though, about any of Widukind's plans.

He'd been burnt before.

'I don't think the king would insist on all Saxons immediately becoming Christians,' said Yoni, 'but he would probably demand that his apostles be allowed to move freely in Saxony, preaching the Gospel. And he would certainly want to build several churches on your lands...'

'Do you really call yourself a Christian, Yoni? I thought you followed all the old Irish gods.'

'I *call* myself one,' she said. 'It's demanded of us. And we have to pray in the new church that Count Simon built for the Auxilla. But what do *I* know about the gods? I used to love Lir, the sea goddess. I worshipped her, but she never listened to my prayers. Father Alwin says if you believe in Jesus Christ you will go to a wonderful place called Heaven when you die. That sounds good. I won't *know* till I die – hopefully many years from now.'

'They baptised me before I joined the Auxilla,' said Bjarki. 'But their religion never made much sense – there was something about three gods in one that was bizarre. And a virgin who had a baby without sex, which is insane.'

Yoni leaned closer in to him. Her lovely eyes sparkled in the light of the wine shop candles. He could smell the sweet wine on her warm breath.

'Tell me something, Bjarki. I want to ask you something private, and you must swear to tell me the honest truth,' she said.

'Ask away,' he said.

She kissed him gently on the mouth. 'The truth, mind,' she said.

Bjarki kissed her back.

'Did you murder Captain Otto?'

'What? No! He was killed by a bear in Thuringia.'

'You swear?' she said. 'There was a rumour going round the Auxilla that he was a spy for Karolus, and that you and Tor…'

'I swear I didn't kill him.'

'That's good,' she said. 'I could never love a murderer.'

Chapter Eighteen

The Iron King of Lombardy

As they walked through the busy streets of Aachen the next day, Tor noticed an air of levity, almost of celebration among the locals.

'Is today some special occasion?' she asked Father Alwin, who had arrived with the news that morning that they had been granted an audience with Queen Hildegard. 'Is it a feast day or something?'

'Since you mention it, it is the feast of St Matthew the Apostle – the twenty-first day of the month of September – he is the patron saint of tax collectors, and in Francia all decent folk are paying their tithes to the Church on this day. But I'm sure that is *not* the reason why the people are so joyful. There has been some good news from Italy.'

'Hear that, oaf? There's *good* news from Italy,' said Tor, too loudly. 'That must surely lift your low spirits this morning.'

Sometimes Tor found it impossible not to tease her brother – and this was one of those days. He was badly hung-over, after a sleepless night of wine and love with Yoni. He had indulged himself, not expecting to be summoned to the palace for some days.

'Good news from *Italy*, is it?' he mumbled. 'Oh, how wonderful.'

'We are told the king has triumphed in his war against the Lombard princes – Karolus was crowned by the Pope with the Iron Crown at Pavia, and all the contumelious Italian lords, save one rascal, have knelt and done homage. Now Karolus is not only King of Francia, but King of Lombardy, too!'

'What is this Iron Crown?' asked Tor. 'Some sort of fancy helmet?'

'The Iron Crown is a relic of enormous spiritual power,' said Father Alwin. 'It was fashioned from one of the very nails used in the Crucifixion; one of the cruel iron nails that pierced the actual body of Our Lord and Saviour. Whoever bears the Iron Crown, men say, can never be defeated in battle.'

'Doesn't sound like good news for the Saxons!' muttered Tor.

Alwin chuckled. 'No, I suppose not – all the more reason for us to try to make peace, as Christ would have commanded us. This news means one other wonderful thing as well. Our king, Karolus himself, is coming home.'

–

The council hall of the palace of Aachen was just as impressive as the last time Tor had seen it three years ago. And the sprawling, half-completed palace complex that surrounded the hall was still a mad hive of ringing hammers, rasping saws and angrily shouting dust-speckled workmen and slaves. However, inside the council hall all was serene. It was a barn-like, red-brick building, with many large windows along both sides, fifty paces long and fifteen times the height of a man. The long, colonnaded interior was further lit with dozens of softly glowing golden candelabra; it was hung with expensive colourful tapestries, and the floor was paved with smooth grey stone.

Now it was filled with more than a hundred people walking and talking, a few even selling hot food and drink from little stalls.

There were dozens of tonsured priests in their plain, undyed robes, with outsized wooden crosses hanging on their chests, wandering up and down the aisles, some disputing theology with their colleagues. There were fine noblemen in silk and velvet, with straight swords at their belts, chatting with friends or admiring the ceiling, which was painted with lurid scenes from the Bible. There were a few common folk, too, wandering around in homespun tunics and cross-gartered hose, gawping like yokels.

They paid Tor, Bjarki and Father Alwin very little mind as they slipped quietly through the door in the north wall of the hall and turned to proceed down the aisle towards the large throne at the far end. *What a difference to last time I was here*, Tor thought. Then she and Bjarki had been swathed humiliatingly in chains, and very roughly handled by a squad of Red Cloaks.

As the trio approached the throne, Tor could see a young woman seated stiffly in a chair that was much too large for her. She was about Tor's age, she thought, about twenty summers, but dressed in uncomfortable-looking, stiff clothes – a long blue and black gown, slashed up to the knee to expose grey silk stockings and a pair of grey silk slippers. She wore a tall ornate white headdress, shining with silver thread, over her tar-black hair.

They were stopped by a royal flunkey, a stooped old fellow, with whom Father Alwin whispered for several moments, the grandsire occasionally crying out, 'What did you say? Eh? Speak up, young man!' before turning to the queen and intoning in a light, querulous voice: 'This is the embassy of Wunderkind of Vest Failure, led by Barking Bloodhound, Jarl with Three Livers and Warden of the First Furnace. He bids you greeting, Highness.'

Tor noticed that, in this horribly mangled introduction, she was not deemed worthy of mention. She didn't care – she was busy trying not to wet her trews laughing. She watched Bjarki straighten his spine, gather his wine-addled wits and step forward a pace, before bowing and placing the heavy cloth bundle that he was carrying on the grey stone floor at his booted feet.

'Highness,' he began, 'it is a great pleasure and an honour to stand before you once more...'

Tor saw Hildegard frown and beckon to the old steward. There was a flurry of loud whispers and much shrugging on both sides.

Father Alwin glided towards the large throne: 'Jarl Bjarki Bloodhand has had the pleasure of residing in our fair city once before. He arrived as a prisoner of war, but fought superbly in the old amphitheatre against a pack of Avars and was pardoned by the king. Later he served with distinction in the ranks of the Auxilla under the late, lamented Captain Otto.'

'Beast-man!' cried Hildegard. 'I remember you now! Back among us.'

Father Alwin coughed loudly and said: 'He is now the emissary of Duke Widukind of Westphalia. He comes with gifts, and authority to discuss a proposal of peace between the Saxon tribes and the Kingdom of Francia.'

'He has gifts, you say?'

Bjarki bent and began to unwrap the cloth bundle on the floor before him. It contained furs, mostly – some beautiful sable skins, several mink, one pure white Arctic fox pelt, even a bundle of velvety moleskins. He passed them, one by one, to the lady on the throne, where they were admired and stroked, with much cooing.

Hildegard summoned several of her court ladies and they too examined the furs with genuine delight. Then Bjarki began passing up the jewels – two cloak clasps with glowing nuggets of amber at their heart; a fine necklace of coins from Arabia and rose garnets; a golden torc with matching arm rings.

It was a veritable fortune in treasure.

'These gifts for Queen Hildegard come with great esteem from Duke Widukind of Saxony,' he said, 'with the ardent wish that a peace can be agreed between our two peoples. The duke sincerely hopes that we may finally set aside all our quarrels and live together in loving harmony.'

'They are so pretty,' said Hildegard, sighing with pleasure. 'You must thank the duke for me in the very warmest of terms.'

'All my lord desires is that you listen to our proposals for a fair peace between our peoples, so that we may put an end to this terrible destructive war.'

'I should be delighted to *listen*,' said Hildegard, with an odd emphasis on the last word. 'But perhaps we should discuss this in a less public place.'

'I should be happy to discuss my proposals here, today, right now – or, or… or whenever Your Highness finds most convenient.'

'Very good – Father Alwin, would you be so kind as to remain for a moment, while we discuss a suitable occasion for future discussions. You now have our permission to leave, Beast-ma… uh, Jarl Bjarki.'

Bjarki stared at her for long beat, then bowed and backed away.

–

'I don't like this, oaf,' said Tor. It was a day after the brief interview with the queen. And the two of them were in the wine shop Bjarki had enjoyed so much with Yoni, but now drinking only a jug of well-watered ale.

'We've given her all that gold and jewellery and furs, and what have you, and we've got nothing to show for it. She could have us kicked out of Aachen. And there is not a thing we could do about it.'

'This isn't some market trade, Tor. We're not buying a goat or a fancy new pot. She's not going to cheat us. She *cannot* cheat us. We gave her gifts. Gifts. Freely given. Not payment in exchange for anything. However, she may now *feel* that she is in our debt, and is obliged to listen to our proposals, and perhaps even be favourably inclined to them.'

'Something is off, oaf, that's all I'm saying. I don't trust her.'

'This is diplomacy – statecraft. It's very new to us, that's all.'

As the days went by, and they kicked their heels in the stuffy little hall in the Auxilla compound, and there was still no word at all from the palace about the talks, Bjarki also began to feel that something wasn't quite right.

After a full week with no news, he went to find Father Alwin.

The weather had changed, becoming much colder, and it now rained hard most days. A cutting wind swirled leaves in the muddy road beside the church, and as Bjarki pushed open the door to the church, he saw lit candles on the altar, and the breeze caused by his entrance made the flames dance. Alwin was on his knees, head bowed in prayer before the cloth-draped altar.

Bjarki waited until the priest had finished his devotions, and then they went and sat together on a bench at the side of the nave.

'I've heard nothing either,' said Alwin, grimacing. 'The queen said, after your audience, that it would be best to meet in her private apartments. She said she'd send word of a time and place. She may have forgotten…

'I have been remiss,' he went on. 'I will go to that fool of a steward and see if I can get this matter cleared up. Do not concern yourself – I shall discover what is afoot. I'll call on you tomorrow, to tell what I've learnt.'

When Father Alwin burst excitedly into their hall, early the next morning, tumbling in for shelter from another lashing autumn deluge, he found Tor entirely absent and Bjarki still snug in bed with Yoni.

After a few moments of naked confusion, and rapid searching for items of discarded clothing – Father Alwin blushing like a boy and turning away to hide his embarrassment – they sat down over a jug of watered ale and some day-old crusts and listened to the priest's tale.

'The queen humbly begs your pardon for the long delay. She has been busy this past week with affairs of state,' the priest began.

Bjarki frowned. He was glad Tor was not present – she had left long before dawn to exercise with some of the Auxilla folk on the parade ground. She would surely have scoffed at that poor excuse.

'Did the queen really beg my pardon?' asked Bjarki.

Father Alwin ignored the question and instead offered him a sad little smile. 'The good news is, Her Highness will be delighted to meet to discuss your proposals in full at noon on the feast day of St Callistus the Martyr. The meeting will be at her private apartments. I shall be more than happy to accompany you there at the appointed time.'

'Ah, so when exactly is the feast day of St Callistus?'

'In two weeks' time.'

'Two weeks!' said Bjarki. 'Winter will be nearly upon us by then. I had hoped to conclude our talks and be back in Saxony before the cold sets in.'

Father Alwin shrugged apologetically.

'These things do take time, Bjarki,' Yoni said. 'You can't expect the queen to dance to your tune. You may have to stay here all winter long.'

Bjarki glanced over at her, noting her coy little smile.

'Father, tell me honestly, swear on your immortal Christian soul, is the queen deliberately delaying this meeting with me? Is she playing a game?'

Father Alwin would not meet his eyes. He stared at the crumb-strewn table and said: 'Who can truly know the mind of another?'

'Father, please. Be straight with me.'

'I do not believe that she intends harm to you, my son,' said the priest slowly. 'But you may also wish, of course, to draw your own conclusions from her actions. My best advice to you – and I mean this in all honesty – is that you stay here and meet her in two weeks at the feast of St Callistus. Put your peace proposals to her then.'

Tor, when she returned to the hall a little while later, was not nearly as scornful as he had imagined she would be.

'It's statecraft, as you said. It's diplomacy. She *is* playing a game, for sure. But I don't know what it is and I doubt we can guess at it. As I see it, we have no option but to stay here and meet her on St Whatsisname's Day. That, or we simply go home now empty-handed, having achieved nothing.'

The next two weeks passed slowly indeed. The weather was atrocious – gales and torrential rain every day. They found that their hall had a leaking roof, and Bjarki spent several days patching it with timbers and turf. There was nothing to do but wait and, in Bjarki's case, spend time with Yoni.

'I wonder what Widukind and the rest are doing,' said Bjarki one morning as they sat in the hall listening to the rain drumming on the roof.

'It's too wet to fight,' said Tor. 'You would drown. I imagine that everyone's gone to ground. Widukind will be back in Verden snuggled up with that Geva. I expect even Livinus's *cabellarii* are back in Buraburg sitting beside cosy braziers, warming their toes. Even if we don't make a peace with the queen, there'll be no fighting at least till the spring.'

'Wonder how big Garm is now,' said Bjarki. 'Huge, I imagine. And Inge is nearly a woman. She's the one who should be worried about babies.'

The feast of St Callistus finally came, and Father Alwin appeared at their door a little before noon to escort them to the palace. For once, it had stopped raining, and the whole of Aachen had a clean, gleaming look, as all the filth of the thousands of folk who lived in the city had been swept away. The complex outside the royal apartments was empty of workmen, too, which meant that it was delightfully quiet for a change. When they had entered the tower that housed the queen's private apartments, and climbed the long stairs, they were met by a slave in the anteroom, who offered them warm wine.

Bjarki who, confined by the weather for days, had been sunk in gloom, felt his spirits begin to lift as the hot wine hit his stomach.

'This is more like it,' he said. 'Some royal hospitality at last!'

'I have already urged the queen to look favourably on your proposal,' said Father Alwin. 'It is not my place to advise her, of course, but I truly believe that seeking peace with Saxony is the Christian way to proceed.'

'I hope the queen heeds your wisdom, my friend,' said Bjarki.

The three of them were ushered, a little while later, into the queen's chamber, and found the lady herself seated on a different, smaller throne, more suited to her size and slender form, in the centre of the room. This time they were all invited to sit.

Bjarki looked all around himself, remembering. He had been in this spacious royal chamber on his last stay in Aachen, but the whole place had been redecorated, and was now even more lavishly appointed. There were thick carpets covering the floors now, and rich wall hangings, embroidered in silver, and several fine marble statues, which Bjarki suspected were of long-dead Roman emperors. There were also, he noted, a dozen armoured Black Cloaks posted around all four walls – big, grim men leaning on their spears and staring at him and Tor with a vigilant, even hostile air of suspicion.

I understand, he thought. *They don't know my intentions. I might be here bent on murder.* But their brooding presence and feeling of menace made the audience room far less congenial than it might have been.

'We thank you for the beautiful gifts you have so kindly made to us,' said the queen, smiling. 'And because of your noble master's generosity, and at the urgings of Father Alwin, we have decided to give ear to your proposals for peace. So, Jarl Bjarki, speak now of the agreement you wish us to make.'

Bjarki got to his feet and cleared his throat noisily.

'Highness, ah, Great Queen... um, Lady Hildegard, we both know that Saxons and Franks have lived in these northern lands together, in this corner of the wide world, for generations. And while our relations have not always been entirely harmonious, I believe that we share more in common than our quarrels of recent times would indicate.'

He cleared his throat loudly again.

'Our language, for example, is very similar, as is the way that the common people dress themselves, and the way, until recently, that they lived, and farmed their lands, went about their ordinary daily lives. The principal difference that I see – and my master Duke Widukind also perceives this – is in matters of the spirit, in matters of our different religious beliefs. We Saxons follow the old traditions, as you know, but you Franks follow the new teachings of the Christ. But I say this must not be allowed to divide us... We will respect your faith as we do our own beliefs, and... and to this end I propose this: that Christian apostles be allowed to travel freely throughout Saxony, under the protection of Duke Widukind. It is true that several of your missionaries have been murdered by our people, and this has rightly angered your great king. But Widukind would guarantee the safety of any travelling priest or monk inside his realm...'

As he spoke, Bjarki's mind went back to the long conversation he had had with Widukind in his tent outside Buraburg, when they had hashed out the details of the peace offer he would make to Hildegard.

'...provided they commit no crimes against our people, and break no local laws or customs. The Christian priests would be considered inviolate in Saxony – and any man who killed or harmed one of them would be severely punished. With death at the very least.'

'I should hope so too,' said a voice. 'Murder is a mortal sin.'

Bjarki looked towards the sound of the voice and saw a tall, tonsured figure in plain undyed priestly robes, with a fine gold cross hanging on his chest, standing by part of the room that had previously been curtained off.

It was Bishop Livinus.

Chapter Nineteen

As you sow, so shall you reap

Bjarki's words died on his tongue and he stared open-mouthed at the bishop. But Livinus smiled genially at him. Father Alwin walked over calmly, bowed briefly, and kissed a huge jewel embedded in a gold ring on the archbishop's right hand.

'Greetings, Bjarki, what a great pleasure to see you again,' said Livinus, ignoring Father Alwin. 'I much missed greeting you at Hedeby, you know, although there was a great deal of respectful talk there of your extraordinary prowess as a *berserkr* warrior.'

'Ah, bishop, um, my greetings to you too,' Bjarki managed.

'Don't allow me to interrupt you – you were outlining a peace plan to our dear queen, I surmise. You won't mind if I hear it too.'

'Do continue, Jarl Bjarki,' said the queen, smirking at him. 'The good bishop and I are eager to hear more of your proposal.'

It took Bjarki a moment to gather his thoughts.

Tor took his elbow and whispered: 'Tell them about the new territorial arrangements, oaf. Tell them about Osnabrucke.'

Bjarki took a breath, lifted his chin. 'My lord Widukind of Westphalia, Duke of Saxony, suggests, as part of the agreement between our two people, that all territory north of the River Ruhr as far east as the Diemel Valley should remain in Saxon hands, to be justly administered by, uh, me as Jarl of the Three Rivers, with the Ruhr acting as the mutually recognised border between Saxony and Francia, in perpetuity, as it has been for decades.'

'But my troops now occupy the entire Diemel Valley,' said Livinus. 'We have constructed several military camps along the river to shelter us from the weather – right up to the foot of your sacred Eresburg. We are also building a *castrum* on the north bank of the Ruhr, a mile east of Sigiburg. Are you seriously suggesting we simply hand all this territory back to you?'

'With the greatest respect, my lord,' said Father Alwin, 'might it not be more constructive if you waited until the jarl has outlined his *entire* peace proposal before you voice objections?'

'When I require your *valuable* opinion, Father, I shall ask for it,' said Livinus, giving him a hard look. 'Till then you will remain silent.'

Bjarki was unsure whether to continue. He looked at Bishop Livinus, then at the queen. Hildegard made a beckoning motion.

He said: 'We do suggest that. We also ask that we retain the territories known as the Stolen Lands – between the Rivers Weser and Ems, which until recently were occupied by your Franks.'

Livinus said nothing – but he shared a glance with the queen.

Suddenly Bjarki realised why the queen had delayed so long before agreeing to meet their embassy. She'd summoned Livinus to her side and it had taken him all these weeks, in terrible weather, to travel from Buraburg back to Aachen. Was there any point in going on, he wondered? Had they already discussed it, and made up their minds to reject his proposals? Perhaps – but perhaps not.

'Furthermore,' he said, 'my lord duke suggests that the town of Osnabrucke – which he now occupies – be declared a free city, governed neither by Saxons nor Franks but open to both peoples. My lord envisions this place acting as a market in which Frankish and Saxon goods can be freely sold, for mutual benefit. The town might also serve as a meeting place for leaders of both folk, a place where grievances might be easily resolved without unnecessary bloodshed.'

Bjarki stopped.

'Is that it?' said Bishop Livinus, his voice dripping with contempt. 'We give you back the Diemel Valley and all the lands north of the Ruhr we now hold? You keep the so-called Stolen Lands – and we share Osnabrucke? Is that all you came to offer us?'

'No,' said Bjarki. 'That is not all. The last proposal is the most valuable, to my mind, one that involves the most sacrifice.'

'How intriguing!' said Livinus with a chuckle. 'You speak of a vast payment in gold, perhaps – or some looted silver coin from Hessia?'

'I do not.' Bjarki looked at the queen. 'Am I correct in thinking that your brother, Gerold of Swabia, is as yet unmarried?'

'He is still young, and he has not been well since he took a wound in battle... but yes, you are correct, he has not secured a suitable bride.'

'My last proposal is that, in order to seal the treaty between us, Duke Widukind will offer the hand of his beauteous sister Edith to Duke Gerold of Swabia, to be his lawful wedded wife, married in a full Christian ceremony, and to raise their children according to the holy tenets of your Church.'

Beside him, he heard Tor's sharp intake of breath.

They had discussed many aspects of the proposals over the past few weeks of confinement – but not this. For some reason Bjarki felt a little ashamed, no, very deeply ashamed, by this offer.

Bishop Livinus was smiling like a cat with a bowl of cream. 'The Saxon Wolf is ready to offer up his own kin as a sacrifice to make a treaty with his enemies? He must truly desire this peace accord!'

Queen Hildegard spoke then: 'You've changed your tune since we last met, Jarl Bjarki. In this very room you berated me for suggesting that you offer up a pretty girl to my brother like – what was it? Ah, yes – like a plate of tasty honey cakes.'

It was Bjarki's turn to blush.

'I offer Edith's hand, with her permission and her brother's, in honourable marriage, as a way of binding our two peoples together.'

'Well,' said Livinus, 'I have heard enough. Highness? Do you have questions for our guests? Should they elaborate on the offer?'

Hildegard shook her head. 'I do not think there is any need.'

'In that case...' said Livinus, '*seize them!*'

Like some horrible nightmare, Bjarki saw that three Black Cloaks had already laid hold of Tor. Two held her thin arms fast, another had dropped his elbow over her throat. He was aware that there was a Black Cloak behind him, reaching for his shoulder. He turned very fast and, using his momentum, slammed an elbow into the man's face, smashing his big nose and dropping him like a stone. A second man in front was reaching for his neck with both hands: Bjarki bullocked forward between the reaching hands and crashed his forehead into the fellow's mouth. He felt teeth splinter under the blow, drew back and butted him again.

His victim collapsed in front of him. Bjarki was now reaching for his sword, but the Black Cloaks were all around him, their own swords out. One man had drawn back his spear for a chest strike.

'Draw a blade, Beast-man, and your sister dies!' said Livinus.

Bjarki found he was humming, a simple four-note tune, the icy expulsion of his *gandr* quite forgotten. But he paused at those harsh words. He looked at Tor – there was a guard with his arm round her neck and a blade to her throat. Tor looked furious.

'Submit or die, it makes no difference to me!' said Livinus.

While Bjarki hesitated for a crucial moment, weighing his and his sister's lives against their immediate deaths, he felt his arms roughly seized and held and his sword belt stripped away from around his waist. Then someone kicked his knees out from under him and he crashed to the floor.

He heard Father Alwin shouting: 'This is an outrage, my lord, I must protest: a breach of both our ancient customs and the law. They came here in good faith, under a flag of truce. What in God's name are you *thinking*...'

Then something crashed against his skull and all went dark.

–

Bjarki's senses returned to him slowly, one by one. The first was a sense of smell: a nasty, rotting stench of damp straw and old dung. He opened his eyes and winced – the orange and yellow flicker of a burning torch, not far away and higher up, was like a red-hot spear blade stabbing through both his eyeballs. His arms were paining him and he looked down to see that they were fettered with iron: two cuffs on his chafed and bloody wrists connected by a short chain. And his right ankle was enclosed in another fat iron fetter, which was linked to another chain that snaked away into the gloom of the room. The cell. He was in a cell – and he thought that he recognised it from some previous life. It was one of the dank cells under the old amphitheatre.

Then sound, in patches: he could hear Tor shouting, and saw that she was standing at the bars of their cell and jabbing her index finger at a figure on the other side. A tall, lean figure with a tonsure – and at first Bjarki thought it must be Bishop Livinus, come to taunt them, but he belatedly recognised the drawn cheeks, lean form and anguished expression of their friend Father Alwin.

Tor was yelling something about '...the sacred white flag of truce... an honest parley... we trusted you... hallowed protection afforded to enemies... symbol of the white shield...'

Father Alwin was replying, apologetic, twisting his hands, but Bjarki could not hear him properly. Then his mind slid into blackness again.

When he next came to, Tor was spooning lukewarm, garlicky soup into his mouth. He choked as a mouthful went down the wrong way, and sat up abruptly and wished that he hadn't. His head swam; he was panting like a spent hound. Tor said: 'Take it slowly, brother.'

He slept again, down into the darkness, and woke and Tor was sitting hugging her knees with her back to the brick wall a few paces away. He watched her silently for a while, then tried to rise.

He failed. 'Are we under the old Roman arena again?' he asked.

Tor leapt to her feet and came to his side. He was lying on a pile of mouldy straw, and he smelt the tang of urine – possibly his own.

'How do you feel?' she asked.

He turned his head away and puked up a few half-mouthfuls of garlicky soup and coughed up some long strings of glue-like saliva into the straw. Then he rolled on his back and wiped his wet mouth with the back of his hand – his heavy, iron-manacled right hand.

'I feel… *magnificent!*' he muttered. Tor laughed.

He was grateful that Tor did not immediately want to talk and, little by little, his mind came back into focus and he began to make some sense of the world again. They were clearly under Aachen's ancient amphitheatre – prisoners of Livinus, who had obviously decided that the rules of parley meant nothing. He assumed that they would shortly be executed, or tortured and then killed, but he felt nothing at this prospect save a vague, dull sadness.

Eventually, they began to talk. They had been in the cell four days now. Father Alwin had come to see them on the second day, Tor said, and brought food and water, and promised he would continue to plead for their release with both the bishop and the queen, who had colluded in their capture.

She had summoned Livinus from Buraburg when the Saxon embassy arrived, not knowing what to do with them. That had been the reason for the three-week delay before the talks – yet, Father Alwin claimed, he had known nothing about the queen's devious plan before they were seized.

'Do you believe him?' asked Bjarki.

'I don't know. I think he must have known that something was not right. But his first loyalty is to the queen, then to Francia. And Bishop Livinus is his superior in their Church. I believe he is a good man, and on our side – so long as we do not ask him to go against his first loyalties. But then again, he may be the world's greatest liar, who set out to trick us from the start. But I don't think so. He says we must not give up hope. He says that Karolus will be back in Aachen soon and we must trust that the king – who is a good, decent man – will do the honourable thing and release us.'

'Hmm,' said Bjarki. 'Are they going to make us fight Avars?'

'Not as far as I know. We are just to be held here for a while.'

–

On the eighth day of their incarceration, when Bjarki was on his feet, feeling more human and able, within the limits of the short iron leg chain, to move about the cell, the king deigned to pay them a visit.

He came to the front of their cell with half a dozen armed and armoured men, counts and captains, all of them warriors. Some of them were joking with each other and jostling; all seemed to be a little drunk. One of them, Bjarki saw, was Count Simon of Herstal – Snorri Hare-Lip. He also noticed that the king's fine cloak and trews were richly spattered with fresh mud. He looked tired and worn as if he'd arrived in Aachen after a long ride.

'Bjarki Bloodhand,' said the king jovially. 'And little Tor Hildarsdottir. I did not think I'd ever set eyes on the pair of you again.'

'Highness,' said Bjarki. 'Despite these circumstances, it is good to see you. There has been an injustice done to us here – we came to Aachen on a mission of peace, under a flag of truce...'

The king held up a hand, sheathed in a well-worn leather gauntlet, to stop him. 'I have been told everything about this matter, Bjarki. I have a full report from Bishop Livinus and from my wife, too, and I even have an account from a priest in the Auxilla who seems particularly eager to help you.'

'Then you must know that we came to Francia in good faith to talk peace with the queen, with our shields painted white and—'

'I *said* I know everything I need to know,' said the king.

'We will need a day or so to clean ourselves up, but I should be most happy to go over our proposals to you whenever convenient.'

Karolus started to laugh.

'Oh, Bjarki,' he said, chuckling. 'You believe I've come to save you, is that right? You think I'm here to release you from your chains. Ha-ha-ha!'

He laughed so heartily the tears were soon running down his cheeks. The counts and captains all chortled along too, slapping each other's backs.

'Poor, slow Bjarki,' said the king. 'A simple fisherman from the North. I am here to see for myself an enemy finally in captivity, a dangerous criminal brought to justice at last. Do you not remember why? You broke your sacred oath to me three years ago. You murdered the King's Shield, my friend Lord Grimoald, in Thuringia, and a score or more of his men. And you thought I would just let you go free, with my blessing, oh, ha-ha...'

'Insult us, if you wish,' said Tor. 'But the truth is that we came here under recognised rules of protection, and your actions – or the actions of the Bishop of Aachen – reveal you as a man of no honour, a tyrant without a shred of shame...'

Karolus stopped laughing. Count Simon sprayed out the words: 'How dare you speak thus to the king – be silent, or I will sew your lips together!'

The king wiped his eyes. 'I sent Bishop Livinus to Hedeby last year, in the spring, under a *genuine* flag of truce,' he said, using a wholly new tone of voice, and Bjarki recognised now that he was truly angry.

'He went in good faith to visit the court of Siegfried to discuss peace with the warriors of the North. Both sides agreed no action would be taken during this time, that no violence should be perpetrated *by either side*.'

Karolus paused. 'I was away in Italy with my army on most urgent business,' he continued. 'Indeed, I have only now returned. But I have been kept well informed of events in these parts in my long absence. And you have no right to claim unfair treatment, in my view. No right at all. When I was engaged in the war in Italy, when my back was turned and Livinus's embassy was *still in Saxony*, while he was making the long journey home, your master Widukind treacherously attacked my new territories west of the Weser, burning *castra*, slaughtering my undefended settlers and taking many slaves.'

He paused as if to master his emotions.

'While my personal envoy was still on the road home, *still* under the protection of white flag and shield, your man Widukind broke the sacred truce, crossing the border and wreaking havoc among my innocent folk.'

There was a sudden painful silence.

'Therefore I shall *not* be releasing you this day, Bjarki Bloodhand, since you are a double-damned murderer and oathbreaker. And your master is equally faithless. Nor will I observe the usual protections of a truce. You'll rot in this cell till you die – or till *I* decide what's to be done with you.'

Karolus glared at him through the iron bars. 'As you sow, Jarl Bjarki Bloodhand, so shall you reap!'

Part Three

Winter 774–775

Chapter Twenty

A bucket of bad luck

They took the chains off, which was something. A farrier came into the cell to do it, with a guard of a dozen alert Black Cloaks with drawn blades and six watchful archers outside the bars with arrows nocked to the strings.

For a day or so afterwards, Tor wondered if Karolus had changed his mind and was about to set them free. But, as the days passed, she realised the king remained implacable in his hatred.

Before long they developed a routine. At dawn, a gaoler would appear with two wooden buckets, one empty, for their evacuations, the other filled with water, which was all they had to drink and wash with for the day. The gaoler, a reed-thin, silent fellow, removed the previous day's waste and empty bucket and provided them with a rye loaf and a hunk of cheese for breakfast.

When the gaoler arrived with the buckets at dawn – and again with their second meal of soup or pottage at nightfall – he always came with at least six Black Cloaks, under their captain, a squat fellow named Drogo, who scowled outside the cell in the torchlit corridor while the gaoler, or sometimes his young son, scurried into their cell with the day's meagre provisions.

After breakfast, they exercised – every day, without fail. Tor had insisted on it from the start, even when Bjarki complained of the headaches from the savage blow he had taken to the back of the head in the queen's apartments. They stretched their limbs and ran on the spot; they jumped up in the air, tucking their knees into their bellies; they wrestled with each other, but carefully to avoid injury. Tor sat on Bjarki's back as he lay on his belly and lifted his plank-stiff body up and down with the strength of his arms.

The exercises began because Tor was convinced Karolus would soon make them fight in the amphitheatre above their heads again, and she wished to be as ready for combat as she could be. But after a month or so, it just became routine. They heard nothing from Karolus, and Tor suspected the king had completely forgotten them.

One evening, a little more than two months after their imprisonment, they heard singing down the dark corridor and later the gaoler's boy came into the cell with a big piece of roast goose and a sauce made from blackberries, as well as the usual fare. As he set the platter down on the floor, he said '*Felix dies Nativitatis*' before fleeing.

'What does that mean?' Tor asked.

'I'm not sure,' said Bjarki, 'but I suspect they are celebrating the birth of their god.' He was eyeing the succulent goose flesh like a hungry wolf.

It grew cold in the cell at night, as they moved further into the depths of winter, and this was when Yoni finally came to see Bjarki.

The skinny gaoler let her into the cell and locked her inside.

'I had to bribe that fool with a whole silver *denier*,' said Yoni, 'to stop his tattling mouth. Count Simon has banned the Auxilla from visiting you on pain of expulsion from the *scara* – including Father Alwin who, by the way, sends his good wishes and says he prays for you both every night.'

Tor regarded the girl with contempt. She was not worthy to be Bjarki's lover. It had been ten weeks now, and not one visit from this platter-eyed ninny. However, her contempt was mollified by the lavish gifts that Yoni had brought for them: two thick woollen cloaks, two clean linen shirts, two pairs of striped trews and a couple of new blankets. She also brought a smoked cheese, a whole ham, some new bread, apples – and a skin of wine.

They ate well for the first time since their confinement, and drank most of the wine, which soon made Tor feel very drowsy.

'What news of the world?' Tor asked Yoni, when she had eaten her fill and was sitting back on one of the soft new blankets.

'Count Simon is rising in favour, which is good news for the Auxilla,' she said. 'He is one of Karolus's closest cronies. He has been named King's Shield, commander of all the Black Cloaks. He is a power to be reckoned with in Francia.'

'He's a treacherous, cowardly goat-fucker,' said Tor. 'That's what he is. I wish we *had* murdered him in his bed, when we had the time to spare.'

Bjarki said: 'What news of Saxony? What of the war?'

'There has been no fighting – or almost none, I think. The weather has been too wet for campaigning. The situation is as it was when you came. Widukind still holds Sigiburg and Eresburg, but our lot haven't made any serious attempts to take them from him.'

'That's good!' said Bjarki.

'It won't last,' said Yoni. 'Karolus is wintering at Quierzy, three days' ride north-east of Paris – but he is getting his Red Cloaks ready for a campaign in Saxony in the spring. I don't know any of the details, Bjarki, they don't tell me anything, but a storm is coming. The king is angry with your folk, with Widukind – his rage is to be feared.'

'I told you he'd forgotten all about us,' said Tor.

'The king is the most powerful man in the world,' said Yoni. 'You can't expect him to be overly concerned with the fate of two prisoners.'

'We're not getting out of here soon, are we?' said Bjarki, gloomily.

'Can you visit us again?' asked Tor. 'To bring more food?'

'Ah, well, that is a bit of a problem... you see, um... the Auxilla has been given orders to leave Aachen in a day or so. Our *scara* is being posted abroad – out of Francia – along with several other royal household units.'

'Where are they sending you?' said Bjarki.

'I probably shouldn't say. It's supposed to be a secret.'

'We're not going anywhere. Who could we tell?' said Tor.

'I suppose it's all right to tell you. We're being sent to reinforce the Black Cloak garrison at Buraburg. Count Simon and the Auxilla are off to join Bishop Livinus's forces down in Hessia.'

Tor went to her blankets soon after and pretended to be asleep while she tried not to listen to Bjarki and Yoni renewing their love on a pile of damp straw. To block out the squelches, she focused on making a plan – there had to be a way out of the cell. Had to be!

In the sickly light of dawn, Yoni bade farewell: 'I'm glad you're in here, Bjarki. No, wait, don't protest, I know this is horrible – but the war will soon be over, and at least I know you'll be safe when the swords begin to sing.'

–

Tor's plan was simple. After so many weeks guarding them without event, the Black Cloaks had become a little lax. Every morning they unlocked the door to the cell at dawn to let the gaoler in with his buckets, and they held the door open to allow him to enter with his burdens. Sometimes they were even talking to each other as they did so, not paying attention, or half asleep.

That was the time to strike, Tor said. She would offer to help the gaoler with his heavy buckets. When the door was fully open, she would attack him with one of his own buckets, knocking him out, while Bjarki surged out of the cell and attacked the Black Cloaks.

'I've seen you take on six enemies before, oaf,' she said, when he expressed doubt about the feasibility of the plan. 'And I'll be with you the moment the gaoler is down. Between us, and even without the help of your *gandr*, I'm sure we can take them all out.'

'Then what?'

'Then we arm ourselves with their weapons and get down that passageway yonder, double quick. If I recall, there's a door that leads to the street behind the amphitheatre – only fifty paces from where we are now.'

'They will come after us. Every Black Cloak in Aachen – and I guess every Red Cloak, too – will be hunting us.'

'They might catch us, yes, and they might kill us – or worse. So what? The greatest test in anyone's life is facing their own death. Perhaps it is the *only* test. And we face it now. How shall we respond? By meekly accepting a long decline, slowly rotting inside this damp cell? Or by taking one wild chance and risking everything at a throw? I say we take that chance.'

'If we did escape, maybe Yoni could hide us,' said Bjarki.

'So, oaf... are you game?'

–

In the half-light before dawn, Tor, leaning casually against the iron-barred wall of the cell, glanced over at Bjarki who lay on his blanket and pretended to be asleep. He had his eyes closed and his breathing was steady. Then she heard the clatter and jingle and low talk of men approaching in the corridor.

Six big burly Black Cloaks and...

'Is the big one still fast asleep?' piped the gaoler's son, jerking his chin towards Bjarki's entirely still form on the floor.

'He's always been a disgusting slug-a-bed,' Tor said as the little boy opened the door of the cell. 'Let me help you with those buckets.'

She had not considered that it might be the little boy today. What was he – nine? Ten? His age was no great matter – he was an enemy. She looked at the Black Cloaks, yawning, sullen, lounging outside the cell's open door.

She reached for the buckets, to take them from the child's small hand. She put them down, one heavy with cold well water, one lighter and dry. She knew she had only an instant to act. She could picture herself swinging the empty wooden bucket; see the curved staves crashing against the boy's head, crushing his little skull, maybe killing him. And, for a fraction of a heartbeat, she hesitated. Could she kill this innocent? She must... she must do it now.

Bjarki surged to his feet, rising from immobility with an ear-splitting roar of battle rage. The boy let out a terrified squeak.

The nearest Black Cloak shouted: 'Hey, you, watch it!'

Tor had her hand on the handle of the bucket, and yet somehow she could not move. The boy darted out of the open cell door and the nearest Black Cloak lunged, seized a bar and clanged the door shut very fast and turned the key, which was still in the lock – just as Bjarki hurled his huge, half-naked body against the solid bars. His big right hand shot forward, and his muscular arm passed through the iron lattice, reaching out to seize the key-turning Black Cloak by his throat; but another guard stepped forward and slammed his weight behind his shield hard against Bjarki's arm, twisting the limb painfully, unnaturally, against the thick prison bars.

Bjarki gave a yell and quickly retracted his massive limb.

'Feeling feisty?' said Drogo, the Black Cloak captain. He stepped in, flipped his spear and jabbed the point through the bars, tearing a shallow gash in Bjarki's side.

Bjarki looked down at the tear in his bare flesh, now weeping blood. He looked up at the Black Cloak – his face slowly changing. It was bright red, anyway, but now it was bulging slightly, his eyes deep pools of hatred.

As Tor watched, frozen by her own failure to act, she sensed the *gandr* come flooding into Bjarki's heart. She heard the familiar droning deep in his throat. The hum. The ancient tune.

And he seemed to be gathering an aura of violence, a red cloud, around him. The big muscles of his arms writhed like mating snakes.

The Rekkr snarled horribly at the knot of fascinated Black Cloaks beyond the stout bars of the cell; he gave an odd kind of barking cough and shouldered forward once more, hurling his whole body at the barrier, and Tor could have sworn she saw the bars bend a little under the massive impact. Her brother bounced off the iron bars, but he gathered himself and surged forward again, and for a moment Tor was sure that he would rip through the lattice as if it were no more substantial than a vast cobweb. He did not. His body mashed up hard against the cell wall – but it held firm.

A Black Cloak stepped forward and stabbed at him with his spear, the tip cutting into his humped right shoulder. Then they were all there, all six of them, slicing steel points through the bars at the huge, blood-maddened Rekkr, poking, prodding, cutting at the half-naked warrior who was now frothing white at the mouth, grasping the solid bars and shaking them, trying to tear them loose of their stone mountings. Bjarki's body was dripping with blood and sweat. The Black Cloaks were crowding closer, wielding their weapons. One spear caught Bjarki on the right thigh; another scored his left cheek...

'Get back, you idiot,' yelled Tor. 'Get away from the bars!'

'Listen to your girl, Beast-man,' shouted Drogo, his spear lancing out once again, passing right between the Rekkr's legs, just missing his testicles.

And Bjarki – or perhaps his *gandr* – knew they were beaten. The Rekkr retreated, and crouched at the back of the cell, snarling, spitting a creamy red froth at his foes, looking this way and that, from one laughing black-cloaked tormentor to another.

'Let that be a lesson for you, barbarian,' said Drogo. 'You get saucy with us, and you'll feel the bite of Frankish steel. You mark this lesson well.'

He and his men, still chuckling with each other, punching shoulders, shoving, jostling, began to walk back down the long corridor. The Black Cloak captain threw an avuncular arm around the trembling boy-gaoler's thin shoulders.

'Fear not, youngster. He can't get out of there. He'll *never* get out of there.'

Drogo glanced backwards into the cell as he walked away, at the huge form of the Rekkr crouched and trembling with rage by the back wall, and said to the boy: 'We've been too soft with them, lad. No food or water for three days. That'll cool their ardour.'

Tor looked over at her brother. He was coiled like a cornered leopard, his skin lacerated by half a dozen bleeding cuts. His muscles were twitching, his face was working, grinding, as if he were chewing leather. The sweat stood out in grey pearls on his brow.

He noticed *her* then – and stood to his full height.

In that instant, she knew real fear. His eyes were red-rimmed, their interiors black and soulless in the gloom of the cell, utterly inhuman. He turned them on her, and took one long stride towards her. His hands were opening and closing, as if he wished to crush and rip her body into chunks.

He took another step towards her. 'You... failed... me!'

'Bjarki, calm down, please – it's me, Tor. Your sister.'

The Rekkr's answer was a snarl of demonic fury. He lunged, leaping towards her with his great mass hurtling at her slight frame. She whipped the empty wooden bucket in her hand round at him, very hard, just in time, shattering the solid vessel against his head in a shower of staves and iron hoops. The blow knocked the Rekkr sideways. He staggered but it didn't put him down. Nor did it quench his rage.

He threw back his head and howled. Then he began to move towards her again.

'Bjarki, don't *do* this. I know you don't want to hurt me.'

Tor looked at the bloody, sweat-lathered creature coming for her, coming close, step by step. And saw this was not her brother, not her beloved oaf. This was the dread monster from all her childhood nightmares. This was her father.

She reached down a hand and picked up the second wooden bucket, just by her left knee, hefting its surprising weight.

She shouted: 'Stop this right now, Bjarki!' And hurled the contents straight at the Rekkr. 'Stop this nonsense *now*!'

A gallon of near-freezing water hit the Rekkr directly in his gurning, bloody, froth-flecked face. Drenching him with its icy splash.

He stopped dead, and blinked. Wiped the water from his dripping beard with one hand, and looked around as if unsure where he was.

Tor saw his eyes were once more back to their kindly shade of blue.

—

'She hasn't left you,' said Tor. 'At least we know *that* for sure.'

Bjarki merely grunted.

'Valtyr has always been a fool, in many ways,' continued Tor. 'But that stupid drowning business in Hel's dark cavern was obviously his greatest blunder yet.'

Tor was tying a bandage made from one of Yoni's new linen shirts around Bjarki's bloody forearm, where one of the Black Cloak spears had slashed him. They were sitting with their backs to wall, side by side, quietly and companionably.

Bjarki had taken six or seven wounds in that mad encounter, but most were shallow cuts, painful and bloody but unthreatening, except this one on his left arm. The spear tip had furrowed deep into the flesh, close to the bone.

'Oh, I don't know,' mumbled her brother. 'Cold water definitely seems to calm her down significantly. She left me when that water hit – immediately.'

He paused and collected his thoughts. 'And remember when you pushed me into the cold sea after the fight with those vikings off Lolland? It was exactly the same feeling – I felt the *gandr*'s presence extinguished, instantly, like a pinched-out candle.'

'You need to keep this clean, oaf,' Tor said, lightly patting the bandage. 'Wounds go bad so easily. Particularly in a filthy place like this.'

'You remember Father's tale?' said Bjarki. 'About him going north to the snows, to the Sami lands, where he met my mother?'

'I try not to think about that mad creature,' said his sister.

'Well, I think that's how Hildar managed to keep a grip on his *gandr* for so long. He was showing signs of going Galálar in the Fyr Skola, as a youngster, remember? That's why they kicked him out. But he was alive, and pretty much sane, for another twenty years or more. I think the secret is the cold. Cold tames them. Thank all the gods you were smart enough to throw that freezing well water on me, otherwise I can't even imagine what...'

There was a small awkward pause.

'It was my fault,' said Tor. 'I couldn't kill that little gaoler-boy, so the plan failed, and you had nowhere to turn your rage...'

'It is not your fault,' snapped Bjarki. 'It is *never* your fault, Tor. Don't say that. It's my *gandr* – I sought her for long enough, I summoned her, I chose to be Fire Born – I must take the full blame for all her actions...'

They sat in miserable silence for a while.

'So you think the cold lulls the *gandir*,' said Tor, 'like... like an insect, like a bee or something, in winter? You think the cold is a way you can actually control a *gandr* – if you can't get rid of it entirely?'

'I think so. Maybe. Don't know for sure. I'd like to think there is some way I can prevent myself ending up like poor old Hildar.'

'Well, we are not getting any more cold water for another three days,' said Tor, 'so you and your *gandr* had better behave yourselves!'

It was not a good joke, but Bjarki was happy to laugh anyway.

Chapter Twenty-one

The wages of sin

Bjarki looked upward at the sky and took a deep breath of fresh cold air. The clouds were low above them, making the world a dull, leaden grey, but he was outside of that damned cell for the first time in more than five months. And that was quite enough for now.

He and Tor were standing in a courtyard outside the amphitheatre, both with their hands tightly bound with rope and surrounded by a score of Black Cloaks, spears levelled, or holding their bows with arrows ready nocked.

'Climb inside, go on, now,' said Captain Drogo, gesturing briskly with his speartip. 'Don't make us force you in there.'

Bjarki looked at Tor and shrugged; he took a step forward and hopped into the vehicle, a big square wagon on four wheels pulled by a pair of oxen, which was roofed in oak planks and had oak bars on all four sides. They might have been let out of their underground cell, but they were a long way from being free. And it wasn't the first time they'd been inside a cage like this.

After their failed attempt to escape, and their enforced three-day fast, cell life had returned to normal surprisingly quickly. The ritual with the buckets had resumed, but now a pair of Black Cloaks with drawn swords came into the cell first, before the gaoler or his son, and the guards, ever watchful, made them stand at the rear wall while the buckets were swapped.

Gingerly, they had resumed their exercises, and Bjarki's wounds had closed up and healed without becoming corrupted

– and quickly, too; he had always been a swift healer – and after more than two months the cuts, even the nasty gash on his left arm, were just purple scabs or fresh new pink scars.

They sat on the floor of the wooden cage and watched the low suburbs of Aachen roll by outside the oak bars. And soon they were in muddy green fields, pastures, with little copses of ash and elm and cows and sheep grazing peacefully. Bjarki stared at everything as if he were seeing it for the first time; it felt dreamlike, as if he were still in the stinking cell and this were all some delightful fantasy. Only the lines of tramping Black Cloaks on either side of the wagon indicated that this was indeed entirely real.

A unit of green-cloaked cavalry, unarmoured horsemen on little ponies, the riders with round shields slung at their backs, cantered past, and the ox wagon halted for a while as the Black Cloaks gave the scouts the road. Looking up at the pale disc of sun, Bjarki reckoned they were heading roughly north-east.

'Hey, soldier-boy, where we going?' called Bjarki to the young Black Cloak standing rigidly to attention next to his cage. He was a pink-cheeked fellow, with a brave wisp of a moustache on his upper lip. 'You can at least tell me that!'

The young guard gave him a nervous glance but said nothing.

'Come on, lad, don't be an arse, just tell us our destination.'

'We're not allowed to talk,' whispered the Black Cloak out of the side of his mouth. 'None of us. Captain's orders. Not a word to either of you.'

'So tell me where we're going,' said Bjarki, 'and I won't tell your captain that you just did speak to me – spoke several words, in fact.'

'We *should* tell his captain,' said Tor. 'This boy doesn't know how to obey orders. He ought to be severely punished to teach him better ways.'

She gave Bjarki a sly grin.

'Shut up!' said the soldier. 'I am *not* talking to you.'

'You are,' said Bjarki. 'What do they do to troopers who disobey orders, Tor? The lash, is it? Or do they just kick 'em out of the *scara*?'

'All right, barbarian, you win – we're going to Duisburg, to cross the Rhenus and join up with the king and his army, which is coming from the south. Karolus is holding this year's Marchfield there. Now, be quiet, both of you. Don't tell anyone I told you.'

The Black Cloak scurried away.

'What is a Marchfield?' asked Bjarki.

'A gathering of Franks in early spring before a campaign.'

'How do you know that?'

'I make it a point of principle to study all the habits of our foes.'

'No, seriously, how do you know?'

Tor laughed. 'One of the Auxilla men told me. I think Brandt mentioned it once.'

'So what's at Duisburg?' asked Bjarki. 'You can't know that.'

'It's where the Hellweg begins,' said Tor, smugly. 'Or where it ends, depending on your point of view. The Ruhr flows into the Rhenus there, I do know that. At the meeting of the rivers is the start of the high road that lunges like a spear into the belly of Saxony.'

The ropes that bound their hands were cut that night and they were fed the usual watery vegetable pottage and given a jug of weak ale, too. But they were not allowed out of the wooden cage, except under guard to visit a recently dug Black Cloak latrine trench. In the morning, stiff and shivering after a chilly night in their rags, they were fed boiled oats and allowed to visit the latrine again.

Two days later, they were crossing the great River Rhenus at a wide stretch of shimmering water that was the site of a traditional fording place. The wheels of the wagon were entirely submerged during the crossing and, at one point, the straw-strewn floor of the cage was awash with brown water.

For the full two hours of the crossing, during which the oxen team struggled nobly to haul the weight of the vehicle against the push of the current, they were accompanied not by ever-vigilant Black Cloaks, but by a swimming herd of black-tailed sheep, tended by a couple of half-naked boys on ponies, who spent the time gawping at the captives.

The evening after that, they found themselves in the middle of what seemed like the entire Frankish nation. The camping ground of Karolus's vast army – the *Exercitus*, they knew it was called – occupied an enormous area of pastureland between the eastern bank of the Rhenus and the north bank of the Ruhr, where it flowed in a grey wash into the larger river. This was the Marchfield, the gathering of warriors from across all Francia.

The Frankish nobles, most of the refined prelates and even some of the richer captains had commandeered the houses and halls of the walled market town of Duisburg, the lights of which twinkled from the south bank of the Ruhr. But Bjarki and Tor's wagon was dragged into the centre of the *Scholares* compound, which was itself the beating heart of the whole Frankish army.

As they passed through the rows and rows of grubby white tents, they noted the many hundreds of campfires and the hordes of young men sitting around them at their leisure, cooking evening meals, drinking ale, cleaning their weapons and kit. There were hundreds upon hundreds of horses, too, loosely hobbled in the pastures around the Marchfield, or tied up in neat lines near the rows of tents of their riders. As well as all this, there were crowds of women and girls, wives of the troopers, or their slaves, and another vast army of their children. Bjarki tried hard to guess at the size of the enormous force the king had assembled here for the Marchfield.

'There could be as many as ten thousand warriors, I think – at least thirty *scarae*. And half that number again of camp followers. What do you think, Tor, how many would you say?'

'Don't know, oaf. Perhaps you're right.' Tor sounded very low.

Bjarki, sensing her black mood, tried to think of something cheerful to say, something to lift her spirits – and came up woefully short.

'Think how hard it must be to feed all these hungry mouths!'

'They plan to forage for food, to live off Saxon land,' Tor muttered.

'And to marshal them all properly in battle – impossible! It must be like trying to get a thousand cats to form a shield wall. Ha-ha-ha!'

'I'm not exactly *overwhelmed* with sorrow at their plight,' said Tor.

Bjarki, taking the hint, shut his mouth. They were fed vegetable pottage again, taken to a latrine, and slept uneasily that night on river-damp straw.

In the morning Karolus, King of Francia and Lombardy, condescended to pay them a personal visit. And he brought the warmth of spring with him.

The sun was already beaming from an azure sky an hour after dawn and, although it was still chilly, there was a wonderful freshness to the air, which made it a pleasure to breathe even inside a cramped, damp, stinking, wooden cage.

The king rode up on a tall black stallion, splendid in a purple cloak edged with gold over a scarlet tunic embroidered with silver. His crown was a bejewelled band of gold that encased his head, above his curved beak of a nose, and his fingers were thick with jewel-encrusted rings. He came with an escort of Black Cloaks and a richly dressed man, of an age with Bjarki, but whose neatly trimmed hair had already turned as grey as a grandfather's.

Bjarki immediately recognised him as Gerold, Duke of Swabia, older brother of Queen Hildegard, and Karolus's most senior military commander. Hildegard, he remembered, had once tried to procure Tor for the duke's bed – she was in fact that plate of tasty honey cakes she had mentioned at the disastrous audience.

The king stepped off his horse, casually throwing the reins to a Black Cloak, and advanced on the cage, staring up at the two scarecrow figures inside.

'Still both alive, I see,' he said. 'Though there's considerably less muscle to you, Bjarki Bloodhand – and you, Tor Hildarsdottir, would make a decade-dead skeleton look overfed!' Karolus laughed heartily at his own tremendous wit.

'I'm disappointed, Highness, that our misery should make you so merry,' said Bjarki. 'I had thought you were better than that.'

The king abruptly stopped laughing.

'You've only yourselves to blame,' he snapped. 'You and your Saxon warlord, the cruel Ravager of Hessia, who is nothing more than a blood-drunk murderer of innocent Frankish farmers, a burner of crops and thief of other men's livestock. But, mark me well, you shall all very soon come to know the wages of his sins.'

Bjarki shrugged tiredly. Tor said nothing, glaring at the two noblemen.

Gerold of Swabia stepped forward and peered up at the caged prisoners. He sniffed and grimaced at the warm stench coming off them.

'I cannot believe I once thought you worthy of my bed, girlie,' he said, looking up at Tor. 'Look at you now. You're perfectly *disgusting!*'

'I *never* once thought you worthy of mine,' snapped Tor.

There was a horrible, dangerous silence.

'Did you come merely to mock our misfortune?' said Bjarki.

'I *came* to inform you of your fate,' said Karolus tersely.

Neither Bjarki nor Tor said anything in response.

'Not at all curious?' said Karolus, puzzled and now clearly very irritated. 'Do you not wish to know what God Almighty has in store for the pair of you?'

'I'm going to go out on a limb here, and guess, ah... death? What do you think, Bjarki? Is our fate to be death? Yes or no?'

'I agree, Tor,' said Bjarki, nodding sagely. 'I'm going to go with death, too – but not a nice, swift one. Something nasty and slow.'

'You find this *amusing*?' said Karolus. He was quite incredulous.

'A few moments ago, you found our abject misery hilarious,' said Tor.

'It *should* be death for you both,' said the king. 'I ought to have you pulled apart, limb from limb, by wild horses, right here, right now...'

'A wise judgment, my lord,' said Gerold. 'My men can easily provide suitable harnesses, and four strong stallions...'

'But, as it happens, much as you deserve such an ending, it suits my purposes better to spare your lives. I have an important function that I require you to perform for me.'

'Are you saying, Highness,' said Bjarki, 'that *now* you wish to discuss making an honourable peace between our two peoples?'

Karolus laughed – but properly this time. A rich, booming, natural laugh, that had anyone within earshot smiling involuntarily.

'It is hard to hate you for long, Bjarki Bloodhand, for all your treacherous heathen ways,' said the king. 'We could even have been friends, you know? I liked you from the first, but then you fled...'

'I liked you, too, Highness,' said Bjarki. 'And trusted you as well. But you tricked me... You encouraged me to speak about matters that were important to you militarily – to reveal the hidden location of the Groves of Eresburg, for example – and you used your kindness to me, a war prisoner, as a weapon against my folk.'

The king frowned up at him. 'How so?'

'You were able to attack the Groves of Eresburg because you manipulated me to speak freely about their importance to us, and of their whereabouts. You dug out my secrets. I was at fault, of course – I was naive – but when you speak of treachery, you should first look into your own heart.'

'I'm wondering now if the wild horses are not, in fact, the far wiser course,' said the king. But he smiled sourly at Bjarki as he spoke the words.

'So… what *is* to be our fate, Highness?' Bjarki said.

'You came to Francia as envoys,' said the king. 'You came as an embassy from Widukind. You shall remain with the army as witnesses of the deeds of my *Exercitus*. And you shall return to your own people, in due course, with my very reasonable terms for their surrender.'

He returned to his horse and stepped easily up into the saddle. As he turned his mount to depart, he called out to the Black Cloak captain.

'Have both prisoners thoroughly washed and issued clean clothes. And flush out that disgusting cage this very day – or you will face my wrath. And, in the name of God, give them something more substantial to eat!'

Then he cantered away without a single backward glance.

–

The *Exercitus* advanced east up the Hellweg that early spring, in all its pomp and power. At its head rode the King of Francia himself, accompanied by Gerold, Duke of Swabia. Behind him came many thousands of warriors from Austrasia, Neustria and Aquitaine; from Burgundy, Provence and Septimania – and in the middle of the five-mile column was an ox-drawn wagon holding two slightly better dressed and nourished prisoners.

As Bjarki watched the world through the wooden bars of his rolling prison, he recalled Tor's recent phrase about the Hellweg, that it was a 'road that lunges like a spear into the belly of Saxony'. That was true, he believed.

He had never really thought of a highway as a weapon before, but the smooth, wide, slightly cambered packed-earth road they were on, with the thick green walls of the First Forest on either side, was indeed a crucial tool of warfare. It allowed the cumbersome Frankish army to move at speed, covering more than twenty miles between dawn and dusk, unheard of for a force of this magnitude, and helped to keep the whole army intact, without slower contingents straggling or getting lost along the way.

There were only two orders a dull-witted captain needed to grasp: stay on the Hellweg, and stay in contact with the unit ahead. When the *Exercitus* called a halt in the late afternoon, each *scara* simply slept in their place in the column beside the road, hacking wide clearings out of the forest to make their camping site.

From time to time the rolling wagon passed gangs of slaves under a squad of Blue Cloaks, Frankish engineers, mending the surface of the ancient road, filling potholes with rubble and earth and tamping it down. Apparently, an endless task. On either side of the road were deep ditches to allow rainwater or snowmelt to run off. And slave teams were seen to be hard at work here too, wielding mattocks under the Blue Cloaks' barked orders to keep the ditches clear of weeds, leaves, stones and washed-in mud.

From time to time, they heard the distant sounds of battle, the clash of steel and the desperate cries of men. Occasionally they passed corpses at the side of the road, men with gaping wounds, and sometimes others still dying.

The Saxons were contesting the Hellweg with Karolus and his mighty army, that was clear – and they were losing. Bjarki scanned the faces of the dead as the cage rolled past, and often recognised some he knew; one of Captain Eckhart's people, perhaps. Sometimes a man he had particularly liked or had drunk with. Tor, wrapped in furious gloom, ignored the dead.

After three days on the road, the column came to a halt one afternoon and Bjarki, looking through the bars to his right, saw the oval-shaped hill on the north bank of the Ruhr, about two miles to the south, and a toylike wooden fortress on the summit of the hill which he recognised immediately.

Drogo, the Black Cloak captain, who had been almost cordial towards them since the king's visit, came to stand beside the bars of their cage.

'Can you see that *castrum* yonder?' he said. 'It is a place called Sigiburg. Or so I'm told. The king said to make sure you've got a good view.'

Bjarki and Tor both admitted they could see the fortress but offered him no further comments. When Captain Drogo had gone away, Tor pointed down to a spot on the hillside, half a mile below the walls of Sigiburg.

'That's where our camp was, oaf, just there. By that big knoll.'

Bjarki grunted something. He was thinking of that terrible bloody day when he had unleashed his *gandr* here – was it nearly two years ago?

There were far more troops down there on this day, so many more of them than the few hundred shields he had commanded then. Now they swarmed around the base of the hill, seven, eight hundred men, perhaps as many as a thousand of them. He could see the distinctive colours of their clothing, a few of the famous Red Cloaks standing out from the mass, but many men under their regional counts, in a motley of greys and browns.

Here and there the bright flash of scale armour or a reflection from a polished helm; the glint of a drawn sword or glitter of a spear point. There were also several hundred Franks to the east of the *castrum*, and milling around to the west of the fortification some Black Cloak cavalry there, too. Not that they'd be that useful in the assault. Probably there as messengers.

'Well, they're investing the place good and proper,' said Tor. 'They have completely surrounded it. How many of our folk are in there now?'

'Used to be a garrison of two hundred. But we stripped it for the attack on Buraburg – now I have no idea. It all depends whether Widukind has reinforced them or not over the past few

266

months. I'd guess not – I have a horrible suspicion that there are fewer than a hundred of our folk in there.'

'Hmm, well, it took us a whole morning to capture the place last time,' said Tor. 'Let's see if these Franks can do any better!'

Chapter Twenty-two

The destruction of worlds

Tor watched through the bars of the cage as the Red Cloaks formed up in their neat ranks and files on the north side of the hill, below the fortress of Sigiburg, exactly where they had made their own dispositions two years earlier. She could see a similar marshalling of the Frankish troops on the western side, too, and glimpse movements right over on the east side as well.

It seemed clear what Karolus had in mind: three attacks on the fortress walls from three sides, almost at the same time. *That is clever*, she thought. If her brother was right, and there were only about a hundred Saxon defenders inside Sigiburg, and they faced three attacks, they could only deploy thirty-odd warriors to counter each one – and each attack would be made by many hundreds of Franks.

On the other hand, with the vast numbers of troops the king had at his disposal, they could just surge up the slope in their thousands and swamp the defences. What could a hundred do against an attack by an army this vast?

But it said something important about Karolus, about the way he thought about warfare, and Tor was determined to learn as much as she could from this defeat – for there could be no other outcome – before they were released. If what Karolus had said had been true – and she did not necessarily trust the king to honour his word – they would shortly be sent back to their friends with the terms of surrender. So if that happened, Tor wanted to be able to furnish Widukind, or whoever was now in command of the Saxon army, with as much fresh intelligence on the Franks' tactics as possible.

There was a faint rattle of drums and a blare of trumpets, and the main force on the north side began to march slowly up the hill. Row upon row of red-cloaked soldiers, six hundred men at least, trudged up the steep slope towards the walls. They carried ladders, she could see that, but also seemed to be moving sluggishly, and all the noise they made was, surely, excessive.

The roaring trumpets were incessant; the constant rattling of the drums drove the men, step by step, forward and upward. Then, unexpectedly, they stopped. The men halted two hundred yards out from the base of the walls and began straightening their Red Cloak lines – neatening their ranks, measuring distances between the men, for no good reason that Tor could see. After a long pause, the riffle of drums began again, and they marched on, up and up the slope.

The defenders waited until they were fifty yards from the foot of the wall before showing themselves. Then, instantly, the top of the palisade was lined with shouting folk and glinting steel helmets.

The barrage began. A lethal rain of spears, javelins, arrows, jagged rocks and other missiles showered down upon their attackers. A brave defiance. The Franks cowered under their big shields, all bunched together, merely enduring the falling death and destruction from above. Some men were skewered, some bones were crushed; there was a handful of Red Cloaks scattered here and there on the slope, lying dead or wounded, but something was wrong with this attack. Tor felt it in her bones.

It felt half-hearted, insincere. It was a feint, she concluded. Rather like Widukind's failed attempt to draw the enemy eye at Buraburg. No one was genuinely trying to scale the walls. A few moments later, the real Frankish attacks went in. From the western side, the side nearest her, Tor saw a running river of red-cloaked men, two or three hundred, sprint up from the bottom of the hillside and attack the west walls. It took what seemed like only a matter of moments before they were at the base of the walls and the ladders were going up, all of them together, each ladder rising at exactly the same time, and now Red Cloaks were climbing, clambering up the rungs – the underside of the rungs, hanging like apes from the bars, and only coming over on to the top at the very last minute. It was skilfully done – these Red Cloaks were *good*. Yet they faced almost no resistance from the distracted Saxons. It seemed the defenders had concentrated almost all their folk on the north wall against the largest, most visible, most noisy and most obvious attack.

The feint.

On the west side, Red Cloaks were *already* over the walls: Tor could see them on the parapet inside, and a second wave of Franks was already on the ladders, climbing up on their undersides with incredible swiftness. Tor could even make out, by craning her neck, that over in the east, another attack was going in on that far side of the fortress. More lines of swift-running men; more ladders swinging upright in perfect unison. And these Franks, too, were now atop the wall, facing almost no Saxon defenders.

That was it: in less time than it takes to boil an egg, the fortress walls were scaled.

'Odin's balls, but these people are competent,' muttered Tor.

'You sound almost as if you admire them,' Bjarki replied.

They had both stopped watching the attack now, and were sitting back on the cleanish straw of the interior of their cage. The sounds of battle could still be distantly heard: horrible screams, cracks of wood and metallic clangs. Neither particularly wanted to witness the final death agonies of their comrades.

'It was very neatly done,' said Tor. 'I'm not happy about it, but it was. I doubt we could have done any better. They *were* skilled today, much better than they were against us at the Dane-Work. Your man Karolus has learnt a trick or two in Italy. He's cautious, but effective. In fact, he's very good.'

Bjarki just shook his head.

Tor put her face to the bars and called out: 'Hey, Drongo, step over here, will you? I have a proposal for you.'

The Black Cloak arrived in a moment, standing just out of reach.

'My name,' he said stiffly, 'as you well know, is Captain *Drogo*.' His face was flushed with anger. 'I will thank you to remember that, prisoner.'

'Yes, sure, Drogo, Drongo, whatever you say, Captain,' said Tor. 'Now, do you want us to go down there into Sigiburg and receive the surrender of the remaining garrison – those who have survived the assault, I mean? We would be happy to help end this pointless slaughter.'

'That will not be necessary.'

'It would save some of the lives of your Red Cloaks, too – those few Saxons will fight on to the bitter end. Bjarki was their beloved commander not long ago. They would listen if he told them to give themselves up.'

'The king has commanded that you barbarians must not be released from your confinement except by his direct personal order.'

'Come on, Drongo, be a sport, let's end this without more bloodshed.'

'It is *Captain… Drogo*,' the officer said through gritted teeth. 'And I see that you don't comprehend this situation at all. The fortress of Sigiburg *defied* the king. It refused to surrender to him. So he has decreed that no quarter should be given to the foe. No surrender. No prisoners.'

Tor looked at Bjarki and, seeing his bleak expression, said no more.

–

Four days later they turned off the Hellweg and headed south-east on a far rougher mountain track towards the Diemel Valley. Both Bjarki and Tor felt a sense of doom as their wagon came out of the shade of a thick band of trees and into bright sunlight on the top of a ridge, and they saw the whole valley floor stretching out below them.

It was swarming with Frankish troops and their followers. They were camped and bivouacked everywhere; the enemy were strolling casually, or building shelters, or exercising, or cooking around fires. Some were just lounging or even sleeping on every patch of grass along the line of the river on both sides – thousands of men, women and children, as well as all their animals.

In the distance they could see the Groves of Eresburg, with a pancake cloud of grey-white smoke sitting above the whole plateau.

'They've already captured it,' said Bjarki. 'And so quickly. In spite of all we did. The Fyr Skola, the Groves, all of it is now theirs.'

It took them the rest of the day to get close enough to see the Groves properly. The crowded track along the Diemel Valley they travelled on felt safe and domestic, as if it was no more than a busy country road in tranquil Francia – not somewhere that had recently been a battlefield. Cheerful women slapped their laundry in the river and beat their soapy linens against the rocks. Children splashed and played in the river shallows – or stopped and stared at the two captives in their strange rolling cage.

Yet, when they got closer to the foot of the slopes of the Eresburg, they saw that it had, briefly, been a battlefield. Bjarki spotted four big siege engines around the base of the almost sheer cliffs, and lazing groups of Blue Cloak engineers around them – mangonels, Bjarki thought these instruments were called, machines that could hurl a head-sized boulder for a quarter of a mile. Bjarki, craning up to look at the plateau above, could see that in some places the wall that surrounded the Groves, which he had so painstakingly constructed, had been destroyed, battered down by their missiles.

There were fresh graves, too. Christian crosses hammered into the earth at the heads of new earth mounds. But not many. Only about a score of Franks had died taking this fortified place, Bjarki reckoned.

And that made him wonder why – why so few?

There were hundreds of Frankish troops now on top of the plateau, moving about. Green Cloaks, as Bjarki knew them: the Swabian warriors of that toad Duke Gerold. With one part of his mind, he recognised the logic of it. Swabians were light infantry, famous for feats of mountaineering in their homeland – *of course* they would have been used to scale the Eresburg.

From the distant top of the plateau, Bjarki could hear the grind of many saws. And the ringing of axes. Much hammering, too. The noises were faint this far away, but recognisable. *They are building something up there*, he told himself. *Something very big*.

Their rolling cage was unhitched from the tired team of oxen that evening as usual, about two hundred paces from the dusty track that led up to the summit of the Groves, but on the far side of the River Diemel. Bjarki was glad they had not carried him up there to view the ruin of the Fyr Skola.

He wondered who was still alive up there. He dreaded that the no-quarter decree of Sigiburg had been implemented here, too.

There was no sign of any prisoners.

He looked up at the vast bulk of the One Tree, the Irminsul, which connected all Nine Worlds of the universe. It still towered over the smoke-darkened Groves, over the valley. He closed his eyes and prayed to Odin.

'Hear me, All-Father. Grant me the vengeance I desire against my enemies, a punishment for what they've done to my people, to your people. Free me from this foul cage and let me visit my rage on these destroyers.'

Tor kicked him: 'Stop mumbling, oaf – look who's coming.'

It was the king, once more surrounded by his loyal Black Cloaks.

He stopped in front of the cage but, instead of looking at the prisoners, he stared up at the summit of the Eresburg, at the One Tree, standing proud, looming over the valley.

'I thought I had timed it better,' he murmured, as if to himself.

'No matter,' he said. 'How do my two envoys fare – Bjarki Bloodhand and Tor Hildarsdottir? You're in better fettle now, I trust?'

'Why did you have to kill them *all*?' said Bjarki. 'They might have surrendered to you. You could have shown them mercy.'

'You mean at Sigiburg, a few days ago? Or here, yesterday, at the Eresburg? There were very few up there in your high, holy garden, you know, Bjarki – some wicked old devil-worshippers, but only about a dozen proper warriors. Duke Gerold's mountain men rolled right over them in *one* single assault. Don't think there were any left to surrender.'

'Did you give them the opportunity to give themselves up?'

'I sent a man up yesterday under a white flag. Told them to throw down their weapons and kneel. Said they preferred to die. I obliged them.'

Bjarki made a disgusted sound in the back of his throat.

'This is *my* war, Bjarki. You no doubt enjoyed your bloody revels in Hessia while I was in Italy. Now it's my turn to make war on you. And when I do so, *I* make the rules. They're simple. You surrender immediately, at the very first asking – or you die. That's it. I do not give my enemies a chance to win. It's surrender or die. Think you can remember the rules?'

'And you Franks have the gall to call *us* barbarians!' said Bjarki.

'You *are* barbarians – and do you know why? Because my monks will write the history of this war, when I have won it, which will be very soon, and in their telling you will be the evil enemy – you will be the barbarians.'

'I see you came here just for another jolly gloating session,' asked Tor.

'By Christ, you like to cross a river on the thinnest ice, don't you, girl?' said the king. 'I've never met anyone who tried my patience so...'

There was a long, loud, shrieking-creaking sound. Almost deafening. Like the anguish of a goddess. Like a mother frost giant who has lost her only child, wailing her enormous sorrow out into the void.

Karolus snapped his head round to look up at the flat summit of the Eresburg. And Bjarki and Tor followed the direction of his gaze.

Neither of the prisoners could believe their eyes.

The One Tree was canted over at a drunken angle. The sawing and hammering had suddenly stopped, but the huge tree itself was still creaking, screaming, calling out in its agony. As they watched the One Tree continued to tip and slide over until with an enormous, earth-shaking crash it was down, and all that could be seen was a few skeletal branches poking up.

'About time,' said Karolus. 'I should have done that on my last visit. That was an error. But I think I've made my point now.'

Bjarki was so shocked he could barely breathe – the Irminsul was the embodiment of the Groves of Eresburg, heart of the Fyr Skola, the sacred symbol of all they revered, all they valued; the living heart of their people, their customs and their lands. The king of the Franks could not simply have... he could not have just... *chopped it down.*

'What point... do you... make by this... foul desecration?' Bjarki just about managed to stammer.

'Like my rules of war, a simple point: that my faith, my Christian religion, is the True Faith – Jesus Christ *is* the Saviour of Mankind – and your beliefs are a mass of superstition, devil-worship and garbled nonsense. I have destroyed your holy garden, I have felled your magic tree – and what will your gods do about that? Nothing. Where is Thor's thunderbolt to strike me dead? Where is Odin's vengeance? If any more proof were needed your beliefs are just a pack of lies, I don't know what it could possibly be.'

Bjarki, and even Tor, were both quite unable to speak.

'Do you know what, my benighted pagan friends? I think I shall build a new church on the place where your big holy tree once stood. Yes, a fine church dedicated to… St Peter and St Paul, I think, the twin architects of the True Faith. One, the Rock on which Jesus built his True Church, and the other a man who saw the holy light of Christ in the wilderness and spread his teachings around the world.'

Bjarki and Tor continued to stare at him, mouths hanging open.

'And since we are talking about spreading the truth,' said the king, smiling horribly, 'it is time for you to do some of that spreading to your fellow heathens. Have I got your attention, Bjarki? Are you listening to me? I have an important mission for you to undertake.'

Bjarki just managed to nod.

'I shall release you from this squalid little cage, give you back your horses and possessions and grant you free passage to go to your compatriots, who are hiding deep in the forest somewhere north-east of here. You will relay to them – to Widukind and all his squabbling petty lordlings – this message from the King of Francia. Are you listening? The message is this: they are all to surrender themselves to me, no later than May Day, two weeks from now. They will humbly accept baptism into the True Faith at the hands of my bishops, kneel before me and do homage for their lands, acknowledging me as their sole overlord and rightful king.

'They will swear an oath that neither they, nor any member of their families, shall ever again rise up against me, for as long as Almighty God grants them breath. From that day forth they shall be my obedient and loyal vassals – have you got that, Bjarki?

'I shall take hostages for their continued good behaviour, of course – twelve prominent men and women, and I expect you and your sister to be among these hostages – but you may tell the Saxon lords that if they do all this, I shall appoint them *Comes*, regional counts, in my new and most *Christian* Kingdom of Saxony. They may keep possession of their ancestral lands, and all their goods and wealth – but under my benevolent rule. Even that cowardly Ravager of Hessia, the brutal upstart Widukind of Westphalia, I shall graciously pardon. He shall be my vassal, but he may retain the title of duke. These are my terms. Do you fully understand them?'

Bjarki nodded. Tor just glared her hatred at him.

'If your jarls will do this,' the king continued, 'Saxony and its rulers, and all its folk, may live out their lives in peace and prosperity.'

Karolus paused and took a deep breath.

'However, if by the first day of the month of May I have not received every jarl's submission, here at the Eresburg, including that of Widukind himself, I shall declare any who refuse my offer a rebel and an outlaw and I will use all my power to hunt them down like mad dogs. I will have all their heads on spikes and paraded before the *Exercitus*. Furthermore, I shall burn all Saxony down to the roots, I shall ravage your lands with a furious anger. I sincerely promise you that I shall do far worse to your lands than anything you ever did to my people in Hessia. I shall cause the folk of Saxony to starve in their thousands upon thousands – those that I do not simply slaughter out of hand. I shall make an empty desert of this land, from the Ruhr to the Dane-Mark, from the Rhenus to the Elbe, as a terrible example to any future fools who might dream of defying my will.'

Chapter Twenty-three

A tyrant and a bully

They drove the horses hard, even though riding felt strange after such a long confinement, and made them puff and pant like sick, hall-bound grandsires.

The king had returned Skinfaxi and Tor's dun to them along with the pack horse and all their possessions, including Bjarki's prized bearskin, and their weapons. All of which, apparently, had been kept safely these past months by Father Alwin. Karolus had ordered that they be brought to the encampment beneath the Eresburg five days ago.

They headed north and east, initially pushing through the entangling woods of the First Forest and then coming out into the more sparsely wooded valley of the River Weser. On the afternoon of the third day, saddle-sore and tired, they were stopped on a narrow dirt track by the sentries of the Saxon forces.

They were archers, a dozen men and two women of the Yew Regiment in dark green tunics and cross-gartered hose, wrapped in long brown cloaks, who ordered them to halt or die – with arrows nocked to their taut strings – and Bjarki felt a deep stab of joy as he recognised their ruddy, grubby, familiar faces, and they welcomed him with equal enthusiasm, with a volley of cheers, happy shouts and much hearty slapping of backs.

'I had given you up for dead, Jarl Bjarki,' said Widukind, an hour later, seizing his right hand and shaking it vigorously. They were in his waxed-linen campaign tent, which was pitched among a hundred others on the west bank of the Weser, fifty yards from the water. To Tor's embarrassment, when the Saxon duke saw her, he exclaimed aloud with genuine pleasure, and wrapped her up in his arms and squeezed till all her ribs squeaked.

They were given ale and bread and meat and cheese, and asked to tell the story of their captivity to Widukind and the other gathered Saxon jarls, *hersirs* and captains, who all listened with a grave, almost funereal attentiveness.

'I cannot believe the King of Francia would break the law of the white shield, which has been observed time out of mind,' said Jarl Hessi of Eastphalia, a brutal-looking lord, who was idly scratching the dragon tattoo that wound round his neck.

'He claimed we broke the truce first when we attacked the Stolen Lands,' said Bjarki. 'That was his excuse, anyway.'

'Nonsense, the Hedeby talks were concluded,' said Widukind. 'The parley was over and done with when our cavalry crossed the River Hunte.'

'According to Karolus, the truce holds till all parties have returned to their own territories. He says Bishop Livinus was still in Saxony.'

'That sneaking toad had left Saxony but he had *not* crossed the Rhenus. He went east!' said the duke. 'The king's just quibbling.'

'It makes no difference now we have been released,' said Bjarki.

'But we do know for sure that we cannot trust Karolus,' said Tor. She had been reluctant to join this council of Saxon leaders – which consisted of Jarl Hessi, Jarl Ulf of Nordalbia and Jarl Bjarki, as well as Widukind and a dozen *hersirs* and senior captains – saying she was no jarl, just a plain and simple warrior of the North.

The truth was, she still felt awkward around Widukind.

'I'd like you to attend, Tor,' he had said. 'You can add your observations to Bjarki's. Your contribution is sure to be valuable.'

When he smiled at her, she found she could not refuse him.

'What are your thoughts on the king's ultimatum?' Widukind asked her, pouring her a cup of ale. 'His order that we all submit to him or face the consequences. What do you say to that, Tor?'

'I say, fuck that! I would treat this blustering as I would any command from a man who is neither my lord nor my king. I'd tell him to shove it as far up his fundament as it can go. Then offer to help him push it up a couple more inches with my boot.'

'Bravely said, lass,' said Jarl Hessi, favouring Tor with a grim smile. 'This king is not my master, and never shall be. Eastphalia is mine, as it was my father's before me, and shall be my son's after me. I'll never bend the knee to a Christ-worshipping Frank.'

'Am I right in thinking he said *nothing* about Nordalbia?' said Jarl Ulf. 'Karolus did not threaten to ravage my lands, did he? Only from the Ruhr to the Elbe, you said, Jarl Bjarki. Not the lands *north* of the River Elbe, not my own territories, is that correct?'

'If the rest of Saxony falls, how long do you think Nordalbia will last?' said Widukind. 'You'll have to choose between submitting to one king or another, between Karolus and Siegfried.'

The Saxon Wolf did not seem angry at this naked display of self-interest, rather, Tor thought, he seemed weary of Jarl Ulf's constant whining.

'If you fight beside us, and the gods favour us with victory,' said Widukind, 'you will rule Nordalbia as jarl for as long as you choose to do so. If you submit to Karolus, and become a Christian, you may call yourself *Comes* or count but he will surely rule in your place.'

Jarl Ulf said no more. He dropped his eyes and began to pick at a piece of bread. Widukind turned to Bjarki. 'You've not given us your opinion on this matter, Rekkr. Only repeated Karolus's words.'

Bjarki took a long pull from his ale horn.

'When is May Day?' he asked.

'According to the calendar they use, I'm told May Day is in ten days,' said Widukind. 'Not long to make up our minds – war or peace, resistance or submission. What say you, Bjarki Bloodhand?'

'How many fit warriors do we have?' said Bjarki.

'I have eight hundred Westphalians or thereabouts with me, Jarl Hessi has five hundred, Jarl Ulf, some four hundred of his stout Nordalbians. Your Yew and Ash Regiments still number nearly three hundred, I believe. But we are widely spread out over a distance of three days' march between Lubbecke and Orhum. But we could muster two thousand shields, if we called in every warrior.'

'Where is Brun?' Bjarki asked. 'Where are his Angrians?'

'A good question, Rekkr. Jarl Brun is still at his hall in Verden, as far as we know, with his eight hundred footmen and two hundred more good cavalry. I summoned him – I sent three messengers. But he has not yet answered my call.'

'Does he know of Karolus's offer?' asked Bjarki, frowning.

'We believe he has been informed of it,' said Widukind, looking away. 'Brun is the most powerful of us all. We know Karolus sent a messenger to him, a young priest.'

There was a long, strained silence. A bluebottle crawled over the sticky, ale-wet surface of the table at which the council sat. The spring sunshine made the big linen tent almost unbearably hot. Bjarki broke the silence. 'Forgive me, my lord, if I speak plainly: do you believe Jarl Brun means to submit to Karolus, become Christian, and do homage to keep his land?'

'I honestly do not know. He swore an oath of fealty to me last year. But who can say what lies within a man's heart? I have sent Abbio, my Master of Scouts, and Valtyr Far-Traveller, too, to persuade Jarl Brun to hasten here to my side, with all his forces.'

'He's no traitor,' said Hessi. 'He would not betray you, lord.'

'His warriors could make all the difference,' said Bjarki.

'You have not answered my question, Jarl Bjarki Bloodhand,' said Widukind, with a strange formality. 'You have spoken of your strong desire for peace at these councils before. You have even risked your neck trying to bring about that peace with an embassy to Aachen. What say you now? Do we submit… or do we fight?'

Bjarki looked round the table. He looked longest at his sister.

'I saw how swiftly Karolus captured the fortress of Sigiburg,' he said. 'His Swabian troops scaled the cliffs of the Eresburg with ease. I saw him cut down the Irminsul with my own eyes – a sight I'll never forget. He destroyed the axel of Nine Worlds: he murdered the Mother of Trees, without hesitation. Like a man trimming his orchard…

'He has,' Bjarki continued, 'as many as ten thousand warriors at his command, who are now along the Diemel Valley, inside Sigiburg and in the Groves, too – in our most sacred places – and he has more troops yet besides that vast host.

'I am a jarl only in name – the swathe of southern Saxony that was mine is lost. And without Jarl Brun, we have only two thousand fighters to pit against his strength…'

'Do *not* say it,' interrupted Tor. 'Do *not* say we must bend the knee to this tyrant, this bully. I cannot bear to hear you say it—'

'Let your brother finish,' snapped Widukind. 'Say your piece, Bloodhand! Speak your mind freely.'

The duke was staring at him intently across the council table.

'Even if Jarl Brun *were* to join us, and stand shoulder to shoulder with his fellow Saxons, we would still be outnumbered by more than three to one. Yet I say this now, in all earnestness: we *must* fight. We must oppose the Frankish king, this Christian tyrant, this bully, as my sister calls him. We must *not* bend the knee because if we submit to him, we die. If we submit to Karolus we will become Franks in all but name, obedient, meek little Christians who all serve the same overmighty ruler. We tried to make a fair and honourable peace with them, one in which we could all live together in harmony. Yet *he* rejected it. He dismissed it out of hand and imprisoned my sister and I – he humiliated us. But that is not why we must fight him to the death. We fight because Karolus will not leave us be until we are all cowed, with each of our necks beneath a Frankish boot.

'There can be no peace. If we submit, we become his slaves. It is as simple as that. So I say we *must* fight, I say we resist the tyrant with all our might – and our guile, and with whatever powers the gods provide us with. And if we fall, *when* we fall – as all must fall one day – at least we die in defence of our homeland… and our freedom!'

'Bravo, Rekkr, bravo!' Jarl Hessi was slapping the table with his palm, making the ale horns jump. Tor could feel her eyes blur.

'Would you mind very much, Bjarki,' said Widukind, through a gale of applause, 'if I were to steal some of your more powerful sentiments? I see I now have a rival in the craft of word-spinning.'

–

It felt very fine to be back among the folk of the Yew and Ash Regiments, and to be reacquainted with the few dozen remaining members of the *hird*. Many of them had elected to remain at the Groves, with a handful of the *gothi*, in a vain attempt to stop the Green Cloaks overrunning the defences.

Bjarki and Tor wallowed in that bittersweet pleasure. They ate and drank with their friends and comrades, they exercised daily with their *lith*, even staging mock battles of the kind they had seen in Aachen. And they praised the skill and achievements of the best, while encouraging the worst.

They also lazed in the spring sunshine, eating, resting, enjoying the feel of the breeze on their pale skins after such a long time inside. They listened to the rustling of leaves in the branches. And behind it all was the knowledge that the reckoning was approaching – Karolus and his huge army, some-where south-west of them, spelled approaching doom, and they were unlikely to survive the bloody day of battle.

Bjarki was happy to renew his acquaintance with Fidor and Fodor – the Wolf twins he had last seen at Buraburg. They had been part of the garrison of the Groves, but were at pains to tell Bjarki that the decision to abandon the Fyr Skola to the enemy, almost without a fight, hadn't been theirs alone.

'Valtyr Far-Traveller *ordered* us to quit the Groves,' said Fidor. 'He insisted on it. He had sent out scouts, and when they saw the size of the Frankish host, which filled the valley from side to side, he said we could not hold the Eresburg with only the hundred or so warriors that we had up there – and it would be far better to retreat and link up with Widukind's scattered folk.'

'I wanted to slaughter them all, of course,' said Fodor. 'But Valtyr said there was no advantage, nor any glory to be had, in throwing our lives away for nothing. He said the Wolf spirit required our great power for another, more decisive day of battle.'

'We consulted with our *gandr*,' said Fidor, 'and he said that this one time we could retreat with honour and fight another day.'

'I'm certain you did the right thing,' said Bjarki, soothingly. 'There will come a time, and soon, when you'll be able to show your mettle!'

He was delighted, as well, to encounter Gunnar and Captain Eckhart, and they spent a raucous evening around the Yews' campfire, telling stories, drinking heroic quantities of ale and recalling old friends. They raised a horn to Captain Kveldulf, who had fallen at Buraburg, and Gunnar told a hilarious story about the mad old Rekkr that he and Bjarki had known called Brokk.

On the last morning before May Day, and the sealing of their fates, Bjarki was awoken by the sweet words that Jarl Brun and his thousand Angrian warriors, both horse and foot, were only half a day's march from their encampment on the banks of the Weser.

Widukind's entire force, very nearly, turned out to welcome the Angrians and their jarl that afternoon. Bjarki and Tor stood on a bank at the edge of a sheep pasture and watched the column of people and horses approaching from the distance. His heart was warmed by the sight. Without Jarl Brun their prospects had been more than bleak. Now that the jarl had kept his word, and come with all his strength, there was a chance, a small chance, that they might be able to stand against the might of the Franks.

'I don't believe it,' said Tor. And pointed to the edge of the oncoming multitude, where a big, dark object had detached from the column and was barrelling towards them at speed. It appeared to be a full-grown bear.

Perched high on the back of the lolloping animal was a blonde girl, waving a hand in the air and yelling out a wild paean of greeting.

—

'Widukind told me he wanted every available warrior in Verden,' said Valtyr Far-Traveller, after hugging both Bjarki and Tor with genuine warmth. 'And that included Ulli and Gerta, who were at your longhouse. I knew that if I collected them, and brought them south to join the army, I could hardly leave Garm and Inge behind all on their own – without Ulli and his bow, Garm would starve in a week. So... well, here we all are.'

Tor had her arms tight around Garm's thick neck and her head buried deep in his soft coat. She sucked his musky bear scent deep into her lungs. The animal, having recovered his excitement at seeing his friends again, was making the soft, half snoring, half growling noise in the back of his throat that meant he was very happy.

'Garm is good-behaved, Bjarki,' said Inge. 'I have told him strongly he must not eat any more stable boys. *No stable boys!* I said. And if he is naughty, he will not be allowed cheese for *one week*. He listens to me. And he shall be good, I promise you!'

'What were you *thinking*, Valtyr?' said Bjarki crossly, dragging the old man aside by one skinny elbow. 'To bring a poor little child into an army on the eve of a great battle. How could you be so stupidly reckless?'

'First, she is no child. Look at her!' Bjarki glanced over at Inge and saw that was true. She was a young woman now, indeed.

'Second, to leave her alone in Verden, a pretty thrall without any protection? *That* would truly have been reckless,' Valtyr said. 'And where in the Middle-Realm could she be safer than under the watchful eyes of two of the North's finest and bravest warriors?'

'It is done now,' said Tor, her face glowing with happiness. The arrival of the bear and girl seemed to have buoyed her spirits.

'If Inge is harmed,' huffed Bjarki, 'I'll blame you, old man.'

–

The air in the council tent that evening was decidedly cheerful. With the addition of Jarl Brun's troops, the army was significantly bigger than it had been before. Indeed, it was almost as powerful as the force that faced the Franks at the Dane-Work three years ago.

'I should like to begin by thanking Jarl Brun for his timely arrival,' said Widukind. The high council were seated once again around the long table. Mead and sweetmeats – nuts baked in honey, and fruit – had been laid out by Widukind's servants for the nourishment of those present: the jarls, with the addition of Bjarki, Tor, Abbio the Crow and Valtyr Far-Traveller.

Looking round the table, Bjarki noticed Jarl Ulf was not with them. He wondered what he was doing that was more important.

'As we know, tomorrow is May Day, the date Karolus laid down in his ultimatum. Since we have chosen not to submit to the tyrant' – there were cheers at the remark – 'I drink to our defiance, I salute you all. However, I must also warn you that we may be attacked at any time from now onward.'

'Let them come,' growled Jarl Hessi. 'We'll show 'em what's what.'

'Where *are* the Franks, anyway?' asked Jarl Brun. 'What news?'

'Our scouts report that the *Exercitus* is still three days' march away to the south-west, with at least twelve *scarae* still spread out along the Diemel Valley, and on the Eresburg – where they are building a new *castrum* inside the old Groves. They are all along the north bank of the Ruhr, too, and they're occupying Sigiburg. Oh, and patrolling the whole of the Hellweg in strength – three *scarae* there, I'm told. There are reports of another force – mainly Black Cloak foot and cavalry – down in Hessia, based around the fortress of Buraburg, commanded by our old enemy Bishop Livinus.'

'So, plenty of foes to go round,' said Jarl Brun, to general chuckles. 'What is the plan, lord? How do we thin out this vast herd of Franks?'

'We are making our line of defence on the east bank of the Weser,' said Widukind, 'with our centre at Braunsberg, which is that abandoned little hamlet by the ford two miles downstream. We believe it is the only crossing place for a day's march north and south, so if they want to come at us at all they will have to cross the river there, where it is shallow enough.

'Indeed, we are hoping they *will* try to come at us there. We can defend the line of the Weser, I honestly believe – and we have enough sharp-eyed bowmen among our force to turn any attempted crossing at Braunsberg into a bloody catastrophe for them. The idea is to funnel them into a narrow front where their numerical advantage cannot possibly help them and we cannot be outflanked. We'll cut them down with our arrows at the ford, and when they finally emerge, dripping, dazed and badly wounded, we hope you'll smash them to pieces with your excellent Angrian cavalry, Jarl Brun.'

'My horse-folk will be more than happy to oblige you, duke!'

'The key to all this is *unity*,' said Widukind. 'We must remain together. This is crucial. Together we are strong. If they can separate us, we are far weaker, and Karolus will gobble us up piecemeal. That is why the king's offer was so very cunning – he appealed to each jarl to make a separate peace deal with him, to safeguard his own personal lands. Each jarl was invited to think of his own people. If we stand together – all the Saxon folk as one – we have a good chance of beating them despite their numbers.'

There was a pause. Bjarki wondered again where Jarl Ulf was.

'Where do you want my warriors to stand?' said Jarl Hessi.

'On my left flank, if you please,' said Widukind. 'Jarl Bjarki and I shall take command of the centre – of my Westphalians, and all his Ash spearmen and Yew archers – and we will be based at the ford at Braunsberg. I want your Eastphalians on Bjarki's left along the line of the river, to the south, and ready to charge the ford if the cavalry, on the right flank, does not succeed in pushing the Frankish attack back into the water.'

'We'll push them back, never you fear,' said Jarl Brun. 'So we Angrians are on the right, the Westphalians and Bjarki's folk in the centre at Braunsberg, and Hessi's Eastphalians on the left,' he said. 'Very good. Now, where will Jarl Ulf's four hundred Nordalbians stand, I wonder?'

Widukind cleared his throat. 'Um, well, it appears... that is, ah, it would seem Jarl Ulf and his force has, ah, unfortunately departed from the army.'

'What?' said Jarl Brun.

'That snivelling little worm...' bellowed Jarl Hessi.

Widukind said: 'Abbio, would you mind very much...'

The weird, raggedly dressed crow of a man leaned into the table. He looked around the faces in the candlelight, one by one, his shadowed eyes seeming like black jewels set deeply into his oddly misshapen skull.

'Jarl Ulf and all hisss people left the encampment late thisss afternoon. He told me that he intended to return to hisss own lands and fortify the line of the Elbe. He says he will *not* sssubmit to the Frankish king. He says he will give usss that much. But he doesss not choose to fight the enemy on the Weser.'

'This is why it is so crucial that the rest of us remain united,' said Widukind. 'As it seems we must fight the Franks without Jarl Ulf's aid.'

Chapter Twenty-four

The third direction

'So much for unity,' said Bjarki, an hour later. They were back in their own comfortable campaign tent – a generous gift from Widukind – with Inge and Garm snoring softly on a pile of straw in the far corner.

Tor poured some ale. 'I don't think it's much of a loss, to be honest. Jarl Brun or Jarl Hessi deserting us would be far worse. Jarl Ulf was always half-hearted about the fight anyway. I doubt his folk would have stood firm in the battle line.'

'Maybe. But his four hundred folk could still have been useful. As scouts, maybe. Watching the baggage. Even holding the Angrian horses.'

Tor gave a grunt of disagreement. 'That Abbio seems to have more than enough scouts. And Jarl Ulf's gone now, anyway. So no point fretting over what might have been. Oh, Ulli says that someone came here calling for you earlier,' Tor said. She used an oddly neutral tone of voice to impart this.

'Who?' Bjarki was unwrapping the strips of cloth around his shins which kept his baggy linen trews from snagging when he rode.

'A lady,' said Tor, pulling off her own jerkin. 'A high-born one.'

'Edith?' Bjarki stared at her. 'I didn't know she was with the army. What did she want?'

'Don't know. Perhaps she wants to know why Duke Gerold of Swabia turned down your generous marriage offer,' said Tor.

'Perhaps she wants to learn to fight.'

Bjarki laughed. 'Perhaps she wants to train as a Rekkr.'

Tor snorted. 'That must be it. Unless she wants you to warm her bed.'

Bjarki stopped laughing.

'I've touched a nerve, I see,' said Tor. 'You like her, then?'

'What could a lovely duke's sister want with an oaf like me?'

'You'd better go and ask her yourself,' said Tor. 'But in the morning.'

-

There was no time for calling on high-born ladies in the morning, for romantic or any other reason. Eckhart, who was in command of the remnants of the Yew Regiment, and a few score of Widukind's Westphalian woodsmen, and who had been on sentry duty the night before, reported to Bjarki a little after dawn that Swabians had been spotted in serious numbers in the First Forest only half a day's march south-west of Braunsberg.

There had been the ringing of many axes behind the Green Cloaks, and Eckhart assumed the bulk of the Frankish army was on their heels and cutting a route through the dense woodland.

Bjarki immediately rode to Widukind to relay the news.

'It would seem that Karolus is wasting no time in fulfilling his threats,' said the duke. 'He also seems to know exactly where we are.'

Yet despite the alarm, there was not a great deal to do after all the Saxon troops had been pulled back to the east bank of the Weser.

The Eastphalians took up their positions in the south, forming the left flank; Widukind and Bjarki held the centre by the wide ford, with the baggage train and tent encampment behind them; and Jarl Brun's Angrians, including their cavalry, occupied the north of their line, the right flank.

The day was sunny, and there was no sign of the enemy at all. After a sweaty morning's work, Bjarki, Tor, Inge and Garm took themselves down to the banks of the wide, green river for a swim after the midday meal. On either side of them, up- and downstream, there were several noisy contingents of the Saxon army who had had exactly the same idea.

Men and a few women warriors were swimming and splashing at the water's edge, or sitting on the bank naked or half undressed. Bjarki reckoned that it would take at least another day, perhaps two, for the enemy to arrive at the Weser in any sizeable numbers, and there were plenty of scouts on the far bank and hidden in the woods to relay a warning of imminent attack.

So he relaxed. He swam a little, then watched Tor and Inge playing with the bear in the shallow water, splashing the creature and trying to push him over and duck his huge head under. The animal was remarkably tolerant of the women, occasionally mock-snarling, his yellow eyes flashing with pretend rage, and gently knocking them down with a massive paw. Bjarki reckoned Garm was now nearly full-grown – this winter would be his fourth.

What should we do with him? A caged enclosure was not the answer – after so long in captivity himself, he could not bear to see the animal confined his whole life. They would have to find a way to release Garm into the wild, surely, into the huge spaces of the First Forest. And get him to stay there. He knew both Tor and Inge would balk, but it was the right thing…

As he sat back on the grass, enjoying the feel of the sunshine on his scarred, naked body, he looked up the riverbank and watched the other Saxon warriors at their leisure. Some of them were painting their round, lime-wood shields with fresh geometrical designs, swirls or lightning bolts, in bold reds, blues and yellows – or with beasts, dragons and ravens. Some warriors were grouped with their friends or lovers, plaiting their long hair into ropes and binding them up so that they could not be seized in a fight. Others were sharpening swords or axes with long strokes of a whetstone.

It was an oddly placid scene for the eve of a battle – Bjarki could hear the sound of merry laughter, and someone was even singing an old country tune further up the bank – and he wondered in a cold moment of clarity how many of these good folk would still be alive on the day after the first clash with the disciplined Frankish *scarae*.

Would he and Tor still live? The odds against were fearsome.

Yet Widukind's plan was a good one, or so he believed. The River Weser was a good seventy paces wide, in some places nearly a hundred, and some parts of the western bank were marshy and treacherous. He knew that the Swabians were famous swimmers, but they could not swim across that distance with all their kit, armour and weapons – at most they might carry a knife or sword across – and they would be slaughtered the moment they hauled themselves, dripping, up on to the east bank. No, if Karolus seriously wanted to come at them, it had to be across the Braunsberg ford, which was a hundred paces to the south of where he now sat sunning himself, marked by rough, muddy tracks on both banks.

As he examined the ford, a narrow stretch of river dotted with large boulders, the brown water showing white as it rushed over the shallows, he saw a woman approaching from that direction. She was very beautiful, he realised, with long golden-brown hair, a small nose and a firm, no-nonsense jawline. As she got closer he saw that she had large, twinkling eyes, and was even smiling at him. It was Edith Theodoricsdottir, Widukind's lovely sister.

'Thought I might find you here, taking your ease,' she said.

Bjarki sat up, blushing, and reached for his shirt. Edith seemed to be unaware of his confusion and unconcerned by his nakedness.

'Such a beautiful day,' she said, and sat down next to him. He saw that she had a large round wickerwork basket beside her hand.

'I got the notion you might be hungry,' she said, taking out a linen cloth embroidered with leaves and flowers and spreading it out in the grass. There was a loaf of fresh-baked barley bread, ham and cheese and a venison pie made with whortleberries, and some sharp spring onions, apples and even a little pot of nuts glazed in honey.

It was, in short, a feast.

There was a skin of ale to wash it all down. Bjarki set to with a will. Even though he had already eaten his midday meal, after such a long time on meagre rations he was perpetually ravenous, and Edith watched him eat with an awed expression on her face.

'Thank you for this,' he managed, remembering his manners and brushing crumbs from his beard. 'It is kind of you to spare the food.'

'We can only take a small amount of baggage with us when we go. I think we have only five packhorses, and this food was to be left behind and shared out between the army. I thought, after your ordeal in Aachen, that some of the best of it should be given to you as a gesture, as a tiny recompense, for all that you've suffered for our people.'

'So kind— Wait! You said, "when we go". Where are you going?'

'I think my brother wants to keep it quiet, if he can, for morale or something, but I suppose I can tell *you*. He is sending us – his household women, Geva and me, the thralls, servants, grooms, and so on – north.'

'North? To Verden?' asked Bjarki.

'Uh, no, all the way north. To Siegfried. To the Dane-Mark.'

'I can see why he would want to keep *that* quiet. Is he not, then, uh, how shall I say it, supremely confident of our victory over the Franks?'

'It's a precaution, that is all. He wants to get all the women and servants out of his hair. It's one less thing for him to worry about.'

'I don't like this. I think we have a good chance of beating them here. I thought Widukind was of the same mind. Is there something I don't know?'

'You'd better ask him,' said Edith, but her voice had an odd tone.

There was a shower of water droplets, and Bjarki looked towards the river to see the young bear shaking himself dry on the bank, with a great twisting, this way and that, of his shaggy black fur. The bear smelt the picnic food and he pointed his snout towards Bjarki and gave a little woof of pleasure.

Tor and Inge were also climbing out on to the bank now.

Bjarki said: 'Will you do something for me – a small favour?'

'Gladly,' said Edith, but she was warily watching the bear approach.

'Will you take the girl – Inge, my thrall – with you and give her your protection? Who is leading the column? Who is warding you on the road?'

'Valtyr Far-Traveller is in command. But we're taking no trained warriors with us. Widukind says he needs every one. Some of the servants will be armed.'

The bear was nosing in the basket now, grunting softly.

'Give him a piece of that cheese,' said Bjarki. 'He likes cheese.'

Edith's face was bone-white, even paler than usual, but her slim hand trembled only very slightly as she cut off a thick wedge from the round yellow wheel of cheese and held it out towards the hungry, snuffling animal.

The bear took the cheese delicately with its front teeth, then tossed back his head, caught the morsel, chewed, gulped it down.

'Now, Garm, you must say thank you to the lady,' said Inge, wringing river water out of her long hair with both hands.

'Inge, how would you like to go on a nice long journey – an exciting adventure to the North?' said Bjarki.

The girl looked at him suspiciously. 'I've just been on a long journey. Now I'm with you and Tor. I'm at home with you two.'

'I have to send you on another one, I am afraid,' said Bjarki.

He caught Tor's look, and she raised both eyebrows at him.

Bjarki explained what he wanted, quietly and reasonably. But Inge burst into tears, weeping as if the world was ending. 'I want be with you, and Tor and Garm! Don't send me away,' she wailed.

'Tor,' he said, 'can you please make her understand? I have to see Widukind.' And feeling like a coward, he went to find his horse.

–

He found Widukind a little north of Braunsberg, inspecting the Angrian cavalry. Jarl Brun had brought two hundred horsemen and women with him from Verden, and these eager young riders were exercising their steeds in a large, marshy meadow a quarter of a mile back from the river. As Bjarki watched, the Angrians wheeled and charged, waving their swords and axes, shouting their war cries, and re-formed again, in a matter of a few moments, and charged back the other way in a spectacular display of skill, their horses' hooves kicking up a fine rainbow spray with each stride.

'They look very fearsome,' Bjarki said politely to Jarl Brun, who was sitting on his noble mount beside Widukind's white stallion.

'If they scare *you*,' said Jarl Brun, lifting one bushy eyebrow, 'imagine what they'll do to the enemy.'

'I've no doubt they will acquit themselves well,' said Bjarki.

Then he said to Widukind: 'If you have a moment, my lord, may I speak with you privately?'

Bjarki and Widukind rode away, back down the line of the river, the duke occasionally acknowledging with a raised hand the captains of the contingents. Bjarki waved distractedly at Gunnar, who had just been given command of the Ash Regiment – more like a large *lith*, at this point – and who was demonstrating to a young spearman the correct use of his weapon.

Gunnar waved back and Bjarki smiled and said to Widukind, out of the side of his mouth: 'Why are you sending all the women and baggage away?'

'No reason. A precaution,' said Widukind, looking sideways at him.

'If you lie to me, my lord, I will never trust you again,' said Bjarki.

Widukind turned in the saddle and looked at Bjarki. 'This must remain a secret,' he said, 'between us. If word got out...'

'I'll try not to tell anyone – but tell me the truth.'

'It is bad news,' Widukind said. 'But not unexpected.'

'Tell me.'

'Abbio's scouts came in last night. They report that Bishop Livinus crossed the River Weser ten miles to the south of here with three full *scarae* – perhaps a thousand Frankish warriors. The bishop came right up the Diemel Valley to where that small river joins the Weser, and found an old fording place north of the junction. Some local Saxons guided him to the right spot, of course, foul traitors, and if I ever discover who it was, I'll...'

'Never mind all that,' said Bjarki. 'So... you are saying that we have, in fact, been outflanked to the south. That an enemy force is on *this* side of the Weser and heading up the river to attack us from that direction?'

'Yes, and at the same time, Karolus and his main force is heading this way from the west,' said Widukind. 'The king means to squeeze us like a pimple, like the pinching of a thumb and finger, between his two armies.'

'It doesn't mean we're lost. We are forewarned. Jarl Hessi is in the south with his five hundred. They're tough, seasoned fighters, those Eastphalians. They know how to set an ambush. If Hessi turns south to face them, attacks them and fends them off for a day or so, we can still beat Karolus here at Braunsberg, with our people and those of Jarl Brun. Our archers will slaughter them in the water and the Angrian horsemen will finish the job. It *can* still be done, lord.'

'I never said it couldn't be done. I only said that I'd received some bad news and made the decision to send the womenfolk away. If I thought we would lose the battle, if I *truly* thought that, I'd order the army to retreat. I know you Rekkar love death or glory, but I'd prefer to fight another day.'

–

The whole Saxon army was raised to a high pitch of alertness: each Westphalian and Angrian warrior was ordered to sleep in their battle position, the cavalry bedding down beside their mounts.

The Eastphalian encampment was abuzz, with Hessi making his five hundred troops ready to head south and confront Livinus. There was much talk of an ambush in the marshes, a cunning trap, which would destroy the new Christian force in one sweep.

Tor and Bjarki shared a bowl of cabbage soup and a crust of rye bread in their tent. Inge had departed, tearfully, with Edith and the rest of Widukind's household. Bjarki felt a sense of relief that the girl was to be far from the horror that would mark the next day.

Tor seemed to be in an odd mood that evening: nervous, irritable. Bjarki could not understand her distress. His sister had never been fearful on the eve of battle.

'Are you quite well?' he asked her.

'Fine.'

'You seem agitated.'

'I'm fine. It's just…'

'What?'

'There is something bad coming. I know it.'

'What?'

'I don't know. It's just a feeling – a prickling in my thumbs.'

'Are you a *seithkonur* now? A witch who sees the future?'

'Don't be stupid, oaf. I just know something bad is about to happen. I *know* this. Listen to me: Karolus attacked and captured

Sigiburg with three attacks, yes? Two assaults would have done it. Odin's arsehole, one big assault could have swamped the place.'

'What is your point?'

'That he's cautious. Karolus doesn't like to take risks. He likes easy victories, not the hard-fought, long and bloody ones. He has more than enough warriors to crush us at the ford, maybe, in one determined assault. If he kept shoving his men over the river, regardless of how many we shot down, he could beat us by sheer weight of numbers. He has ten thousand men to throw at us!'

'I don't know that he would necessarily win...' said Bjarki.

'You're right, it isn't a certain victory. And Karolus doesn't want to take that risk. He wants an easy victory, as I have said. So he sent Livinus across that forgotten ford to the south of us. Just so that he could attack us at the same time on two fronts. So he could outflank us. Win an easy victory.'

'I still think we can win tomorrow,' said Bjarki, stubbornly. He wondered if it had been a mistake to tell the secret of Livinus's crossing to Tor.

'You are missing the point, oaf,' said Tor. 'As usual.'

Bjarki scratched his blond beard quite hard but he said nothing.

'At Sigiburg,' said Tor, 'when he really did not need to, he attacked the fortress from *three* directions. Three. Not two, or one. Three.'

'What are you saying?'

'Karolus has something else, some other plan in his devious mind. He'll be coming at us at Braunsberg from a third direction.'

'From where?' said Bjarki.

'That's the problem. I can't work out what that direction is.'

Chapter Twenty-five

'There is nothing more to be done here!'

The five hundred battle-hardened Eastphalian troops of Jarl Hessi pulled out mid-morning the next day. Tor and Bjarki, Widukind, Abbio and Jarl Brun sat astride their horses by the chuckling waters at the Braunsberg ford and watched the dust cloud of their departure. Yet, the Eastphalians did not march south, down the riverside road towards the oncoming threat of Bishop Livinus and his three Frankish *scarae*. Instead, they turned about and headed north-east across the marshy fields back towards their homelands.

'I could not ssstop the newss ssspreading, lord,' said Abbio. 'My sscout told one Eastphalian, a cousin of his, and that was it.'

'You knew it was coming, didn't you?' Tor accused the duke.

Widukind gave her a chilly sideways glance but said nothing.

'That night in Verden, after I had been wounded, you asked me about our time in Rerik, Bjarki and me, and the huge stores of grain held in the warehouses there, and about Prince Witzlaus of the Obodrites. You knew they were preparing to make war on us. Then you discovered that Livinus had made a secret visit to the Wendlands. You knew, didn't you, that Karolus would make a pact with Prince Witzlaus to invade Saxony when the time was right.'

'I didn't *know*,' said Widukind. 'A possibility, sure. But how could I *know* that a horde of Obodrites would choose this moment to cross the border into Saxony and begin to ravage an undefended Eastphalia?'

'Because this is *exactly* the right moment – you and all the Saxon forces are massed here, and facing west, and Karolus knows that well enough. It's a perfect time to have his allies in the east make their move. And you should have known that. Odin's arse, with only a quarter of the information you get, I knew something bad was coming – the third direction. The third *fucking* direction.'

'Tor,' said Bjarki. 'He is our duke, show some respect...'

'Why?' she snapped at him. 'He shows *me* no respect!'

She turned her horse and galloped back towards the river.

'I apologise, lord, on her behalf,' Bjarki began. 'She's...'

'Let us speak of it no more, Rekkr. She is upset by something else – apart from the Obodrites' surprise attack and the Eastphalian desertion. It is a private matter. None of your concern. We need to think on what to do now. Jarl Brun, I shall need your horsemen to harry Bishop Livinus on his southern approach. And, Jarl Bjarki, if you could extend your lines a little further and set up some sort of...'

'My duke,' said Jarl Brun.

'I will need your Yew archers, Jarl Bjarki, to accompany the Angrian horse on the march,' continued Widukind, 'light, fast-moving...'

'My lord,' said Jarl Brun, more loudly. 'I must speak now.'

Widukind looked at him. 'What is it, old friend? What now?'

'We cannot stand here and fight without Jarl Hessi. I must say it to you bluntly. Between Karolus in the west and Livinus coming up from the south, we will be crushed. We must go, while we can.'

'You too, Jarl Brun? First it was Jarl Ulf who left me, then Jarl Hessi. Is there no loyalty, no faithfulness, left in all Saxony?'

Brun stared at Widukind, one bushy brow cocked in contempt.

'I must inform you, my lord, that my Angrians shall depart this very day. We will be on the road within the hour. I wish you luck in your struggle against the foe, but my people are quitting this place.'

'Wait! Jarl Brun, forgive my foolish words. Stay and we will beat them together. Stand, and we'll see them off, I know we will.'

'There is nothing more to be done here, lord,' said Jarl Brun. And he turned and headed back towards the Angrian encampment.

'It is just you and me now, Bjarki,' said Widukind. 'And my brave Master of Scouts, Abbio! We three men against the world!'

'What did you do to my sister?' said Bjarki. His words held a sword edge of menace. 'What have you done to upset her?'

'It is a private matter, as I said. If your sister wishes to confide in you about our relationship, fine, but I do not choose to do so.'

'If you have hurt her, Saxon, then I swear to you...'

'We do not have time for thiss now,' said Abbio, 'we mussst prepare to march north, and quickly, too. Look yonder, lord!'

The strange little crow-like man was pointing over to the far side of the River Weser, no more than a hundred paces away. Bjarki could see a lone figure standing at the edge of the woodland, a tall, lean, long-faced man, fair-haired, wearing a dark green tunic and cloak, an ash-wood spear in one hand and a shield in the other.

He looked like a forest elf, a sprite, one of the hidden folk, a being from another realm somehow magically transported into this one. Except for one thing: his round, green-painted shield was decorated with a large white Christian cross.

–

Stupid, stupid, stupid, thought Tor. How could she have been so stupid? When Bjarki was fast asleep the night before, she had lain awake in her cot, thinking about the third direction, and what Karolus might have been planning. Then she had decided to rise and share her thoughts with Widukind – he would surely be awake at this hour, on the eve of a battle. A problem shared, Valtyr used to say, irritatingly often, was a problem halved.

Was that true? Was she, in fact, lying to herself? She had known, had she not, that Geva had gone north with the other non-combatants. She knew there would be no one in Widukind's bed that night. It didn't matter, really. She had gone to his tent, telling herself her only intention was to share with Widukind her suspicions of Karolus's third direction. And he had indeed been alone when she arrived, save for Abbio, whom he'd soon banished.

They had shared ale and honey cakes while they discussed her fears.

Tor could not remember how it happened. One moment they were looking into each other's eyes in the soft yellow candlelight over a crumb-strewn, ale-splashed table, and the next they were kissing; then they were on his soft sleeping pallet, and their clothes were coming off by themselves... And it was perfect. Magical. Better, in fact, much better than the last time they had done this in the sacred groves outside Verden after the *blot*.

Then she made her mistake. In the cold, predawn light, after they had made love for the second time, she confessed she loved him. Had loved him since she first saw him in Hedeby. She could not stop thinking about him. And she would surely love him for ever. He had not replied in words, but had, instead, kissed her tenderly, and began to stroke his hand down the length of her naked body once more. Then she made it so much worse.

'You must let her down softly, my lord,' she whispered. 'You must tell Geva, as kindly as you can, as gently as you can, that you cannot be married to her any longer. That you are mine now.'

He had not replied, but merely continued making love to her.

She stopped him. 'Did you hear what I said?' she asked.

He smiled lovingly at her. 'You're a wonderful girl, Tor. One of the finest people I have ever met – as a warrior, as a lover, as a friend, you are a unique woman. But I cannot leave Geva. Ever.'

'Why not?' said Tor. 'I love you. You love me. You cannot love Geva, even if you ever truly did. It's simple. We belong together.'

'It cannot be, my sweet.'

'Why not?' Tor knew her voice had taken on a strident tone.

'I enjoy being with you like this,' said Widukind. 'A stolen night, here or there. I feel close to you when we meet like this. But Geva is my *wife*. We made solemn oaths to each other. And more importantly, she is the tie that binds Saxony to the Dane-Mark. Do you think I would abandon Saxony for love? Do you think I would risk the anger of King Siegfried – Geva's father – and perhaps cause a rift between Saxon and Dane just for a little happiness with you? If you think I would do that, you do not understand me at all.'

'So you would rather sneak about like a thief, ashamed of our love, lying to Geva about our relationship? *That's* what you want?'

Widukind gave her a boyish smile and said: 'No. I would have you in my life, and in my bed. I cannot take a second wife – Geva would never allow that. But a great man might take a concubine.'

'You would make me your whore?'

'No, my sweet, you would be recognised by all as my woman. But not as my wife. We could have a little ceremony, if you like.'

That's when Tor hit him.

–

It wasn't much of a blow, now that she thought about it: a hard, ringing slap around the side of his grinning face. She seemed in that after-love moment to have lost all her battle skills.

And she would need to regain them, fast.

304

She peered over the top of the dead tree at the empty clearing in the woods before her. This was a little patch of the First Forest that occupied a wide loop of the River Weser, ten miles north of the Braunsberg ford.

The road – a rutted track was a more accurate term to describe it – left the river here and cut across the neck of the loop, and for the first time it was possible to position her folk on either side of the road in thick undergrowth.

'On my word, Eckhart,' she whispered to her companion.

The old Eastphalian grinned at her. 'As you say, lady.'

Tor and the *hird* formed the rearguard of the Saxon army, with Eckhart and half of his Yews. They were at the tail of the column of warriors, who had followed the course of the Weser, tramping north all that sweltering hot morning.

Jarl Brun had wasted no time in withdrawing from his position north of the ford and, as he had said, an hour after his conversation with Widukind, his warriors were marching up the road beside the river, the Angrian horse leading the way, the foot eating their dust.

Widukind's remaining troops had been slower off the mark, but they hadn't dawdled either. Once it became clear they could not hope to face the Franks at Braunsberg, they abandoned much of their food and kit, tents, fodder and livestock, and set off with whatever rations they could carry – and all their weapons, of course.

Tor had been one of the last to leave the position by the ford and, as she hurried after the retreating Saxons, she glanced back to see a dozen Green Cloaks already halfway across the river, probing delicately with their spear butts to test the firmness of the riverbed.

She reckoned in about two hours, or even less, the lead elements of Karolus's main force – ten *scarae* strong – would be this side of the water.

Widukind halted them all at noon and, by then, they had lost all contact with Jarl Brun's people. They had eaten a few mouthfuls, refilled their water skins from the river, and it had been decided that Tor and Eckhart should set an ambush for their pursuers.

'We just need to slow them down, Tor,' said Bjarki. 'Make them wary of catching up. We need to put some distance between us.'

The plan, if you could call it that, was for the Saxon army to make for Minden, a town with a bridge over the Weser about fifty miles to the north and east of Braunsberg. Once over the water, they would be in the region of Westphalia, Widukind's homeland.

'And what then?' Tor had asked.

'Widukind believes he can scrape up some more of his own loyal people to rebuild his forces. It is his home turf, after all.'

'Does he truly think he can find enough folk in Westphalia to beat Karolus's massed legions? To face ten Red Cloak *scarae*? I thought we had already called up every spearman in Saxony.'

Bjarki said nothing for a while. 'Do you want me to command the ambush this afternoon, Tor? I'm happy to do it, if you like.'

'I'll do it,' said Tor. 'I'm in the mood to kill some stupid men.'

—

Tor felt a gentle hand on her arm and jerked round to look at Captain Eckhart. The veteran silently pointed a finger towards the south side of the clearing. At first, Tor could see nothing, and then, like shy fawns exploring the world for the first time, she saw them, two Green Cloaks, armed with bows, pushing aside a frond of greenery to step forward into the empty arena. They were very cautious, watchful, clearly experienced troops.

In a moment of silent panic, Tor wondered if this were too obvious a site for an ambush. Of course they would suspect the enemy to be waiting for them – of course they would, *stupid*!

She took a hold of herself.

The two green-cloaked Franks stepped out into the clearing, gave it one long, sweeping glance, then looked behind and beckoned. A few moments later, a dozen spearmen were marching confidently across in the grassy space. One of them, Tor noticed, was an officer, an older man with a green plume on his helm.

'Take the plumed fellow alive,' she breathed in Eckhart's ear.

There were more Green Cloaks behind the initial group of twelve, two score more men, some with bows slung over their shoulders, but most armed with ash spear and sword and dark round shields, all marked with the Christian cross. They were Swabians, Gerold's men from the dark, looming mountains south of Hessia. They were elite light troops, famous for their toughness and ability to climb steep hills at speed, to run for miles without tiring. But when it came right down to it, they were still flesh and blood.

'Now,' said Tor. Eckhart stood up and loosed his bow.

On the western side of the big clearing, thirty Saxons stepped out from behind trees and began to shower death on the Swabians.

In a few instants, the clearing was a scene of carnage, of frightened, shouting men, the hiss and thump of arrows hitting shield or flesh, blood spurting, weapons clattering. Screams, appeals to God, vile curses and threats filled the air. The Saxon archers nocked, drew back their strings and loosed, again and again, plucking out arrows, speeding them into the foe.

They poured their lethal shafts into the unsuspecting mass of the Franks, a black rain, a killing rain. Green-clad men were falling here and there and lying bloody on the turf. The plumed officer was trying to get them to form a shield wall, bellowing, 'Form up! Get those shields high. Bowmen on the flanks! Move it, move it!'

With astonishing speed, the well-trained Green Cloaks formed a wall, the front rank kneeling behind their shields, the second rank behind them, covering the front men with theirs.

Archers on both ends were now replying to the Saxon arrows. Tor saw one of her Yew women fall with a Frankish shaft in her belly, and another man shouted and clapped a hand to his left eye, from where a dark yard protruded. But the Franks had taken a fine mauling. More than a dozen of their men were down, bleeding on the green grass.

That was when the second contingent of Saxon archers, on the farther, eastern side of the clearing behind the Frankish shield wall, stepped from their places of concealment behind the trees and loosed their shafts into green-cloaked backs.

The initial volley dropped six unsuspecting men; a moment later, a second barrage felled another four. The shield wall, assaulted from both sides, front and back, crumbled. Some Franks were running back to the trees, some were looking around wildly, madly, uncomprehending, terrified as the lethal shafts hammered them.

'Run!' shouted the green-plumed officer. Tor saw he had a bloody shaft through his leg, skewering his thigh, and was down on one knee.

'Back to the *scara*! Warn them, warn them of this. Flee!'

Tor led the attack. She charged with a hand-picked score of the *hird* behind her, wielding axes, swords and shields. Yelling wildly, they crashed into the remnants of the shield wall, immediately swarming all over the Green Cloaks.

The rush of Saxons overwhelmed the surviving enemy. But Tor killed only one man, a swarthy fellow with a shield and sword, who snarled and cut at her as she came at him.

She caught the blow on her shield rim, shrugged it off and lunged her own blade up under his guard, stabbing through the thin leather armour he wore and burying her sword in his guts. He looked at her in utter amazement – and slumped to the ground.

The Green Cloaks who could run had fled. And the Saxons were busy executing the wounded without compunction. Those who begged piteously for mercy were given a one-word response: 'Sigiburg!' before being quickly dispatched by their blood-grimed foes.

Captain Eckhart was standing guard over the Green Cloak officer, who was whimpering with pain from the arrow through his upper leg.

Tor crouched down next to him. She examined the wound, pushing the groaning man over on to his side. The shaft had gone all the way through his leg and poked bloodily out in front of his knee. She grasped the arrow and in one quick movement she snapped it. Then she roughly pulled it free of his sucking flesh. The man yelled out and Tor looked calmly at him: 'Stop being such a crybaby. You'll live, Christian – at least, for a few hours.'

She stood and looked around the blood-spattered, turf-torn clearing. There were forty Franks lying dead on the field of battle.

She turned to Eckhart and smiled at him warmly.

'A fine afternoon's work, captain,' she said. 'I congratulate you on it. That should slow them down a bit. Now, let's get this big Frankish baby bandaged up – we're taking him with us.'

Chapter Twenty-six

One stout-hearted warrior of the North

Bjarki could clearly hear the awful screams of the poor Green Cloak officer. They grated horribly on his nerves; and on and on they went. He tried to block the noises out and concentrate on what Widukind was saying; something extremely dull about a lake he had swum in as a boy and how the water had been a particularly vivid shade of blue.

He stopped listening and beckoned to Gunnar, sitting with half a dozen other Saxon captains, inviting him to throw over the half-full ale skin from the other side of the fire. Out in the darkness somewhere, the Green Cloak gave another gurgle of anguish, which was abruptly shut off. Bjarki took a huge swig from the ale skin. *What were they doing to the poor man?* He discreetly grasped both his thumbs in the ancient sign to avert evil.

'On a still day,' said Widukind breathlessly, 'you could see a reflection of the mountains in the surface, and the oak trees round the edge, a perfect reverse image, as if there was another magical, upside-down world beneath the waters of the lake...'

They had eaten a lot of dust that day, Bjarki reckoned, and their small Saxon army was now, they believed, a good half-day's march ahead of the enemy. Tor's well-executed ambush had caused the Franks to pause a while, take stock and temporarily halt their reckless and speedy pursuit.

The Franks were still following them, of course, but a little more cautiously now. And Widukind had driven his people along the river road with a febrile energy that had exhausted every warrior except, apparently, himself. Around them in the Saxon camp, a very few fires still glowed in the darkness but most of the folk – those not on duty – were already fast asleep, wrapped up in their furs and blankets under the stars.

'...and the fish in there, I swear by Thor's mighty hammer, some of the rainbow trout in that astonishingly beautiful lake were *this* big!'

Widukind held out his palms an improbable distance apart.

Bjarki felt a sudden mad urge to punch the Duke of Saxony in his handsome face, to knock him tumbling off the log he was sitting on. Then the fellow might shut up for a brief moment or two.

Yet, he reflected after only a moment, he really must try to be more understanding. Only a couple of days ago, Widukind had had a proper Saxon army behind him – more than three thousand shields – a disciplined force capable of challenging his enemy and perhaps even beating him. Now he had fewer than a thousand spears, and Bjarki knew some of them would be slipping away in the darkness, going back to their farms and families to pretend they had never left them. *How quickly the wheel turns*, he thought.

The Saxon Wolf had finished his boring lake story. Nobody spoke.

'When we get to Minden, what then?' Bjarki said, yawning.

'You blame me for this, Rekkr, don't you?' said Widukind suddenly, and Bjarki was surprised at how angry the duke sounded.

'Who do *you* think is to blame?' said Bjarki. 'Your departed jarls?'

'Do you know how difficult it is to keep even a small group of strong-minded, independent Saxon jarls together in one place – all seeking personal advantage, all with their own private plans? Do you understand how impossible even the *idea* of a united Saxony is? Soft, rich Nordalbia has always hated and feared wild and woolly Eastphalia. The Angrians have been stealing Westphalian sheep and cows for centuries – the blood feuds go way back. We hated and feared the Danes until recently. And your lands, Jarl Bjarki, were under Frankish control in my grandfather's day. My father took them from Karolus's father by guile and force of arms.'

'So you're saying now it is too difficult a task to accomplish?' Widukind stood up. He brandished a hard finger at Bjarki.

'I had a vision,' he said loudly. 'I had a dream one night when I was a boy, after a Jul-tide feast with the Nordalbians, that one day all of Saxony could be united into one mighty nation. That Nordalbians and Eastphalians, Westphalians and Angrians would one day regard each other as one people, as brothers and sisters. And do you know what? My Westphalian elders all laughed at me. They said I was a childish fool. What could a lordly Angrian horseman galloping across his sweeping grasslands have in common with a drab Eastphalian fishwife, her bare feet still damp from the Havel marshes?'

Bjarki kept silent. *What do I have in common with this duke?*

'Then the Franks came – the Christians. And they started encroaching on our lands, building their foul churches, their *castra*, chipping away at our ancestral territory. They sent their missionaries into Westphalia and Eastphalia, teaching their religion, dispensing food and alms to the poor, healing the sick, telling our people that their god had a place for them in Heaven if only they would forgo their bad ways, renounce the old gods and worship Jesus.'

Widukind's eyes blazed blue as sapphires in the firelight. Bjarki could see the captains round the fire were now paying full attention to his words.

'The Franks came, our traditional enemies, our mortal foes, every year more powerful than before. And all of a sudden Saxony – a united Saxony – became less of a Jul-tide joke. This enemy made us realise that we had more in common with each other than we had first thought. My father Theodoric was a duke *in reality*, rather than just in name, as *his* father had been. He managed by bribery, by cajolery and, more often than not, by threat of bloody war, to unite the jarls under one banner. They fought for him. All of Saxony fought then and, united with our brothers north of the Dane-Work, we triumphed over the Franks. We came together and we defeated them. You know this too, Bjarki – you were there.'

Bjarki nodded slowly. He could see all the captains were enthralled by the man's words. He was moved too, despite himself.

'We beat them at the Dane-Work, and I believe that we can beat them again. So I will answer your question, Bjarki Blood-hand, Jarl of the Three Rivers and Warden of the First Forest, in this manner. What will we do when we get to Minden? We will do what we have always done. We will gather our forces, come together and resist the enemy with our combined strength.

'I will continue to fight for my dream of a united Saxony, for my long-ago vision of Westphalians and Angrians, of Nordal-bians and Eastphalians – yes, and Danes and Norse, too, should they choose to join us – enfolded in fellowship as one people. And I swear that I will fight until I can fight no more. We may have to retreat, we may suffer hardship and setbacks, but I shall *never* surrender.

'What was that you said to me, Bjarki Bloodhand? When we met at Hedeby? "As long as one stout-hearted warrior of the North stands with his feet planted on his own lands, ready to defend them against all, ready to die for them, then we are not defeated. We will *never* be defeated". Those were *your* words, Bjarki. But you know what? I, Widukind of Westphalia, I am that stout-hearted warrior. And though I may fall in battle one day, I shall never be *defeated*.'

There were roars of approval from around the campfire, even some warlike cheers, and while Bjarki was pondering his response, Abbio came into the circle of firelight, wiping his wet, bloody hands on a piece of filthy old rag.

The black-clad Master of Scouts went over to Widukind and whispered into his ear. Widukind looked at him: 'You are sure?'

Abbio nodded. Bjarki noticed that he had a spatter of blood across his forehead. 'The Frank believesss it. I am sssure of that.'

'This is good news – tell us all now what you just told me.'

Abbio turned to face the fire. He looked around the circle of tired but expectant faces and said: 'It ssseems that Karolus is *not* pursuing usss any longer. He has taken the majority of hiss army *east*, after Jarl Hessi. He hass taken Duke Gerold with him and decided to crush Jarl Hessi between his Red Cloak *ssscarae* and the Obodrite army which is now ravaging eastern Eastphalia.'

'So nobody is chasing us?' said Bjarki.

'No,' said Abbio. 'Bisshop Livinuss and hiss Black Cloakss, some of the Swabians and others, are sstill behind uss. But the oddsss against us are far better now, that iss all.'

'You got all this from that poor Green Cloak?' said Bjarki. Abbio nodded.

'Did you have to kill him to get it?' asked Bjarki.

Abbio frowned, then shrugged.

'I made him ssspeak to me. Then I offered up his life to Odin as a sacrifice. We will sssurely need the godsss' help in the dayss to come.'

–

The news that Karolus had divided his forces and that the king of the Franks himself was heading east after Jarl Hessi and his Eastphalians spread swiftly throughout the camp and put heart into the whole of Widukind's army. As they set out the next morning, a little after dawn, there was singing to be heard in the columns of marching warriors, and the Saxon Wolf rode up and down the lines, smiling at his people, slapping shoulders and exchanging loud, jovial remarks and shouts of encouragement with those he knew well.

They came to a small village called Hamelin at noon, where the river turned sharply north-west, and Widukind bought all the spare food he could from the handful of terrified inhabitants with the coin in his war chest, and warned them the Christians were coming, suggesting they take refuge in the First Forest, which was thick and almost untouched outside the boundaries of their fields.

Karolus might not be on their heels, but, in the middle of the afternoon, Bjarki, who had command of the rearguard that day, spotted a full company of fifty Black Cloak horsemen emerging from a sun-dappled patch of woodland not a hundred paces away.

He gave orders for his *hird*, plus a score of the Ash Regiment spearmen, who made up his rearguard, to form a hasty shield wall across the width of the road. The Black Cloaks formed ranks, and for a while Bjarki thought they meant to charge the hundred-strong wall, braving the double line of spears. Fidor and Fodor, and their gang of acolytes, began to howl like wolves; a wild, eldritch sound.

'Not now, lads,' called Bjarki, down the line of shields. 'Keep your *gandr* at bay. These Christian cowards won't dare charge us today.'

The howling died away and the shield wall stood firm for the best part of an hour, looking at the lines of Frankish cavalry, before a trumpet rang out and the horsemen all turned and trotted back down the road the way they had come. When the shield wall broke apart and they resumed their march – hurrying to catch up with the main force – Bjarki slapped Fodor on the shoulder and said: 'I truly think you and your brother scared them off today, lad!'

The Wolf Rekkr looked at him, blinked and said: 'Our *gandr* is close, all the time. When shall we be loosed to the great slaughter?'

'Soon, lad, soon,' said Bjarki, suppressing a shiver of apprehension. The thought of unleashing his own *gandr* on the day of battle made him queasy. Could he do it? Would his *gandr* come to him? Did he want her to? Did he have the stomach to summon her?

He honestly did not know the answer to any of these questions.

They pushed onward and made good time, Widukind urging greater speed from all the parts of his little army. Yet because so few of them were mounted – Bjarki rode Skinfaxi, Widukind was astride his magnificent white stallion, and a handful of Abbio's intelligence-gathering scouts were mounted – the army moved at the pace of the slowest walker. From time to time, they saw Frankish scouts – not Black Cloak cavalry but lighter-armed men, lancers in green or brown cloaks on fast, scrubby little ponies. They kept their distance, well out of long bowshot, and Widukind decided there was no point in trying to challenge them in battle.

'Haste is what we need,' he said. 'Not wasted Saxon lives.'

Three days later they arrived at Minden, footsore and hungry. And there they rested. The unwalled market town lay astride an old wooden bridge over the Weser. They had seen no Frankish troops for the past two days, and Bjarki wondered if they had broken off their pursuit, or forged off in another direction for some unknown reason.

Over a suitably humble meal of leek pottage and ale in the largest hall of Minden, Widukind revealed to him the latest news.

'They have gone after Jarl Brun – Livinus and all his Black Cloak *scarae*. Apparently, the Angrians have concentrated their troops at Buckegau – Brun has a big fortress there, and Livinus and his force is heading straight for it with all his men.'

'Where is Buckegau?' asked Bjarki.

'About half a day's march east of here, and a little south.'

'So we are still not off the hook, then?'

'No,' said Widukind, 'but we do have a moment to breathe. With luck, Jarl Brun will occupy Livinus for a few days – I can't imagine he will beat him. Livinus has some two thousand troops, and Brun only half that number. But his fortress might delay them for a little while. I would say we have three or four days in hand.'

'Three or four days to do what?'

'I'm going north,' said Widukind. 'Abbio and me, and no one else. I'm leaving you in command of the whole army.'

'What?'

'You have charge of the Saxon army – what's left of it now.'

There had been a steady stream of desertions the past few days.

'Where are you going?'

'Across the old bridge here is Westphalia – my homeland, the sacred soil of my tribe since before time began. I will go to see the folk who did not come out to fight before, and raise them for battle. The shy men and those who thought themselves too old to fight, the faint hearts, the lazy ones, girls who can shoot a bow and skin a deer but never thought to slaughter a Frank.

'I'll put heart into them and bring them to you. And you, my friend, must hold the ones we have together, and prepare to face Livinus...

'I entrust my folk to you, Bjarki. Their fate is in your hands.'

'You are leaving the army?' Bjarki still couldn't quite believe it.

'For a few days, a week at most. But I'll be back soon, I swear to you, with more stout-hearted folk, with enough spears to see off these Franks for good. Will you do this, Bjarki, will you take my people, hold them in your strong hand, and keep them safe until I return?'

–

'He's going *where*?' Tor was incandescent. 'He's running away, that's what he's doing, and leaving us to face the Franks alone.'

'Widukind promised he would come to our aid, when he has sufficient reinforcements, at Lubbecke – you remember, the village we stayed in on the march south from Verden. It's on the edge of the First Forest, a boggy little place. That's the meeting ground. He told me to take the whole Saxon army there and wait for him.'

'Where's he going to get "sufficient reinforcements", eh? Is he going to raise the dead, call an army of ghosts to fight the Franks?'

Bjarki sighed. 'You championed him, Tor. In Hedeby you said you believed in him and in his cause. Have you changed your mind because the tide has turned against us?'

'That was before... that was when I thought he was...' Tor was suddenly at a loss for words. They sat in gloomy silence for a while. The bear was on his back and snoring in the corner of the fisherman's hut they had commandeered on the edge of Minden.

'I said I would accept command of the army,' said Bjarki. 'I swore to protect his warriors as best I could. But *you* don't need to stay. If you like, Tor, you could go... go north to the Dane-Mark, or even home to Svealand and safety. Remember what Hildar used to say? When in doubt, go north.'

Tor indicated her derision by making a rude farting noise with her lips. 'I'm not taking advice from that brute – especially now that he's dead. Besides, I need to look after the *hird* – and if I left you alone, you would no doubt do something spectacularly oafish. No, I'm staying with you, brother. We'll go to Lubbecke together.'

They had eaten well that evening – hot, cooked food and fresh-brewed ale for the first time in days – and both were sleepy. But as they were getting into their blankets, Bjarki said: 'Widukind told me something else – more bad news. Want to hear it?'

'I do – *now*. Otherwise I'll just lie awake wondering. Go on...'

'Jarl Hessi has submitted to Karolus – he and his Eastphalians surrendered at some little place on the River Oker called Orhum.'

'It's where Hessi built his hall,' said Tor sleepily. 'His home.'

'Is it? Anyway, they were trapped between Karolus and the Obodrites, it seems, and painted their shields white and went out to meet the king. Didn't even try to fight. Probably the wisest thing to do. They would have been slaughtered. They gave up their weapons, Hessi knelt before the king and did homage. They're to be baptised, and Hessi will become a count.'

'I really thought *he* would hold out to the bitter end – even after he left us in the lurch at Braunsberg,' said Tor, rolling over and pulling up her blanket to her chin.

'It's never the ones you think, is it,' she said, 'who show themselves cowards when it comes to the clinch.'

Chapter Twenty-seven

'This is where we stand'

It *was* defensible, Tor thought, with enough determined warriors to hold the line. Indeed, it was not so terrible a place to make a glorious last stand, this low, treeless ridge that ran north-east to south-west across the Minden road a dozen miles west of the town.

On the left flank, to the north-east, was a large area of smelly marshland, criss-crossed with streams and dotted with dark places where a man or horse could easily sink down without trace into the sucking mud. It was a stinking, treacherous, impassable bit of land, and it warded their left flank admirably.

On the right, to the south-west, was the beginning of the First Forest; the land rose sharply to a mountain ridge, thickly forested with pines and oak, elder and ash, with impossibly tangled undergrowth that had to be chopped through, yard by sweaty yard.

Tor knew this from bitter experience – she and Bjarki had hacked their way up this same slope two years ago with an army on the way to capture Sigiburg Fortress. There was no sign now of the route they had cut then with so much effort. The First Forest had effortlessly healed the wounds they had inflicted.

So, little chance the Franks could come from that side either.

Standing on the crest of the ridge, Tor looked east half a mile along the dusty road to the abandoned village of Lubbecke, a drab huddle of muddy shacks and flat fishing punts on the lip of the wide marsh. If you took that road and followed it on eastward for most of a day's march, you would reach the old bridge at Minden over the River Weser.

A stiff north breeze on top of the ridge ruffled her unkempt red hair, and the day, though bright and blue, was chilly for the time of year. Summer could not come soon enough for Tor. But would she live long enough to see it? She doubted it. She turned around and looked west. That was Westphalia yonder – the rolling grasslands, wide pastures and cosy farmsteads of Widukind's homeland.

The Saxon Wolf had departed three days ago, with Abbio the Crow, and now he was out there somewhere, no doubt using his silver tongue and silky words to persuade some idiot farm boy with barely a whisker on his lip to take up his father's rusty sword and come south to his certain death.

Well, that was the boy's lookout.

It was quite possible, she thought, that Widukind had simply ridden away with Abbio, his closest friend, and that he had no intention of returning to die gloriously at Lubbecke, despite all he had promised Bjarki. Perhaps he had tricked her oaf into staying to face the foe simply so that he'd have time to escape.

She did not want to believe that, but she saw the Duke of Saxony more clearly now – a great talker, but not a great warrior; a man of imagination and with buckets of charm but possessing far less determination and sheer, honest grit than she had ascribed to him in the beginning. Did he have the courage to face his end like a warrior? He made a fine speech – could he make a good death?

She sighed. Only time would tell. In the meantime, she had a ridge to defend. It *was* a good, defensible spot. But then it ought to be – she had picked it.

–

At the bottom of the slope she joined Bjarki and a group of grim-faced captains of the *lith* of the now much-shrunken Saxon army.

'We can hold this hill, I'd say, even if we *are* outnumbered,' said Tor. 'They cannot come round the sides – we have marshes on our left…' she pointed north-eastward, 'and the First Forest to our right…' she waved at the green wall and the mountain slopes to the south-west. 'That means they have to come at us head-on, straight up this road, up the hill and on to our spears.'

Bjarki nodded. 'I only wish we had some decent cavalry,' he muttered, and then took a grip on himself. 'Right, then. I want archers on both flanks. Divide your men, half and half, Captain Eckhart, a hundred bows on each wing. When you have your Yew folk in place, get them started on digging horse-traps in front of their positions. Simple holes in the ground, one foot wide and one foot deep. Dig as many as you can. They *do* have cavalry, and I want our bowmen as well protected as possible. That's where the enemy horse will probably try to come at us, the flanks, and we need to be ready for them.'

'Ash Regiment – where are you, Gunnar? Oh, there you are! You will hold the centre-right on the ridge. Up there! See? And I'll want a good tight shield wall, no gaps, when the time comes.'

Gunnar nodded gloomily.

'Captain Wulfric – you will uphold the honour of the duke on the centre-left with your Westphalians. I know I can rely on you to stand like a mountain against the foe.'

'As you command, jarl,' said the one-eyed Saxon, one of Widukind's veterans.

'I shall be in the centre with half my *hird*, under the banners.'

'Wait, Bjarki,' said Tor. 'Where am I going to be…?'

'I want you, Tor, to command the reserve. Fifty of the best fighters, stationed on the reverse slope, and you can pick them from any regiment. I'll give you half of the *hird*, and Fidor and Fodor and all their Wolf Lodge crew – but you will need to guard our baggage, and to keep Garm tethered and out of trouble as well.'

'I want to stand in the shield wall,' said Tor. 'I don't need coddling.'

'Your role is vital, sister,' said Bjarki. 'The most important one on the battlefield. When they come at us, you must stand ready to reinforce any point in the wall that looks as if it might break. If you see our warriors being pushed back, you come forward with your fifty spears and plug the gap. If they break through our wall, we are all dead. Do you understand, sis?'

'I do know how battles work, oaf,' said Tor.

'Do you think they will come today, Bjarki?' said Gunnar nervously.

'Today, tomorrow, or maybe even never, if the gods smile on us. But this is where we shall stand until Widukind returns to us.'

'What else should I be doing, Tor?' said Bjarki. 'I feel sure I've forgotten something.'

They were both sitting on the grass of the reverse slope of the ridge with the small amount of army baggage, a few dozen yards behind the detachments on the summit, eating bread and cheese and drinking ale with Garm. Tor was tossing small lumps of cheese in the air for the bear to catch in his mouth, a favourite game of theirs. They had been able to commandeer a large amount of fresh bread and other foodstuffs in Minden market, and at least the army was in no danger of having to fight on an empty stomach.

'Have you thought about praying?' said Tor, snaking the ale skin from Bjarki's hand. 'Or perhaps you should select a young spearman or two and sacrifice them to Odin to ensure our good fortune in the coming battle!'

Bjarki stared at his sister. 'I'm not going to do *that*!'

'Why not? Many will die when they come. What's one more or less?'

'You *think* you are joking,' said Bjarki. 'But you're not being funny.'

They were interrupted by a shout from the ridge; Gunnar was waving and yelling something at them.

Bjarki levered himself to his feet.

'I suppose I had better go up and see what he wants.'

At the top of the ridge, Bjarki joined his friend and together they looked out over the road that led towards Minden. A few miles away, beyond the silent hamlet of Lubbecke, they saw a cloud of dust, and something dark and massive moving underneath it. A few moments later they saw that it was a company of horsemen; a mass of cavalry approaching fast down the road towards them.

'Shield wall,' bellowed Bjarki, 'Form up! Shield wall.'

–

'Where is the duke?' said the cavalry captain, a grizzled fellow called Hammarolf. 'We thought Widukind must be here with you.'

He gestured up at the two banners that were fluttering on poles above the very centre of the Saxon line. One was a bright yellow with an image of a bear depicted in brown – it had been sewn by members of Bjarki's *hird*, in his honour; the other a grey wolf standing on hind legs on a blood-red field, Widukind's personal battle standard.

Gunnar had recognised the horsemen as Angrians at a distance and, warily, they had allowed the riders to walk their horses up the hill before being ordered to halt before a spear-bristling Saxon shield wall.

Only this fellow, Captain Hammarolf, had come forward to the summit, dismounting and leading his chestnut horse by the reins.

'He's gathering reinforcements in Westphalia,' said Bjarki. 'He ordered the rest of us to make a stand here. Where's Jarl Brun, is he nearby? Will he be joining us soon with his forces?'

Hammarolf hawked and spat a gobbet of phlegm on the green turf.

'I piss on Brun,' he said. 'He has submitted to Livinus. He went in person to kneel before him at Buckegau, the moment the Franks arrived. He has received baptism. He's a mewling Christian now, something called a *Comes*.'

'But *you* did not surrender?'

'The moment I heard the news of Brun's betrayal I gathered up as many riders as I could and came west, looking for Duke Widukind.'

'Why did you not obey your jarl and surrender too?'

'My only son was in Sigiburg. He was slaughtered when the fortress was taken. He was eleven summers old. Eleven. Only there to tend to the horses. Now I would rather die than bend the knee to Karolus.'

'You are welcome to fight with us,' Bjarki said. 'How many are you?'

'Sixty horse, a dozen women and children. How many warriors have you?'

'A little more than six hundred.'

'So few?'

'Widukind will bring us more when he comes, in a day or so.'

'We are going to need them. Livinus is heading this way – we saw his dust on the road to Minden. He has more than two thousand.'

–

When it got dark, they cut wood from the First Forest and hauled it up on to the ridge and built three huge bonfires. Then they feasted.

They slaughtered the remaining livestock, with Bjarki sacrificing a pair of goats to Odin. They ate heartily, keeping little in reserve, knowing they might not taste food again until they dined with the gods in the Hall of the Slain, should they be so honoured. They guzzled their ale and mead late into the night and gorged on roast goat and sang old songs around the bonfires.

The next morning, feeling thick-headed and irritable, Bjarki and Tor inspected the scores of horse-traps which had been dug on either side of the ridge before the two blocks of the Yew archers.

Captain Eckhart had dug the holes deep and scattered handfuls of twigs and grass over the top to disguise them from enemy eyes.

'You think they'll work?' Tor asked. 'Surely even the Franks know better than to charge over ground that's been prepared by the enemy.'

'I don't know. But if these holes kill a few Frankish horses, or stop them riding over our archers, that's a victory of a kind, I'd say.'

In the afternoon, Bjarki addressed the gathered troops. He got on Skinfaxi's broad back and rode along the front of the battle line.

'I do not have Widukind's golden hoard of words, nor his skill in spinning a jewel-bright phrase,' Bjarki began. 'But he's trusted me to ward your lives and see off the enemy this day. So I place a similar trust in all of you, to ward the lives of your comrades, and to send the Franks reeling back from this ridge in confusion and disarray.

'We *can* beat them here. We can stop the foe from advancing further into our homelands right here, on this hill, and we can send him back to Francia in defeat. We can win – we *shall* win. But only if you trust in me, and each other. Do you trust me?'

Bjarki's question was met with a roar of assent.

He is far better at this than he realises, Tor thought.

'Widukind is coming,' Bjarki continued. 'He is coming to us at this moment, with hundreds of brave warriors of the North, a new army that will aid us in driving back the Franks. So, hear me now: stand firm, keep your shields up and look out for your neighbour, and we shall prevail. Soon we shall have victory. It will be ours because we know what we fight for: for our lands, our families, for Saxony – and for our glorious leader, Widukind!'

'Wi-du-kind, Wi-du-kind!' The answering roar split the skies.

If only Bjarki's words were true, Tor thought.

–

In the evening, the Franks came to Lubbecke. The first signs were horsemen in green cloaks, lancers on scruffy little ponies, coming up the road from Minden, and who cast impossibly long shadows behind them from the declining sun in the west.

Swabian scouts, Tor assumed, as she watched from the brow of the hill. About a dozen came trotting up the road towards the ridge on which the Saxon army waited in their battle line. At five hundred paces, they gathered in a huddle, only briefly, then three of the riders turned their ponies and galloped back down the road.

They know we are here now, Tor thought. *What next?*

The rest of the scouts fanned out and cautiously approached the low ridge. They took care to remain at a distance of more than two hundred yards, out of the range of the longest Saxon bows, but Tor saw two of them on the left by the marsh, poking and prodding at the black water with their long lance butts, estimating the watery depths. On the right, by the forest, another pair of scouts were talking and pointing at the long sloping area in front of the archers.

One of them picked up a fist-sized stone and hurled it high towards the area of horse-traps. The stone landed and skipped on the grass once and plonked into one of the deep, narrow holes, disappearing from view, and the two scouts exchanged a glance, nodded at each other, remounted and went their separate ways.

Tor heard a trumpet squeal behind her, and the shield wall in the centre split open to allow Captain Hammarolf and his sixty cavalry to ride out on to the top of the ridge. They did not waste any time but, with shouts and cries, waving their swords and spears, they cantered down the slope towards the enemy scouts, who took one look at the wave of Saxon cavalry thundering towards them and immediately made off as fast as they could spur their ponies back down the road towards the village of Lubbecke.

Hammarolf clearly had his men well under control, for they reined in after only a quarter of a mile, and turning, grinning as if they had secured a victory, and patting their horses' necks, they made their way back up the slope and through the lines to their position in the rear beside the remaining stores and baggage.

Oh good, Tor thought bitterly, *now they know we have cavalry*.

Bjarki came to stand beside her in the last of the light and together in silence they watched the Frankish *scarae* march on to the field, one by one, and take their positions: so many *scarae*, so many fighting men.

In the vanguard came the Black Cloak cavalry, dozens of squadrons of fifty mounted men – *cunei* – all trotting in neat ranks. Behind them came the *Scholares* infantry, marching in step along the dusty road. Big spearmen in glittering scale mail with viciously spiked shields, iron helms and two swords apiece. Many hundreds of them, too. Then Green Cloaks, but not so many, three *cunei* at most, perhaps a hundred and fifty shields, and Tor recalled that Gerold, their master, was with Karolus in Eastphalia.

'You see that big group of horsemen in the rear,' Bjarki said, pointing. 'Under the red, blue and gold banner with the big black cross? That's Bishop Livinus himself, surrounded by his Black Cloak cavalry.'

'And you see all the multihued clowns round them on foot, in furs and shiny armour, and those extravagant helms?' Tor replied. 'It's the Auxilla – our old unit. Still playing at being a ceremonial guard, I see. Luckily for them.'

'Must be more than ceremonial if they're on campaign with Livinus,' said Bjarki. 'I wonder if Snorri Hare-Lip is with them.'

'I'd like to come face to face with that cunt-faced traitor in battle,' said Tor, spitting on the turf. 'I'd cut his fat head clean off and claim the reward silver from Siegfried. A chance to do that would almost be worth dying for.'

'You are *not* going to die, Tor. And I don't suppose we'll ever have to face the Auxilla over the shove of the shields, anyway. Not with a thousand Black Cloaks between them and us. I believe Jarl Snorri – or Count Simon, or whatever stupid name he calls himself now – is quite safe from your righteous fury, Tor.'

As they watched, the various units split off the main road on either side and found themselves patches of ground to camp on, marking them with ropes and wooden stakes hammered into the turf, and soon, as the darkness grew heavy, all they could see was a field of twinkling lights, a good mile distant, where the foe had made their campfires.

'It would be beautiful, I suppose,' said Tor, 'if that glittering sight was not a portent of our doom.'

'Widukind will come, Tor. I've sent out riders looking for him, telling him to come *now*, with whatever troops he has.'

The look she gave him was, fortunately, invisible in the dark.

329

Chapter Twenty-eight

A black wave of death

Bjarki barely slept that night. He wandered across the low ridge and behind it like a ghost, moving from campfire to campfire in the darkness, sitting and accepting a sip of ale here or a bite of food there. He sang some of the war songs of his homeland, and they told stories of heroes and giants, of elves and dwarves. He checked that the cold sentries down on the slopes and on the flanks were awake, and watched with them a while. To everyone he gave the same message: Widukind is near. Stand fast; all will be well.

He snatched an hour's sleep just before dawn beside Tor and the bear and was up again before the sun was even a hand's breath above the eastern horizon. The morning light clearly illuminated the extent of the enemy camp, which was already stirring. It was a mighty host: two thousand men, a daunting sight for Saxon eyes.

Bjarki could already tell it was going to be a hot, dry day. Almost summer now. So he went to ensure all the skins were filled with a mixture of ale and water, and that, when the battle started, the few women still with the army – mostly Angrian mothers – were ready to pass them out to the thirsty fighters.

In the middle of the morning, a group of riders set out from the enemy camp and came down the road towards the Saxon lines. A sentry yelled the news across to Bjarki, who was in the middle of fitting a sliver of wood into the iron socket on the head of his bearded axe, to make the fit a little snugger.

He left the axe with the carts and baggage and went to the centre of the lines, underneath the two banners. The shield walls were not formed. Most of his folk were just sitting on the ground in their lines. No alarm had been given, no brash trumpet sounded. The enemy came only to parley.

As they came closer, Bjarki recognised Snorri, resplendent in a long purple cloak, scarlet trews and leather riding boots. He wore a thigh-length leather coat of mail on to which small iron squares had been stitched, and these had been polished until they shone like tiny mirrors. A sword with a jewelled hilt hung from his left side and his balding head was covered with a magnificent helmet, shined to a dazzle, like his coat, and crowned with ram's horns.

Snorri's moustaches were thicker, too, and looked as if they had been waxed, but they could not disguise his ugly divided upper lip.

Beside him, on a massive carthorse, rode one of the largest men Bjarki had ever seen – and he was himself no minnow. This huge fellow was bare-chested, his tanned skin oiled or greased, beardless, bald as an egg – even the eyebrows had been stripped away – and he wore a perpetual pout. There were a dozen mounted *Scholares*, the king's black-cloaked bodyguards, riding a few paces behind this extraordinary pair, their eyes ever watchful.

The group halted well down the slope, and the huge bald fellow rode out a little way and shouted up at the raggedy Saxon line that his lord, Count Simon of Herstal, the King's Shield, sought parley with Widukind of Westphalia and no other. The big man's voice was oddly high-pitched, and looking closely at him Bjarki realised the big fellow was younger than him.

Bjarki stepped out of the lines and took several paces down the slope towards the Frankish embassy.

'Widukind of Westphalia is indisposed,' he shouted. 'And so I shall speak for Saxony in his place.'

Behind him Tor edged out of the lines, too; she had a bow in her hand and an arrow already nocked on the string. A couple of members of the *hird* also stood ready, with drawn swords and nocked bows, should there be any attempt at trickery by Snorri.

'You there!' sprayed Jarl Snorri, kicking his horse forward a few paces. 'You, Bjarki Bloodhand, are you saying you speak for Widukind? There is no great lord in your army? No man of noble birth or worldly experience? I do not parley with mere *nithings*.'

'What do you want with us, Snorri?' said Bjarki tiredly.

'I have told you before, Rekkr. You will address me as Count Simon, or my lord count. I have long since renounced all my heathen names.'

'That's it? All you want today is for me to get your name right?'

'I come to accept your surrender,' said Snorri. 'You'll be treated fairly if you lay down your arms and submit to my justice. You must also agree to undergo baptism and swear an oath to—'

'No,' said Bjarki. 'Do not waste my time. We have been ordered by Duke Widukind to stand fast on this hill. So here we stand.'

'The king has been merciful to the other Saxon rebels, the jarls Brun and Hessi. He would be inclined to be generous to you, too, I have no doubt.'

'I said no… *Snorri Hare-Lip*,' said Bjarki, feeling a hot spurt of anger at this corpulent, split-faced buffoon.

'I have told you, I am Count Simon of…'

'I don't care for your new names. You'll always be Snorri the Traitor to me.'

Snorri sneered, his lip twisting open to reveal his big, grey teeth.

'Do not disrespect the count,' piped up the giant in his little-baby voice.

'Or what?'

There was a long pause.

'What will you do, big man, if I insult your beloved count?' said Bjarki. 'If, say, I call him a maggot-ridden, cowardly lump of dog shit? Which is exactly what he is.'

'There will be *consequences*...' squeaked the giant. 'I shall look for you in the storm of battle, Bjarki Bloodhand, I shall seek you out and you shall feel my wrath. My name is Adalhard of Dorestad, and I am the count's champion, and I challenge—'

'I'm even less interested, sonny, in learning *your* stupid names. But enough of this nonsense! Go back to your lines, all of you, go before I lose my patience!'

Bjarki turned his back on them and stumped back up the slope.

–

The Black Cloak horsemen formed up a good five hundred yards away, three blocks of men in dark clothes on dark horses. Bjarki remembered a scrap of information about them then, something he had been told in the Auxilla: the *Scholares* chose their mounts based on the colour of their hides, not skill, stamina or warlike temperament. It was another reminder of the power of the Frankish realm – they had so many herds of suitable warhorses to choose from that their cavalry could afford this display of pointless vanity.

The *Scholares* were formed up in three squadrons of about a hundred men each, with fifty paces between each dark block, and for a long time they just stood there, doing nothing at all, the only movement the intermittent twitching of the horses' tails.

Bjarki had the shield walls formed: Wulfric's Westphalians on the left, about a hundred and fifty warriors in three ranks, adjacent to one contingent of the archers under Captain Eckhart. On the right flank a slightly smaller force of Ash Regiment spearmen under his friend Gunnar, again in three ranks, again supported by a wedge of archers on their extreme right; and in the centre, formed tight and linking both larger shield walls, stood Bjarki and half the surviving members of his *hird* – thirty of the most experienced, and often older, fighters – under the two flapping banners, the grey Standing Wolf of Widukind, and Bjarki's own shaggy brown bear.

Behind them to the left was Tor and her reserve – fifty men and a few women, who were standing or sitting next to the piles of baggage, a few boxes and barrels, the upturned carts and the few draught horses, donkeys and mules that the army possessed. To Tor's right stood Captain Hammarolf and his dismounted men. Bjarki had given him instructions that he was not to engage with the enemy. 'Let them wear themselves out on our shields first. If they break our lines and scatter us, you may then charge. Not before.'

The enemy were moving now. The first block of Black Cloaks coming on at a stately walk, up the rise towards the crest of the hill. Two *cunei*, Bjarki estimated, in this first squadron, which was just coming up to the trot.

'Keep your shields tight!' Bjarki bellowed. 'Front rank just stand firm, let the second and third ranks do all the bloody work.'

The Black Cloaks were at the canter now, a hundred yards down the slope, and Bjarki could feel the drumming of their hooves on the dry earth through the soles of his leather shoes. A horrible tickling vibration. Down the hill, the second and third squadrons of *Scholares* were already moving forward.

His mail coat was tight under his armpits, too tight, and the thick bearskin cloak he wore was making the sweat trickle down from under his steel helm into his eyes. It was past noon now, and very hot. The sun was relentless.

He hefted the long, bearded axe in his right hand and locked his shield rim against the *hird*-man standing to his left. The man on the right did the same to his shield. Behind him he could feel the press of a round *hird* shield in the small of his back, setting him in his place, fixing him immobile in the very centre of the long shield wall.

'Stand firm,' he bellowed. 'Stand firm for Saxony!' A roar went up along the line. He glanced left, looked right. The shield wall was solid.

The cavalry were just heartbeats away now, the dark horses seemed impossibly huge, the dark-clad, scale-mailed riders grim under their steel helms. A wave of death. Each rider grasped a nine-foot spear in an overhand grip, the wooden shaft resting on the right shoulder, steel point extended forward ready to be plunged into the faces of the folk in the line.

The Franks were shouting now, yelling their battle cries: 'For Jesus Christ!... For God!... For Karolus!' The first horses crashed into the wall of Saxons, the Frankish spears hammered down and down again, ripping into flesh, and the Saxons began to die.

Bjarki felt the impact of the cavalry as a ripple all along the wall. He could hear his *gandr*, somewhere near him, chitter and squeak with the excitement of the hour. *She's with me again*, he thought. *But I cannot loose her yet.* A Frankish horseman, vast and black, was towering over him, lunging down with his spear.

He felt the thud of the horse's whole weight against his shield, shoving him backward. But he could not move his axe arm to respond. He tucked his helmed head in beside the rim of the shield and felt the jab of his enemy's steel against his helmet, and the point scrape noisily over the metal.

He heard the Saxon behind him yell, 'For Odin!' and lunge forward with his own long spear, and suddenly the pressure was gone from his shield and the horseman too. Another heavy black shape took his place. Something scraped right across his shield rim, then that weight was gone.

He looked up and snatched a glance left and saw that all along the shield wall the horsemen were still surging up against the line, spiking their spear points down at the Saxon heads, some lashing the line with swords.

The wall held firm.

The noise was quite astonishing – screams and yells, the clash of metal on wood, the neighing of wounded horses. The Saxons in the second rank were hacking at the enemy vigorously, striking with axe and spear. There were riderless horses here and there, and dark-clad bodies too. Just beyond the end of the wall he saw that the Yew archers on the left were methodically loosing their shafts into the enemy flanks – *fft, fft, fft*. Franks were shouting out in pain, their arms, ribs, thighs and their horses' rumps feathered with shafts.

The second wave of cavalry hit the wall, another hundred *Scholares*, spurring their horses up against the line of shields. Another great shimmy of impact through the tight-packed wall. A Frankish horseman was galloping all along the row of shields, striking at all the helmeted heads he could reach with his sword, like a child noisily dragging a stick along a wooden fence.

A hand axe flew out from the mass of Saxons and took him dead centre in the chin, splitting it cleanly to expose his bloody tongue, and he sagged back, dropped his sword and slid out of his saddle. There was a general pattern to the attack, Bjarki saw, as he ducked and shrugged under the blows of his foes, who were like a wash of great black waves on the shore, with Frankish cavalry coming up the hill the left side, crashing into the shield wall and fighting their way all along the length to the right, before retreating down the slope on that side. As they retreated, they were pecked at by the wedge of archers on the right of the line, dozens of horsemen falling victim as they withdrew.

But the shield wall was looser now – gaps were being made by fallen Saxons – and some of the Black Cloaks were trying to force their horses into the holes in the line. Bjarki saw a rider stab down with his spear at a blond, bearded Saxon face and catch the man in the side of the neck, blood spurting, the man collapsing. The Frank had his horse almost halfway into the crush when Bjarki found his right arm was suddenly freed and he was able to make a long, looping cut with his axe that thudded into the rider's thigh.

The Frank yelled; at the same time two spears punched out of the mass of Saxons and took him back and side. He fell, disappearing into the crush of struggling folk.

'Close up, close up!' Bjarki was yelling desperately, but the loose, struggling, boiling wall of warriors paid him little heed. The third squadron was now on the hilltop and the press of horses and Franks was heavy and heaving all along the surging line. Swords were ringing down on the defenders' shields and helms, clanging, screeching, thudding home, dropping many a warrior. The arrows whipped like swallows across the face of the wall, skewering flesh, both horse and man, embedding in scale mail or shield. The grunting, howling, screaming and calling on gods was incessant.

Bjarki felt a wounded man slump heavily against him, pushing him sideways out of position. His foot slipped in a puddle of blood; he felt a hammer blow against the back of his steel helm – and his *gandr*, very close now, chattered deafeningly, gleefully in his ear.

'Kill them, kill them all,' she whispered inside Bjarki's reeling mind. 'Let me loose, man-child, and we will slice them all into meat.'

And suddenly it was over. The remaining horsemen were cantering down the slope with a few Saxon shafts whistling after them.

Bjarki straightened his helmet with a shaking hand and, shrugging loose of his comrades, he stepped forward out of the wall. There were bodies everywhere in front of the churned-up strip of earth that marked the line of the Saxon shields – plenty of his own men and women, hacked and torn, but two score or more of the Black Cloaks, too, and half a dozen of their horses. Some of the Saxons were hurrying out of the lines carrying naked seaxes, eager to finish the enemy wounded – and Bjarki felt too tired to go and stop them. Here and there he heard the mocking calls of 'Sigiburg! Were you a great hero at Sigiburg, eh? Take that, you murdering Frankish bastard!'

Tor was beside him. 'Looks like I missed all the fun,' she said.

'They'll come again,' he said. 'You can be sure of that. This was just a probing attack. Testing our mettle, to see if we'd stand.'

'We did that, well enough,' she said, looking along the line. Warriors were hugging each other; some cheering their victory. Others, wounded or exhausted, were sitting on the bloody, torn-up turf with their heads bowed.

'We lost a hundred shields,' said Bjarki, 'maybe more when some of the wounded die tonight. And it was just a test. But we stood firm here. We held them.'

–

Summoning all his strength, Bjarki set about making sure that every warrior had food and something to drink. He did not allow them to move out of their positions unless they were wounded, in which case they were carried to the rear with the baggage.

He reorganised the two main shield walls – moving folk from Wulfric's Westphalian left to Gunnar's right. His friend had done well, he thought. He had a sword cut under his left cheek that was bloody but not serious; it would make a handsome scar. He was filled with manic energy, having personally speared a Black Cloak rider to death.

'Can you hold them when they attack again, Older Brother?'

'Let them come,' Gunnar growled. 'We've got the measure of these foreign bastards. If they want another spanking, let 'em dare to come at us again.'

He praised his friend lavishly. 'Stand fast, Captain, hold the line and all will be well. Remember: Widukind is on his way!'

'We don't need him to beat these cowardly *nithings*!' yelled Gunnar.

–

The shadows were lengthening, and Bjarki was sitting down with Tor in the baggage area with a horn of ale and a bite of bread and sausage, the first food and rest he had had all day, when the bronze voices of the wolf-horns sounded: the signal

338

for alarm. He swallowed his ale and shoved the chunk of bread in his mouth and, chewing, levered himself to his feet.

'You know what to do when the time comes,' he said to Tor.

'Will you unleash your *gandr*?' she asked. He thought he detected a little whisper of fear in her voice. Or perhaps just awe.

'No. I shall not. Not if I can keep her out. Not till I *have to* let her in,' he said. 'Not till all is lost and there's no other possible recourse.'

She nodded, understanding.

It was the Frankish infantry this time. Great, fat columns of black-clad men plodding up the slope towards them. They were steel-helmed and clad in scale mail beneath their cloaks and carried spears, round black shields with a white cross and two swords apiece. Bjarki could hardly believe their huge numbers – many hundreds, perhaps even a thousand men, all now coming forward in one concentrated attack on his already weakened shield walls. And in front of the black columns were scores of Green Cloaks: lithe, lightly armoured little men running forward in pairs, clutching javelins and shields, pausing every few yards to wait for the ponderous marching columns to catch up with them. The swift-moving Swabians formed a screen of skirmishers in front of the marching Black Cloak *scarae*, a cloud of tiny running figures.

For the first time in this battle, Bjarki felt the true, bone-numbing dread of death. They were outnumbered here at least two to one, and these troops were fresh – his were wounded and weak and tired from their hard, bloody bout with the *Scholares* cavalry.

The Swabians started to take casualties from a hundred yards out, with both wings of Saxon archers loosing their wicked shafts into them at more or less the same time. Many advancing green-clad men dropped, a dozen, a score, two score, stuck through with arrows, but the slope in front of the shield walls was dotted with shafts that missed.

The Green Cloaks responded by giving a great shout and charging the last fifty yards at full pelt. They skidded to a halt ten paces out and hurled their javelins at lethally close range into the shield wall, arcing the light spears over the front rank to plunge into the warriors behind. As Bjarki watched, once more immobilised by the press of shields, a pair of Swabians came right up before him and launched their javelins. He felt the wind of one of the spears on his cheek, and heard a cry behind him. The first green-cloaked man smiled – he actually smiled right at Bjarki, a cruel, horribly intimate expression – and hurled his second javelin from ten yards directly at Bjarki's face.

Purely from instinct, Bjarki jerked his shield up, and he felt the solid blow against the wood as the javelin landed and the dragging weight as it became stuck in the shield's flesh. He lowered the rim again and watched as the man turned on his heel and sprinted away. But a second Green Cloak was now in the act of launching his missile. Bjarki saw it coming, a streak of grey; he twisted his head to one side at the very last moment, and felt a burning touch against his neck and heard a scream of pain from behind him.

The whole shield wall was looser already. Bjarki could feel a little free movement all around him. Space, where there should be none. Saxon spears were whistling over the top of the wall, aimed at the Swabians, most of whom were running back down the slope. Pursued by arrows from the flanks.

Then the Black Cloak infantry struck them.

The first *scara* crashed into the section of the shield wall commanded by Wulfric, thirty yards away to Bjarki's left. He felt the shock once more all along the locked shields – but a slower, harder pressure than the cavalry. Three hundred Black Cloaks plunged up against the shields of Westphalia, grinding painted wood against wood, snarling, hacking with spear and sword, shoving their weight against the line, forcing it back, and back.

The Westphalians buckled under the immense pressure from the Frankish horde; strong warriors forced back against their will, their shoes slipping on the blood-wet turf, scrabbling to stay upright and keep their shields locked, as the spears and swords of the foe battered their helms.

'Stand firm!' Bjarki yelled. 'Hold – now push back. *Push!*'

The second *scara* surged up against his part of the shield wall. The massive impact knocked him back a full yard, despite the press behind him. Bjarki felt bruised, breathless and squeezed, and a furious, unshaven face was inches from his own; the man in helm and black plume was screaming something at him. Bjarki did not comprehend it.

He dug his feet in and shoved hard, and felt the scrum move forward a fraction. Something was hammering painfully on his helm, from the right, again and again. A sword sliced into the top of his shield, kicking out splinters of lime-wood, needle-sharp against his cheek. He could smell the shouting Frank's hot, fetid onion breath; and the oily reek of shit, blood and fear rising from beneath his shoes.

A Saxon spear lanced past his face on the right, inches away, and took Onion Breath full in his open, roaring mouth, and just as the foeman staggered back, Bjarki gave an enormous heave, using his colossal strength, and shifted the whole line forward a few feet.

He got his axe hand free at last and swung it over the top of his shield, hacking deep into the shoulder of a new Black Cloak, who popped up – and just as suddenly reeled away. He was able to take another half-step forward. And felt the tangling of a body beneath his shoes. It was still moving, so he stamped down hard. His *gandr* was hissing in his ear: 'Yes, yes, kill them all.'

He could feel the vast, ancient power of the Bear spirit growing, swelling inside his chest, noticed a blood-red tinge to his sight.

He bellowed: 'No. Not yet, you foul bitch. Not yet!'

A wedge of *Scholares*, a dozen big men all tightly crammed together, charged as one, and forced their way into the line of Saxon shields just a few yards to Bjarki's left. The wall bent backward, Bjarki saw Saxons falling, then he was himself tumbled back and half turned by the massive force of their thrust. The Saxon line buckled, but held, then a fresh surge of Black Cloaks powered forward, joining their force to their comrades' and suddenly, shockingly, the Saxon shield wall broke and there were Franks to Bjarki's left, a knot of shouting black-clad men, and yet more *behind* him, and one was lunging at him with a sword.

He twisted and took the sword point on his shield and, as the blade scratched across the painted surface, he countered with an overhand axe blow. He knew the shield wall was gone now. They were all finished. It was only a matter of moments. He deflected a lightning spear strike, stepped right and split a Frankish skull with another massive downward chop, hot blood and pink matter back-spattering his own face. Someone shoved him hard in the back, a blow of some kind, but it was muffled by the thick fur cloak, and he whirled round to see that he was now detached from the rest of the line.

The wall had been shattered in several places and now, instead of one long, unbroken barrier, three men deep, standing firm with locked shields against the enemy, there were three or four blocks of struggling Saxons, huddling together, fighting for their lives, surrounded by a seething mob of *Scholares*. Bjarki gave a snarl of rage and hurled himself, axe swinging, into the nearest knot of his foes.

Chapter Twenty-nine

'Widukind is not coming. We all know it'

With her heart in her mouth, Tor watched the Black Cloak attack from on top of an empty rye flour barrel amid the baggage.

From this vantage point she could see over the heads of the shield wall as the huge black blocks of Frankish infantry swept up the hill and smashed into the thin Saxon line.

She could make out Bjarki from his height and the thick black fur cloak that covered his broad shoulders, in the very centre of the press. And she could hear his booming commands echoing across the field. But when the enemy struck the line, she lost him in the swirls of dust and flashes and crashes of steel, the crack of wood.

She looked down to her left at the small group of warriors, fewer than fifty folk who made up her reserve.

'Make ready,' she said loudly. And immediately the twins Fidor and Fodor began their wild, mournful wailing, mimicking the calls of the wolf, summoning their *gandr*. Their followers, a dozen men – and it was all men – took up the call, drawing swords and seaxes from sheaths, hefting their shields. The other remaining thirty-odd folk of the *hird* maintained a grim silence, but they too drew blades, or took a firmer grip on their ash spear shafts.

Tor looked to her right and then gave a long, piercing whistle.

Captain Hammarolf turned his head. He and his sixty troops were already mounted. 'Make ready,' Tor shouted across to him.

Hammarolf merely lifted a leather-gloved hand in reply.

When Tor turned her head back to observe the shield wall, she knew immediately all was lost. Just in that short space of time the battle had turned. The scrum of dark bodies on the far side of the wall was now too thick; the Saxon lines, thinned by the Green Cloaks and now battered by the Black, were being pushed here and there, rippling like a flag in a breeze, under the constant pressure of the surging foe. The air was filled with the shouts of men killing, dying, calling on their gods, and the stench of blood and liquid shit coated the back of her throat like a poisonous oil.

It could only be a matter of time, she thought, before the dam broke.

Then it did. A wedge of a dozen *Scholares* poured into a gap in the line made by two fallen Saxon warriors and forced their way forward, dividing the defenders, severing the shield wall in two. She caught a glimpse of Bjarki laying about him with his axe like a mad butcher, bloody streaks flying in the air. She heard his furious bull-bellow as he cut down another Frank. But a fresh breach was made in the shield wall over on the right. She saw Gunnar try to rally his Ash Regiment troops, saw him smashed down with a sword, try to rise, and sink beneath a rainbow of steel.

'Now, Hammarolf,' she shouted. 'For Sigiburg! For Saxony!'

The captain gave a fierce little yip, bellowed 'Charge, for Sigiburg!' and kicked back his spurs, plunging them into his horse's flanks. And he and his sixty riders flowed forward like a tide, a river of horses, accelerating into the bloody chaos on the hill.

Tor looked to her left. 'Your jarl needs you,' she shouted, to the expectant faces of the *hird*. 'Let us go to his aid.' She hopped off the barrel, scooped up her shield and, sword in hand, she charged towards the summit of the ridge, with the folk of the *hird* and the howling Wolf Lodge hard on her heels.

Hammarolf's horsemen struck like Thor's thunderbolt. The Angrian cavalry smashed deep into the mass of Black Cloaks on the ridge. They used the weight and momentum of their mounts to physically bowl the enemy over, and the galloping hooves of the riders that followed to trample the fallen Franks into bloody ruin. Their spears licked out, driven from the height of the saddle, slicing open the faces of the Franks, punching through their armour and torsos, snagging limbs, cracking ribs, ripping bellies.

When the spears were all broken, they drew their swords and slashed their way deep into the surging black tide of men on the hill. Riders were soon surrounded by throngs of furious Franks, the spears punching upward, and many bold folk were dragged from their saddles to their doom beneath chopping blades. Yet the Angrians fought with the ferocity of their ancient Saxon heroes, battering their enemies down, hacking, slicing the foe into bloody meat. Many had soon cut their way clear of the churning press, before turning, with impossible bravery, to ride back into the fray.

The cavalry charge utterly disrupted the Frankish attack. The tide was turning again. There were Black Cloaks dropping their weapons and staggering back down the slope, many bloody and wounded, but not all.

Some had simply had enough of the fight.

Tor's small force smashed into the struggling masses on the ridge, crashing into the backs of the Black Cloaks gathered around the small knots of Saxon defenders. Tor rammed her sword into a black-cloaked back, the man squealing in agony as the sword ripped through his kidneys, and she whirled smoothly and slashed another Frank across the face, half severing his lower jaw. She hacked at a big fellow, who blocked with his white cross shield, and saw Fodor behind him swing his axe and take the top off his head like a soft-boiled egg. The twins were in full Wolf fury now, froth showing white on their lips, and they howled and gibbered and slew; they were tireless, swift as the wind and truly invincible.

Working as a pair, they swarmed whole groups of Black Cloaks, a dozen men at a time, cutting and hacking, lopping limbs, axes now long gone but doing their bloody work with sword and seax. They disdained shields, taking wounds but disregarding them, and they left a trail of bloody, reeking mayhem behind them.

Tor dropped a fellow with a lunge to the throat and, taking a tiny pause to catch her breath, she watched with panting awe as the twins hurled themselves into a seething mass of armed Black Cloaks and emerged, only moments later, slathered in gore, with the bodies of their enemies slowly falling to the ground all around.

She saw Bjarki, seemingly calm, hacking at a lone Frank, swapping cuts, absorbing the blows on his shield and finally battering the enemy down with the hammering power of his axe. A wild-eyed fellow barged into her, knocking her sideways, but he ran away down the hill before she could react. She saw that the enemy was now in full flight.

Bjarki was leaning on his axe, breathing heavily, exhausted, and staring down the slope at the mass of retreating *Scholares* – hundreds of them, more than half of those who had come up against them that day.

By Odin's favour, the Franks were quitting the field.

The ground around was thick with dead, Saxon and Frank, sometimes piled two or three deep, entwined in their final anguish. The ploughed-up turf on the ridge was sodden with fresh blood.

Horses nuzzled their slaughtered owners, neighing softly as if to awaken them. But Bjarki was whole and hale, as far as she could see, thank the gods, except for a deep cut along the left side of his neck, which was clotted but still dribbling gore, and a gash on his left hand. She came to stand beside him. He glanced down and gave her a half-smile through his blood-spotted features.

'Good timing, sis,' he said. 'Perfect, in fact. Thank you.'

In that moment, she felt a surge of pure love for her brother, an emotion so intense it dwarfed any of the feelings she might once have had for Widukind. She knew, in that burning instant, that any man she might love in the future – if there was a future – would always be measured against the big oaf standing beside her now.

–

They piled the Saxon dead on the reverse slope, near the baggage. The Franks they threw into the stinking marsh, and with each heave and dull splash, the throwers merrily shouted out: 'Sigiburg!' A call that was repeated more than three hundred times during that grim night.

Despite the heavy toll taken on the enemy, and the drubbing they had endured, the Franks had clearly not abandoned the field. Tor could see the twinkling of the campfires down below, so many of them, in fact, that she wondered if it was actually a ruse, a trick to intimidate the Saxons in the coldest reaches of the long night.

Their own casualties were horrendous. Hundreds were dead, and a similar number wounded in varying degrees of severity.

Fidor and Fodor, while exhausted, and battered and slashed in many places, had avoided any crippling wounds. Although the gash in Fodor's thigh made him hobble like a grandmother – Tor worried it might go bad.

'They'll come at us again tomorrow, oaf,' she said. 'You know this, don't you?'

They made one huge bonfire with their remaining firewood, also burning all the barrels and boxes they could spare. The last of the food was greedily consumed, the best given to the wounded, although any warrior might eat or drink whatever he or she chose. They all knew this would be their last night on this green and pleasant Middle-Realm.

'Widukind will surely come tomorrow,' said Bjarki, sleepily. 'I am certain of it. He gave me his solemn word.'

He was sitting with his broad back against a large boulder near the bonfire, a half-empty horn of mead in hand, his freshly cleaned axe lying beside his thigh, but he could barely keep his eyes open.

'Oaf, it's me,' whispered Tor. 'No need to keep pretending. Widukind isn't coming. You know it, I know it – we all know it.'

'He *will* come,' mumbled Bjarki. 'He *has* to come to our aid.'

The horn was slipping out of his hand. Tor gently took it and set it aside. She reached for the bearskin and spread it on his body.

Then she swallowed down his mead and went to check on the sentries.

–

The next morning, a little before dawn, when she was feeding Garm a few scraps of dried venison and a chunk of hard, stale cheese and giving him some much-needed attention, the Swabians attacked.

They came out of the First Forest to the south of their position, their movements obscured by the thick veils of mist that rose from the marches and drifted like smoke across the whole battlefield. Their charge surprised the right flank of sleeping Saxons on the ridge, where scores of archers were lying blanket-wrapped in their battle positions.

They exploded out of the trees in a screaming mass, a hundred Green Cloaks armed with javelins and spears, a few with bows, too, and they obliterated the Yew Regiment bowmen of the right flank before many of them were properly awake. Saxon folk were skewered half-naked, half-conscious by javelins and arrows as they rose from their warm blankets and reached out for their weapons.

Tor's first thought was, *They must have murdered all my sentries.* Her second: *It must have taken them all night to work their way through the thick forest to the ridge – in darkness and silence. Such a feat!*

Then she was too busy for thoughts. She was bellowing the alarm, trying to remember where her shield was, kicking Bjarki awake – yelling at him to stand to, stupid oaf – shouting at the *hird* and the remnants of the Ash Regiment to form a circle of shields around the baggage and the wounded – *now, right now, move, move!* Her stomach filled with ice water as she heard the drumming of horsemen on dry turf – and saw, bursting out over the top of the ridge, like demons emerging from the mist, Black Cloak cavalry.

She could hear trumpets and the distant cheers of infantry.

'They are throwing everything at us,' she called to Bjarki, who was fastening his bearskin with one hand, his long axe gripped in the other.

'All the way round, a tight circle,' she yelled at a confused Saxon, naked from the waist down. 'Where is your shield?'

Captain Hammarolf was in the saddle, along with a score of his people, but he valiantly spurred forward to engage the oncoming Black Cloak riders – absurdly outnumbered. A handful against hundreds. Nevertheless, they charged into the Frankish horse, calling on Odin to witness their deeds, and all were enveloped, swamped, speared within moments.

'It's barely dawn,' mumbled Bjarki. 'It's still fucking night-time. They might have waited till a decent hour to come up here and kill us.'

Captain Eckhart and his remaining men were inside the circle now, which was very shakily formed. But, crucially, it was *formed*.

All shields faced outward and were locked in a continuous ring, the badly wounded and a few mounds of kit and spare weapons sat in the centre of the circle near the smouldering ashes of the bonfire. The Saxon archers inside the ring were shooting over the heads of their comrades, lobbing shafts down on the mass of black-clad troops that surrounded them. Tor glanced over at Garm, who was looking in bewilderment at the rushing, shouting humans.

The enemy cavalry was cantering around the perimeter, occasionally leaning in and hacking down at the Saxon heads they passed. The Green Cloaks were all round them, loosing shafts and hurling javelins – finding targets inside the circle. The Saxon ring braced, gritted its teeth and endured.

'Infantry,' Tor said. 'Livinus will be coming up that hill.'

'I know,' Bjarki snapped. She looked over at her brother – he was making a curiously flat droning noise, deep in his chest and throat. She realised he was humming, making the ancient four-tone tune, rhythmic, hypnotic. Gathering his awful power once more. It was time.

She looked around and saw the twins Fidor and Fodor nearby, and called out to them: 'Time for you, too, to summon your *gandr* again!' They stared at her, appalled. They both looked exhausted, utterly spent. One made a half-hearted wolf's howl, then he stopped.

There were enemies swarming over the ridge now, a thick, boiling mass around the outside of the tight circle. Individuals and groups of men surged in and struck; steel clattered again and again on wooden shields, and Tor could hear the shrieks of the wounded, loud and pitiful. The swords battered at the perimeter. She saw Saxons falling, one by one, skewered by Green Cloaks, or hacked down by the rearing dark horsemen, and the sad ring of shields tightened, shrinking as it grew less with every passing moment.

Garm was acting strangely – he was growling and tossing his big black head, jerking hard against the stout rope attached to his leather collar, which tethered him to a spike driven deep into the turf – and barking and mewling at Bjarki, looking away and then coughing at him. He seemed to be speaking, arguing with the man.

Tor saw that Bjarki's face was horribly contorted; his scarlet cheeks were bulging and writhing. The sweat stood out on his brow, and he was making a low, rumbling, growling noise now, the very same pitch as the bear, no longer humming the ancient tune.

She looked up at the ridgeline, fifty paces away, and saw a line of black-clad infantry just cresting the hill – many hundreds of them – and a wide flag in the centre of the line, a standard of blue and red and gold. A tall, golden man on a fine horse, gorgeously dressed, with an enormous pointed white hat marked with a cross, sat surrounded by scores of his warriors – not Black Cloaks, nor Swabians. Proud warriors in leather armour and furs, with impossibly shiny helms, elaborately decorated with wings or bull's horns.

The Auxilla had come to the battle.

Bjarki Bloodhand threw back his head and roared at the sky.

He turned on his heel and hurtled towards the ridge, axe in hand, bearskin cloak flying out behind him like a black banner of doom.

He swept the shield line of Saxon warriors from his path with one massive hand as if they were a curtain of gossamer, and burst into the ranks of the encircling Swabians beyond. He screamed again in his *gandr* rage, his axe swinging like a red pendulum. The blood spurted high.

Bjarki made short work of the nearest enemies, howling and snarling and tearing the foe apart from within their ranks.

Tor turned to Eckhart, who was gaping with astonishment at Bjarki's assault on the Green Cloaks. She seized him by the arm.

'Get archers and follow your jarl,' she said. 'Protect him!'

Eckhart stared at her. 'What is the plan? What are we *doing*?'

The ring of Saxons was disintegrating by now, punctured in several places by the enemy. There were green-cloaked Swabians inside the crumbling circle, by the last few boxes and barrels. Garm gave a low growl, jerked his shaggy head once, very hard, twice, jerking against the rope and peg that tethered him to the earth. It held firm.

He chomped down on the rope and severed it with his sharp front teeth.

'What are we doing?' said Tor. 'Simple. We're *attacking*.'

She saw that the young bear, now freed from his rope, was lolloping after Bjarki, heading towards the ridge and the black line of foes.

'Garm,' she called, 'wait, boy, wait for me!'

She sprinted after her bear.

Garm charged into a pair of Green Cloaks, who foolishly had their backs turned to him. He hit one Frank with his huge shoulder, knocking the fellow flying a dozen yards, and while passing, he slapped the second man with his claws, ripping off his astonished face. The bear bounded onward, with barely a break in his stride.

He barrelled up to the ridge on all fours, occasionally giving a sky-splitting bark of sheer joy, and tore exuberantly into a pack of cavalry, scattering the terrified horses, eviscerating one mount with a sweep of his claw. Next, he bowled into a shield wall of Black Cloaks, hurling men this way and that, like a whirlwind hitting a pile of loose straw. There was something elemental about his assault, Tor thought: nothing could stop him.

She followed in his path. She barged into a bewildered Black Cloak, who hacked at her wildly. She took the weak sword blow on her shield, and her blindingly swift counterstroke half severed his neck. Then she ran on – looking ahead, she could only glimpse Bjarki from the big flapping black fur cloak and the bloody sheen of his swinging axe in the crush of his enemies.

He was unstoppable too, she thought. The bear seemed to be heading towards her brother, pausing only to rip the sword arm off a *Scholares* who was foolish enough to stand and challenge the bear.

There were Saxons round her now, folk who had burst out of the circle at the same time. There was Captain Eckhart with a dozen archers, nocking shafts and loosing, dropping enemies left and right as they steadily advanced. The Franks seemed to have been surprised by the eruption of the frothing Rekkr and the wild bear from the defensive ring of shields and were stumbling backward, looking about uncertainly for fresh orders.

Tor's blood was now pumping hot and fast, and she felt clean and pure as fresh snow. As strong as Bjarki – or even her Garm. She clashed swords with a Green Cloak, knocked him down with a feint and shoulder barge, and dug her blade deep into his neck.

She ran on. *If this be the day I fall, All-Father, watch me and mark my deeds – mark my deeds, great Odin!*

It became clear to her what Bjarki, in his madness, was attempting to do. Ahead of her on the crest was the tall man on the big horse in dazzling gold raiment, with a mace in one hand and a shield in the other. It was Bishop Livinus riding fearlessly into battle.

Now Bjarki was thrashing away furiously with his gory axe at a thick, writhing wall of Black Cloaks in front of the mounted prelate. He was besieged, surrounded, and struggling desperately to smash his way through to the bishop. And he was still inexorably moving onward. Gobbets of flesh flew in the air. Bjarki was trying to kill their greatest enemy and he was now only a dozen yards from the Christian lord.

The growling bear smashed into the line of Black Cloaks to the right of the Rekkr, sending three men flying. Garm snarled and slashed at one fellow, clawing his shield out of the way and surging forward to bite down on his helmeted head, crunching easily through steel and skull. A Frankish spearman lunged and struck his spear point deep into the bear's side. Garm yowled and turned, quick as a whip, ripping the man's belly from his spine.

Tor shouted: 'Don't you hurt my poor little boy!' and charged into the Frankish line behind the bear. She killed one spearman, a straight lunge stabbing him through the eye, and slashed another across his overextended forearm, nearly lopping off the limb.

Now the Black Cloaks were falling back, retreating from the onslaught of the wild animal, the furious girl and the huge, froth-lipped, blood-covered warrior with his swirling axe. Eckhart was there too, now, loosing lethal shafts into the ranks of the astonished foe.

The Franks before Livinus crumbled, split and dispersed. And there was the Anglecynn bishop himself, astride his fine horse. Magnificently attired in gold, under the gaudy flag, with a double line of warriors before him.

There was Snorri Hare-Lip, standing in the centre of the line, his baby-faced champion looming like a mountain beside him.

On Snorri's other side, his right, was a small figure – a girl, blonde plaits peeking out from under her helmet, in scale mail and sword-girt for war, a stern expression etched on her pretty little face.

It was Yoni.

Chapter Thirty

With the dawn's early light

His fury was like a constant hot pressure inside his chest. Like a pig's bladder inflated with breath to its maximum capacity. He felt as strong as a fortress, fierce as a lion, fast as a falcon, and best of all, there were always more enemies as fodder for his axe.

Hot joy bubbled up inside Bjarki Bloodhand's pumping heart as he hurled himself towards the line of fur-covered foes that stood before the tall man, the holy man with the mace on his high horse. A bad man.

He knew he had taken wounds; he could feel a wet stickiness all over his itching skin, but he cared not one jot. The first victim fell easily to his axe, his head leaping from his shoulders. And Bjarki gave a full-blast scream of rage and victory and swung again, the gory blade thudding delightfully into fresh new flesh.

'Kill them all, kill them, man-child,' his *gandr* hissed. 'There can be no rest until all of them are made into meat!'

There was one before him – a big, bald, baby-faced fellow, naked from the waist up, who seemed to want to speak with him.

'No talking,' his *gandr* told him sternly. 'Do the work. Finish the task. Kill him quickly, then slaughter all these other folk too...'

The bald one took a step forward and swung a sword at Bjarki's head, fast. But the Rekkr was even swifter: he ducked the blow, bent his knees, losing a foot in height, and the blade just hissed over the top of his helmet.

Bjarki giggled, then tapped the axe against the big fellow's ankle.

The axe struck deep and almost chopped the foot clean off. And the big bald one was down now, sprawling on his back, crying in pain. Bjarki stepped back and swung the axe high again, and the blade thudded deep into the centre of the funny man's oiled chest.

Something smashed into his back; he turned, snarled at a new man, and leaving the axe buried in Baldy's ribs, he pulled out his seax and, seizing his attacker's head with one huge hand, he jammed the blade into the side of the fellow's neck and waggled it.

There were many others all around him, battering at him, trying to hurt him. But Garm was there, his baby, his bear-child, and Garm knew just as well as he did how to open up these lovely meat bags. It was in his mother's blood, of course it was. He slashed at a new man who flinched away, and now there was a small one in front of him – a girl, he suspected. She was trying to speak to him too – he could not make out the first few words, but now she was simply pleading, 'No, no, please. Bjarki, it's me!'

He shouted, 'No *talking*!' and slashed at her with the bloody seax. She stumbled back and tripped. He leapt on top of her, landing like a cat, knees and elbows straddling her prone body, and now his blade was punching into her belly, into her sweet loins, again and again, and he was snarling and snapping at her face with his bloody froth-flecked teeth. And panting. Suddenly very, very tired.

Was it over now? It was, apparently. He could feel the *gandr* slipping away, leaving him, leaving him wholly emptied in spirit. Spent.

He got up with some difficulty, stiff, hurt and swaying with exhaustion, but there were no enemies nearby trying to kill him, none as far as he could see. There were many Black Cloaks on the slopes of the ridge, true, but they were all running, retreating – why?

There was that gaudy holy man, halfway back down the slope on his wildly galloping horse. The bishop. Running away. The coward. There were torn bodies all around him. Groaning wounded, too. And there was his Tor, a dozen yards away. A bloody sword in her hand, a look of grim triumph on her small, tight face, standing over the body of a fat, moustachioed man with bold stripy trews and a silly horned helm.

She looked over at him.

'Are you back with us, Bjarki?' she said. It sounded as if she were many miles away, or down a deep well. As if the battle had made him deaf.

He nodded. 'Why are they running?' he whispered hoarsely.

'Look yonder, oaf,' she said. 'There is your answer.'

Bjarki lifted his eyes to the top of the ridge.

With the sun just rising in the east, Bjarki could see a figure on a horse, a huge, shining white stallion, brightly illuminated on the top of the ridge. The big horse was rearing up on its hindquarters. The mounted warrior held a long, gleaming, silver sword triumphantly in the air, as if celebrating a great victory.

He wore a golden helmet, which was adorned with a pair of eagle's wings, extended upward as if in flight. And all around him were the outlines of other warriors, the shapes of shields, the slim shafts of spears, hundreds of them on foot, some on horses, too, with more coming forward every moment, filling the skyline.

Widukind of Westphalia had come to battle with the dawn's early light.

–

Bjarki's legs failed him and he slumped down on the greasy grass. All the rage and strength had seeped out of him and he was left with a cold, grey feeling of utter despair. He had summoned *her* again and she had eagerly come to him – and they had done terrible things together. He looked to his left and saw the ripped corpse of Yoni in a lake of blood, the girl he had made love to. The girl he had loved. He knew what he had done. Her lower body was a glistening ruin, entrails poked and looped through the torn flesh. Her little face was strangely untouched save for an expression of astonished horror.

He leaned forward and vomited, bile gushing from his belly.

There was a thudding of hooves, and looking up, he saw it was Widukind, shining, handsome, virile, as yet untouched by any of the filth of war, and dozens of spearmen all around him. The Saxon duke looked down at Bjarki from the high saddle and smiled.

'You did well, Bloodhand. I knew you could hold the line for me.'

Then he was gone, waving his troops forward to complete the rout of the Frankish forces. Bjarki watched him depart in a scatter of hoof-thrown clods – and vomited massively again. He looked once more at Yoni's little corpse and began to crawl slowly, painfully towards her.

When Tor came to him, he was cradling the Irish girl's head in his lap, her mangled body lying across his legs. The tears were running freely down his bearded cheeks. Tor crouched down beside him.

'How badly are you hurt?'

Bjarki shook his head. He could not speak.

'Can you stand? There is a lot of blood on your back.'

Bjarki dropped his eyes; he gently stroked Yoni's cheek with one filthy hand. 'Look… look what I did to her,' he managed at last. 'To my Yoni.'

'She's dead, oaf. But you are not. Now I need to see your wound.'

Bjarki looked at her. 'I can't go on, Tor. I can't… look at what my *gandr* has made me…'

'Let's get you up and away from here.'

Bjarki looked up at her; his eyes were massive. 'No, I can't do this any more. *I have become my father.* I am Galálar. Kill me,

358

Tor. You must do it now. End my agony, I beg you. I beg you. If you love me, sister, strike and end my suffering this very day.'

'You're being particularly stupid, oaf. That Irish girl was our enemy – sure, you may have bedded her – but she was our foe. She stood in the line of battle against you. And took the consequences.'

–

Over the next few weeks, the usual feelings of shame and self-disgust, the oily foulness in his lower guts when he contemplated the terrible deeds he had done when the Beast was inside him, became almost unbearable. Far worse than it ever had been before.

Far worse than the wounds he had received, all the random cuts and blows; worse even than the arrow that had pierced his back, that had punched through the thick bearskin, through his mail and had entered the rope of muscle to the right of his spine.

And that was *extremely* painful, agony, even, and meant he could not now lie on his back. Instead, he must lie on his belly in the jolting ox cart that bore him north along the rutted tracks of Westphalia, north towards the safety of the River Elbe.

He saw again and again, in his mind's eye, the terrified face of Yoni as she stood before him in the line, her sword limp in her hand, and begged piteously for her life. He saw again her dead blue eyes staring blindly up at the sky as he had held her in his lap when the battle was done.

Each time he had to fight the urge to throw up.

What he wanted most of all was to end this nightmare – this endless round of fury, death and blood followed by horrible, heart-shrivelling shame. When Tor refused to kill him on the field, he had thought about cutting his own throat, in the days afterwards. But Tor's company and thoughts of Garm and Inge, people he loved, stayed his hand.

I have become my father. The words he had spoken to Tor echoed in his mind. Her brutal reply was seared in his memory, too: *She was our foe. She stood in the line of battle against you. And took the consequences.*

Widukind said something similar to him about Yoni's death, a day or two after the fight on the ridge. 'When you think of all of our people we loved who perished at Lubbecke – your friend Gunnar, my captain Wulfric, Tor's *hird*-woman Gerta – weighed against those, the Auxilla girl's death, that *enemy soldier's* demise, isn't such a tragedy.'

Bjarki glared at him. He had still not forgotten the night of the *blot*, when Widukind had calmly executed nine helpless prisoners of war.

'You did your duty, Bjarki, you held the line until I came, as I knew you would. You kept our army together and gave Livinus a bloody nose into the bargain. I honour you for it. I'll always be in your debt, Jarl Bjarki Bloodhand. And when the battle for Saxony is won, you shall possess all your lands once more, and receive a splendid reward from me, as well.'

When the battle for Saxony is won... it was now Widukind's most commonly used phrase. Yet it completely ignored the harsh reality.

The warriors who had come to the Saxons' aid were Frisians, under the command of the elderly Raedbad, grandson of the last king of Frisia. Widukind had scooped up a handful of old men, girls and boys from the farms of Westphalia, but the bulk of the five hundred spears he had brought to Lubbecke in the nick of time were Frisians, folk who had been persuaded that he could win a war against Karolus and restore the North to its religion.

Yet cracks in that new Northern alliance were already starting to show. Raedbad had been astonished that the survivors of the Saxon army – which he had been told by Widu-kind was so powerful – now only numbered about two hundred warriors, many of whom were wounded or exhausted. The first thing the allied force had done, after chasing Livinus and his Black Cloaks back to Minden, was retreat into Widukind's homeland.

Abbio's scouts reported that Karolus himself was approaching the Weser with a fresh army two or three times the size of Livinus's force – perhaps five thousand men, in perhaps fifteen *scarae*. There was nothing to do but run north for the safety of Nordalbia.

'Jarl Ulf will give us succour beyond the Elbe,' Widukind said breezily, 'while we heal our wounds, rest our tired bodies and recruit more brave warriors to our cause.'

'He's completely mad,' Bjarki whispered to Tor, when she was in the ox cart one evening a week later changing the dressing on his wounded back, and cleaning up the lesser cuts and scrapes on his battered body. 'He still thinks he can beat the Franks.'

'So what do you want me to do about it?' Tor said grumpily.

Bjarki was silent for a while.

'Did I tell you that Garm spoke to me during the battle?'

'Spoke to you?'

'Spoke to my *gandr* when she was in me – he said: "Mother, why do you make a den inside this man-child?" And my *gandr* replied to him: "This is my plaything. When you grow older, my beautiful son, you may be strong enough to have a plaything, too".'

Tor started at her brother, unsure what to say.

'I have to get her out of me, Tor. After what she, what *I*, did to Yoni… I cannot do this again. I must rid myself of the *gandr*.'

'How would you do that? More drowning yourself in icy pools?'

'I'll go to the far north, to my mother's people – the Sami. They helped Hildar, remember. Maybe they could help me.'

–

One month later, Tor and Bjarki stood in front of the long table in the King's Hall at Hedeby. In front of them sat Siegfried, Lord of the Dane-Mark, and Geva, his smug, well-fed daughter, with two of his senior Danish jarls, neither of whom they knew well.

'What news of Widukind of Westphalia, my daughter's husband?' said the king, gesturing over at Geva. And Bjarki, whose back was still paining him considerably, felt certain that the old man already knew all the news from the south, and was in truth asking a quite different question – what are you two doing here?

'Widukind is in Treva on the Elbe,' said Bjarki, 'a welcome guest in the halls of Jarl Ulf. He intends to bide there for the rest of the summer.'

'He means to rest his forces in Nordalbia?' said the king.

'His plan is to lead a series of small, swift raids into Frankish-occupied Saxony, striking hard at *castra*, ambushing columns of Red Cloaks on the march, harrying the enemy whenever he can. That sort of thing.'

'Indeed. And has he a sufficient number of warriors for this glorious task? I hear that Raedbad of Frisia has returned to his lands in high dudgeon. I have heard, in fact, that they had a bitter disagreement, a parting of—'

'I cannot speak to that,' said Bjarki shortly. The king looked surprised to be interrupted, but he bore the discourtesy with grace.

'But my sister and I *have* parted company with Widukind – we parted amicably, but we no longer serve the Saxon duke. And I have renounced my claim to be Jarl of the Three Rivers and Warden of the First Forest.'

'Why is that?'

Tor watched Geva as a triumphant little smile spread over her face.

'To be blunt, my lord king,' said Bjarki. 'I have renounced the title of jarl because it is a nonsense – an empty title. Karolus and his Franks occupy all the territory that I once so briefly held. And there seems no prospect of recovering any of my lands. The Groves of Eresburg are filled with a garrison of more than a thousand Red Cloaks, I am told. The Fyr Skola is no more. The Irminsul has been destroyed, cut down, and its sacred flesh turned into timber planks to build a new Christian church. Most of Saxony, in my opinion, is lost for ever. Even Nordalbia will fall soon, I believe. My sister and I have chosen to refrain from the pointless shedding of yet more blood.'

King Siegfried looked at them for a very long while.

'You're wise,' he said. 'I think Widukind is a great fool if—'

'Father,' protested Geva. 'That is not fair to poor Widi—'

'Be silent, daughter. I am speaking. You are wise, Bjarki Bloodhand and Tor Hildarsdottir, to sever your connection with my impulsive young ally. He is a good man, I think – but a fool. And he will surely be destroyed by Karolus. He will also drag many a fine warrior down to Hel's cold realm with him when he falls. I have told him this to his face and insisted that he recruit no more young spearmen from the Dane-Mark.'

Bjarki bowed to the king, as low as his poor, wounded back allowed.

'May I ask you what you plan to do now, Bjarki Bloodhand?'

'A man once told me that when he was in doubt, he always went north. I shall do exactly that. I would seek out my mother's people in the frozen wastes beyond Svealand. I have been grievously wounded in body and in mind in recent months. Perhaps I shall find healing in the soothing snows. My sister will accompany me north, part of the way, but she has decided...'

'But I plan to build myself a hall in Svealand, in the deep forests of my ancestors, somewhere where my pet bear can roam about freely and live the life he was born to. I intend live out the rest of my days up there quietly and in peace,' Tor said. 'Or until I grow too bored. But I do have some business to conduct with you this day, O King!'

She walked forward towards the long table. In her right hand was a bundle, damp and stained. 'I present you this,' she said.

She set the large, soggy bundle on the tabletop in front of the king and untied the cloth knot at the top. Then she peeled back the wrapping to display the partly decomposed severed head of a man. A fattish, oldish, balding fellow with long ginger moustaches, which only partly covered a big split like a hare's in his upper lip.

Geva gave a shriek of horror, a hand flying to her face. King Siegfried leaned forward and peered closely at the foul, stinking object on the table before him.

'I claim the reward, O King,' said Tor. 'Behold the traitor's head.'

Historical Note

It is sometimes difficult to describe to the uninitiated what, exactly, historical fiction *is*. It's not history – no one should read a novel as if it were a textbook on the period in question – but neither is it entirely fabricated like, for example, a fantasy story.

So the purpose of a note like this at the end of a novel is to help the reader distinguish between historical fact and authorial fiction. Sometimes it's obvious – if I were writing a story about Agincourt, I wouldn't have to tell people that Henry V was a real English king – but sometimes it is not. *The Saxon Wolf* takes place during a period that used to be known as the Dark Ages, and about which we still know very little. The illiterate, pagan Saxon tribes left no written records of their deeds and the 'histories' of the Christian Franks, their enemies, are often close to propaganda, extolling the virtues of their hero Charlemagne and his triumphs over the forces of, as they saw it, the Devil.

Widukind of Westphalia was a real warrior, a young Saxon nobleman who led the resistance against Karolus (the future Charlemagne) and his Frankish warriors for several decades in what is now northern Germany in the late 8th century. However, his story is surrounded by a thicket of myths and legends – he is a Robin Hood-type character, to my mind, a brave man who led a peasant army in dense woodland, including many bowmen, against the invading Christians and using what we would now call guerrilla tactics, or asymmetrical warfare. His support was mostly drawn from the lower ranks of Saxon society, farmers, woodsmen, cattle herders, and so on, while his fellow noblemen were more easily persuaded to accept their Frankish overlords.

Widukind made a lasting alliance with Siegfried (Sigfred), king of the pagan Danes in the traditional way by marrying his daughter, and several times the Saxon warlord was forced to retreat north into the Dane-Mark, behind the protection of the mighty Dane-Work, to seek sanctuary with his ally. He also managed to convince the Frisians (a decade later than this story) to rebel against their Christian lords and return to the old ways.

Widukind – whose name means 'Child of the Woods', a Saxon euphemism for a wolf, hence the title of this novel – is recorded as the Saxon leader in the *Royal Frankish Annals*, a contemporary account written by Charlemagne's monks. But almost nothing is written about his personal characteristics.

I have imagined him as an inspired public speaker because he must have had considerable powers of persuasion to induce his countrymen to fight on against impossible odds for thirty years. He also must have been stubborn, perhaps even a heroic figure.

The *Annals* record Widukind as being followed by his great friend and adviser Abbio (or Abbo) – his 'constant companion'. I have, however, arbitrarily embellished the character of Abbio, making him a weird-looking sorcerer and spymaster, to create a more compelling actor in future books in the Fire Born series. Abbio's bizarre way of speaking adds, I hope, to his sinister aura, but there is also good archeological evidence that people in the Viking Age often filed grooves in their front teeth, or even removed some of them, perhaps as part of some magical ritual.

The *Annals* also mention a chief called Hessi, naming him as the leader of the Eastphalian tribe, and a man called Brun, meaning Bushy Eyebrows, identifying him as warlord of the Angrians, who were famous for their horses and horsemanship.

Bjarki Bloodhand, Tor Hildarsdottir, Valtyr Far-Traveller, Snorri Hare-Lip (Count Simon) and Bishop Livinus are all inventions of mine. Although Livinus is an amalgam of several

Anglo-Saxon clergymen who crossed the English Channel to serve Charlemagne or who bravely went into the wilds of pagan Saxony on proselytizing missions. These include Alcuin of York and Saint Boniface. Neither of these two holy men exactly fitted the time period I was writing about, so I decided to give Karolus a fictional chaplain and chancellor (a role equivalent in clout to a grand vizier or prime minister), and also make him the Bishop of Aachen and putative Archbishop of Saxony. I also wanted the freedom to have my fictional baddie satisfyingly slaughtered by Bjarki or Tor, in due course, without distorting historical truth.

In charting the progress of the war in Saxony between AD 773 and 775, I was, as far as possible, guided by the original Frankish records. One of the things I enjoy most about writing historical fiction is that you are often gifted storylines from the time. You get verisimilitude – no one can say something is far-fetched if it actually happened – and, if the events in the novel take place in an obscure period, the reader is unlikely to be familiar with them, and you can more easily keep them guessing.

The Saxons did surprise and capture the Frankish fortress of Sigiburg (a site now occupied by the ruins of Hohensyburg Castle, near Dortmund) in the spring of 774. They also occupied and fortified the fortress atop the Eresburg (now the sleepy town of Obermarsberg), where I placed my fictional berserker academy, the Fyr Skola, then campaigned southwards in to Hessia (Hesse) where they fought a battle at the fortress of Buraburg, which they failed to take. The remains of iron stirrups and horses' bits have been found by archaeologists at Buraburg, which indicate that it was garrisoned by Frankish heavy cavalry.

The Saxon army ravaged most of northern Hessia in the summer of 774, pillaging farms, burning crops and gathering booty and slaves. They sacked the Abbey of Fritzlar, near Buraburg, slaughtering the monks and removing many treasures before retreating back north of the Ruhr into their own territory.

The following year Charlemagne, who had just returned victorious from a long war in north Italy – where he had indeed been crowned King of Lombardy with the Iron Crown in Pavia – marched his vast army up the arrow-straight Hellweg, the great highway, into the very heart of south Saxony.

The Hellweg was built by the Romans during their long wars against the Germanic tribes across the River Rhine. The road was used to march the Legions into the heart of the Teutoburger Wald (called the First Forest in this novel), where famously, in AD 9, they had their arses handed to them by the Germanic warlord Arminius. Eight centuries later, the cultural descendants of the Romans, Charlemagne's Franks, used the Hellweg to attack the descendants of Arminius, the Saxon tribes. The name 'Hellweg' means the Road to Hell – or the Way to the Goddess Hel's Realm, perhaps because of its military applications.

Admittedly, some scholars believe it may also mean the Salt Road – *hal* is a Celtic word for salt – because local people may have transported this most valuable commodity along it. Yet another etymology is the Bright Road – *heller* means bright or clear – because it is a space in the gloomy forest. I think of it as the Hell Road, mainly because that is a fine, dramatic name for a highway. A good chunk of this route, which ran from Duisburg to Paderborn, is now prosaically named *Bundesautobahn 44*.

Shortly after his triumphant return from Italy, Charlemagne recaptured the fortress of Sigiburg, then attacked the Eresburg settlement and easily took the cave-riddled prominence that rises out of the Diemel Valley. The King of the Franks did cut down the Irminsul, the holy World Tree of the Saxons, which was probably atop the Eresburg plateau. The original wooden church of St Peter and St Paul in Obermarsberg is said to have been constructed on the site where the mighty Irminsul once stood.

The Saxons retreated north in the face of the overwhelming might of Charlemagne's forces but made a stand at Braunsberg, a defensible ford on the wide River Weser. There they waited stoically for Charlemagne to come at them. The *Royal Frankish Annals* describes it thus (with my comments in square brackets):

775 AD

Then the pious and illustrious lord king Charles [in my novel Karolus] *held the assembly at the villa called Düren* [near modern-day Cologne], *from where he undertook a campaign into Saxony. He captured the castrum of Syburg* [Sigiburg], *rebuilt Eresburg and reached the River Weser at the place called Braunsberg, where the Saxons, who intended to defend the bank of the river, were arraying themselves for battle.*

By the help of the Lord and the exertions of the Franks, the Saxons were put to flight; the Franks seized both banks and many Saxons were killed. Then the lord king Charles divided his army and himself advanced with the men whom he had chosen to the River Oker. All the Saxon Eastphalians came there with Hessi, gave hostages as he was pleased to demand and swore oaths of fidelity to the above-said lord king Charles.

Similarly, when the king returned from there, the Angrians came with Brun and their other optimates [leaders] *to the district called Bucki* [Buckegau] *and there gave hostages, like the easterners* [Eastphalians].

On his return from there, the aforementioned king joined up on the River Weser with the other part of his army, which was holding the bank as ordered. The Saxons had fought a battle with them at the place called Lidbach [Lubbecke] *where, by the will of God, victory had fallen to the Franks, who had killed a great number of those Saxons.*

Despite what the *Annals* say (they were written by Frankish monks), most historians think the battle at Lubbecke was inconclusive rather than an outright Frankish victory. But, either way, Widukind and what was left of his Saxon army after the surrenders of Hessi and Brun (Jarl Ulf of Nordalbia is fictional) were forced to retreat north after the battle to beyond the River Elbe, and Charlemagne was left in control of much of Saxony.

Yet the war was far from over. Widukind and his now ragtag army continued the fight on against Charlemagne for many more years, and he even managed to win some notable victories against the Christian Franks. But that is a story for another day.

Acknowledgements

Many people have a hand in the making of a novel, and I would like to take this opportunity to thank just a few of them. My wife Mary has been brilliantly supportive, running our house and educating the children during various lockdowns, as well as holding down a demanding job, and allowing me the time and space to write. I also owe a large debt of gratitude to my excellent literary agent Ian Drury, of Sheil Land Associates, for his unfailing encouragement of my works over the past decade and for introducing me last year to Michael Bhaskar and the good folk of Canelo, the publishers of the Fire Born series.

Craig Lye (of Canelo) has been a superb editor of these books, correcting my excesses and helping me to create the best novel that I can. His meticulous copy-editor Jenny Page has also been excellent, saving me from many an embarrassing mistake.

I'd like to thank my older brother John Brodie Donald for creating such a brilliant map of Old Saxony; and, finally, I'd like to give a special mention to Professor Neil Price of the University of Uppsala, whose erudite but extremely readable books *The Viking Way* and *Children of Ash and Elm* have been my go-to reading on the pagan cultures of northern Europe.

Yet it goes without saying that all errors and failings in the novel, historical, grammatical and other, are entirely my doing.

Angus Donald
Tonbridge, 1st September 2021